ELENA'S SMILE

ELENA'S SMILE

HENRY TEROL

Back cover:
St Fernando Cloister- Monastery of Las Huelgas, image courtesy of Burgos Municipal Archives.

*To Rus, my wife and to my daughter Irene,
the two princesses in my life.*

Any resemblance of the characters in this novel to real people is purely coincidental with the sole exception of those who have expressly consented to be mentioned by their real names. In other cases names and places have been altered.

As for Montanilla del Alarzón, it is a place that can easily be found after the second star on the right.

— "AT THE PRIMA HOUR, FROM LIGHT WILL
COME LIGHT"

Truth is stranger than fiction because fiction is bound to be plausible. Real facts are not.

— MARK TWAIN

CONTENTS

PART II
FOLLOWING THE CLUE

EPILOGUE

POEM OF THE PRINCESS

I have heard that a princess lived on the banks of the Arlanzón.

Small of figure, of agile step,

Green eyes like emeralds, warm voice like a winter campfire.

Born in distant lands they say that on the day of her arrival the cathedral bells tolled twice.

And the pious knelt and prayed for her happiness.

Many have been the travellers who wanted to know about her, her name and ancestry, but they were only told she was the Princess of Arlanzón.

PART I
THE DISCOVERY
QUESTIONS ARISE

CHAPTER 1

MONTANILLA UPON THE ARLANZÓN

Of Pipe smoking, regattas, and other outdoor activities.

Once upon a time, there was a quiet and guarded city in Spain covered in fog, scattered rain, and snow, with a river of silky water running through it.

The cathedral spires rose proudly and majestically above the low roofs, providing welcome shade and hiding places for the seedy areas beneath them.

Burgos was the name of this city.

A few kilometres to the east of it, on the banks of the Arlanzón River, was a small and tranquil town. The river had come to bathe it after paying its respects to the Grande Dame and her towers.

It all started here, on this cool October day.

Montanilla upon the Arlanzón had a small population, but its few shops and several bookshops set it apart from the neighbouring villages. The town, with its thick stone homes, had been a cattle-rearing centre for generations. After years of internal squabbles, the current town council added the hydronym "upon the Arlanzón" to its noble original name to give it more dignity. Following the settlement, one was faced with a densely packed forest of trees and dwellings. The whole thing looked like they were posing for a family portrait.

Every day, delivery vehicles and large lorries from the nearby industrial area of Burgos East drive this route, bringing various items and spewing urban and profane pollutants over this lovely setting.

The night before, a snowstorm had blown through the area, blurring the street contour and making it more difficult to find this secret entrance. Only one sign indicated that one had arrived at this new seat of learning: the University of Montanilla.

A single man was walking through the woods by himself, following the long shadow cast by his body in front of him.

As he walked through the falling snow on the trail, he kept his head down, focused on putting one foot in front of the other.

Judging by his appearance, he appeared to be a university fellow.

The university stood triumphantly on a hill in front of him, dreaming of the nearby capital on this cloudy evening. From this high vantage point, he could see the river as it twisted and turned through the village, as if in a fairy tale, sending painful reflections into his eyes.

The current structure, which had previously served as a sanatorium in the 18th and 19th centuries, had been renovated for the twenty-first century, transforming it into an educational facility with academic aspirations at its core. Its founder, Don Eusebio Mogueroles, an ardent supporter of traditional educational systems, had intended to give it a special touch of classic patina, or more precisely, British and traditional scholastic practises.

However, there was much more to this educational institution's story than met the eye. After serving as a health center—or, more accurately, a prevention centre to which people flocked to find relief from their ailments—it was eventually transformed into a casino and hotel owned by a certain Baron de la Cost. The elderly baron, according to legend, lost his entire fortune at the casino's gaming table having squandered the rest of his fortune on ladies and speculation in Dutch Guiana—both of them overseas—in a single dizzying spin of the roulette wheel. A spin as fast as fate turns a corner. He had had included his hotel and casino in the final bet in a masterful *tour de force*.

Don Eusebio Mogueroles had achieved his goal, but not without first enduring the wrath of bureaucracy against his own person, without first twisting the university law in force, No. 6/2001. 6/2001, thus eliminating the critical point that ultimately made the institution's existence possible. Unfortunately, he had to leave this world before completing his dream.

His legacy, the Mogueroles Foundation and his initiative, had outlasted him.

Since the previous semester, according to his initial instructions, plans had been in the works for an annual regatta on the river modelled after Oxford and Cambridge. The first one was scheduled to take place the following term.

Given the river's lack of navigability and shallow depth, this was no easy task. However, after lengthy negotiations with the authorities, it was possible to relocate some obstacles and waterfalls on the Arlanzón to create a passage long enough for the event to take place.

When the project was first announced, the renowned creator imagined the cathedral's two spires towering over the trees in resemblance to those of Magdalene College in Oxford. This was, of course, a romantic fantasy given the distance between Montanilla University and the city of Burgos, which made such a sight impossible. Nonetheless, his vision was recorded in a painting that today sits in the office of the present rector, Patricio Noguer, courtesy of his close friend and *amateur* painter, Count Dabrowski.

The walker, lost in thought, had arrived at the Faculty of History building after traversing the gardens and frozen pond. This was another reality, concealed in a wooden outbuilding that looked more like an old Arkansas logging shack than a university academic building. Long corridors ran throughout, and small windows let in light. There was something eerie about the entire place, worthy of future archaeological discoveries over the millennia. The man took a long look around at the snowy landscape. He appeared to be in no hurry, his walk no destination. It was five o'clock in the afternoon, just the right time for his daily walk.

As he stood here, taking in the distant structures, a sense of contentment washed over him. The man's thoughts could have been elsewhere, perhaps in the vastness of an unknown past teeming with planets and chimaeras beyond his comprehension.

He'd also gone for a walk and smoke a pipe, just for the sake of it. Each step he took was deliberate, as if it were a hypothesis to be tested before being put into practise.

From his vantage point, he could also see the central library's long rows of windows and the student dorms in the west wing. He could easily picture them sitting in each of these rooms, heads bowed over their books, just as he had done in the past.

Pigeons perched on the sloping rooftops, covered with mould and wind-blown tree leaves. Beneath their flapping wings, the resident academics—a different kind of bird—sat close to their stoves, their eyes obscured in the faint light of the lamps, hunched like their backs, bowed inwards, rusty like their joints.

He recalled curling up with a book on similar days, listening to the crackle of the nearby stove while snow and rain pelted the window panes outside! He recalled reading texts that had nothing to do with his studies on such evenings. On such a day, he began to read Emily Bronte's *Wuthering Heights*. He'd noticed the resemblance to those windswept wastelands.

The man continued to stare in awe at the sparrows and the occasional thrush scurrying across the grassy glades where the snow had already melted. After years away from the city, this had been an unexpected blizzard. This year had been especially prosperous.

A wall confronted the walker. Boston ivy had moved in and taken over before winter stripped it bare, leaving a creeping, skeletal path on the wall.

Two snow-covered bicycles were leaning against it. They appeared to be dozing off, daydreaming of long walks along seemingly endless highways, a well-filled wicker basket on the front, occasionally containing a philosophy or linguistics book.

On days like these, when he had a lot on his mind, he would walk around the campus in this manner, past the pond and the small temple atop a hill, before crossing the bridge and returning.

He eventually took a pipe from his pocket and struck the bowl on the bridge—the sole purpose of this walk. He filled the pile with the same care he had taken on his stroll, lighting it without regard for the snow. He inhaled the tobacco pouch. The air was filled with a distinct aroma of Virginia-cut tobacco.

Then, and only then, was he prepared to return to his office, having imagined the faraway city of Burgos among the campus's tree-tops. His figure moved through the snow-covered bushes that lined the walkways. Because of his odd gait, crows came to a halt and hopped in small leaps across the grass to investigate him. As soon as they noticed that this strange monster was blowing smoke out of its mouth, they went back to their task.

The walker's shape eventually vanished and merged with the forest.

In this dry and white environment, he appeared to be the last pipe smoker on the planet.

CHAPTER 2

A WALK BY THE RIVER

A student carrying an oar approached him from an adjacent route. A clear indication that he had been rowing on the river.

'Good day, Professor!'

'Ah, Trevelyan, how was the river today? Wasn't it a little breezy out there?'

'Outstanding, Professor! Those two Americans in our team this term will certainly be of help. Burgos University will be no match for us. You know our motto: No time is too valuable for Montanilla students,' he said, resting for a few moments on the bridge.

'I see. Still, the UBU people will continue trying to make the river appear impenetrable,' the professor said. 'Old mindsets cannot be changed by a river victory!'

'It's a great shame, but if they're looking for an excuse to fail in the first regatta between the two schools, they'll certainly find it.' Trevelyan said. 'By the way, you were present at the rowing medal ceremony, weren't you?' Noticing the professor's affirmative nod, he continued, 'Absolutely stunning, isn't it? That Blue Burganda trophy would look great with the rest of my memorabilia in my room. It appears I will have to wait a little longer than expected.'

The difficult rowing in the chilly water had indeed thrilled the student, even though he was clearly exhausted as a result. The boathouse and changing room were one hundred metres behind them, next to the jetty. A few kids were already there, taking off their gear and rubbing their hands together to warm themselves up.

'And how's your French Revolution essay coming along?' the professor inquired.

'Well, I can't say I'm complaining. It's just a slow process, you know. There are days when everything goes smoothly, and others when I'm at a loss for words. By the by, I'd also like to thank you for lending me the book. It's an amazing piece of work! You were right about using literature as a lens through which to examine historical events. I'll certainly never look at the French Revolution the same way again after reading *A Tale of Two Cities*.'

'But don't get too carried away with the romantic aspect of things, Trevelyan; that wasn't the plan either. I simply hoped it would provide you with a broader perspective and a fresh set of eyes to examine data from a different perspective. May I tell you something? Mind you! should this information become public, your grades will suffer greatly.'

'That is not going to happen! I' assure you The young man's laugh sparkled as brightly as the stream he had just left. 'What's the deal, Professor?'

'Well... when I first heard about Napoleon in school, I imagined him as Marlon Brando,' he said. Before proceeding, he waited for his student's reaction. 'Don't laugh, don't laugh. I had just seen a movie in which this actor played the Emperor, and I can honestly say that historical facts took on a whole new meaning for me, one that went beyond the dry facts and dates provided in my textbook, wrapping them in an aura of adventure and mystery. It was as if a switch in my head had been flipped on. The names in my history textbooks had become the names of real people like me. As a result, I continued to watch films based on true events. Dates and names had a mystical allure when viewed through the lens of Hollywood grandeur.'

'Wow, Professor! What a brilliant idea. I never imagined it from this angle. However, it makes sense. Every person should have a life philosophy. Would you be interested in knowing what mine is?'

'Certainly.'

'Are you familiar with the concept of meaningful synchronicity?'

ARTHUR TREVELYAN WAS UNDENIABLE A HANDSOME young man with a brilliant mind. This English boy, coming from somewhere in the Costwolds was certainly one of the best among his students. He had an exceptional ability to think on his feet, was attentive, and demonstrated a strong sense of initiative.

However, the professor noticed some oddities about him from time to time. Despite his best efforts, he couldn't come up with a name for it. He always wore a half-knotted tie, which is an absolute must for a young man. However, because his hair was all over the place, he always appeared to have just rolled out of bed when you first saw him. In other words, he resembled the alter ego created by the professor in his mind.

It was evident that the young man possessed voracious curiosity and contagious zeal, making it difficult to imagine him as a future history professor, let alone a university researcher sitting in front of books for hours on end. But this he did, by combining the study of history books with the study of other, less traditional literature such as esotericism, ancient faiths, and cultures. Several books about the Rosicrucians and the Templars could be prominently displayed in a small library in his rooms.

A group of students of both sexes, well-protected by their woollen jumpers and earmuffs, marched laughing past the bridge where the two of them stood.

'See you later, Arthur,' said a girl with an Argentinian accent, beaming enthusiastically at the young man and greeting the professor in passing.

'Hi there, Camelia! Arthur said, 'See you in Hall.'

Their laughter lingered in the air, their bright eyes filling the void left by their departure.

Was it a well-known person or another academic who said that phrase that the professor remembered? It honestly did not matter. It was something along the lines that the most painful aspect of teaching was the realisation of getting older while students remained the same age. Perhaps this was the only way to discover the fountain of Eternal Youth, which Ponce de Leon was unable to find?

The boathouse and changing room were one hundred metres behind them, next to the jetty.

'See you later, Professor,' the young man murmured, as he glanced at the group of departing girls, adjusting his cap and picking up his oars, before walking towards the boathouse. The professor remained there, watching him walk away. He had battled for a world like this. Certainly, the rector of the university was no saint, but the professor was well aware that there was no perfection in the academic world either, despite a few indications of a few scrapes here and there in his everyday life.

'Oh well, there's always been a devil in paradise!' he exclaimed.

He realised then that he had left a tiny notebook on his desk in class. He decided to go back for it, making good use of the stroll.

Without thinking twice, he reversed the path he had already travelled.

Any delayed student leaving the library at this hour could be startled by the sight of this skinny man in his forties with erect but well-combed hair ambling incoherently through the History Department aisles in the twilight.

His long arms and piercing gaze through his glasses gave him an unsettling appearance. To some, it looked as if he could see into the soul of the person standing before him. Some of his less affable coworkers compared him to a modern-day Faust. However, a curl on his brow defied the order of the rest of his hairstyle, providing him with the much-needed air of human imperfection and dispelling any doubts.

As the professor entered classroom number twelve, a cool neon light illuminated his gaunt form. His desk was bathed in the same light. He carefully extracted the notebook that had prompted his visit.

He raised his eyebrows. He had never been here at this time of day before. The combination of the hour and sunset made the classroom felt a little different.

The rows of seats in front of him, which had only a few hours before been occupied by about forty students, were now empty.

In these modern facilities, Nordic-style benches arranged in symmetrical, clean rows contrasted strikingly with the outside of the building, leaving nothing to chance. Knowledge per square metre. A few volumes were stacked on the professor's table, in stark contrast to this picture of order and cleanliness. Next to them were some notes and markings indicating the progression of knowledge, half-formed thoughts arising from a day's work, and the overwhelming explanations, hypotheses, and data, as if he could revive the facts and deliver them to his students in this manner.

From the windows, he could see tree-lined gardens with benches. This was a popular hangout for students who would spend the first few hours of the day, either seeking or avoiding the sun, depending on the season.

The professor was struck with an odd feeling as soon as he walked into the classroom. Was it the feeling that something was missing or forgotten? He rummaged through his memories but came up empty-handed.

'I am such a fool!' he grumbled, 'I am always obsessed with something.'

As he exited the classroom, he almost bumped into a dark-haired woman of medium build with long hair who was making her way to an office two doors down. On her left arm, she was carrying a pair of green file folders. When she saw him, she performed a military salute by placing two fingers of her right hand on her forehead.

'Good evening, Carlos! Still working?' she inquired before unlocking the door with the magnetic card she was holding in her mouth. Her wide grin spread across her face, giving the professor the impression that the corridor was becoming brighter as she walked down it.

He responded with a barely audible nervous sound that sounded like 'hm... um... hmm' as he walked in the opposite direction, squeezing the keys into the inner pocket of his jacket with some difficulty.

Only a single lamp lit the long corridor. He neglected to flip the master switch. He had learned to appreciate the conspiratorial silence and shadows that this corner of tranquilly offered.

Elena Serna, his colleague with whom he almost bumped in the hallway, was also a professor in paleography, a newcomer from the "other" university, a fact that could not even be whispered on campus without risk of immediate expulsion. She was, without a doubt, a friendly, dedicated, attentive, and warm teacher.

Once the professor reached the first floor, he came to a halt in front of an oak door on which hung a carefully carved sign,

Carlos Lafuente, M.D., Paleography Department.

He entered his PIN, which controlled the door's opening. A

gentle sound rang out, and the door opened gently, giving way to a white cat that jumped out of the room and rubbed against his legs.

The professor's office appeared to be crammed with various scrolls and papers of all kinds. There were books all over the place, covering the walls and lining the shelves in double and even triple rows.

A spiral staircase near the front door led to a small upper room, a tower, with a narrow window at the top in which a coffee pot kept guard. Below the stairs, additional volumes were strewn across the floor, making it necessary to walk a short distance to reach the desk on the opposite side of the room. The volumes even reached the adjoining toilet, which had become completely useless for anything else.

A large window at the back of the room provided a view of the campus and flooded the entire room with light.

The professor had two passions; one, of course, was history; the official one, to be precise. The other was a collection of butterflies that he had meticulously classified and described in detail in a black-bound book tucked away in an old chest of drawers, hidden from all but the closest confidants who had the privilege of being invited home.

Ishmael, his cat, growled slightly when he saw that he was occupied with this task, neglecting the caresses that were his due as the oldest inhabitant of the place. On his flanks, there were some strange patterns: a heart-shaped figure on the right side, and a Mickey Mouse head silhouetted on the other.

That was, indeed, his office. Old paintings, darkened, without light, sunken into corners that Lovecraft would have loved to describe; corners where no cleaning lady, for money or love, would have dared to use a feather duster.

On one of the shelves stood a warrior in armour —an antique passed down from his grandfather—holding up a spear that showed its old golden patina. It had been a book steward for more than one hundred and thirty years and pretended to continue in that capacity for a few more years. A duplicate of this warrior was kept at home.

Sometimes Arthur Trevelyan assisted him in organising and preparing documents entrusted to him for examination. He felt young as he listened to the questions of his student, whose exclamatory gestures at every minor detail he came across made him look more like a participant in a television show than a researcher, a member of the academic tradition of knowledge. He smiled.

But now he was alone. With some disgust, he cast a suspicious glance at the manuscripts he had yet to review. He had been forced to interrupt his work on the essay he had been writing for the international congress on the history of the navy and its relationship to the historical novel, which was set to take place in Valladolid in a few weeks.

All in favour of an egomaniac count who appeared to have sprung from a 19th-century novel character. The wishes of the aristocracy still counted.

He sighed and carefully put on his gloves before taking the magnifying glass in his hand. According to the first information he had received, what he had before him on the table were some apocryphal letters attributed to a thirteenth-century monk, discovered during recent excavations in the village of Silos.

Silos. He remembered the old monastery. That sliver of the Middle Ages that has survived on the earth's surface.

Every time he faced a similar task, he was reminded of Mónica, that girl with the googly eyes, the only fellow student he had dared to date in Santander that distant summer of 1977. Water had overflowed the bridge.

'Why don't you put your books down for an afternoon and act like a normal human being? We could take walk, to the movies, or just hang out like other couples! Watching you flip through your books late into the night is all well and good, but it's not exactly my cup of tea.'

Yes, his two passions had destroyed any chance of love. Sometimes a certain itch boiled up inside him when he thought of Monica, but he drowned it immediately by taking refuge either in his books or butterflies.

The entire academic community was aware of Professor Lafuente's scientific care and attention to his research, as well as his extensive knowledge of palaeographic studies.

Only Mr Noguer cast a shadow over his joy, as he was always on the lookout for more funds from the Mogueroles Foundation. His ambition was to improve the university's infrastructure as well as its academic competitiveness. He insisted on devoting more hours to teaching and less to research. He believed that researchers' relentless pursuit of the Nobel Prize or similar awards would lead to nothing — the moron!

Lafuente thought of his students. Nothing bad could happen if you tried to impart some knowledge to them, could it? His students! Those empty heads who did not see the relevance, the difference between one historical period and another, or the glitter on the horizon of an incomparable figure like Alphonse X, the Wise. But he hoped one day to be able to prove Mr Noguer that he was in the right.

The photograph on the opposite wall revealed something else. There, a butterfly wing, viewed through a microscope, was framed, revealing thousands of veins of coloured scales. It was a picture by photographer Linden Gledhill, another crazy butterfly enthusiast. Lafuente had even attempted to replicate these stunning photographs, going to the extent. He even went so far as to purchase the same microscope as the artist, an Olympus BH2 with that accessory called StockShot. He was fascinated by the thousands of colour fans, patterns, and unrepeatable textures captured by the microscope's light, invisible to the naked eye.

That reminded him of the manuscripts he had to examine that evening and he first time he saw them.

~

CHAPTER 3

THE COMMISSION

When the professor entered Patricio Noguer's office, he found the principal playing absentmindedly with the large wooden globe placed on the right side of his desk. As we said before Count Dabrowski, son of Russian immigrants and a great admirer of art, frequently invited to the rector's official occasions, had decorated the office with a breathtaking landscape that hung on the wall opposite the window. The image, inspired by the works of the Romantic painter Caspar David Friedrich, depicted a few strollers in the foreground of a modern university campus. The cathedral's towers could be seen rising in the background, behind the curvature of a meandering Arlanzón. This provided a magical touch and compensated for the fact that neither the people who built the city nor the land itself had had the courtesy to make this perspective attainable in the current world. 'Lafuente, the result of your report must be submitted to National Heritage in a timely manner,' the rector began 'If at all possible, prior to the end of the term. It's necessary to assess whether or not the count is the rightful owner of the documents. To the best of my knowledge, he intends to auction them at a Sotheby's.'

'Considering how much research and restoration work has been done on the monastery so far, it's really remarkable these writings had not been unearthed before,' Lafuente replied.

'Professor, surprises are the norm in our field. You should know that without my telling you so. Silos is and will remain a shining treasure. But I'm not going to waste any more of your time. It is limited, and I expect you to make an effort.'

No doubt the fact that Don Patricio's brother-in-law held a key position within the National Heritage had not been a trivial consideration when entrusting Montanilla University with the responsibility of examining the manuscripts. It should be taken into account, as the rector himself would have suggested.

The professor leaned back in his chair and pondered this new assignment.

What he had in front of him at this moment was relatively insignificant. A small wooden box, almost completely rotten inside of which lay a few scrolls of a yellowish colour. On their surfaces, pale characters stood out, in the same amber colour as the box they had been in. It was evident that only with patience and the use of appropriate material could any light be cast on them. A manuscript was already stretched across the surface of the desk. A worn-out notepad stood next to it, neither digital in design nor content, but equally useful. It could be transported anywhere without concern for battery life or harsh sunshine obscuring the display. On its pages, in dense handwriting, barely perceptible to the naked eye, was the laborious reconstruction of the half-erased text.

The professor carefully removed a new parchment from the box, being cautious not to expose it to the chemical products that had been strewn on the desk in an attempt to restore the more severely damaged pieces.

A cursory examination with the magnifying glass revealed that its condition was fairly good. It appeared to be an old chronicle. He set it down and took up another piece of parchment. On it he noticed a laboriously illuminated text under a capital "K."

It only took the professor a quick look to ascertain it was an old story about Princess Kristina of Norway, the daughter of King Haakon IV of Norway and Margot Skulesdatter, of the royal line of Sverre.

Kristina.

The legend was filled with romance and passionate overtones. However, the reasons for the princess's visit to Spain differed depending on which historiographical sources one might read. It was generally believed that the princess had passed away not more than a few years after marrying one of Alfonso X's brothers.

There was one line of text in the margin, very close to the bottom of the page. Contrary to the rest of the parchment, written in Old Castilian, this line appeared in Latin. Perhaps this had been done to ensure its contents were not forgotten? For some, Old Castilian was considered a transient or ephemeral language. Or was this a way to keep it from being read by prying eyes not familiar with the old language?

A simple phrase. One line, clear and short, which, in his opinion, rendered the Latin translation unnecessary,

> "May the Brethen continue to guard the sacred mystery
> of the Flower of the North."

Nothing very remarkable. Due to her youth, the princess was sometimes referred to as "the girl from the north."

The lamp's light threw Professor Lafuente's shadow on the back wall, stretching it to the ceiling, thus creating an ominous atmosphere in the room.

There was another paragraph in the margin. At first glance and based on the variable intensity of the strokes, it appeared to have been written by a different hand in a different ink. He took a closer look. Yes, the calligraphic style of shaping particular consonants. Despite the fact that ink tones were distinct, they were remarkably similar. It was most likely written at the same period, or a few years later, at most:

"Quodam frate vel sorpresa insigniter auxiliante Quoque obvenient, cuius."

His years of Latin study—under the tutelage of that curly-headed professor nicknamed "Caligula" by his students due both to his subject matter and physical appearance—bore fruit in this translation,

"It will be easier to find meaning with the qualified support of a brother readily available and quick to respond."

Or something along those lines. An odd place to use such jargon. Carlos reviewed the passage and compared it to another sentence in the same folio.

His interest was attracted by some words written in gothic characters,

"At the prime hour, from light will come light."

And further down,

"Whoever desires to see another letter will see it; whoever can tell the difference between day and night will have eyes to view God's writing."

What exactly did that mean? Where was the connection with the previous lines?

A little below he could read,

"The Virgin Mary is cleaned by the Sun while she sits in her temple."

And finally, the closing words,

"Master Johannes will fix it."

There was no doubt. An academic game of Cluedo was at play here. A second opinion on the matter was required. The image of his colleague Elena immediately sprang to mind; but he was too hesitant to ask for aid, but Elena was the best palaeographer he had ever encountered.

CHAPTER 4
PATRICIO NOGUER

Not far from there, unknowing of Professor Lafuente's plight, Patricio Noguer toiled along on his bicycle across a snow-free area that, concealed behind the hills, surrounded the tranquillity of the old buildings.

He did this on a daily basis to ward off the ghost of old age. He tried, if only for a little while, to relive his days as an Oxford student, when, cycling across the English countryside with his pals, used to carry a fine bottle of Chateau d'Armignon or de la Motte in a wicker basket.

Throughout those years, he had retained a sense of persistence and tenacity, as well as a strong resolve.

It was rumoured however that he had also retained a certain excess of liquids, considering his obese figure.

His bike came to a halt at the start of an unnamed trail. It was the same one that Professor Lafuente had taken moments before in his smoking and meditative mood.

With a certain a sense of arrogance in his gaze, he inspected the reddish tinted lettering and the distinctive university logo that exhibited a coat of arms. This was not surprising, as he had given precise orders for its placement at this particular location, five metres from the road to be precise.

After a run of futile employments, the inheritance of an old tutor from his boyhood, for whom he had immense affection, had a profound effect on his life. Soon after, he reencountered one of his classmates from his salad days, now a respected member of the elite Mogueroles Trust. As a result, he became the most ardent and unwavering supporter of the founder's ideals. He was now in the midst of the university expansion project that Mr Mogueroles had suggested when he formed the Trust.

The main structure, built in the early 1900s, had been extensively renovated with new paint and electrical and plumbing systems. The nearby countryside, formerly farmland, had been added into the campus after an unwelcome redesign. This had been made possible not only thanks to the foundation's efforts, but also to the support of the local government.

Weeping willows split the neoclassical and neogothic chapels on an artificial hill in this area of the campus.

Those at the nearby Burgos University, scoffed on the other hand at the idea, claiming it was ridiculous to create an institution so far from the city centre. Others however stated that this was due to the resentment of those who had been turned down in the examinations for resident professorships five years ago.

Whatever the case, Patricio Noguer had an unwavering belief in re-creating the British academic paradigm, even this was done a bit extravagantly. Perhaps it was a bizarre concept, but stimulating nonetheless. Neither the currently vilified traditional values nor the Hispanic heritage itself would be harmed.

Didn't past British colonies, such as Hong Kong, have similar cultural relics? Didn't the local culture remain solid and steady, yielding such a remarkable outcome—not to mention the aesthetic effect of witnessing schoolchildren with oriental faces emerging from neogothic churches?

CHAPTER 5

AN ARTISTIC APPRECIATION

Holding a cup of tea, Elena Serna stood in front of the portrait hanging in her workplace admiring the artwork. She loved the cloud formations that appeared in it; the way they encircled and wrapped the terrain, the houses, the structures, the odd bridge, and the mill by the river.

She loved Constable's skilful incorporation of meteorological phenomena into his painting. She had had this copy framed, especially for this place... She was unable to tear her eyes away from it. At the bottom of the frame, the name and year: *The Hay Wagon, 1821.* She would have loved to enter it like a modern-day Alice in order to discover what was behind the house depicted on it, to inquire about the shepherd's day. Perhaps also to ask the ox-driver where he had acquired such magnificent specimens. The young professor longed for the feeling of being enveloped in this deceptive light, witnessing these cloud patterns. It was at moments like these that her father's words came to mind:

"You should have studied Fine Arts instead of ancient history."

But she perceived, if you will, an aesthetic hidden inside the pages of history itself. She was enthralled by the everlasting connection between past and present. Of course, she could always pursue her second interest and even combine the two, as she had done in several of her publications, namely *The Mediaeval Art* and *The Roman Forum in Art,* both of which had recently been published by Arlanzón Press.

Elena's office was a world apart from Professor Lafuente's. A collection of books bound in leather and fabric stood out with gusto on a white lacquered shelf the focal point of the room. The upper volumes could be reached through a ladder easy at hand. Had Professor Lafuente been present while Elena was so engrossed in the Constable picture-and should painting have been his passion, which it was not, he could have noticed a resemblance between the delicate curves of Elena's face and Johaneesnes Van der Meer's paintings. Perhaps he would have also discovered in her face an absolute brilliance emerging from an odd place that poets such as Wordsworth or Coleridge would not have hesitated to place in the light of setting suns. At that precise moment, it bore an striking resemblance to the renowned artist's masterpiece, *The Young Girl with the Pearl,* should the lady in the portrait had worn her hair down to her shoulders instead of pulling it back into a bun like we are used to seeing her. Paradoxically, true beauty is seldom aware of itself. Perhaps that is as it should be, another of its mysterious components.

However, as things stood, her profile and the clear gaze of her eyes, the exquisite slope of her nose from root to tip, and her golden cheekbones were orphaned and unappreciated from the outside that afternoon. There are times when beauty, like the paintings in a museum after it closes for the day, takes a retreat into itself, yet don't losing its essence, existing outside the more or less vain appraisal of the outer world.

Elena regarded her work as her most valuable asset. With this goal in mind, she had remodelled and outfitted her large office. Her intention had been to create the most relaxing environment possible, reflecting its new use as a private study or living room. When she wasn't hanging out with her friends Alberto and Sonia at art galleries, she spent much of her time here.

In the words of Virginia Woolf, it had taken her a long time to finally be able to state that she had "a room of her own" after growing up in a modest household with three brothers. This had been crucial both for her and the British author to gain a foothold in the world. The fireplace behind her validated that.

She had worked previously for several years in an optician's shop in her hometown. Then, one day, out of the blue, she decided to study history after reading a book that moved her deeply, becoming eventually one of the youngest palaeographers in the country.

A knock shook her out of her trance-like state. With regret, she placed the cup of Horniman's red tea down and turned her attention to the door.

'Come in!' she said resignedly. Perhaps a student who needed tutoring or a change in the direction of his work.

Instead, Professor Lafuente's head appear from behind the door. She would never get used to the unexpected intrusion of her peculiar colleague into her inner sanctum. Although this annoyed her a little at first, she quickly got used to it when she realised that he had the same passion and dedication for research as she did.

'Wow! I thought you were shut away in your office working on your enigmatic manuscripts. How are you doing? What ever happened to your one-of-a-kind Watson? '

'That's precisely what I wanted to talk to you about, Elena,' Lafuente said. 'Are you busy right now or should I come back later?'

'I was just about to have some tea. Would you like some? '

'No, no, thank you very much. Nonetheless, Elena, I have something to show you, though,' he replied gruffly, without looking up, as if the pattern on the floor were of the utmost importance to him.

It didn't take him long to choose an armchair by the window with rose embroidery and sit opposite her. The seat was next to a side table, where the kettle and tea service had been placed. The professor assumed an unconcerned posture and a cavalier air, as if the thought of sitting in this precise spot had been only an isolated, anecdotal event, like the many vicissitudes of history, the final consequence of a battle that hinges on one last decision, one last haughty gesture. The truth was that as soon as he had entered the room, he had checked noticing the spot nearest to the fireplace, the only one he longed for, making it appear as if everything had been an afterthought.

The river bend and the weeping willows could be seen from that vantage point.

Carlos Lafuente admired his colleague, but not even among three people could elicit this truth from him. One of Elena's former colleagues at the "other" institution referred to her as a "hinge" professor, meaning she had got her education in accordance with one curriculum but forced to use her teaching skills in a completely different one as the professors newly arrived to Montanilla were expected to conduct research in their first term.

Elena had a vast knowledge of the thirteenth and fourteenth centuries, as evidenced by some of her recent publications, such as *The Calf of Illuecas*. The only "but" in their relationship was her systematic refusal to listen to the professor if he so much as hinted at wanting to discuss the most recent Lepidopterus he had acquired, or, even worse, attempted to show her a photograph of it.

In such situations, she used to remember she had a last-minute appointment or simply declined the invitation by using the shortest approach possible: the practical and quick method of ignoring the question, as if it had never been uttered.

'Now, what do you think?' he said gruffly as he opened his black notebook and flipped to the page where the translation he had made a moment before could be read alongside the rest of the cryptic phrases.

Elena glanced at the contents that lay before her. She opened her eyes shifting her gaze from the note in the book to his colleague.

' I'm assuming it refers to the manuscripts you're reviewing, right? Well, I must admit it sounds delicious, even poetic, but what makes it so special? I must admit though the use of the term "prime hour" is intriguing in this context. It was used by monks to refer to the portion of the day between the hours of Lauds and Tercia.'

'Have you ever heard the story of Princess Kristina of Norway? And the way she arrived Spain to marry Alfonso X the Wise in order to establish an alliance between the two kingdoms?'

'Well, read about it in my varsity years. I know some of the facts, as does everyone in Burgos, to be sure' Elena said with her usual modesty, brushing her hair out of her face. 'I think even some of my old colleagues from Burgos University—well, from the other university—have written something about it.' Here she looked over her shoulder upon realising she had uttered the forbidden name. 'And what if the purpose of the trip to Spain had been motivated by something other than marriage? What if it had been something else?' questioned the professor.

'Well, to be honest, if it was something else, we will never know for the very reason you just pointed out: there are hardly any chronicles. And the Codex Frisianus appears to be the most reliable of them.'

'And don't you find it odd that these manuscripts in which her name is mentioned were discovered in or near Silos monastery? Could there not be there another chronicle containing additional information?'

Elena looked at Carlos. She had learned to identify those moments in which her colleague spoke with deep conviction, when the certainty of a concept reached him to the core. This was a well-known fact among the rest of the faculty members. When this happened, once a certain theory had taken possession of him in this way, awakened the academic beast that dwelt in him, nothing in the world but a stone wall could stop the professor. Twilight seemed to bathe the scene in unreality and he bend in the river frozen in time. Elena had the sudden feeling that the outside world had turned into a wintry landscape painting by Constable or Van der Mer, strange light pouring through half-open doors.

'Do you truly want me to tell you what I think?' Elena finally said.

'Yes, please. I am very interested in hearing your professional opinion.'

'I believe we would need more tea,' said Elena, standing up and fetching the kettle beside her.

~

THE ENTRANCE TO THE DINING HALL WAS FLANKED BY TWO massive stone pots standing on either side of the big gates.

Upon reaching the top of the stone stairwell after having waited by the balustrade for the doors to be opened, both the resident professors and students entered the building in an orderly manner.

There were three long rows of tables in the spacious hall.

The pupils sat down, silently perusing the menu cards placed in front of each chair, sincerely hoping against hope that broccoli or veggies would not be prominent that day. They heaved a quiet sigh when they realised their expectations had been dashed once again.

Some encouragement came from the Hispanic waiters, well aware of what the students were going through.

'Today's dessert is simply delicious,' said Rosa, a pleasant Mexican girl who had only been working there for a few months. 'If you behave, I'll bring you an extra helping!'

On an elevated platform at the other end of the dining hall, and away from these academic intrigues, in the middle of the long table reserved for the fellows, sat Elena and Carlos Lafuente. In a prominent place behind them was a large, faded portrait of the founder, with the school's motto written below it,

Et in Arcadia Ego.

Patricio Noguer had chosen it due to his passion for Evelyn Waugh's work, *Brideshead Revisited.*

'Please, should they serve you duck, would you kindly give me some so I can keep your secret to the grave or until the end of time, whichever comes first?' Elena said, a twinkle in her eye.

Lafuente grimaced as he gestured for his companion to lower her voice.

'Something occurred to me last night,' said Carlos. 'Something to do with... well, you know.'

After that, he fell silent, fixing his gaze on his plate. He appeared to have lost track of his prepared remarks.

'Well?' said Elena, placing her cutlery on the table and pushing aside the dish of soup to make way for the salmon and meatballs that followed the first course against Virginia Woolf's dire predictions on the matter.

'I apologise, but this is so bizarre... Have you ever heard of the theory of significant coincidences?'

'You mean in a completely different sense from what we mean by coincidence, don't you? Because I do not believe you have put on that mysterious and absent face for an elementary school subject.'

'No, no, of course not. Carl Gustav Jung wrote about it as you know. In his daily life, coincidences like this happened frequently. Things walking down the street, thinking about an old friend you haven't seen in twenty years only to run into him as you turn a corner; or thinking about a book or a memory, only to find that same information in a store window a few minutes or hours later.'

'Yes, I remember hearing something similar. Wasn't he the same who wrote about the beetle in the window? Yes, I do remember now. He was consulting with a patient who was describing him a bizarre dream involving a beetle with extraordinary wings. Jung heard a noise at the window, and when he approached to shut it, this very insect was on the sill.'

'Yes, that's it, Elena. I am glad you remember.'

'And what triggered this reflection *ex tempora*, my dear colleague?'

The professor's response was cut short by the sight of Don Patricio walking up towards them, halting and placing on the table the Diario de Burgos he had been reading minutes earlier.

'How is the research on the manuscripts coming along, Professor Lafuente? Any advances?'

'Yes, I hope so, Mr Noguer. In fact, I would like to inform you about something I found in them.'

'Is that so?' he said it with little enthusiasm, looking at his watch as if his personal agenda could be found there. 'In that case, come to my office tomorrow after class and tell me all about it. But please, do not come later. I have an appointment in Burgos at noon.'

'Do not worry, Mr Noguer. I will be there.'

The rector nodded gravely after this brief conversation and, without saying another word, stepped down from the podium and walked to the door with the movements of a contented squirrel, greeting a colleague here and there and disappearing through the gate as if it were a burrow.

'THE MANUSCRIPTS COULD BE FRAGMENTS, A PART OF THOSE existing in the monastery, lost fragments' —repeated Carlos Lafuente noticing the rector seemed to be swimming in deep thoughts while he had been making his explanations for the last ten minutes. He appeared to be looking with excessive interest at the globe in front of him— 'after all, as you yourself said, we must be sure beyond any doubt whether or not they belong to the looting of documents that the monastery suffered at the end of the 19th century. That reference appearing in them, "to the brothers", « could well point in that direction.

His interlocutor listened absently, assenting now and then to Professor Lafuente's explanations. His right hand slid automatically between the pages of the book by his side, *The Fall of the Roman Empire* by Gibbons, a volume that he liked to reread from time to time listening with special glee to the sound it produced when deposited on the table.

During this exchange of words Elena had been hiding behind the large globe that occupied such a special place in the office, a silent witness attempting to remain unnoticed.

'I sincerely believe that if we could examine some of the manuscripts kept in Silos, we would certainly find one written by the same hand,' said Lafuente.

'Well,' said the rector, nodding in agreement and clearing his throat. 'Going to Silos seems like a brilliant idea, anyway. It's something to behold! Something to behold'—here he stopped relishing the sound of his own words—. 'Surely we could benefit from greater recognition in such places. We could be at the same level as those at Burgos University, you know. Find a niche there and in similar places. Our research presence needs to be felt, no question about that. By the way, I met the former Silos abbot only a few months ago and made him aware of our interest in all aspects of the monastery.'

He sank into his chair after saying this and retrieved a cigar from an ebony box that stood in front of him, preciously decorated with Hindu motifs. He regarded it with a calm, possessive gaze, enjoying the front's exquisite craftsmanship, which featured an elephant deftly guided by a mahout perched atop the box.

'Would you like one?' he offered. 'Sorry, it's just a habit. I'll never get used to the fact that you are an avid pipe smoker and that the lady here dislikes them.' He shrugged, unable to relate to these classical teachers. They belonged to a different species.

He examined the cigar, twisted it between his fingers, and snipped off the tip.

'However, I do not want you to abandon the job you have been preparing before the appearance of these texts. You know, the Valladolid Congress is less than a month away, and you have done excellent work on the history of the Navy in relation to classical literature. Your idea in the last congress of presenting the life stories of every sailor who boarded along Juan Sebastian El Cano was particularly appealing. Oh, that human touch! The memory of that circumnavigation deserves it. Such a good idea to bring it up!'

'Thank you very much, Don Patricio. Don't you worry! I am sure the paper will be ready by then.'

'Fantastic, wonderful! And remember, professor Lafuente that we are dealing with a decisive issue here,' he grunted, leaning against the stone fireplace in a casual way, 'Time, dear Professor Lafuente, time! Please allow me to reiterate that point. These manuscripts were lent to us for a brief period of time. Only two days ago, Count Dabrowski inquired again about the progress of the case.'

'Wow! That really is throwing coal into the machinery. But I am aware of course that to the outside world, the myth still prevails we labour without pressure and slouch lethargically over our books.'

'Do not believe a single word of it! The Mogueroles Trust is likewise exerting pressure on me over the outcome of the analysis. No need to remind you that the initial plan was not to pursue any leads, or "clues", as you so elegantly suggest. But if you want to look around here and there, I recommend you to take advantage of the opportunities provided by the monastery itself through the use of its hostelry. You could make it that way better use of your time and avoid travel expenses. It is worth considering. Obviously, I do not need to inform you that Professor Elena must remain at her post, you know. The term has practically started already, and someone will have to take care of your classes in your absence while you play Indiana Jones. Take with you, if you will, that one-of-a-kind student, this Roberto or Ricardo, I believe his name is.'

'Arthur' His name is Arthur Trevelyan,' Lafuente ventured to correct.

'Maybe he'll learn a thing or two, that is, assuming you can get him out of the water and leave the oars behind.' He made a face that was meant to be a smile before continuing. 'And you know, please stick to the research budget and not the one meant for the royals.'

'Of course, Don Patricio. We will certainly do that. Thank you very much.' Then he caught Elena's gaze. She shrugged, somewhere above the North Pole and behind the wooden globe where she had been hiding. She had properly interpreted her colleague's look as the palaeographer she was; it was necessary to flee this office before a counter-order arrived. Elena understood the limitations of her work and she would not be the one to answer back the big man.

~

CHAPTER 6

OF FAR AWAY LANDS

How Arthur heard a fairy tale one winter afternoon.

Arthur and the professor were at the campus temple. They were seated on one of the stone seats that lined the structure's perimeter. The view encompassed distant trees, the main buildings, the entire campus, and the back gardens.

This temple was a duplicate of the famous one in Munich's Englischer Garten, following a commission by the founding patron. The sole witnesses to their conversation were some distant treetops at dusk that resembled a fading landscape sketch.

'Well, Trevelyan, you are a grown-up student by now, so I have no choice but to tell you a fairy tale to finish up your education. Actually, it's more of a princess tale. Unfortunately it lacks any Disney flavour. To get to the heart of the matter, let's take ourselves to the Lord's year of 1256. To top it off, we could even say, "It was the year of the Lord of 1256," thus enhancing the tone of the statement, as you are after all a man of letters.' After noticing Arthur's astonishment, he added, 'So far, so good! At the time, King Haakon of Norway deemed it expedient to arrange a marriage of convenience between his second daughter Kristina and Alfonso X, named the Wise, King of Castile.

The latter was much in need of an heir to the throne of Castile. Remember that, thanks to the Pope's intercession, Alfonso had every chance of becoming the next Holy Roman Emperor. The princess was gorgeous, blonde, and tall, Arthur. We still remain within the boundaries of tradition here. I am aware that I am not really original, but please be patient; we are getting there. Her entourage included numerous Norwegian knights, among them the ambassador of the king, Lodinn Nepur, Bishop Peter of Hamar and a number of ladies-in-waiting. All of them accompanied by an amazing dowry of jewels, relics, and furs.'

Arthur and the professor were at the campus temple

The professor paused before continuing: 'The journey took so long, however that by the time Kristina appeared before the king, Queen Violante of Aragon had already given the monarch that much-needed son. Therefore, he chose to continue his marriage, and had the princess married to one of his brothers instead. Thus, one of the numerous versions of the saga was created. Her only solace was that she was able to choose her husband among the King of Castile's brothers.'

'Blimey!' Trevelyan added in a quiet voice, still visualising that remote Nordic country, 'It certainly sounds intriguing.'

It was easy for him to become engrossed in the story, owing in no small part to the chill he felt due to the recent snowfall.

'The worst was still to come, though, Arthur. According to the majority of chronicles, the princess died of melancholy in Seville, three years after her arrival to Spain. She is buried in Covarrubias, a small village not very far from here. Sometimes endings are like this, you know, and in this specific case, there was no special drama, no dragons or crossing of swords involved.'

Despite the professor's somewhat caustic and mocking tone, the student thought he had detected a note of grief in his voice.

Arthur looked then at the remains of the ivy that had once covered the columns of the temple. The creeper had left signs of its growth all over the treetops, colouring them with autumnal hues before departing till spring. This gave the scene the appropriate framing, that ochre and bright tone that is often found in stories of this nature.

CHAPTER 7

IN CUSTODY OF THE BRETHEN

How palaeographic research is compatible with gardening, wine appreciation, and croissants for breakfast.

It was a frigid morning when the tiny green Volkswagen T-Cross parked in front of Silos Monastery, after having traversed the La Yecla gorge, rich in natural caverns and hidden corners that speleologists, those natural palaeographers, diligently investigate.

The vehicle entered through an unexpected alley and traversed these calm alleys, flanked on one side by old stone homes and on the other by the ancient monastery walls, which seemed to be part of the hamlet itself.

The small vehicle proceeded slowly through the streets, its occupants mesmerised by some unusual trees in a park close to the monastery; trees with gnarled branches as a result of a winter that had stripped their structure refusing to leave without leaving its mark.

The driver searched for a parking spot. He eventually discovered on a little esplanade outside the monastery's gates, which, by its emptiness at that hour, seemed to entice strangers to enter this hidden location.

Two figures descended, slowly and silently, from the car. After closing the vehicle doors, they stared at the wall surrounding the venerable building. These were none other than Carlos Lafuente, followed by Trevelyan, his palaeographic shadow, an extraordinary witness in an investigation that was confusing at best.

TWO DAYS BEFORE, LAFUENTE HAD ASKED HIS PUPIL TO COME TO his office. There, after a half-hour of tutorial, the professor remained silent. Finally, he revealed his plans for his trip to Silos.

'Let me recap, professor.' Trevelyan paused while staring Lafuente in the eye without blinking. 'Are you asking me to stop preparing for my upcoming essay and examinations, as well as my training for the boat race? You propose instead that I accompany you for a few days to Silos Monastery in quest of ancient manuscripts stored there. Am I right?'

Carlos Lafuente shifted in his seat uncomfortably. Hearing the repercussions of eliminating one of the brightest pupils from his daily assignment did not reassure him and made the concept seem completely absurd.

'Are you aware of what you are requesting from me? To leave my books,' Arthur continued, 'the lamp in my room, the university routine, and everything else, in order to spend a few days studying the past, old buildings and tales, hunting for any trace left by a mysterious monk on a piece of parchment from centuries ago? Oh, I forgot to mention it! All that regarding a distant princess virtually unknown' and after a brief pause, the young man abruptly rose from his chair, and shook Lafuente's hand:

'Count me in, professor!'

Lafuente remained seated, looking at Arthur as if his pupil had gone bonkers. He was unable to suppress the smile that begun to form on his face.

ONLY A FEW DAYS HAD ELAPSED SINCE THE PROFESSOR CALLED the monastery to request permission to conduct research there. That morning, a muffled voice had mumbled "monastery" into the receiver as the only greeting and information in response to the call. The word had been uttered in a terse manner, as if the person who answered the phone had been cut off in the middle of ardent and concentrated prayer.

Perhaps it was his way of forewarning them that they were about to enter another age, another dimension.

As directed, they had reserved rooms at the monastery inn, a modern construction meant to reconcile the modern world with the isolation and religiosity of the place.

'Ready?' said Lafuente as he slammed the trunk shut after extracting the two little suitcases they had brought along.

'Ready!' answered Trevelyan, as he adjusted his tie with a broad smile that did not conceal his uneasiness, or rather his concern for the future of the trip.

They approached the main gates after this brief exchange of words, leaving the car on the esplanade. Some distinguished architect had built it under the false misconception that it was a happy combination of parking and playground.

Perhaps it was the frigid morning, the puff of frosty air from his mouth, or the fact that the season had changed dramatically since his first visit to the monastery years ago, but Arthur was shocked by a weird sensation: the sense of being in the wrong place.

Sometimes we do experience something similar when, heading to work, all the usual chores done, we feel something has been left unfinished, pending. Perhaps it is merely a past-due payment, an errand, or an upcoming task, or perhaps it is only a phone call; in any case, a feeling we cannot put a label on.

He shrugged.

Both walked in silence, appreciating the privilege of being in that place. Right there.

The St Domingo Inn was located at number 5 on St Domingo Street. It was a dead-end alley, with that excess of imagination that those responsible for the nomenclature of street maps usually squander between two substantial stone structures, as were practically all of the other buildings in the village, acting as a natural link between the outside world and the concealed realm represented by the monastery.

Before entering the inn, the professor wiped the bowl of his pipe with a wistful expression. He knew it would be a long time before he could use it or feel it in his hands again. In both the guesthouse and the monastery, smoking was prohibited. That information had clearly come along with the brochure.

The only furniture in their rooms were a crucifix placed at the head of the bed, a narrow wardrobe, and a wooden table with a white telephone placed near the window. Unfortunately, the cloudy glass prevented them from seeing the sky through it. Nonetheless, the comforting company of a radiator on such a day was certainly cause for gratitude.

Carlos had perused in the past few days with particular envy the brochure of the other inn located in the old St Francisco Convent. It had been recently purchased by the Silos monastery itself and had preserved its former name as well as a Booking web page listing. The brochure featured images of the hotel's elegant rooms and huge lobby. The professor had been forced to settle for the most humble accommodation in St Domingo in order to comply with the rector's directions about their academic budget.

'Getting out of here and spending the day in the library will be incredibly stimulating,' sighed Arthur as he surveyed his room before throwing his suitcase onto the bed.

When they arrived at the monastery's main gates half an hour later they were greeted by a prominently displayed poem on a wall next to the ticket counter, bearing the eloquent title "To the Silos Cyprus."

Perhaps encouraged by its presence in that location, Trevelyan—more prone to literary ecstasy than his mentor—recalled the poems of Gerardo Diego, who had sung to that same cypress tree and felt compelled to recite a few of them aloud:

Vertical source of shadow and dream
Your spear disturbs the sky in this manner.
Cypress both smooth and silent.
From the pond, depict your imposing figure.

'How about getting a little serious, Arthur?' said the professor with a disapproving tone in his voice, not very given to his pupil's poetic ramblings.

'I'm sorry, I guess I got carried away by the place,' Arthur blushed.

After the first formalities, they proceeded to the lower cloister and, more specifically, the chapter house. Since ancient times, monks had gathered there with the abbot to discuss the management of the monastery and its daily operations.

The professor surveyed his surroundings for several minutes.

'Trevelyan, could you imagine for a moment that time in 1835, when the abbot, against his will had to gather the monks in order to send them to the diaspora? Likewise, he was forced to abandon monastic life here.'

'It must have been painful,' Trevelyan said, looking first at the ground and then around him.

'"Painful" is the very word. When one sees this, infected by this apparent calm and estrangement from the world, if you allow me to use the easy topic, it's hard to believe that life can find its way into its nooks and crannies. History is not a fixed thing in a book. Here people suffered, yearned for, and pursued the same things we do today.'

'Love, work, and health,' recited his companion on the run without thinking, repeating the lyrics of a well-known song.

At that hour of the morning, the old cypress appeared to be guarding the cloister, shading the cultural heritage contained within the monastery walls, within its branches. Even though there was no monk present at that moment, the tree was sufficient to command respect and silence.

Carlos quietly turned and walked a few steps toward the end of the old cloister. Trevelyan was so absorbed in a distant bas-relief that he didn't realise he was missing until he heard the professor calling him from a distance,

'Trevelyan, you have to view this. Come here, if you please!'

The lanky professor was pointing to a corner near the exit door for tourists. Some of them had already entered the place, heads bowed, camera in hand, ready for a quick and urgent selfie, transmitting that transgressive WhatsApp on their smartphones. Others frowned upon the professor as he passed and paused among them, preventing many magnificent photographs from being taken in front of the lower cloister reliefs. The professor seemed to stay away from any circumstance other than his train of thought. Trevelyan arrived to the spot with some embarrassment. Lafuente kept triumphantly pointing to a spot on the wall.

'Take a look at that, and please don't tell me that our ancestors weren't farsighted!'

"Do you mean those stripes?'

'Pay more attention, please! Otherwise, I will begin to doubt if your last-term essay was yours or copied from that rascal Meseguer. As you know, when the monastery was built, paper was unthinkable as an instrument to draw or plan anything. So the workers used any surface in its place, any! In this case, they used the wall itself to trace the design. It was like a draught to be cleaned up later—the mediaeval equivalent of a blueprint. You see, the design itself corresponds to the very door in front of us.'

'History never ceases to amaze me! Behind any daily explanation, it seems always to be another, other meaning besides the expected,' Arthur replied in admiration, placing his hand on the wall.

'That's right! Isn't it so? These little things, these tiny details, are the ones that humanise a place like this. Here we see the genuine, human effort, not of supermen, not of an amorphous entity building these monasteries, but of actual people, like you or me. People who would sit here for a quick snack or a tiny pause from their building efforts. And now, let us visit the library! The days awaiting us are going to be crucial ones,' said the professor.

'I see this is going to be a long ride,' Trevelyan mumbled before rejoining Professor Lafuente.

THE LIBRARY.

The word itself appeared sparse and hollow; a mere word compared to what their eyes beheld upon reaching the upper cloister.

This location contained one of the access doors. Carlos Lafuente had repeatedly heard about this place from other colleagues who had consulted, researched, or catalogued its numerous manuscripts. Nevertheless, his expectations had not adequately prepared him for this. Behind that seemingly innocuous door, he found himself atop a staircase, presiding over a vast room surrounded by books. The atmosphere seemed almost sacred and religious. It was a path to the world of intellect and introspection.

Wood dressed that splendid room—one place of worship within another. On the opposite wall, they could see more stairs leading up to two higher levels, similar to the one they were standing on. Some fortunate bookworms were carefully examining the winding mountains of books already stacked on the tables.

A Christ against a black background dominated the entire learning space. At his feet stood a smaller virgin carved in wood, and immediately beneath these two, and protected by them, several voluminous codices lined up on a special shelf.

The rest of that spacious space resembled the nave of a church. Two additional floors comprised the entire nave, presided over by the two figures previously described, occupying the upper portion of the staircase on which they stood, the place of an imaginary pulpit.

They quietly descended the stairs.

After introducing themselves, they were told to wait for the head librarian.

On the opposite wall they could see a wooden door with a semi-circular arch and the word "Library" emblazoned across its entire upper outline.

A central skylight resembling an inverted pyramid allowed for the passage of diffuse light.

The door at the top of the upper cloister gallery reopened, and a monk with solemn expression descended like a lizard seeking knowledge.

'This place would never fail to impress me,' Lafuente whispered, 'no matter how often I returned. The best ancient copyists and illuminators of antiquity worked in the scriptorium! There was even a goldsmith workshop dedicated to the creation of liturgical objects and other items, and that without counting the many craftsmen who gathered here!'

Arthur noticed a particular spiral staircase at the other end of the long room resembling an elegantly folded DNA helix. Higher up, some books were perched precariously near the skylight, as if they were attempting to cling to the wooden beams that supported the ceiling. Volumes too large to fit on the lower shelves occupied some of these. They seemed to have reached the highest level of evolution within the library. The student could see that the lower levels still had some gaps in them.

Wood dressed that splendid room—one place of worship within another.

They noticed then that the monk who had descended the stairs so quickly minutes before was now occupied with a photocopier near the main entrance. A young priest stood behind him with appropriate Benedictine patience, awaiting the delivery of the material being printed. The image reminded Arthur of a priest and a choirboy attending the beginning of a silent mass in front of a few parishioners who, seated instead of kneeling, might be deeply immersed in inner prayer.

''Here you are then' he said finally, giving the printed material to the young priest 'and please tell Father Rufino to be careful with his eyes. He should go out for a walk now and then.'

After the young priest had disappeared through the arched door, the monk librarian —for such was indeed the newcomer's identity—, remained motionless for a few more seconds, arranging the remaining pages in his hands with parsimony and care. He was was ready to face the researchers.

'Good morning, gentlemen. I am Fray Anselmo,' he said,

addressing the professor while avoiding eye contact with the young man standing by his side. To be sure, one of those students in practise that would leave sooner or later some chewing gum stuck under the seat. He would have to keep a close eye on him lest he forget to put on any gloves prior to examining the manuscripts. 'You come from Montanilla University, right? How can I be of any assistance?'

The vivacious and talkative-looking monk moved with celerity, glancing around as he spoke, checking with a quick and shrewd glance that table lights were off, that no one had left a forgotten book on a table, a pen or a piece of paper with some note scrawled in that sacred and classified place, ensuring that the chicks were nearby so he could be able to come quickly with the worm in his mouth at the slightest sign of danger.

'I see that you are technologically up-to-date,' Carlos said, attempting to create an appropriate environment.

"Well, professor, Silos's is a serious library. History and progress should not be in opposition' the librarian replied sharply.

Trevelyan gazed silently at the high ceiling and the double row of wooden shelves that ran the entire length of this enormous room. It was indeed a cathedral of knowledge. His attention was drawn to the central skylight. The young investigator could feel on his neck the breath of many centuries. When he lowered his gaze, Lafuente was displaying their credentials and authorizations to Fray Anselmo.

'What codex are you interested in? In your request, you did not specify anyone in particular,' he said raising his head, the pen ready in his hand to complete the research inquiry form.

'Well, none in particular, really,' and Lafuente then proceeded to explain the purpose of the visit in general terms before the librarian's bewildered gaze. 'That is, we would like to determine if additional manuscripts by the same copyist might exist in the library. And if so, to examine the quality of the parchment, you know. Perhaps there might be some gloss written by the same author, such as marginalia and the like. Our fragments are quite incomplete. I believe they are part of a codex or manuscript that could be discovered here.'

'Don't you think that's a little bit irregular?' Father Anselmo reexamined the authorisations bearing the university's seal stamped on them. He seemed tempted to hold them up to the light to confirm their legitimacy. 'So, you want to determine if any of the copyists could have written some of the manuscripts you found, you say? Allow me to explain and save you such a lot of trouble. An inventory of all the volumes and papers in the monastery—particularly the codices—was compiled in the thirteenth century. The codices in particular have always been part of it and kept in a closet in his private rooms as if they were the relics of St Domingo de Silos himself. I do not particularly believe that any strange parchment by that copyist or any other could exist here.'

'But, I believe... the name at the bottom of it... the colophon...' he professor insisted, hesitating somewhat in light of the archivist's assurance.

'I reiterate that everything has been meticulously catalogued. Nevertheless, what you intend to investigate seems a bit...'

Here, the librarian paused while searching for the appropriate word. He was a master of this art and a very professional man who took great pleasure in managing information by using the elementary technique of denying access to anything that could be requested. The delight in delaying the answer was proportional to the applicant's desire to obtain it. He thus examined a thousand and one ways to deny or postpone at most the contribution of a single drop of knowledge regarding the existence of a particular piece, book, or codex. He had honed this skill to unexpected heights because what he disposed of most at the monastery was time.

Satisfied with the anticipation created in this way, he blurted out his answer, dropping it without a net into the conversation:

'Your research seems somewhat fictitious, wouldn't you say?'

And at this point, he smiled, a smile that cut a thin line across his face. 'You should be especially careful when examining the original scroll, you know.'

The closing time of the library was approaching. After determining with the librarian which volumes would be examined the following day, they left the monastery.

'Stupid self-reliant idiot!' Lafuente said as soon as they were outside its gates. 'He has questioned in so many words our professionalism as palaeographers! What a moron!'

Carlos Lafuente made no attempt to conceal his rage. He stopped after a few steps and inhaled deeply. The inn could be guessed in front of them.

'Professor, please forget it. It's late, and yes, you are right, he's a moron, but nothing will convince him to change his ways, and we still have to return here for quite a few days.'

And so, throughout the following days, their first impression of the place would be recalled whenever Fray Anselmo made one of his mysterious apparitions on top of the stairs that resembled a makeshift pulpit, offering them a false flattering smile. He remembered his student's words and squinted intently at his task, looking with meticulous care at the miniature illuminations or Latin text in front of him, as though his soul depended upon it.

That first night, once alone in his room, Carlos opened the window and contemplated the illuminated cloister of the monastery. He could hear from there the Gregorian chant of the monks during the Compline Mass. The voices appeared to get lost in the starry night. The final mass of the day, marking the moment for the monks to put themselves in God's hands. The silhouette of the tall cypress towered over the adjacent rooftops in front of the professor.

He inhaled the night's coolness, the tranquillity that flooded everything. He had not felt that nocturnal silence for a very long time. A silence he had come to cherish when, as a child, he and his mother would cross the train tracks on the outskirts of Santander, going on some errand or other to a neighbour's house. Oh, those "errands" mothers were so fond of! At the time, he had been particularly attracted to the yellow lantern of the switchman's booth, the isolated light in a nearby window, and the distant barking of a dog, all of them announcing mysteries in the darkness, as he walked with his mother's hand in his, bound to a vague destiny.

Upon seeing the cypress and night lights of Silos, he felt somehow close to home. He could even imagine, a few metres away, the silhouette of ghostly train tracks appearing in the darkness.

'Well, here we are,' he said to himself. Tomorrow, my friend, we'll see if we can discover something about you and your secret.'

∼

CHAPTER 8

LAUDS MASS
ORA ET LABORA

Arthur felt someone was shaking his left arm.

'Come on, get up!' It was the voice of Carlos Lafuente, full of urgency, somehow breaking through the haze of torpor that invaded him. when he finally opened his eyes, he looked at the clock on the small bedside table. It read 5:45 a.m.

'But it's only six a.m!'

'An ideal time to attend Lauds!' the professor said as he opened the windows, throwing a scarce light into Arthur's small room.

'Lauds?' Arthur asked, spinning around and staring into the room and then back into the professor's face, trying to discover something he might have missed. However, there was nothing new there. They were still at the inn where they had arrived the previous day. He felt rather relieved. For a brief while, he had believed he might be in a Russian gulag about to endure some kind of interrogation.

'Yes, that's right. We will integrate into the community as far as possible,' added the professor. 'Isn't that what you always tell me? Don't you said that you must engage with the spirit and matter of things in order to comprehend them? Now show me that wasn't just drug-induced rambling!'

And so Arthur Trevelyan headed for the bathroom, prepared to start the new day as a hero or perish trying, cursing himself for expressing his viewpoint so eloquently.

Shortly afterwards, the two left the inn to attend the religious service and immerse themselves—as the professor had cleverly indicated-- in the monastic atmosphere and environment of a bygone era.

As soon as they entered the church, they could see through a fence some monks walking silently down a parallel dark aisle, their black hoods pulled over their bowed heads.

The bells chimed loudly. There was no need to talk. They were already doing so for everyone present. They represented permanence, habit, and the tenacity of centuries, but also patience and the reminder that one day more the garden needs care, the need to water the lettuce once more, and that it was urgent to tend that vine newly planted.

A chorus of men's voices reached their ears through the air, filling their minds with its beauty.

They stopped.

'Listen, Trevelyan, listen. Isn't it marvellous? Gregorian chant drains every last drop of blood out of me.'

The sweetness of those voices permeated the air. Arthur nodded. This was a privileged moment. Just the sound of human voices singing, no orchestral accompaniment, theatricals, or fanfare; just beauty over the waves.

The doors were still closed to tourists at that hour, so the two researchers found themselves in a different universe without having to embark on a voyage to distant or exotic lands.

AFTER THE SERVICE, HAVING LISTENED TO GREGORIAN CHANTS with half-closed eyes, Lafuente and Trevelyan proceeded in search of another morning coffee, one that would switch on their explorers' minds--or at least the grey cells dedicated to the work in progress. To the chagrin of their slumbering minds, the coffee at the inn was closer to Heaven than Earth.

They found their destination just a few metres away, right at the intersection of Calle St Domingo and the village main street. They had not noticed it previously, due to their having risen early, no doubt. This was undoubtedly a strategic location that acted as a counterpoint to the adjoining inn's menu and made the crossing of the valley of tears a bit more tolerable.

On the façade facing the two streets and above the entrance a wrought-iron sign read "Adolfo's" in sober letters. Besides it, a noble sign carved in stone and a couple of wrought-iron balconies curving inwards, gave the place a charming appearance. The presence of a tobacconist nearby—a few metres to their right—prompted the professor to enter the premises without hesitation.

They observed the establishment was nearly deserted at that hour, save for a few guests who glanced up momentarily before returning to their *carajillos*--that essential coffee and brandy concoction--, and their whispered conversation.

They found this was a cosy place after the sobriety of the inn. Several lights made in the Castilian style hung from the ceiling. The walls were coated in the same native stone as the façade, offering an immediate sense of warmth and protection.

Arthur and Carlos selected a window table and ordered two coffees.

A fat man with a broad smile—likely the Adolfo on the sign—approached them followed by a young man in his twenties struggling to bring their breakfast to the table on a tray he could only balance with some difficulty.

'Here you go... A cup of strong coffee, a latte...' and at this point, the man made a deft and unconcerned movement with his left arm taking the tray from the table, pretending not to notice the young man's manoeuvres and efforts to prevent the whole from falling to the floor. He repeated the same process, placing carefully a plate with two croissants on the table. 'And here, the specialty of the house.'

The two men were comparing notes, the older on a black notebook the younger intent on the screen of his iPhone, both with the same level of concentration and focused silence.

The innkeeper, recognising the exceptional self-absorption of his patrons, signalled to his young companion to follow him leaving them to their scholastic fate.

Carlos Lafuente placed the coffee cup in front of him and examined its form. It was a sturdy, heavy one.

He made little turns with the teaspoon, stirring the sugar. It pleased him to witness how the cube, following unchanging, unalterable rules, was unhinged by this simple movement when, once the lump was thrown, this cubic and perfect shape ceased to be, changing into something else before vanishing.

Trevelyan silently let him go. He was already used to the professor's impromptu manias, both in and out of class. They had been the targets of jokes and remarks from his classmates. Now, on this foray, he was dealing with a new person he had to discover. He already knew that Carlos Lafuente needed these intervals of isolation and absence, possibly to sort out his mental processes, to order his thoughts, or who knows what else. The fact is that this was quite convenient for the young man as he also required some time alone to organise his notes, even if he had to do so at the table of a bar while holding a cup of steaming coffee.

Yes, the repetitive phenomenon of pouring a sugar cube into his cup was comforting to the professor. Suddenly, the bitterness of coffee was gone, facilitated by the introduction of a single element, aided by a few discreet hand movements.

In Silos, he had discovered a beautiful and tranquil spot, a place where he felt at ease. He had so much to observe here, so many hints... Indeed, so many clues to a mysterious past surrounded him that he was keen to find out those that may have been overlooked during the initial examination of the recovered manuscripts.

After a few minutes of been busy on this task, the professor spoke:

'Have you ever noticed, Trevelyan, what a daily miracle a cup of coffee is?' he asked with a smile, fully aware of the bewilderment this would cause in his student.

But the latter had paid no attention to his words, for he was busy scribbling something on a piece of paper while gazing at his cell phone.

'Excuse me, Professor, but I was looking at the list of volumes kept in the famous cabinet indicated by our helpful librarian. Despite his best efforts, it appears that there are more original Silos books outside the monastery gates than within.'

The professor nodded, rising from his chair, his thoughts elsewhere.

'Yes, that's right. And now, let's go. It's time to get started,' he said.

Fray Anselmo was already at the library when they reached the library, waiting for their arrival. After a brief "Good morning!" and a slight nod of the head, he escorted them to a long table prepared in the furthest corner of the large room.

After a few minutes, the librarian returned with one of the requested codexes, which he placed on the table with great care. It was the celebrated *Codex Calixtino*. Both professor and student approached to examine it, regretting that they could not touch it by reason of the protective gloves they were both wearing by now.

So they began their research across the centuries in the solitude of the library. They traced the lines, the souls of the scribes who had left these intricate illuminations, these pigments that had fought against the passage of time.

An unusual paragraph highlighted in a different ink and with a slightly different tone and shape at the end of it took their attention. The handwriting resembled that of the Montanilla manuscripts, but the professor recognised a younger hand in it, as if it were a postscript written months or years later:

Please pray for my soul, O reader.

Lafuente was surprised at the wording.

The monk who had copied the scroll in Silos for future generations begged for forgiveness. A supplication for his soul. What justification might he have for such a request?

For a brief moment, Arthur envisioned this ery monk hunched over the scriptorium, painstakingly blending the colours of the illuminations, risking not only his sight, but also his time, his entire life in order to copy a few volumes.

This examination was followed by detailed digitisations on their computer screens. In this way the incunabula was not tampered with unless it was deemed absolutely necessary and justifiable by an assessment of the paper or ink used.

'How I would love to hold these volumes in my hands! This is inhuman!' the professor said, pointing at the unflinching computer screen. The small icons representing an equivalent number of actual manuscripts held somewhere in the library seemed to mock their efforts.

They continued to stare at their screens, at these images that, however clear they might be, lacked the scent, weight, and tangibility of a book in hand, a centuries-old work poorly portrayed by a few pixels on a screen.

Time went by. Periodically, they shared glances, an occasional gesture indicating their relative progress in regard to the material at hand. A few priests passed by, wearing those long cassocks that had long ago departed from everyday Spanish life. They appear to be perusing the shelves, putting down a new volume, leafing through them or consulting a new tome. Should one of these volumes awaken a certain intellectual itch or pique their minds, they proceeded then to carry it to their study table. Contrasting with the gloomy spines and incunabula, nearly all of these had sleek, shiny, state-of-the-art computers. Some fellows in white coats were moving slowly from one corner to another carrying books.

'They are part of the staff responsible for cataloguing and digitising the archives.' Lafuente explained 'These fellows are the ones to blame for you and me being glued to these screens.'

Sometimes Arthur spotted Fray Anselmo behind them when they went outside for fresh air. He believed he had seen him before peering out from behind the Romanesque columns in the cloister, watching and monitoring every one of their movements. He stared at them briefly before resuming his forward movement, as if he had not noticed them.

It was easy to find him in the corridors of the monastery, his hood tilted forward. Only his keen, piercing hummingbird eyes betraying his presence.

But even if they went out for a brief respite, the feeling was oppressive and suffocating as soon as they returned to the library.

And whenever Arthur looked up from the book he might have in his hands or shifted his sight away from the computer, there he was the small man again, lazily lifting his gaze to meet Arthur's. This had the feeling that every time he exchanged a remark with the professor, the librarian would be at the ready to detect any change, any shift in the tone of their voices. Was he perhaps trying to perceive some nuance of excitement, something unusual? "Could these two guys finally discover what they are seeking?" his gaze appeared to imply.

'DO NOT TO PAY TOO MUCH HEED TO THE LIBRARIAN,' ADVISED the innkeeper after their return to Adolfo's for lunch after listening to their concerns. They were seating in the same place by the window. 'You know, he believes he owns the library. According to what I've heard, he has standards and theories for virtually everything. It appears that considering the numerous recent visits from renowned experts and personalities, the position of Father Librarian has gone a bit to his head, giving him an inflated sense of self-importance.'

'Yes, I had a similar thought' remarked Lafuente with a smirk on his face. 'It must have something to do with him being a possible descendant of El Cid, the great Spanish hero in the struggle against the Moors.'

Adolfo laughed out loud at his guest's response, congratulating himself for the professor's willingness to engage in a little conversation, an attitude so drastically different from the one he had displayed the first day.

'My son here knows more than meets the eye, although he prefers to keep a low profile. He once told me that monasteries used to lend each other unusual books. Also that our king at the time, Alfonso X the Wise—may God preserve him in his glory!—saw fit to exercise his royal prerogative not returning many of the books borrowed from the monastery. I have no doubt our brothers in Silos remember him occasionally in their prayers.'

'It's reassuring to know I wasn't the only one to conduct such deeds! And that King Alfonso behaved like a modern library patron,' Arthur confessed with a guilty grin. Perhaps the librarian believes we are king's envoys in search of books.'

'If you want my opinion, the job these copyists did over the centuries was nothing short of extraordinary, patient and that stuff. But if you ask me, the one with two bullocks was the last Silos abbot before the Order was dissolved. He bore indeed a burden before history. Nothing less than that. He carried the whole task, taking on his shoulders the entire responsibility of protecting the monastery's cultural heritage like a ship's captain perishing with the vessel. How unfair life is! The irony of fate was that the monastery, which had safeguarded these riches for more than forty years, reopened its doors after the arrival of new monks from France. Then, precisely then, some sons of bitches devised a plan to exploit the circumstance. Their greed was stimulated. They had had all these treasures at home, collecting dust. Now ambition ruled. And they would have to hurry, because otherwise... I can't explain the urgency in any other manner.'

The man repeated his own words to emphasise his thoughts. His son, more at ease now as he did not have a tray in his hands, nodded, marking his father's arguments.

'Rodrigo Echevarría,' the innkeeper paused after these words, as though to emphasise the name. 'Remember that name, young man. That was the name of last abbot of the monastery prior to its confiscation and a truly wonderful figure in my estimation. Noble, that's the proper word, isn't it, Pedro?' he asked his son, who nodded enthusiastically. 'Instead of leaving Silos, he remained in it for over twenty years as a plain priest until he was named Bishop of Segovia. Before leaving he relocated the monastery's valuables to a secure location. In houses of trusted families, in hidden places, who knows where else? So they remained protected from prying eyes for more than forty-five years. The amazing thing isn't that some of its contents were lost after being sold; no, no! nor that some of it was dispersed over England, France, and Germany, to say the least, but that something remained in the library. As I said, the virtue that had ruled in the town under the charismatic presence of the old abbot seemed to have vanished when, against all odds, a new brotherhood of Benedictine monks seized control. French monks, if you please! One has to see this in the context of its time. After the recent War of Independence, this was nothing to sneeze at.'

'It seems those clever fellows wasted no time in destroying the good man's efforts in preserving the monastery's heritage,' the professor said.

'There are always a handful of them around every corner, ready to ask you the time before running away with your watch.' After that the innkeeper remained silent passing a cloth over the table and setting in front of his customers two cups of coffee.

A thought struck him at that point. He scowled and asked quietly to the two researchers, 'Did you say the manuscripts you found showed up in Count Dabrowsky's house? If I may say so, that smells fishy. A dubious marquis at Madrid purchased the majority of the incunabula that arrived in those turbulent times. He spent his time selling antiquities, supported by an illiterate named Jesusa.'

They continued conversing in this manner, oblivious to the passage of time, accompanying the conversation with renewed coffee and some apple liqueur. They ended the repass talking about the over a hundred and eighty books that had once been classified at the monastery, not to mention the plundering by French forces under the orders of José Bonaparte himself, who had carried the very Beato de Lieabana Codex under his arm.

Arthur, who had been playing chess with the innkeeper's son at a neighbouring table, looked from one to the other from time to time, assisted in this task by his new friend, pondering the culture of Alfonso and the professor's responses.

It was already eleven o'clock when the two left Adolfo's and headed for the inn.

'And don't you worry, Trevelyan, we won't be up for Lauds tomorrow,' the professor added as they stood in the street while he lit his pipe.

～

CHAPTER 9

AT THE LIBRARY

Of studies, fountain pens, and midnight musings.

The following days followed a similar pattern. After arriving to the library around nine o'clock, they sat down in front of a computer to examine the high-quality digitisations of manuscripts or documents, their eyes analysing every page, every detail, grappling with one mark or another. The two armed themselves with the enormous bibliography of authors like Professor Clark who had followed the inventory conducted by Father Ferotin when the French Benedictine community seized control of the abandoned monastery.

They continued their work with this routine until one p.m. Then, after a quick meal, they would continue from four to eight p.m, ending each working day with an odd mixture of regret and relief. On certain occasions, and after having applied certain amount of pressure on Fray Anselmo, they were fortunate enough to hold a real jewel in their gloved hands, and being able then to examine more closely the ink's quality, the parchment's components, its craftsmanship, the script, and the page lettering.

They felt somehow trapped here, prisoners of another era, like the very codices they were examining, like folios bound to the nerves, gripped by an inexplicable uneasiness.

Sometimes they would traverse the cloister at noon. The professor rummaging through his jacket pocket with mechanical gestures for a pipe that could not be smoked. When they looked up at the upper gallery they would occasionally see some of the monk passing from one side of the gallery to the other. Passing by would perhaps be too inaccurate a word to describe their meandering glide from one door to the next, which opened and closed silently on opposite ends.

Even the smallest sound, such as the twig of a plant brushing against the stone base of the low wall in the inner garden, captured their attention, distracting them from the monotonous and focused work.

After several hours spent in this way, Arthur sighed and said, 'I don't know what we're looking for, nor if it's worth the effort to be searching here day after day for something that, as our friendly monk suggested, may be just a romantic notion.'

'Have you ever considered that someone must perform this task a thousand times before seeing results? Do you believe that the desired result, the signature at the end, will suddenly appear as a brilliant "cum laude thesis"? You are certainly aware that the results, if any, cannot be purchased in department stores. There is no way around that,' the professor stated, attempting to persuade himself of that very reasoning.

They were passing once more the north side of the cloister, the very side where Lafuente had shown Trevelyan the stone outline their first day here. Only two days had passed since then, but their frequent walks, the twists and turns of the columns, and the careful observation of the bas-reliefs under the changing effects of light and shadow, gave Arthur the feeling they should have been in this place for months.

He had began to identify himself with these silent monks.Would he turn into one of these figures, one of these monks who appeared unable to walk? Would he be perceived similarly from the outside by tourists frequenting this area?

He dreamed of the capitals and the miniature codices, of the red ink that had silently been poisoning the monks for centuries without their knowledge. Death had defeated them with the same strategy at their solitary labour, much like the Red Death in Poe's story.

After a few days sitting in front of those scrolls, Silos was revealing its true nature. A place rife with secrets. Ancient, holy, an architectural masterpiece, that was certain, but also a jealous protector of its privacy.

Arthur sat that evening at the small, dark table by the window, captivated by these thoughts.

He turned the lamp on.

He carefully extracted then a slim white case from his jacket inside pocket. On its red lid, the words "Mont Blanc" appeared written in white letters, next to the brand's well-known, distinctive six-pointed star and a miniature aeroplane logo created for this edition.

He opened the box with exquisite delicacy. Therein was his treasure, a fountain pen asleep in the slight indentation that replicated its shape, waiting to be awakened.

A beautiful fountain pen in maroon and gold.

This was more than just a Mont Blanc. It was the Meisterstueck Doué Classique model. Le Petit Prince Edition for *connoisseurs*.

It had been a gift from his parents when he received the Montanilla scholarship. A scholarship for barely twenty places out of over fourteen thousand applicants. From that point forward, the fountain pen served as his reason for being there. Every time he felt discouraged, he only needed to glance at it to recall his mother's words,

"You are truly unique. Do not miss this opportunity. If you try, you could write your life with it."

Memories aside, it was an experience to use it while gliding the

M-size nib across the paper like a dancer on the ice rink, making unexpected turns, finishing a line, doing a pirouette, writing a letter.

And that's what he liked to call her.

The little ballerina.

From now on, he would carry it proudly in the pocket of his blazer.

He retrieved a small notebook from the drawer. A simple note-book with a rigid cover. He fumbled with before starting writing,

On November 24th, at Silos Inn...

I have had a strange feeling since we arrived. Not just the fact that I suddenly find myself constricted in a library after being used to moving freely around campus and paddling vigorously in the river. No, it's something else. Perhaps the professor could be more specific about it. However, he does not exactly concur with my views on the magical reality of things. There is undoubtedly the Silos struggling to survive, coexisting with modernity in order to secure a place in the contemporary world while maintaining its image of seclusion, spirituality and peace.

But there is a second Silos, this one belonging to the occult and mediaeval worlds, concealing the secrets of a privilege perhaps known only to the monks who have inhabited it through the ages. Perhaps only a few of them know them, those who guard the secrets of the manuscripts, the secrets that accompany the enclosed life of the monks, devoted to God, complete with their anxieties, fears, and hidden sinful deviations. To preserve that knowledge only a selected few can have access to it in its entirety, while the rest—longing to possess it too—work, keep the fire burning, polish the doorknobs, and open the windows to let in light and dust into the room.

Arthur, exhausted from writing these fanciful ideas, closed the notebook and climbed into bed with a gesture of weariness, but not before looking out the window overlooking the front gate and observing the streetlights that illuminated the narrow alley. Adolfo's, located at the opposite end, had just closed its doors. Only the silhouette of the metal sign, barely visible in the darkness, gave away its position.

He drifted off to sleep.

CHAPTER 10

STUDY CONTINUES

Of codices, serpents, librarians, birds of prey and other silently moving things.

Arthur was examining a volume that the professor had shown him.

An exquisite copy of the *Beatus of Liebana*.

'Here it is, Trevelyan,' Lafuente said, 'copied around the year 1100.'

'Even if it is not the original codex, it's a faithful reproduction, both in size and quality. Without a doubt, a masterpiece.'

'And where is the original?'

'At the British Library in London. I would love to see it one day,' the professor stated. 'But just look at it, Trevelyan! Observe how precisely the miniatures are rendered! No fewer than one hundred and six of them!'

The beautiful and artistic images, the colours of the various inks, and the intricate details of each stroke, were evidence of what could be accomplished with effort and time over the years.

'At the British Library, you say? And how did it end there?'

'Do you recall what our innkeeper friend told us about the abbot's management of the monastery property? What happened the books that were kept in St Domingo's private closet that were later sold to the highest bidder? This one has the unfortunate distinction of being one of them.'

The facsimile displayed a green leather binding with dry-embossed text housed in a case of the same material.

Arthur's interest was sparked upon picking up the book, and he proceeded to examine it more thoroughly. It was preceded by a monographic essay signed by Father Clemente Serna Gonzalez, the former abbot of Silos.

The professor pointed to the abbot's name repeatedly: 'Such a good illustration of modernity. He was the one who popularised Silos Gregorian chant, bringing it to an international level. No one could have done more to preserve and promote the cultural heritage of this place.'

The preface had been written by Miguel C. Vivancos, head of the Department of Medieval Antiquities at the National Archaeological Museum and former librarian of the monastery. "The former librarian" Arthur mused. 'I wonder whether we would have fared better should had encountered him instead of Fray Anselmo here.'

When Arthur reached folios 147 and 148 in the codex, he discovered there a peculiar illustration.

It depicted a snake. Upon examining the artwork closely, he believed he had uncovered its significance. It was without a doubt that iconic emblem, the fight between the reptile and the Son of Woman. He jotted down a note in his notebook—an additional element for his doctoral dissertation.

While examining the codex Carlos Lafuente recalled a sentence from an engraving he kept in a little frame in his office,

"Whoever you are, use this book well, and do not forget the scribes, so that the Lord will forget your crimes. Writing causes blindness, hunches the back, fractures the ribs, and upsets the stomach, causing discomfort and annoyance to the entire body. This is why, O reader, you should turn the pages gently and keep your fingertips away from the letters; just as hail kills the harvest, an inefficient reader blurs the text and destroys the book."

This comparison between a reader exerting his mind and a copyist tiring his body was well-known among palaeographers.

The time the two researchers had spent so far in the library was making itself felt.

IN THE DAYS THAT FOLLOWED, FRAY ANSELMO REPEATEDLY approached their table with a smug smirk or, more closely, as a knife-like slash on his face. Arthur could not deny that the monk appeared delighted by the everyday inability of the two historians to extract any information from the texts.

'Good morning, gentlemen' he said by way of greeting as they entered the library. 'Are you prepared for another day of research and study? God bless you! ' And in an aside to Trevelyan, he added: 'Young man, I apologise for pointing this up so bluntly, but your tie appears to be a tiny bit wrinkled.'

'May Satan devour you!' Arthur murmured less cautiously than Professor Lafuente, always attentive of his etiquette.

'I think we are missing something, but I have no idea what could it be,' Lafuente stated. 'Perhaps the archivist is right and we are, like so many others, dealing with an apocryphal text. On the other hand, it is just possible that the copyist, exhausted and on the verge of death, created this jest for posterity in order to irritate poor morons like us. I should be preparing my speech at the conference in Valladolid, instead of being were. We are both wasting our time here!'

It was inappropriate for Carlos Lafuente to speak in such a manner. His pupil regarded him with curiosity. After a few seconds of hesitation, he said:

'Professor, please! I am confident that we will find something in one of these volumes. Wait and see!'

'And how are you so sure? Ah, But of course!, I had almost forgot. It's because of this foretelling of the future that you speak and read so much about. It's know as clairvoyance, am I right? How could I have forgotten something so simple!'

Arthur became aware of a peculiar sensation and looked up. No, he had not been mistaken. At the opposite end of the library, Fray Anselmo lowered his head quickly. Certainly, he had been observing them like a jealous bird of prey guarding its nest. In this regard, there was no doubt. He was guarding the hidden secrets of Silos.

DURING THE LUNCH BREAK, THE PROFESSOR FOUND THE student particularly talkative.

''I do believe there are people in the world who live on silence, secrets, and hidden things,' he said, dividing the loaf of bread he held in his hands into three pieces to better illustrate his point. 'They are offered to us gradually, as one would with a child, so as not to spoil it. Just a little bit of knowledge every few years, nothing more, nothing less,' he said as he arranged the cutlery on the table-cloth in different places even at the risk of some of it falling to the floor. 'And if it becomes dangerous, if it could alter a certain perspective of things, the information is condensed and concealed a bit more. Nothing mysterious or intriguing as depicted in certain novels. They simply distract you while they remove the card from the sleeve or the rabbit from the hat. Tcha-tchan! It only takes that little gesture for us to miss the point, and then it's another moment, another day,'

'Very interesting, very interesting indeed, this bunny metaphor, but frankly also quite movie-like,' the professor said. 'Certainly, more in your line of work than mine, my friend. You see, this involves more than simply deciphering the meaning of an obscure clue on a random piece of parchment, Arthur. It is not enough to examine the past, rearrange it, and give it meaning for the present. Although I believe I just stated something that is at least partially pertinent. That word is order. Without a structured representation of history, only chaos can be communicated. It's the idea, the principle, that interests me. The idea and the respect that following the traces someone has left us over the centuries means. These experiences teach you not only to be humble, but also to respect the past.'

With these words, he stood up and declared dinner to be finished.

THAT EVENING, LAFUENTE DEPARTED ALONE FROM THE INN. HE required a stroll to gather his thoughts. He recalled with irony how long before him wandering philosophers and Einstein himself used to walk in this way, aimlessly, waiting for creative bursts of creativity to ignite their minds.

The streets of Silos appeared to be playing hide-and-seek with him all that evening. The facades of the city, which had appeared so welcoming and open during the first few days of their arrival, now presented a closed, hostile face, receding to avoid being seen, their windows lying in darkness, refusing to acknowledge, like eyes squinting under closed blinds, seeming to say, "We have never met before."

After crossing the small stream, he looked back down at the silent Silos.

Only a few scattered lights illuminated the houses and streets he had just traversed.

In one of those streets was the inn, and in one of its rooms Trevelyan slept, oblivious to the worries running through his mentor's mind.

～

CHAPTER 11

A TALK WITH FRAY ROMANONES

Or, how religion and wine are delightful soul-relieving companions.

It was the third day of their stay. The professor was extremely focused. That was obvious. What didn't seem so clear to Arthur was what his mentor was doing on that piece of paper where he was repeatedly drawing scattered circles. They lacked any discernible pattern; they were just mere circles. When he had executed a good number of them—around fifteen, according to Trevelyan's quick calculation—, he meticulously connected them with lines as if they were Venn diagrams.

The peculiar thing was that Professor Lafuente seemed unaware of his own artistic achievements; to be outside of all that strategy, his mind intently focused on the task at hand.

They had just occupied their usual seats at the table. There were few people in the library that morning. After a few moments and a moment of hesitation, Lafuente left the intricate circle drawing, rose from the chair, and approached Fray Anselmo, who was standing near the photocopier.

'Fray Anselmo, I was wondering if I could speak to the abbot,' the professor said, gathering his courage. 'Perhaps he may know an additional unclassified source, one he would be especially familiar with due to the history of the institution.'

He was unable to say anything else.

Fray Anselmo's alarm level would not have been the same if, at that moment, the Solomon Temple had once more been divided in two.

After inhaling for a few seconds, the librarian exclaimed, 'Look, the abbot would tell you the same thing as I do. In addition, as I mentioned you on the first day, I have worked in the library for over twenty years as the former librarian's assistant. I am intimately familiar with the institution's catalogue and its history. I believe I may know a thing or two, don't you think?' he continued, with a poorly disguised tone of hostility in his voice. 'In any event, the abbot does not receive visitors in his office unless they are personally invited by himself. In that case it is he who comes down to greet the distinguished visitors to the library, I'm sorry to say' he said with a particular nuance in his voice that seemed to imply the opposite and then, as if he had remembered a funny story he said 'Several months ago, a gentleman came here and told me he was documenting himself for a novel. He directly asked me if I knew which floor the abbot was on. The abbot himself!' Such disrespect! Such audacity! I explained to him the history of the monastery, but he must not have found it particularly romantic because he hardly paid attention. Do you know what I told him next? Should he attempt to include my name in his books as the current librarian or even that of Father Vivancos, the previous one, he would be sued for image rights. Obviously, it all would have been different should the book had been supported by extensive study, on actual events, a major matter in lieu of this. But a novel? A novel is entirely fictional!

'All lies then, you mean?' said Lafuente with a smile, the purpose of which was to encourage the little man to finish expressing his anti-literary sentiments.

Fray Anselmo chewed his lower lip while placing his left hand on his earlobe.

'I only say there are some things that should be kept away from the monastery. This is not an Umberto Eco book, you know, nor a museum; it's a real monastery, a place of worship. We are not here to have the place populated by sinister monks in dark cells, or galleries, or to have our daily habits altered in any way' he added, turning to the copier in the same manner as a confessor entering a confessional, his eyes inspecting the papers in his hands with great attention through his bifocals while pressing the "copy" button. As a final thought, an apostille—he was a librarian after all—, he turned to the professor and said, 'If you want to see the remainder of the manuscripts, you can always go to the British Museum, Paris, or Leipzig to see them. Perhaps the English or Germans, with their customary pragmatism, will perceive your idea with new eyes,' concluded Fray Anselmo with a sly twinkle in his eyes, having already recovered from his original outburst of rage.

Upon leaving the library that evening, shortly after seven o'clock, they encountered an elderly monk walking in front of them. Carlos had noticed him the first day they arrived. He used to sit in the library's far corner, intent on his reading since early in the morning. They had never observed him doing anything specific or with a clear objective while being there. In contrast to the other users, he would leave the table and computer after an hour or two with a smile that never appeared to fade from his face, but only after he had set the table and books he had hardly consulted in perfect order.

As they left the library, they came upon a bulletin board advertising upcoming activities in the nearby Assembly Hall. Above it was a large banner depicting a priest standing next to a computer surrounded by books, looking straight ahead.

Below the picture were written the words,

Seminar
Fray Romanones, Abbot
Silos's Modern Scriptorium and New Technologies. Wednesday,
November 27, at 19:00.
St Francis Hostelling Association Assembly Hall

'By Jove, Trevelyan, I attended one of his conferences in Madrid years ago,' Lafuente said, pointing to the poster. 'How highly captivating was the way he delivered his lecture to the audience! He described the entire process of creating parchment, from the time the lamb was skinned until it reached the copyist's table. You can imagine his explanations were too detailed for some attendees, but they were accurate nevertheless. So he is the current abbot!'

His eyes shone brightly. He furrowed his brows and pursed his lips.

He turned after a few seconds, observing the board.

'The date of this lecture is tomorrow!'

And without further ado, he strode with resolute feet towards the monk they had seen minutes earlier, who was making his way slowly towards the cloister.

'Excuse me, father. I wonder if it would be possible to talk to Father Romanones?' asked the professor boldly, attempting to give an air of authority to his voice while simultaneously pointing to the photo on the poster, bolstered by his interlocutor's smile as he raised his head, 'I'd simply like to say hello. Years ago, I had the pleasure of attending his presentation on the history of the scriptorium.'

The compassionate monk appeared to pause briefly. He scanned his surroundings, and after twice adjusting his hood, he smiled again.

'Sure thing, please follow me!' he exclaimed, as if he were used to performing this task daily.

Their new guide led his shocked guests up a flight of steps that went to the superior cloister via dimly lit passageways they had never noticed before.

Once they got there and walked a few metres, the monk knocked on a low-key, dark door on the wing opposite the library door through which they had entered the first day. Trevelyan, who did not fully comprehend the professor's manoeuvres, observed them with wide-open eyes, astounded by the apparent easiness of the former.

'Come in, come in, please' pleaded a polite, measured voice, muffled by the thick wooden panel.

Upon entering, they found themselves in a whitewashed, almost bare room, as one would expect from a good Benedictine. A mahogany table, a few bookcases, a crucifix, a calendar, and a modern Ives computer, made up the whole furniture. Yet, among the books, Carlos could effortlessly distinguish the works of Fray Vivancos and Father Serna on a prominent place.

'Have a seat, please be so kind' said the same voice.

Fray Romanones sat back in his chair, and displayed a broad, white smile.

As the picture had shown previously, the abbot was a cheerful-looking man whose smile lit up his face as he spoke. His was a dark-skinned face, the face of a priest who wished to convey to the world the impression, the illusory assurance, that a place as solemn as Silos could contain people as joyful as himself within it. People who could both share their enthusiasm for learning and for life.

He couldn't help but compare that smile to those of priests he had known at the Marist, Salesians, and Jesuit Brothers schools.

He knew well enough that, when confronted with such a smile, there was no hope, no chance at all; you were in uncharted territory. As if years had not passed, he once again felt like a student who had been caught skipping class.

'Allow me to welcome you both to Silos. It is a privilege to have two representatives from Montanilla University here. Oh, don't display that shocked expression, professor! Mr Noguer, informed me of your arrival in advance. His brother and I studied theology in Orihuela. Unfortunately, my obligations have prevented me from meeting you in the library as I would have liked. I beg your pardon.'

Fray Romanones locked his clear, penetrating eyes on the historian, prepared to hear the visitor's complaints regarding the elusive library aide-de-camps. His head nodded in agreement now and then throughout their entire conversation.

The fact that he knew the rector caused the professor to take a deep breath. For some reason, the more the father nodded and smiled, the more uncomfortable Professor Lafuente was finding himself as he began,

'Occasionally, while inspecting books, manuscripts, and other incunabula, he...'

He finally stumbled over his words and concluded his speech with a bewildered mumble.

'He hasn't left us alone for a second, that's the simple truth' Trevelyan said bravely assisting his mentor. As soon as he was through, he was completely flushed.

Fray Romanones laughed loudly upon hearing this. The laugh seemed almost sacrilegious coming from him and considering the setting in which they were. The professor mistrusted this joyful outburst more than Fray Anselmo's perpetual frowns.

'Professor, young man... You are totally right! The library is open to you whenever you desire. Please forgive the overzealousness of Fray Anselmo. He has spent many years in Silos and treats the books and manuscripts as though they were his own family. You see, there are so many people using the library these days, you have no idea, so many hands want to inspect facsimiles and antique documents that some safeguards must be taken. Obviously, as a palaeographer, you are aware, professor, that the fewer times an original is handled, the better. The history of the monastery has already been marked by a great deal of sorrow and darkness, by many shady areas. On the other hand, this monastery's tradition has always been to unite the past and the future. You have witnessed the incorporation of new technology as a result of the most recent investments made by various public and private organisations for its preservation and maintenance. Yes, the monastery is remodelling itself. We are receptive to knowledge and willing to share it with the world, while also providing peace to those who visit us, even for a few days. By the way, I understand that you are staying at the inn. How are your accommodations? Are they to your satisfaction? According to what I've heard, it lacks the same amenities as the Convent St. Francis Inn. Is that so? It is unfortunate that you were not able to remain in the latter, where our guests like to stay. I believe its cuisine to be exceptional, not to mention the luxury of its accommodations.'

'Sure, yes, we've been OK,' Lafuente answered in a weak voice, recalling the glossy images of the brochure he had seen days earlier, evoked in such flagging colours.

Fray Romanones rose slowly and discreetly, like everything that was done in this place. In contrast, Trevelyan and Lafuente's chairs creaked significantly, breaking the silence with their noise as they both imitated the abbot by standing up. Carlos turned around, almost expecting to hear disapproving whispers from a non-existent audience.

When both professor and student realised it, they were standing by the door towards which the priest had been imperceptibly propelling them by the simple method of advancing gently forward as they retreated. Fray Romanones was reconquering his office's land.

It was impossible not to notice that they were being expelled with impeccable gallantry.

The interview had been ended by the abbot with grace, courtesy, and a completed and measured Benedictine grin.

This time, the professor felt, this time their parents would not be notified of their little misdeed as long as they apologised and pledged not to do it again. There would be no reprimand that afternoon, nor they would be denied a stroll or snack.

'Please let me know should you find any additional material, professor, or a fresh string to pull. I would be delighted to learn more about it', the priest stated naturally, as if he had no role at all in the move forward they had just been witness to.

After a pause, he lowered his head smiling, before raising his gaze again to his interlocutors. He was enjoying the farewell with more of a Jesuit than a Benedictine spirit, as if they were a couple of students who had made a mistake but were nevertheless still fine chaps.

'In addition, your theory is quite excellent, incredibly brilliant! Keep following it. I will look forward to its publication. Please send us a copy when the time comes. And should you want to attend my conference tomorrow, it would be a pleasure to see you there again.' he added, shaking hands with his visitors.

The door closed behind them with a barely perceptible click.

· · ·

THEY ENTERED THE TAVERN IN SILENCE, TAKING THEIR customary seats by the window.

Once seated, Carlos Lafuente picked up his napkin and pondered it for a moment before folding it into a four-fold and laying it on the right side of the table. Then, after a few seconds, perhaps uncertain of the outcome, he unfurled it again.

Adolfo approached cautiously while displaying a kind yet concerned demeanour. Too much time had passed for him not to notice the difference between the end of a good day and a terrible one. On days like this, his professional side felt moved towards his guests.

'Good evening, professor,' and then, noticing the grim face of the former, asked Arthur with a friendly tone 'Kid, how was your day?'

Carlos ceased folding the napkin and looked upward.

'Let's say in a good romance that Real Madrid did not win the day' he said briefly.

'Well, in this scenario, I feel compelled to tell you something. Have you completed your daily lot? You don't have to drive or do anything else, do you? Well, things being like this...' he repeated while staring at them. 'I may not have a well-furnished apartment on the top level as opposed to my father who served in the mayor's house. He read anything he could get his hands on, was a man given to accounting and clever things. My talents have been more along the lines of walking around the block with my friends. You know, chasing after girls and such stuff. But I can tell you one thing for certain..'

The innkeeper remained silent while peering intently into their eyes.

'I've seen so many people pass by, some of them for just one night, while others stayed for weeks or months, all of them fascinated by the monastery's treasures. It's not uncommon to see here art students, journalists looking for a story, and scholars like yourselves and, yes, occasionally masons performing much-needed restoration work. However, from the first to the last, they all had one thing in common. Every one of them was a real person who had to deal with the hardships of bad weather and a demanding schedule. My son, Pedro, who possesses such a poetic soul inside, might better articulate this thought. Why does he appear so timid and quiet? because he's continually rummaging through his stories. Perhaps he'll say they pursued a different dream. In any event, when these people from such diverse backgrounds grew weary, despondent, and came to my counter seeking a chair to snort on at the end of the day, I offered them my solution, our house solution... the traditional Silos rotten pot! Casa Adolfo's rotten pot, to be precise! What do you say to that, Amelia? Am I right or not?'

The woman so addressed stared at him from behind the counter.

'You fool! Always bothering customers with your stories.'

Adolfo arrived at the table a few minutes later with a steaming platter of food.

'Come on,' said the excellent man, a smile crossing his face, 'Try this and let me know how things turn out,' said the good man, a smile crossing his lips. 'Remember that our celebrated Calderon de la Barca referred to this dish in his writings as "the princess of stews." I would even go so far, getting into deeper waters, to assert that Cervantes called it "The Big Dish" due to its consistency.'

The two men gave the dish a thumbs-up after tasting it; maintaining a surprising silence as they enjoyed their meal, sprinkled with the young Cillar de Silos wine that the innkeeper had brought along.

'So what? How do things go now? Have we found a way to raise our spirits a tad?' asked the hospitable innkeeper, continuously rubbing his hands over his apron, which presented a pitiful appearance due to so much manipulation. 'Is research now on a better track?'

'You were right. I can now view things from a different angle.' Here, the professor paused, sipping from the glass he had raised to his mouth, unable to suppress a smile. 'Thank you very much, Adolfo. We needed it. That's the truth.'

'The Romans had previously expressed something similar... "*In vino veritas.*"'

The good man was overjoyed at the prospect of having contributed to the happiness of his guests.

'Don't leave just yet, as they say in the circus; for there's more to come! You have to try Grandpa's dessert made according to my top-secret recipe. It has been passed down from generation to generation, and now my son prepares it with those student hands God has given him.'

A few minutes after this, the above-mentioned appeared through the kitchen door, grinning and carrying two plates of delectable Burgos cheese, walnuts, and honey.

'I believe I'll enjoy it the most!' said Trevelyan, uttering these words without a moment's hesitation as he grabbed the nearest spoon.

The two young people sat down after dinner in a nook near the fireplace to play chess, as they had been doing over the past few days. Pedro removed the pieces out of the box and petted the pawns, smiling.

As he lay in bed later that night, Arthur mingled in his mind the image of that distant Nordic princess gazing at the Arlanzón waters with the memory of the delicious stew they had tasted that evening. He drifted off to sleep, slowly and peacefully. His jacket was slung over a nearby chair and clinging to it, remnants of the excellent dinner that good old Adolfo had given them could be clearly seen.

~

CHAPTER 12

ARTHUR DEDICATES HIMSELF TO GARDENING

Or how Arthur Trevelyan could testify that helping others both enriches and strengthens the spirit.

Arthur had left the inn early that morning to take a walk through the town before entering the library.

On his way back, as he strolled along the road that encircled the monastery, he passed the gate reserved for monks and providers of goods. There was no one around there at that hour. It was only natural that he felt like exploring this part of the monastery.

He remembered having seeing two monks crossing this courtyard an hour earlier when he began his stroll. This encouraged him to approach the place cautiously, discovering in doing so a gate to his left.

There was a figure in that spot. The man had not noticed him.

It was an old gardener, wheelbarrow in hand, although by the angle of his curved back and the the weight he was hauling, it gave the impression that the thing was pulling the old gardener towards the gate and not the other way round. But if he accurately recalled his high school physic classes, he knew this was impossible.

Inside the wheelbarrow, fallen leaves, faded flowers, hard ground, and the occasional brick. And on the floor surrounding it hundreds of autumn leaves patiently awaiting to be collected. The shape and colour of this year's leaves, different ones yet identical to those of previous years in shape and colour. The same crimson hue, the same form that had endured for generations, the same cell arrangement.

'Excuse me, can I help you?' said Arthur, before the very thought of helping the gardener had entered his mind.

The man raised his head slightly in disbelief at being addressed in such a peculiar way. He had been performing the same tasks automatically for so many years that the sound of a voice in the midst of his routine had surprised him.

'Now that you mention it, could you please take the wheelbarrow from that end so we can get through the gate?' he said, rapidly recovering from his surprise at this unexpected assistance as if the young man were a new apprentice.

It appeared that scholastic tradition, the accumulated knowledge of several centuries in the monastery, had not yet discovered a solution to the prosaic and mundane chore of avoiding an old gate's lower crossbar.

'Were you looking for someone?' the old man asked, once the wheelbarrow had been deposited on the floor within the monastery's boundaries, not without performing a series of more or less heavy breaths of varying intensities, punctuated by a few coughing fits. At that point, he had already realised that the apprentice's idea, though a brilliant concept, sound in theory, had been but a mere illusion.

'Well, I wonder if I could enter the library from here, if that is possible.'

The gardener looked at him like someone used to hear this very plea all day. He opened his lips to speak, but before he could utter a word, he coughed again and flailed his arms violently, with an intensity that Arthur found astonishing for a man of his age. During one of the breaks, he looked at the boy pointing to a location beyond the fence they had just passed.

'If you ring the bell over there, the father porter will lead you to the library.'

Above the doorbell was a small monitor and camera. Modern technology to the service of monastic life.

Arthur grinned inwardly. Sometimes he had imagined the professor and himself were the only ones who still believed that ancient monuments, abbeys, churches, schools, and castles retained the same dampness, moss, and tapestries that had covered their interiors, walls, and floors since the dawn of time. Theirs was profession of romantics who refused to leave.

The gardener behind him blew his nose loudly.

After pressing the indicated button, a voice responded.

'What..?' Some static noise ensued, interrupting the transmission, as if a swarm of bees had decided to nest behind the intercom lines. The sound concluded with a high-pitched tone resembling a goldfinch being crushed to death by a doorjamb with a precise sharp blow, showing no mercy.

He felt foolish shouting his plea repeatedly into this contraption. The more he heard himself doing it, its believability appeared to diminish. What a silly idea! They had already spoken to the abbot just the day before! What did he believe he could accomplish in the consulting room after spending over a whole week in front of the computer?

A chubby-looking monk opened the door for him.

'Follow me, boy! I will take you to the library. You can speak to Father Prior there. Fray Anselmo is not here today.'

And so they walked through a lengthy corridor and then a stone staircase leading to the upper floor.

The gate keeper appeared to walk with an odd rocking motion, possibly due to a hip condition. This, combined with his pace, gave his figure a reassuring, almost hypnotic aspect.

'And please tell me,' said Arthur, both nervous and glad that he would not be meeting Fray Anselmo at the end of their journey, although he was not so sure about meeting the Prior himself. 'Have you noticed a significant change since the times of Father Vicente, the former abbot?'

The monk turned slightly when he heard the question.

'Fray Vicente was an abbot like few others,' he replied without breaking the increasing rhythm, revealing to the student a face that spoke of deep compassion. 'Many of us here lament his departure from office. Alzheimer's is a terrible thing. Terrible!' he exclaimed, falling instantly silent, as if someone else had spoken.

He shook his head several times as they continued their climbing routine.

Arthur wondered at the apparent ease with which he had got there and could not help but wonder how his companion would have reacted if, instead of asking for the archivist, he would have applied for a 7.62 calibre Dillon machine gun, similar to the one used in the capture of "Chapo" Guzmán, or even some first row tickets to the Mamma Mia! show. Would he have responded similarly? Would he have made a different decision? Or would he perhaps have volunteered some VIP tickets due to his position?

He would never know, because while he was thus contemplating the matter they had reached the top floor. For a moment, the young man felt the urge to stroll past the porter and offer him his assistance for the remainder of the journey. But when he raised his eyes, he realised the familiar library could be seen through an open window in the inner wall.

At that moment, the person who seemed to be the prior was standing in front of the photocopier machine. When Arthur glanced at him again, he realised that he was not other that the very enigmatic and friendly monk who had accompanied them to Fray Romanones' quarters.

'Fray Lucas!' said the father porter 'This young man would like to speak to you.'

And without further ado, he retraced his steps, straining his body to the utmost in order to negotiate the stairs, preparing himself for the adventure that his return would bring.

Fray Lucas smiled upon seeingthe young man, as though he had been anticipating his arrival.

'Good morning... I assume you got off on the wrong foot by walking behind the monastery. Is that correct?'

'Yes, sorry, I did not mean to disturb you. I am aware the library is not yet open, but I saw the gardener outside with...'

'Ah! Jerónimo! Always so obstinate! What a rebel! He insists on not requesting assistance. He's been warned a thousand times to do so when he should carry something heavy, but he doesn't give up easily. It is difficult, don't you agree? To give up?'

Arthur sensed something strange in Fray Lucas' gaze as he uttered this question.

'Yes, I suppose it is' he said weakly.

'Well, you could very well be right. You could have a point there. By the by, while you were here, did you take the time to look at the old archives?'

'Yes, of course, the volumes at the far end of the library, right?' said Arthur, perplexed by the query, as he was sure the prior had noted their presence in the library day after day. 'We are already consulting them, you know.'

'No, no, I meant the real archives. Oh! 'I see' he said, observing Arthur with the same smile as if this were a board game between grownups whose only purpose was to locate the starting square. 'Fray Anselmo... I understand, I understand...' he kept muttering while looking at the tips of his shoes. 'You see, the previous Father Archivist —Fray Vivancos—, was quite unique, so kind, so generous! He did not impede anybody. For him, what you did with the results of an examination or the time spent in the library was something you had to carry on your back for the remainder of your life. The present one is quite different. He has become a consciousness that filters, distributes, grants and denies everything.'

And after chewing these words with emphasis, he beckoned Arthur to follow him through the very pointed door the young man had entered a few minutes earlier. A few steps later, Arthur was shocked to see the archivist stop in front of a wooden door on the opposite side of the stone passage. Without uttering a word, the priest extracted a key from his right pocket and inserted it with a certain air of conjurer.

The door opened to a large, dim room.

The archivist flipped a switch and suddenly the room was awash in bright white light. It was completely filled with shelves and more shelves as far as the eye could see. The only indication of modernity was a fire extinguisher located to the left of the stairway that led to the basement. The light switch previously mentioned and a sign marking the location of books in the aisles according to subject were the only other signs of progress.

'There are three floors here. These are the books that were removed from the main library because they were too large and bulky. Here, they are kept at a temperature-controlled environment and are only brought to the main area only upon request.'

'Of course, and I presume they are mentioned in the general catalogue.'

A momentary pause from the monk.

'Yes... Well, obviously, not all of them are listed in the catalogue, you know. Many are still being digitised, and others remain under the custody of the father librarian and, of course, the abbot.'

'I see,' Arthur remarked, his eyes fixated on the tangle of volumes.

Here, the young man felt he had discovered the monastery's bowels. The heart of the monster, the thing that made it beat. There were no visits here, no consultations, no quick steps through the corridors.

The monk shut the door and the labyrinth of texts, codices, and manuscripts vanished behind it. For a moment, Arthur thought what the professor would have given to be present.

'Thank you so much for showing me this. It's really fascinating' he said as he prepared to leave.

The prior showed no sign of having heard or perceived the young man's intention to do so. Instead, he walked towards another door, slightly to the left of the first. Once there, he removed another key from his pocket without saying a word, as if he were showing a new employee his workplace.

The interior of this additional room was considerably different from the previous one. On the right wall was a wide bookshelf, some thirty metres long, covered with books from floor to beamed ceiling.

Large windows on the left side of the room bathed the area with light. A few black lanterns spaced at four-metre intervals completed the design.

'This is where the repeated books are kept,' Fray Lucas stated.

'The repeated books?'

'Yes, all the editions that have not been lent to other monasteries, for some reason or other, are kept in the main library. Of course, these are not the actual codices, but facsimiles, analyses, etcetera.

'But the vast general archive we have just viewed contains codices as well.'

'Of course, and there is where they ought to be. Particularly the most sensitive ones. It is easier to protect them there than in the library.'

Arthur stared at this place. A question surfaced in his mind. Weak and improbable, but a query nonetheless. And like all questions, it might or might not have an answer.

'I simply hope you can make the most of what you have seen.' were Fray Lucas' final words to the young man upon the departure of the latter. The young man made his way to the library's main hall to meet Carlos Lafuente, a thick volume under his arm.

CHAPTER 13

GONZALO DE BERCEO-THE LIBRARY CLOSES

Of how Literature classes on a rainy day help to comprehend the threads of Fate.

The professor sighed. Arthur hadn't come yet. The stack of books on the table had grown into an impassable barrier. A wall that seemed to prevent his access to knowledge. He glanced at the manuscript that had been his lot that day, then at the neutral screen in front of him, promising everything, giving nothing.

'I believe we have it, professor, I think we have it!' Trevelyan said in a nervous whisper approaching the table where Lafuente was sitting and setting down a thick volume upon it. He was making great efforts not to raise his voice.

Lafuente winced when he saw Arthur arrive in this excited state, and once he regained his composure, he examined the codex his pupil was showing him.

'How did you get this?' Professor Lafuente exclaimed, awakening some hostile glances from the nearby tables with a face in which astonishment was painted in the purest impressionist style.

'The invisible threads of the universe, Professor. The invisible threads I am always telling you about. From time to time they move.'

Carlos opened the volume. He immediately recognised the text.

The same hand that had illuminated the manuscripts kept in his desk at Montanilla. Indeed, this was it. At last.

The famous manuscript listed as number two in the Ferotin inventory.

He looked closely at the illuminations.

He found it peculiar that this manuscript, of all things—also catalogued in Grimaldi's book as manuscript number 12, *Gonzalo de Berceo and Pedro Marín*—, should have the clue, should be the one copied by the very monk who had written the manuscripts from which everything had started. And he thought it strange precisely because it was the most romantic of them all, composed between the 13th and 14th centuries in half Latin and half Spanish.

'Arthur, this is the manuscript I was telling you about. The one discovered in 1914 in the nearby village of Carazo by the librarian and parish priest of St Domingo de Silos, Father Mateo del Alamo.

'The one that had been stored in a kitchen?'

'Wonderful memory, Arthur, excellent! The priest, a well-known collector of antiquities, enquired at one of the houses about any old books that might be on the property and discovered that many of them were stored in the kitchen and attic. Among them, he discovered this book, whose pages had been used as fuel for the fire over the years, though not in a spiritual sense.'

'Are you serious? Let me see it, please.'

The part of the MS corresponding to folios 1 to 20 was displayed in double column in front of them.

'Gonzalo de Berceo' the professor said in a calm voice as he placed his gloved hands carefully on the volume.

The name alone brought to mind the lessons taught by Dona Eugenia, that gaunt teacher with pointed nose and glasses extolling the renown of the Spanish author in a high-pitched voice while, through the tilted windows, the pattering of rain could be heard. She must not have done her teaching too badly, for she instilled in him an almost mystical appreciation for the Spanish Middle Ages, the priesthood itself, and yes, even the rain.

He shut his eyes. He might easily put himself back in that class. His mind recalled the verses he had first heard long ago. It seemed to him like a miracle, one of those *Miracles of Our Lady* that the distant poet had had described in rhyme.

'It is a pleasure to see you after so long, my friend,' the professor muttered.

After experiencing the unique sensation of having these pages in his hands, he examined the abbreviations, the variances between the f's and t's. However this codex seemed to convey something else to him. He looked around, trying not to notice the other scholars in the library, heads were bent over the texts, over the computer white screens, in stark contrast to how the ancients had conducted their work. A state-of-the-art scriptorium.

In the evening, as Arthur returned to the task and the sun began to set, he felt saliva thicken in his mouth after the first illusion, the first impression of having discovered the book had been left behind. Suddenly, his mind went blank. Despite the wealth of the volume and the significance of its discovery, there was no remarkable note or gloss from the "jocular copyist"—as he was now called. The student realised this with some bitterness. There were no hints, nudges, or any information offering a glimmer of hope.

The typewriter still worked, but the paper roller was empty.

'How can the manuscripts we are examining be connected to this?' Arthur declared to Lafuente, 'I do not see anything here that could help us in any way.'

'Well, at least we know the mysterious copyist worked here in Silos, or at least his shadow passed over here one time or another' said Lafuente. 'Now if he belonged to the scriptorium besides working in it, there is no evidence. No relationship or reference to the cryptic passages observed in the Montanilla manuscripts.'

"In the prime hour, from the light will come light" Arthur recited in a
hushed voice from memory.

They were surrounded by reality. The clock announced the
library closing time till the afternoon. The photocopier's low, muffled
sound reached them. The distant cough of a rakish monk and the
turnings of their own legs crossing under the table gave the moment a
sense of unreality. They had been living in a dream, hunting for the
fine line linking the circles like Lafuente had done on the tablecloth
days earlier. However, they had discovered none. The professor was
not a naïve man. As a historian, he was aware this was to be expected.

'In the Montanilla manuscripts it was mentioned that a copy of
the them along with the princess's secret had being left "with the
brothers,"' Trevelyan added in an effort to encourage the professor.
'Now, if they were discovered in the village, in the properties of
Count Dabrowski's, the monastery would be the logical location,
right? 'I am certain it is either here or in one of the missing volumes.'

'Trevelyan, do not be fooled. There is nothing here. We've
reached a dead end. From what we have seen so far, it must be all a
copyist's hoax. Certainly, it would not be the first time someone had
the brilliant idea to add an aura of mystery to their work after being
hunched over a scroll all day, exhausted from the day's work. Despite
this, his work has still considerable merit, don't you think so? None
other than the author of the very first detective novel' he exclaimed,
snapping his notebook shut and placing it into his leather wallet.
'And we've been the lucky ones to discover it!'

The closing time finally arrived, signalled by tense coughing, restless feet, and ever emptier seats.

THE INNKEEPER APPROACHED QUIETLY.

They had spent many nights conversing in the inn's backyard
while gazing at the moon, the neighbouring mountains and the tranquil countryside. Now they had nothing more to say to each other.
Nothing other than trivial words.

Carlos Lafuente took out his pipe while Adolfo extracted a fine cigar from a secret drawer. Apparently, and judging by the looks on the innkeeper's face, the origin of the cigar was a complicated family secret that needed to be solved.

The innkeeper inhaled deeply after completing this delicate procedure.

'I think you will have a good road ahead tomorrow' he remarked. 'Last night it rained heavily, but today the sky is bright and all indications are that this trend will continue.'

Carlos nodded. They finished their ritual as if they the chiefs of two Indian nations gathering for a powwow. The white man's land had conquered them; there was no place left to hide.

A resolute embrace sealed the parting.

'Come on, we must leave!' Lafuente said to Arthur, with words that were meant to encourage himself rather than his pupil.

Arthur bid farewell to Pablo who was at the moment returning the chess pieces to their small wooden box. When he finished, he got up and carried the box into the house, shuffling his feet with the eloquence that had distinguished him throughout their stay.

~

CHAPTER 14

ARTHUR'S PROPOSAL

The presence of minor puddles on the streets indicated that it was going to be a rainy day after all.

Two coffees chilled on the table as professor and student solemnly regarded the old walls in front of the tavern where they had gone for breakfast that day, lacking the courage to return to their old friend after the farewells of last night.

The waiter came by twice and stroked the adjacent tables with his cloth. The absolute stillness the two customers kept in front of their coffee mugs partially startled him. He already knew that the nearby quiet monument drew to it oddballs and unusual folks who frequently went without leaving a tip.

Trevelyan gave the professor occasional glances. There was something strange about his attitude today.

'Well' said Lafuente finally 'There is nothing left to do here. We should pack our belongings and return home.'

Trevelyan nodded silently without speaking. He stood and paid the tab. They had agreed to take turns in doing so with the money that sweet Sofía, the rector's secretary, had given them for that purpose.

Arthur immediately realised what he had missed about Professor Lafuente over the past few days, excluding last night. Not for a single moment had he looked for his pipe, not even outside the monastery gates. It had remained in the inside pocket of his jacket all this time.

'Let us go, Trevelyan,' the professor repeated in what appeared to be a last-ditch effort, as he reached for the keys laying next to the unfinished coffee. 'Let us leave this place.'

The student followed him, adjusting his tie. On that day, the knot was nearly flawless, but the deft manoeuvre restored everything to their usual state.

THE GAUNT LIBRARIAN DISMISSED THEM WITH A DISTINCT relief in his eyes and swivelled to the photocopier as if he were in the final minutes of a countdown to the launch of a space rocket. Perhaps he had confused the initials of SILOS with those of NASA, so concentrated he seemed. In any event, he disliked these newcomers from this upstart university, this young man's arrogance, who surely masked his lax habits under a veneer of academic curiosity.

'At least two conclusions can be derived from our journey,' the young man said, breaking the extended silence as they pushed the two suitcases towards the car park.

'Yes? And what could it be so positive about that, Trevelyan?' said Lafuente.

'Well, on one hand, we've established the originality of the copyist and the era, correct? On the other hand, we know for certain that it was here where the scribe worked on the manuscripts.'

'That's peanuts! However, you were talking about a second conclusion, weren't you?' he said after a little pause as they passed the old stone fountains, no longer in use.

'Yes, no other surviving manuscript in Silos matches the time period, the type of calligraphy, or the technique used so well, either because they were completed works or because they were written earlier.'

'A great conclusion, Trevelyan, a great finish' murmured Lafuente, pausing and staring at the mediaeval square they had crossed each day as if seeing it for the first time.

Silos was the end of a chapter. It had retained its secrets, just as its old copyists hunched over the scriptorium, sacrificing each passing day before their scrolls. Something of them certainly had remained in those very scrolls, part of the secrets and mysteries of the old monastery and, most importantly, part of the patience that inhabited it. In a sense, they were still there, hidden within the walls without knowing it, to be unearthed perhaps centuries later.

They walked quietly, slowly, like fugitives, like thieves trying not to attract attention, having obtained no prey.

As the car engine started, the monastery, now busy with a coach full of tourists that had just arrived at its gates, appeared to have forgotten them already.

Through the rear-view mirror, St. Domingo de Silos seemed to go backwards, as if it were a film in reverse, returning to its roots, disappearing over the horizon. And with it, the codices, manuscripts, and documents it contained until finally disappearing from view.

On the way back to Montanilla, silence reigned. The two men looked at the road that stretched ahead of them. Behind every bend there were new paths, new routes to follow. Once more, they traversed the twisting road across Mataviejas River, leaving behind La Yecla tight gorges and solitary caverns.

Trevelyan looked from time to time at the notes he had been writing these days, interspersing this activity with drowsy reflection through the car windows. The young man —possibly in symbiosis with the copyists of the monastery—had, like them, sunk into a hypnotic stupor, that stupor in which all sort of images occupy the consciousness and appear unexpectedly before us. Only when Burgos emerged on the horizon, the two towers of the cathedral sewn to the sky, did the young man open his mouth, perhaps moved by the vision.

'I don't know about you, Professor, but I believe we should try something else before giving up.'

The professor paid no attention, his gaze fixed on the road. He appeared disheartened, although deep down he knew it was absurd to feel this way. Yes, this was part of any formal research, wasn't it?—the walls, the locked doors, the abrupt change of direction, the orientation, the protocol, if you will, the formulation of new hypotheses and yes, also the realisation of human incapacity, the impossibility of knowing everything or even a tiny fraction of what one would like to know. He must be glad, though. He would release the damned report so that the equally damned Count Dabrowski could do anything he wished with it. Then he could return to his regular routine, prepare his lecture for the coming symposium, and continue writing his book on the Invincible Armada.

'I repeat, Professor, there's something we must do.'

Carlos eventually turned and stared at him.

'Yes? Really? Maybe inspect another scroll? Because if that's the case, we can turn at the next crossroads. Canas Monastery is not far away.'

'No, at least not yet' replied Arthur, oblivious to the professor's ironic tone. 'I believe you have awakened my childish streak.'

'Your childlike streak?'

'I'd like you to tell me more fairy and princesses tales. Particularly about the latter.'

'Huh?'

This time, Lafuente shifted his attention to his partner. Had the boy become insane after sitting in front of the computer for so many days?

'I'd like to visit that place you mentioned the day you told me about the manuscripts for the first time. The place where our main character fell asleep, namely where Princess Kristina is buried.'

'Covarrubias?'

It was just another tiny query asked in a tiny green car lost on the road, its occupants trying to get home as the sun was setting on another day and time.

~

CHAPTER 15

AN HISTORICAL MEETING

Regarding fairy tales and other related matters.

Dawn revealed multiple visitors approaching the legendary city of Valladolid. Its melodious name alone suggests stability and heritage. Despite Madrid's last consonants being the same in the old Castilian conflict among Spanish cities for fans of light banter, the latter did not convey the same heroic and chivalrous vigour when uttered, that image of troops at the ready, flags raised.

Valladolid, cradle of Castilian nobility, lay dormant, awaiting the advent of the scribe, of the troubadour who would speak of its previous glory to a world that had forgotten it.

That day had finally come that November 17th.

Hundreds of foreign historians and authors from every imaginable field had gathered here.

They were greeted upon their arrival with the vision of the contemporary Miguel Delibes Cultural Centre, located on the outskirts of the city, just a few feet from the highway and other congested highways. The place might be labelled as "well linked" if one desired a positive and affable adjective. A site that could be easily reached using GPS or similar navigational aids.

It made sense that this convention of historians and authors be held in this location. Some, unaware of the significance of the event, might wonder why people from different countries and cultures with vast, traditional histories had decided to gather here of all places, on the outskirts of Valladolid, to discuss history in a place devoid of it.

It was a cold and impersonal place, empty, desolate of life and foliage and distant from the city. Distant indeed from that urban centre whose surface had been imprinted by the footsteps and footprints of generations, where mythical people had raised their heads and gazed upon the roofs of those identical buildings, street lighting, parks, and fountains.

It was an unbearably cold morning and those who dared to open their mouths experienced a flushing of the cheeks and the formation of tiny clouds in front of their eyes. On their way to the entrance, however, the assistants were disinterested in such metaphors as they vigorously wiggled their feet and rubbed their hands. Clouds of mist had been gathering on both sides of the road since early morning, as if they too wished to participate in the event.

Exiting the air-conditioned buses, rental cars, and private automobiles and navigating the parking lot to the front entrance was quite an adventure in itself. More than a few reflected on the circumstances that had led them there and berated themselves for taking part in this journey. The sun would be pleasantly lighting their classrooms at that hour had they remained in the hot south. The idea that they were following in the footsteps of previous explorers brought no relief.

Yes, tales of pirates and explorers in the case of lovers of fiction; of kings, soldiers and conquerors, in the case of historians. One could not cease lamenting this change, this pervasive chill. The scarce birds had not yet begun to sing, many of them were still in their summer destinations. During their absence, they had allowed these other species to take over the city squares and the wide esplanade in front of the Cultural Centre. It was not surprising that the sight of so many birds might could have inspired the city's most famous son, Miguel Delibes, to write so extensively about hunting and engage in it so frequently.

It was nine o'clock in the morning. Above the large glass facade hung a large notice board, reminding the absentminded of the meeting's purpose,

Literature and History in Spain, the mediaeval novel or the novel of the Middle Ages

In view of how many folks were already making their way to the entrance, the hall's vast capacity, which could easily handle over one thousand people, did not appear to be sufficient. Visitors from all over the world continued disembarking from coaches, taxis, vehicles, and minibuses and crossing its doors. Small groups began to form as they got off, in pursuit of the long-awaited Middle Ages.

Some of them were already arguing with the driver about the fare charged between points A and B, probably asserting ancient transport rights in the same manner that old barons did before King John.

Desolate groups scurried indoors to escape the frigid air and fog that dominated the broad esplanade.

One of them, however, appeared to be in no hurry. He had just parked his car and seemed to be observing the pavilion's glass doors with a familiar expression. Professor Lafuente was delighted to have returned to Valladolid.

He registered at the front desk, hastily collecting his identification card, pinning it to his lapel and waiting for Trevelyan near the main entrance. The latter in the meantime had succeeded in leaving his car at the farthest end of the expansive parking lot.

'I wasn't expecting so many people,' said the young man in apology when he arrived in front of the professor and witnessed the logistics that had been set up around the main gates. The location briefly reminded him of a ski resort's entrance during high season.

Arthur had come prepared for such cold weather indeed. He was wearing a huge grey scarf that appeared to curl around his neck like a boa constrictor, insulating him both from the chill outside and inquisitive eyes attracted both by his youth and lack of intellectual appearance.

'Trevelyan, a city that was once home to the famed Samoa pools on the banks of Pisuerga River, deserves at least one visit,' the professor stated as they entered.

'You intrigue me every time you speak, professor. Don't be shy now and tell me all about those pools!'

'There is nothing much to say, Trevelyan; or almost nothing... Just one of those things that time alters,' he said with a shrug.

'Don't play games with me.' Arthur muttered as he followed the professor's lengthy stride to the reception desk.

'Well, since I am here as an official storyteller and in order to open up our imaginations to what awaits us inside there, I might as well tell you,' the professor added, pointing to the auditorium hall. In 1935, the riverside of Pisuerga River was turned into a little beach, complete with sand and all the trimmings. After a few years of success, the phenomenon receded in the late 1990s, as is typical for such successful endeavours. I'm unsure whether the municipal council no longer cared about its continuation or if it had simply fallen out of favour. But I recall visiting them whenever my family and I came from Santander for the long vacation. It was an unusual sight.

'Outstanding professor! A beach in Valladolid!'

'Unfortunately, that is not the only thing that has vanished. I believe here is when historians enter the picture. To remind its citizens that their city, or at least their neighbourhood, was once an entirely different place. Perhaps a modernist palace or the city's first wheat mill once stood where people are currently piling trash. Such inconsequential minutiae,' ended Lafuente in a curt manner as he rearranged for the hundredth time the documents in the folder he had been handed along with his accreditation.

They carried their briefcases under their arms. Papers and notebooks were in their pockets alongside the tablets that had just been charged. Everything was prepared for the event.

'Where is Elena?' Arthur inquired, staring at the enormous glass. 'She ought to have arrived by now.'

'Trevelyan, If by "Elena" you mean Professor Serna, I believe she has already parked,' the professor grimaced.

The censorious gesture of Carlos Lafuente did not stay for long as he looked at the sprawling metropolis that could be seen in the distance through the windows of the convention center.

The discreet notice of a *WhatsApp* rang on the professor's phone.

'She's already here,' he said, as if his theory had been confirmed by the reading.

YES, THIS WAS HIS SECOND TIME ATTENDING A CONFERENCE IN this city, the eternal capital of Castile. The first had been year ago, in commemoration of the 500th anniversary of Magellan's exploration of the globe —that event the rector had referred to the day he allowed for their joint visit to Silos. Yes, it had been a memorable congress attended by prestigious historians from all over the world, such as Dr Sally Alexander from England, Maurice Agulhon from France, and Han Assmann from Germany, as well as local talents such as Professors Sánchez Conesa and Pérez Adán.

On this occasion however, prestige had diminished a little — according to an opinion he kept very much from sharing with others —. He had let himself to attend a gathering of authors of the misnamed historical fiction. These conceited individuals justified their entire narrative's craziness by quoting three or four unreliable Wikipedia articles or, worse, Google results.

And now, due to one of those scholarly coincidences, he would be surrounded by them in this utilitarian area, cut off from the city, with no means of escape—a rare witness to some sort of street rioting.

He attempted to create a mental refuge, to envelop himself in an imaginary bubble. He had heard Arthur say that since Stanislavski's times, actors have created their own secret worlds away from the public in order to get into character and shield themselves from the outside world.

He could observe Elena and Arthur through the windows exchanging greetings. From that vantage point, he got an excellent view of the city's skyline; the old town, which had been so familiar to him years earlier, was there somewhere. The wedding of that enigmatic princess whose trace they were following, took place there in some distant past. The church where she married Felipe de Castilla no longer exists. The cathedral arose over it. At times like this, he doubted that the Catholic Kings, Magellan, Quevedo, Colón, Cervantes, and Zorrilla, among others, would have gathered in this city at various points in its history, not to mention Princess Kristina.

While waiting for his colleagues to return from the reception desk, he perused *North de Castilla*, the dean of Spanish newspapers, which had been distributed here and there for the solace of congress assistants along with several other national and international magazines. He would have loved to take out his pipe out and fidget with the bowl and chopped tobacco to calm his anxiety, but he couldn't do that right now.

Elena and Trevelyan approached at that moment, the former proudly exhibiting the ID card she had just received. The professor continued to ramble, his mind elsewhere.

Elena had chosen for the event a navy blue double-breasted jacket and a light grey scarf that wrapped around her neck. The back of her long hair appeared to be almost concealed by a bonnet, while the front fell loose and gorgeous, beautifully framing her cleavage. The corners of the handkerchief had been tied with exquisite care turned to one side with millimetric precision, in a ten past two position, thus diverting attention away.

'Have you noticed, Carlos? They have worked miracles with the photo they took for this!' she exclaimed, pointing with pride at the card pinned to her chest, as if she were attending a weekend picnic instead of a convention. 'It was high time you included me in your Boy Scout outings. In any case, this is my first congress!'

'Indeed, yes,' replied the interpellated, averting his gaze and trying to occupy his attention with something else. He searched for aid throughout the lobby, founding it at last it under the form of a coffee machine that, discreetly out of the way, was at that point being besieged by a small group of people. Its members fumbled busily through their wallets, in search of a way to revive their minds.

Trevelyan observed with certain glee the scene from one of the few seats that surrounded the infernal machine.

'Well, I suppose... would any of you like a cup of coffee before entering?' Carlos murmured with a sigh of relief as he approached the vending machine.

It was the first time that Veltin, —a new Valladolid firm— had been hired to organise the event, and they found their hostess cheery and welcoming. After verifying their credentials, she asked,

'Are you a group?'

'Well, yes and no. I mean...' began the professor.

Elena smiled and said, 'Yes, the three of us go together.'

Arthur demurred briefly before accepting a few programmes from the hostess, which allowed him the opportunity to offer her a wink that was neither totally scholarly nor completely professional.

The professor, seated between his companion and his assistant in one of the first rows, looked around getting now and then several of the attendants. The vast majority of them familiar faces, recognisable from the last congress. A short, round-eyed, glasses-wearing man with a round beard sat nearby. He responded to his greeting awkwardly. In their youth, they had shared a faculty seat in Santander. "God, I hope I haven't changed as much as he!" The professor thought while going over the lecture schedule one hundred times.

, Arthur appeared entirely immersed in his notes, oblivious to the professor's intermittent signs of uneasiness. It was only after having put his cell phone in airplane mode, that he noticed Lafuente seemed unable to decide what to do with his hands.

'Easy, professor, easy. I'm sure your lecture is very well prepared.' he said, believing this was the reason for his tutor's agitation.

'No, Trevelyan, it's not that. At least not all. With the preparation of my speech and things like that, I cannot help but feel we are drifting away from what truly matters, what is genuinely important. I mean, we put the investigation on hold a week and a half ago. Isn't it? It's quite irritating having to interrupt my work in this manner to listen to gibberish precisely when we are pressed for time. Besides, I promised you we would be visiting princess Kristina's tomb soon.'

'However the university also requires our presence here,' replied Trevelyan not quite convinced by the professor's argument. 'Don't worry and try to enjoy the moment.'

While they were talking in this vein, Elena came to the conclusion she no longer needed to continue wearing her ID card after the initial identification process. Her jacket pocket would be the best place for the item. She considered she could handle the resulting anonymity. After cataloguing manuscripts, books, and other material, she did not like to appear like another shelf item herself.

From Ernesto Santos' notes

When I began writing this story as a journal, I had no idea where it would take me. I had read incredible tales, fantasising about impossible adventures and stories like any average son of his time. I never anticipated, however, that I would be both the protagonist and witness in one of them.

No, there was no storm to darken the sky that day. The wind was not sweeping through the streets, nor had the light on the horizon gone out; situations always favourable for narrating stories of this nature. In my city, the sun shines all day through —or almost always—and yet...

7:20 a.m.

The clock alarms on our two cell phones rang simultaneously. Luckily, and after several days of exploring ring tones, Clarissa and I had been able to find a pair of tracks that perfectly matched each other.

Since *Out of Africa* was my favourite film soundtrack, I chose Mozart's *Concert Adage for Clarinet and Oboe in A K 622*, which had mesmerised me from the moment I first heard it. Clarissa had selected *Feeling Good* by Michael Bublé, a song we had previously heard.

'Sleepyhead, up and shine!' said Clarissa throwing a pillow at me before kissing me good morning. 'You are going to leave them dumbfounded today. Wait and see.'

'I feel as if my pijamas does not fit me.' I retorted, returning the pillow in the same manner.

Indeed, such was the case. Everything was happening too fast. The book had only been released a few months ago. Desiré, my editor, had just informed me that according to the most recent data she had, sales were increasing. It was a significant leap, though, to be invited by one of her literary friends —whom, by the way, I had barely met at the publishing house and had coffee with—, to offer a lecture on nothing less than Novels and History.

Instead of driving ourselves to the conference site, we choose to leave our car at the hotel and take use of the chauffeur service organised by the conference organisers. The name of our chauffeur was Pietri. At least, that is what he informed us, along with other information provided in the twenty minutes it took the car to negotiate the city streets. A native of Turkey, he had an outstanding knack for synthesis. He had just arrived from the States, where he had first immigrated, and he had not missed, until precisely this morning at 8:30 a.m.—so fortunate had we been, such had been our privilege—, the summer afternoons spent by his front door as the sun set, listening to the shouting of children in front of the store he used to run. Similar anecdotes would never have arisen in our private car, and being this such a special day for us, it certainly added interest to the occasion. We gave him instructions to pick us up later.

At the main desk, we were given our badges. Strangely enough I didn't feel odd. Throughout my lengthy career, I had gained some experience in the export world, moved in a multicultural atmosphere, organised events, booked and altered stands, and so on. So, although this was a unique event, it was also oddly familiar.

When I saw the identification cards bearing our names on our laps along with other personal information, I felt a pang of nostalgia for my college days.

I stopped at a stand to peruse some magazines while Clarissa completed the registration process.

'Well, let's go over there. I believe that's our door,' I remarked, placing my hand on Clarissa's arm and pointing her in that direction.

A woman walked with a fast gait in front of us, carrying a pair of sodas in her hands, perhaps to make the first lecture more enjoyable.

Lights gradually dimmed, plunging the entire audience into darkness. A few last-minute anxious coughs were the only indication the event had begun.

It was to be opened by Mr Rufio Colmenar of the History Dpt at Ohio University. The introduction was followed by the predictable hollow speech of the authority on duty. Once it was over, she would quickly leave the audience and return to her official automobile or private plane as the case may be, to her secluded, cosy office. The remainder would become history in turn.

After the introductory presentation, the MC Mr Clemente Násera, introduced the speaker from the University of Murcia.

The time arrived to announce the third participant. Less time before my turn came, less time to cease observing the upholstery in front of me, the wall coverings and the lighting distribution of the space.

'And now, ladies and gentlemen,' continued Mr Násera, 'I have the pleasure of introducing my friend and colleague Carlos Lafuente Lázaro, professor at Montanilla University.'

Upon hearing this a lanky figure emerged from one of the rows in front of us. The guy, who reminded me of a middle-aged James Stewart, marched confidently with a firm stride towards the steps leading up to the dais.

The professor spoke with fervour and conviction about palaeographic research in general and the scholar's work in particular, focusing on the daily task of battling time only to discover the smallest unit of significance.

Finally my turn arrived. I climbed the steps two at a time and positioned myself behind the long table set up for the speakers, a table which unavoidably reminded me of the Last Supper one. However, its length seemed to serve no purpose, as after being introduced by the MC was used by only one of the speakers at a time.

I had a glass of water in front of me. Behind it, the audience waited expectantly. I cannot recall the exact moment I broke the silence, but this I did after changing the position of the glass several times while my introduction was being made. I did not drink from it though, but the manoeuvre certainly helped me to relax. Neither was I aware of the audience despite the auditorium's PA system, I could listen myself speaking only through what appeared a misty atmosphere.

I had done some theatricals in my youth, so I should have been used to addressing an audience on stage. What a mistake! There was a difference now. I was not hiding myself now behind any of the roles I played. Now I was being myself, expressing my beliefs. That was it! There was the rub! I talked about the subject because Clarissa's smile and words had just given me conviction, passion, and strength before going upstairs.

You could tell I was in my environment. And yes! It was my first time speaking at a conference, so I was naturally anxious. I was, after all hardly a published author. My closest experience had been the English linguistics conference held in Malaga during my last term at university. I recall this vividly because I found there the same amount of enthusiasm in other students of my age and mostly, the love and thirst for knowledge shown by the students of Deusto University at Bilbao.

This congress also brought to my memory the adventurous nature of my undergraduate years. It was comforting to see that many of the people who now filled the corridors and conversed in the neighbouring chairs before the event began appeared to be in the same mood as I recalled from those times.

I started with a gentle throat clearing. Certainly, that always adds a professional touch. It might be considered a rhetorical tactic.

'According to my fellow historians, we storytellers are in our environment here' (muffled laughter was heard in the audience). 'But I do not see it that way. Contrariwise, I believe it is precisely my erudite fellow historians who enjoy the authority and benefit of depending on hard facts. There is, however, a shaky ground where we both meet: the grey area of unverified facts. This is both the pinnacle of the historian's skill and the source of his aggravation.

On the other hand, this same dissatisfaction is a novelist's delight. For it is here that the door opens, when the option of fictionalising history and putting a concept into context arises. Those of us born in 1958 and subsequent years will definitely recall with fondness and nostalgia the feeling of adventure that pervaded the streets at the time.'

Here I took a short, planned breather in order to see its effect on the audience.

'The old television shows and the children's novels we read and learned by heart, such as those of Enid Blyton and similar others emphasised this feature. We read Jules Verne and adventure stories as if our lives depended on it. Almost with the same zeal as some young people today fight with their Play Stations.' (new laughs). 'We novelists create our own stories and adventures. Others, however, had experienced them in the first person and, with their courage and personal dedication, made real a previously imagined world beyond the horizon, far from the known lands. I am frequently asked what our source of inspiration is, the legendarily naughty and enigmatic unconscious that, according to legend, walks behind us. The storyline is always something more or less technical, just as war is nothing more than the continuation of politics through other means and art might be nothing more than the expression of grief through other methods. This is the objective of all art, and the reason why it has captivated us throughout the centuries.'

THREE INDIVIDUALS IN ROW SEVEN APPEARED TO BE PAYING THE uttermost attention to the speaker's words. One of them was Carlos Lafuente, who was pondering having heard something similar in the past. Yes, there was some justification for this man's words.

He believed nonetheless these were impracticable concepts. Could this be the author who wandered around Silos? The cause of the librarian's persistent gloomy disposition? It was a possibility. He smirked as he envisioned the scene. He looked at his companions. Elena and Arthur appeared to share the same feeling. The latter, following his custom, was scribbling ceaselessly in his small notebook. More patiently, Elena licked the point of a pencil as she took the occasional odd note, displaying a grimace of complicity or assent to some of the topics stated at various times. That scarf really fit her quite well.

The author was concluding his speech:

[...] 'Therefore, sometimes during our everyday work, whether derived from the study of old codices, archaeological remains, works of art, and such in the case of historians, or by a crazy idea that connects two previously unconnected points, creating that scene we novelists were looking for, we both have something special that is typically referred to in my field as a "Epiphany" —in the same sense that James Joyce used the term—. That something is the key to our work. That's the central element of our work. Others, more pragmatic or less idealistic, could suggest it's a form of intuition. And this is how, my friends, we shall rediscover our sense of adventure in studying the Spanish Middle Ages.'

With this words and with a certain sense of relief, having put away the few papers he had prepared for the occasion, the novelist left the platform among the applause of the audience.

Carlos stood up along with his companions.

'Professor!' said Arthur with scarcely concealed enthusiasm. 'That was directed at us, haven't you noticed? Tell me if that's not surprising, a true epiphany!'

'It has been a very emotive and sincere speech' said Elena.

However, Lafuente was less receptive to the articulated viewpoint.

'Yes, of course, just like the horoscope in today's newspaper,' he replied with a grunt.

Obviously, he had read about epiphanies, a term that literature students used far too frequently for his liking. He had always referred to it as the "Newton phenomena" and the scientist's dubious anecdote concerning an apple. He rejected all of Trevelyan's colourful pseudoscientific beliefs. It was not sensible to seek explanations for odd happenings outside of the scientific approach. It irritated him that his student didn't shy away from improbable explanations.

Yes, doing so was the sensible thing to do. The most consistent and rational.

Possibly the most tedious as well.

Ernesto felt someone was observing them. When he turned around, he noticed that the tall professor who had previously reminded him of James Stewart was slowly approaching. He was in the company of a young man and an attractive brunette with long hair. Judging by the boy's yellow identification, he must be a one of the few postgraduate student who had attended.

The professor seemed to hesitate for a moment, and after whispering something to his companions, advanced towards Ernesto, his right hand extended.

'Congratulations on your speech! I especially liked your reference to the world of adventure and maritime exploration. It's unfortunate you did not attend the last congress. You would have cherished it.'

'Well, it doesn't have great merit, really. I am a novelist, remember? We get paid for making stuff up and spewing so many words. Besides, I believe it's necessary to periodically assert the old values so that they are not readily forgotten.

The man smiled. Despite his timid demeanour, his brilliant eyes expressed a connection that made them both feel immediately at ease.

'Allow me to introduce you to my colleague. She is... '

'Hello there! I'm Elena! How are you doing? We thoroughly enjoyed your speech,' said the aforementioned, interrupting the professor's formal introduction.

'And my name's Arthur Trevelyan,' the student smiled, continuing in the same vein. 'I'm one of Professor Lafuente's students.'

'He is not a mere student; please disregard his extreme modesty,' said Lafuente when the boy could not hear him. 'He possesses a unique talent. But excuse my manners, I'm Carlos Lafuente from Montanilla University,' he added, offering his hand, glad at the chance to finally introduce himself.

'Do you write fiction as well?' Ernesto inquired, once they had been properly introduced. 'Some references in your lecture led me to believe you had authored something along these lines.'

'No, I'm afraid I'm from the enemy camp. However, after attending your talk you'll find me flying the white flag at our campus.' At this point, he lowered his voice and said with a scowl, 'At least in the history department.'

While his companions were discussing the lectures and events schedule for the current day young Arthur approached Clarissa and Ernesto.

'Excuse my asking, Mr Santos. It may seem odd to you, but after listening to your lecture, I consider it absolutely necessary. Have you ever heard of significant coincidences before?'

After recovering from the initial shock of such an awkward question, Ernesto was about to respond when a soft warning buzz was heard above their heads. It was a call for assistants to return to the auditorium. They proceeded to their seats while muttering and glancing at the small group that impeded their entrance. The brief intermission had ended.

ARTHUR WAS SEEING THE SUNRISE IN FRONT OF THE WIDE windows of the cultural centre. It was the congress second day. Lafuente found him there after having gone to the coffee machine. He was holding a cup in his hand from which he drank in little swallows.

With his badge hanging proudly, Arthur reminded the professor of those magical days when he had attended his first history convention. It had been held in Santander, a year after completing a postgraduate programme in Paris.

The young man turned upon hearing him.

'Welcome to a brand-new morning!' Arthur stated, gesturing toward the city centre visible behind the glass. 'Do you know, professor? Yesterday after supper, I wandered among the old alleys in the city centre. I really liked it —all those stately streets! You already informed me that you spent several summers here. Surely, you must have many memories of the place.'

Before responding, the professor averted his sight and fixing his gaze on the countryside beyond the glass.

'Yes, I came several summers with my parents. We owned a house on Mirlo Street, very close to Patricia Park. Do you remember I told you yesterday that Valladolid is full of surprises? The Cafetín is one of them, one of the few remaining bars where it is still possible to extend an afternoon till the following day. My friend Benito and I used to go there every morning before exploring the streets in search of employment or simply wasting time, meandering aimlessly in search of something to do. I was still undecided as to what studies I wished to pursue. And when I finally did, our lives parted ways.'

Carlos was thoughtful. For a brief instant, just a few seconds he once again saw Benito's face in front of him. That slightly carefree look on his lips that gave him the appearance of being constantly smiling and attentive.

'I wonder what might have become of him,' he said. 'He was a stubborn fellow, always ready for a good fight. In spite of that a part of me will always remember the walks we took around the city in those long summers when I was about your age, Trevelyan. Good heavens! To think I was once your age... Anyway,' he added, raising his head and patting the student on the back. 'End of nostalgia for now. Trevelyan, we live too much in the past; trust me, don't follow my example. Run away while you can.'

CHAPTER 16

A MEAL FOLLOWED BY DINNER

How restorations, epiphanies, and coincidences arouse the appetite and thirst for knowledge Or how to organise an exploration trip in an art déco setting.

The group that had gathered at the cafeteria was, to say the least, strange. The historians, Carlos Lafuente and Elena Serna, sat to the left of a long table near to a huge window facing the expansive view of the parking lot. In front of them, Ernesto Santos and Clarissa were accompanied by Arthur Trevelyan who seemed to have traversed the chasm separating the two specialties in order to join them and next to Rus Bermejo, a renowned art curator from Burgos University (UBU).

At the opposite end of the table and paying the utmost attention to everything that was occurring sat the M.C, Mr Clemente Násera. The latter had a face framed by a grey goatee and round glasses that resembled that of the famous Spanish physician Ramón y Cajal. Like him, he appeared to be searching everywhere for morsels of microscopic knowledge. Mr Rufio Colmenar on his part displayed an abundance of gestures, of toasts offered left and right, something that perhaps he was missing in his daily routine at Ohio University.

'Would you like to know something, Mr Santos?' Lafuente said to the novelist.

'Please, professor, call me Ernesto. We have long since passed the Middle Ages, haven't we?'

Carlos looked down. He was changing many customs too quickly.

Before continuing, he glanced at the tabletop and altered his tone:

'You know... Ernesto?' he said at last, not without some effort.'What you mentioned in your lecture, that pertaining to epiphanies and the like.'

'Yes, yes,' Ernesto said encouragingly.

'My student Arthur Trevelyan, always on the lookout for similar occurrences, refers to it as a "significant coincidence"'

'Yes, I know... good old Jung! As a matter of fact, Arthur has already asked me about it earlier today,' Ernesto said, winking at the student. 'We do study some psychology at the Literature Dpt if only to interpret what our professors do. I am sorry, but I must disagree with you. Those of us writing fiction cannot afford to rely on significant coincidences to advance the plot. Not even to tell a story. It's the simplest and most obvious approach that comes to mind. I apologise if I sound a bit pedantic, but...'

Occasionally, one discovers a major link among a group of newly-met individuals. Suddenly everything looks familiar, near, and we feel as though we could bare our souls and even our diaries to these folks. The tune eventually changes, we relax, lower our guard and to alter our everyday pattern.

Carlos had experienced such a feeling since the very beginning of the meal and this relationship had been building and taking shape unnoticed. It didn't take long for the professor to share his studies on Princess Kristina to the new acquaintances and table companions he had just met. It was inevitable that it would be thus, infected by this intellectual yet casual milieu.

'What you say is simply amazing!' said Clemente Násera when

he finished, 'So it is possible that the purpose of the princess journey might have been something different than the one described in the chronicles, correct?'

'Not only that,' Carlos said, elated by the interest aroused. 'It is certain that right now, we are unquestionably at a dead end. The authenticity of the discovered manuscripts is uncertain. They could be simply the product of an elaborate prank. We believe that because something is old, its substance must therefore be correct, forgetting in so doing that our distant ancestors also played practical jokes and made fun of each other.'

'Well,' Ernesto Santos intervened, addressing no one in particular, but glancing quizzically at Arthur, 'if coming to Valladolid and meeting someone following a clue concerning the journey of this mysterious princess through these lands, is not one of those significant coincidences of yours, I do not know what it might be then.'

'Would you like to continue this pleasant conversation over a delicious dinner?' said Clemente Násera. He had remained silent throughout the entire lunch, attentively listening to both the professor and the author. He seemed pleased at the success of seeing interest leap from both sides as he fiddled with the seal he carried on one of his left-hand fingers, Elena and Arthur exchanged looks, surprised at this outpouring of kindness and hospitality from the master of ceremonies.

'Come on, my friends! Please don't give me "no" for an answer.' insisted Mr Násera. 'I would like to take you to a fantastic restaurant in the Gutiérrez passage. Don't let me enjoy its Beauxartian architecture alone. And you, Rus, kindly plead on my behalf' he said, addressing the attractive art curator who was busy sipping her champagne.

'We would undoubtedly be contributing with our modest contribution to the preservation of a portion of the historic centre of Valladolid. I would be incredibly privileged to have you as my companions, besides being this, if I may say so, a combination of a historical and literary meal in order to please everyone in terms of vocabulary.'

. . .

IT SPREADS SLOWLY OUT OF NOWHERE STRETCHING OUT ON THE ground. A furtive shadow, almost invisible, follows and hides behind the columns of the old city's corners. It peeks out, perverse, mixing with the cobblestones, the ornaments, the portals of the old tenements. It enters them and remains there long enough to pass unnoticed only to remerge minutes later, victorious and threatening, looking for its prey.

It approaches the cobbled alley, saving as best it can the puddles that have formed among the stones that make it, dodging and jumping over some of them. Finally, it reaches the lighted window at the passage corner and looks up at the unmistakable wooden sign hanging there.

It belongs to the Olid Restaurant, that place with an unsetting old look. But nothing can deceive that shadow that looks and stares, that digs beneath the surface of things. Slowly approaching and peeping inside, discovering there the presence of the group of strangers arrived in the city the previous day by different routes. They are now seated at a table together, amid laughter and raised glasses.

The antique street lamp sways slightly as a result of the wind that has just begun to blow. The shadow pauses for a minute, stares up at the sign moving beneath the post that supports it, trembles at the dim light provided by the lantern. After that brief pause, the shadow continues down the street towards the passage exit leading to Castelar Street. A thin drizzle begins to fall. It does so gently, washing the pavement with a dull sound that only a knowledgeable rain enthusiast with a sharp ear could perceive, raising that familiar smell of ozone all over the place. And so, just like that, listless, with bad manners, without a single kind gesture, the shadow, which many continue to refer as fog, spreads until until vanishing completely, allowing the street lights in the passage and especially those outside the Olid restaurant, to rule supreme.

The Gutierrez passage, located between Fray Luis de León and Castelar streets is one of the few in the country that pays homage to the first commercial passageways that emerged in Paris in 1799 during the industrial revolution, along with the galleries of Victor Emanuel II in Milan, Umberto I in Naples, and the small but charming Burlington Arcade in London. We're talking about passages like the Verdeau, the Joffrey, and the Panoramas, which can be found in different Parisian streets.

Inside the Olid restaurant, Arthur is looking at the oak wood affixed to the wooden walls. The time is thirty minutes past midnight.

He has been looking at it throughout all dinner, as if he wanted to confirm that the restaurant existed and occupied a physical location in space and time.

It belongs to the Olid Restaurant, which has an unsetting old look.

THE EVENING HAS PASSED PLEASANTLY ENOUGH. ON ONE SIDE of the table sit the members of Montanilla University, the novelist and his girlfriend. The latter have fallen under the fatherly protection of Professor Násera. They are unable to find cover or retreat from his insatiable curiosity and interest in all aspects of human activity.

The passage is frequented even at this hour by a few solitary pedestrians and several groups engaged in quiet conversation on its terraces.

These have taken refuge there from the fog and the rain, sipping coffee or beer under the light of Mercury-shaped lamps placed at regular intervals that illuminate the entire area with their spheres of light.

The Gutierrez passage is a journey across time. By looking at the windows and lanterns that graced its walls, anyone might have believed to be oneself in the late 19th century. The space has been designed with a distinct sense of style and flair, harmonious with its surroundings.

Professor Lafuente and his companions enjoy it very much, and Rus Bermejo has expressed his admiration for the careful adaptation and restoration of the premises.

'I had no idea such a place could be found today. It's charming!' says Arthur enthusiastically as he gazes at the art nouveau décor, matching the passage outside. A large number of mirrors, lamps, faux-Greek statues, replicas of paintings, and seascapes adorned the walls, creating the illusion that they were in a museum rather than a restaurant.

He can see at his back velvet curtains framing the stairs they had descended hours earlier.

'Few people are aware of its existence,' Clemente Násera volunteers over his glass after noticing the enthusiasm on the faces of both the young man and the curator. 'A little over six months ago, there was nothing here. The owner is a French hispanophile. Yes, yes, indeed do not laugh! There are several of these among the frogs. The man had the idea of restoring here in Valladolid one of those places in the style of the Gijón coffee-house and some other nineteenth-century cafés in both France and Spain, among others. As you can see, he is doing rather well.'

Yes, such is the case; elegantly dressed people are constantly crossing its doors, with that natural elegance and *savoir-faire* that needs such an adequate frame to stand out and move around. Ladies wearing costumes fashioned of inconceivable materials, their moves similarly sophisticated, leave their coat in the closet and place an order for a fine wine, menu in hand, waiting to be assisted by the *sommelier*. In short, a place where the worship of elegance is not ashamed to show itself.

Santos is in conversation with Professor Lafuente. A waiter approaches and offers to refill their cups.

'According to my knowledge, at least four novels have been published about the figure of princess Kristina,' the novelist is saying.

'A story with such few elements, little-known facts, and few hints gathered almost at random over the course of at least eight centuries lends rise to conjecture. As a writer, I can't help but realise this is a story full of possibilities.'

'In my experience,' interrupts Rus Bermejo 'It's comparable to discovering beneath an old painting being restored an even older piece. That always reminds me of the novel Julia by Lillian Hellman and the film of the same name. She referred to it as "pentimento": when the artist repented. What do you do in such a circumstance? What work should prevail? Restoring the new means discarding the one humanity has known for generations. What would happen, for instance, if we discovered, beneath the Mona Lisa we all know and cherish, another picture by Da Vinci? Which shall we retain? Just contemplate that!'

'Certainly, I do understand' says Ernesto 'It would be like restoring Notre Dame or the British Parliament with their original whitish tones instead of the black ones we are used to. Is that it?'

'That's it! I see you get the point.'

At this moment, Arthur drops his head and speaks in a low tone to the professor. Upon hearing him, the latter smiles slightly and nods multiple times before standing up while maintaining his customary grave expression.

Beethoven's *Moonlight* sounds softly on a piano in the background beneath the rapid and nimble fingers of the Jamaican pianist.

'Friends,' started Lafuente, 'you must have realised by now after telling you these facts that we are attempting something quite tough in Montanilla University. It involves putting the scarce information we have into a historical context. Possibly then, everything might acquire a new significance. And should the day come to discover another Da Vinci underneath..., mind you, at least we will have the conviction that it exists! ' Here the historian lowers his voice before continuing 'Our friend Arthur here is responsible for an upcoming cultural tour in search of his own Excalibur, so to speak. He has convinced me to visit the nearby village of Covarrubias in the coming days, the place where Kristina of Norway is buried. So, What do you say to that? Will you join us?' he asks, addressing Ernesto and Clarissa. 'You are not returning to Valencia until the day after tomorrow, correct? Perhaps we should discover nothing ' and as he says this, he clenches his teeth, still resentful of the days spent in Silos. 'It's possible that, as our novelist would say, everything would result in fog amid the grass, but it's not every day that one visits a princess, wouldn't you agree?'

The author and Clarissa smile in amusement. Clarissa, who has been nearly silent during supper, stands up raising her glass.

'To significant coincidences!' she exclaims, with a big smile that wonderfully matches the environment.

Everyone finds their glasses with certain effort due to the effect of so many libations.

Ernesto, swayed by the general enthusiasm, says in turn 'Yes, and may Arthur's wild Epiphany bring us to a successful finish.'

'I hadn't seen it exactly that way,' Trevelyan says, 'but if it's about providing any excuse to go to Covarrubias, it's good enough for me.'

Rus Bermejo deeply regretted not being one of the party, as she is now fully occupied with the restoration of one of the chapels at Burgos Cathedral.

It is now time for Clemente Násera to rise, doing so with a grin as he takes in his surroundings, looking around with pleasure.

He never anticipated, even under the best of circumstances that his initial suggestion for this meal would result in such an outcome. For a few hours, he has escaped the ostracism of his office and the monotonous conversations he is accustomed to, both at the university and the local Chamber of Commerce.

Nobody dares to verbalise it clearly, but a peculiar aura of mystery floats in the air.

The small group designated for this exploration is formed by the promoters of the initial idea, Carlos Lafuente, Professor Elena, and the eternal pupil, Arthur Trevelyan. Ernesto Santos and Clarissa have been designated as official chroniclers of the expeditionary force, with the explicit promise that they would provide Mr Násera with a thorough report of their exploits. The whole thing reminds Ernesto of the beginning of *The Posthumous Papers of the Pickwick Club*, the first novel written by Charles Dickens. More specifically, the chapter in which the famous club members begin their thrilling voyage.

The little assembly bid farewell at the exit of the Gutierrez tunnel in the wee hours of the morning, leaving the passage filled with echoes and devoid of human presence.

November 19, 20th

We have just got out of the most bizarre meeting I have ever attended. I came to Valladolid invited by some friends of Desiree to speak about the adventure novel. I leave this city now with new friends and a unique invitation to study the secrets of a princess who—until a few days ago, I had never heard of. But there was no way I could have resisted something like this. Everything seemed cut up for me.

The hints, the scent of a mystery that someone had left behind, whispered to me in enticing and intriguing tones. Clarissa was as ecstatic as I was and she obviously enjoyed seeing me in that state. She smiled at me during dinner and the ensuing talk at the table, displaying that self-assurance that I admire so much in her. On the other hand, I found the comments of this boy, this *cum laude* student, *Laudy*—a benevolent nickname I like to use when talking to Clarissa—both fascinating and disturbing, paired with his philosophical and esoteric thoughts and the story he has revealed us.

So, here I am at the entrance to this fantastic universe that has stumbled across my path. So much so that I am thrilled to embark on this adventure of exploration if I am not a hindrance. It may not be Magellan's global journey, but it would be a Castilian tour in historical terms. We may uncover an alternate reality. This has always intrigued me. Not to mention that there could be material here for a novel.

Everything is different here. I don't have to search for a storyline, plot, or motive. It is unnecessary to pursue a pretext to build an argument, a justification to express my hell, nightmares, and flee from myself. I merely have to take that legend, any legend or story in the world, and sign it. Make it mine. That's all there is to it! Then I would have time to battle with metaphors, embellish the language, and finish sentences and paragraphs with my thoughts. I had read somewhere that beliefs are living beings existing independently of us, awaiting recognition as the fruit of the Tree of Good and Evil, at its proper point of maturity. Once our attention is captured, we will be mercilessly devoured.

The ship had been chartered. The expedition already been organized. Everybody is in earnest. The crew recruited from a variety of ports. Hundreds of people have visited Admiral Benbow's inn, but no one has got hold of the map. The trail written on it by a faraway scribe from centuries past, floating through the air of history.

One could only hope that a gale wouldn't break the sails, that the crew wouldn't revolt, and that Treasure Island would be located where it was depicted on the sole map we could find.

～

CHAPTER 17

THE ARLANZÓN PRINCESS

Of our heroes' visit to the viage of Covarrubias, their discovery of a princess there, followed by a reflection concerning brothers and sisters.

From Ernesto Santos' notes

Burgos, November 23rd

When we exited the Hotel Rice Reyes Católicos at 9 a.m, we were faced there with Arthur Trevelyan at the wheel of a classic yellow Volkswagen van. The inscription "Scooby-Doo" on its side reminded me of the old cartoon series that my brother and I used to watch on Saturday afternoons on our tiny tv set.

The similarities between those heroes of my salad days and the present circumstances made me smile.

'Welcome!' Elena said with a smile, sticking her head out the window. 'Are you up for an adventure?'

'Whose van is this?' Clarissa said. 'I was under the impression that none of these existed outside of modest collections and exhibitions.'

'It belongs to a classmate' Trevelyan stated, feigning to spin the steering wheel at full speed. 'I borrowed it in exchange for some extra lessons and diagrams; you know, the usual student stuff. He's memberof a rock band and use it to transport the equipment. Therefore, beware; you may discover cables or similar objects in the back seats!'

'Ok then' said Clarissa as she mounted aboard and, following the instructions received, moved aside a pair of microphones from the seat. Then, noticing the rest of the passengers inside the van, she said, 'We absolutely require the dog! Because we already have the mystery.'

Thus, with such vigour, we began the journey we had outlined that evening at Pasaje Gutiérrez in Valladolid. After all, this was more to my liking than attending conferences and listening to boring lectures, but one cannot have everything, can one?'

Yes, equipped with a cell phone and a notepad to record whatever transpired from our trek, I felt like the reporter of an expedition across uncharted territories. Like countless explorers before we took with us only the bare essentials: a few drinks in the trunk and plenty of pencils and paper, in addition to our various electronic devices. A mysterious black leather suitcase sat on the lap of Professor Lafuente. I was aware of the moment's significance and my role as chronicler. I rolled down the window and breather in the fresh air, which I assumed had already visited our destination. Although, given the circumstances, I would have preferred the smell of saltpetre blown by the wind hitting our faces, I would have to settle for the scent of the fields and crops we passed on our way.

We traversed in this manner the slopes in our small van, contemplating the grion vultures' ceaseless flight across the sky. I had allowed myself to sink into a state of drowsiness, observing the landscape from the backseat. A panorama that naturalist Félix Rodríguez de la Fuente had already toured in quest of images of that elusive scenery.

The Montanilla group barely uttered a word during the journey. Arthur or Elena occasionally pointing out a strange feature of the landscape, such as a cliff or hill with an irregular rock formation that might have been there since the Universal Flood. However,

Lafuente only responded with mute nods, his eyes locked on the road.

A FEW KILOMETRES BEFORE REACHING OUR DESTINATION, WE spotted on the left-hand side some imposing ruins in a state of upcoming restoration, a few metres below our level. The main facade, echoing its illustrious history, stood out prominently among the others. They were the only remnants of the former San Pedro de Arlanza monastery, at whose feet flows the river by the same name. Fortunately, the massive portal was still standing, as stubborn as it had been since its erection on that hill above the stream. Nearby there were clear signs of the reform and repair works that would prevent the historic building from collapsing. We finally arrived at the little town of Covarrubias, that little hamlet forty kilometres southeast of Burgos. I had heard a great deal about it and read a few details in books, but that was it. Even in this age of Internet and Google, nothing can equal the feeling of finding oneself in a real location.

I never cease to be amazed at the capacity of us humans for astonishment. The kind of astonishment that allows us to continue marvelling at a new scenario, a fresh experience.

After passing a pub bearing the name "La Serna" on its front, we parked the van on a small esplanade at the road shoulder as no vehicles were allowed inside the hamlet.

'Look, Elena. Your forefathers arrived here before the very Vikings did!' Arthur remarked grimly, pointing at the pub's sign.

Elena responded by sticking her tongue out in silence. A gesture of sheer pragmatism.

So we entered the settlement via those cobblestoned, automobile free streets. A number of its stores remained closed at that hour in keeping with the slumber of similar businesses away of the daily rhythm. The street we were walking on was lined on both sides with planters every few metres. Some black lanterns protruded from its facades, enhancing the scene's picturesque quality. A discreet sign hanging from a store to our right announced with some modesty that shortbread was sold there.

We found ourselves at the end of the street a little square with a stone cross in its centre. Next to it stood the Galin bar-restaurant and, supported by its historic arcades, a pension with the same name.

In this same square, intersected by houses with exposed beams reminiscent of the Middle Ages, was the town hall guarded by the above-mentioned pension and a few other bars. I was struck by how appropriate it was that theone across the street was named "The Vicky."

The peculiar perspective of the square houses seemed to be fighting against symmetry, leaning forward as though to observe who might be walking down the street. They filled everything making it impossible to escape an unsettling feeling of unreality.

I imagined for a second how Carlos Lafuente felt when he first opened the dilapidated box in the peace and quiet of his office for the first time. That evening that now seemed so far away.

The town hall was easily identified by the Spanish flag hanging from its facade as well as by the clock placed at the highest point of its facade, showing that, although being constructed in the Middle Ages, the town kept up with the times.

When we walked in, a friendly young woman with mother-of-pearl glasses and eyes who had been fixed on a computer screen greeted us.

'Good morning, we have an appointment with the Tourism Councillor, Mr Ramón Valverde,' said Carlos.

Before she could say a word, a man with a big smile emerged from one of the ground-floor offices.

'Welcome to Covarrubias,' he said. 'Professors Serna and Lafuente, right? I'm Ramón Valverde. A real pleasure having you here.' Then noticing the two of us who, along with young Trevelyan, had remained a little further back, looking amused through one of the windows that overlooked the square, said—'Come all of you this way, please, we'll talk better in my office!'

He made a gesture with his hand to the girl with mother-of-pearl glasses, and said,

'Please don't pass me any calls for the next few minutes, Rebecca.'

'Of course, Mr Valverde.'

'Sorry about the mess,' he said as soon as we entered the office, tossing what appeared to be some forms he had been carrying in his hand onto the table. 'Until yesterday, we've had numerous visitors, including the Minister of Education and Culture, among others. On top of that, we are in the middle of the preparations for the festival and the many Norwegian cultural missions... sometimes this gets a little out of hand when the computers go to the dogs!'

'Don't fret, you should see my office on a typical day' Carlos said.

'On the other hand, it's rather unusual for us to receive a visit of this sort... A group of palaeographers seeking information about Princess Kristina is sufficient to raise curiosity... but if you add to that a novelist searching for

documentation..., this is already something exceptional!'

'Well, You know, that's not totally accurate,' I said. 'You are undoubtedly aware that numerous novels have been written about Kristina.'

'Yes, by God, we know that! Historical fiction is gaining popularity.'

'Actually we have been taken aback somehow,' the professor began.

'I did send multiple emails to the manager of Princess Kristina Foundation but have received no answer at all.'

'Well, I can't answer on behalf of the foundation, you know. But keep in mind that, as far as I know, the presidency is largely a symbolic role with minimal compensation, if I may say so. I will, however, introduce you to a person here who will certainly help to make your visit a profitable one ' he said, smiling as if he was about to give each of us some sweets. 'At least that's my intention. He is a young man by the name of Hans. He is a sort of *aide de camps, a cultural attaché of sorts* to the Princess Kristina Foundation. I am certain he will be thrilled to be of any assistance to you. He is constantly travelling from one place to another'—and then, lowering his voice to avoid being overheard by the ladies present—'a lucky son of a bitch who can live as I would love to--.' And then he added aloud 'Follow me if you please. I'll lead you to him. It is not far. Well, everything is close here,' he stated with a grin that resembled a fiord after being used to so many Norwegian visits.

Thus, we emerged into the street. The councillor and Lafuente leading the small group.

I enjoyed the sensation of strolling along those streets, looking at nothing in particular, listening to the sound of our feet on the cobblestones. There was however an unnatural quality to the atmosphere. After all, in the councillor's words, the hamlet was nothing more than a model set that came to life during the summer, with two or three points of interest. Unfortunately, it gave off the appearance of having become another another theme park. Be that as it may, I suspended my critical judgement and allowed myself to be carried away by the cacophony of shapes, beams, and dwellings swirling about me in whimsical silhouettes. I hadn't seen a village like this for a long time since I discovered in my childhood the old Disney classic *Pinocchio*, which featured a lonely Tyrolean village at night as the camera slowly approached Geppetto's window to reveal its cosy inside.

The hamlet was nothing more than a model set that came to life during the summer

We located the residence we were seeking a little further on, between Los Olmos and St Tomás streets. It was nearly identical to the one replicated in the strange wastebaskets that appeared in abundance across the village. It was a house with three or four geranium-filled balconies and exposed beams adorning its outside. There was no indication whatsoever that the individual we were searching for resided in this inconspicuous location, in this secret alley identical to so many others in the city.

A tall, blonde girl with long ringlets of hair and one of those impossible smiles that only blue-eyed Scandinavians girls can show, opened the door. After welcoming us inside, she led us to a tiny parlour where we sat.

She reappeared shortly after with the same smile, increasing Arthur's heart rate.

'Come with me, please,' she said in a thick Nordic accent.

We entered a bright office where, sitting in front of a Macintosh computer, was seated the person we were looking for.

He was a handsome young Norwegian wearing black paste glasses. Long blonde hair hung on either side of his face, making him look like a Viking version of Clark Kent.

'This is Hans,' remarked the councillor, the current coordinator of Princess Kristina Foundation in Covarrubias.'

Hans stood up smiling, thus exposing his final weapon: a height of around six feet, which made everyone present feel out of place and Elena and Clarissa speechless.

'I will leave you now in his very capable hands. If you would excuse me, I must return to the city hall, but should you need anything else don't hesitate to stop by my office before you leave,' the councillor said shaking hands with a tone that appeared to imply this wouldn't be necessary.

After this hasty departure, Lafuente spoke, feeling the ground,

'We were expecting to find here the official headquarters of the foundation or something of that kind.'

'Well, it's difficult to explain,' Hans replied, with a big smile. 'Although the foundation has its official headquarters in Madrid, it is physically housed for practical reasons within the Norwegian embassy, you understand. In the end, it's merely a commercial-cultural mission, more or less covert between the two countries, helped by the story of the princess as a conduit. Please accept my apologies for my Spanish.' Here, he said something in Norwegian. 'I'm still trying to improve it. You see, I've just returned from my holidays in Norway. That doesn't help much.' Here he let out a loud chuckle that sounded as if it emanated from a fiord in his native country while sipping a beer at sunset.

Hans spoke with confidence, used to addressing the same questions about Kristina over and over again. He did not, however, relinquish his genial demeanour or deep voice for a moment. Instead, his limpid stare enveloped us whenever he responded to one of our inquiries.

Hans, with his stunning and piercing blue eyes, was the ideal ambassador for his country, supported in this task by his meticulous and refined manners. Everything on his part seemed calculated to divert the attention of his interlocutor. He elevated conversation to an art form; comparing cultures, languages, and ways of perceiving life. Not without some effort, and only after having looked first at their respective notes, Carlos, Elena, and Trevelyan asked him many questions.

Clarissa and I used our cell phones to record the conversation.

'But, follow me please!' he finally said after a few minutes, aiming to change the subject: 'You've also come here to view Princess Kristina's burial site in its original location, right? It will be my pleasure to accompany you to St Cosme and St Damián Collegiate Church and introduce you there to the parish priest. He's fed up already with seeing me bringing people around and pestering him with questions. Shouldn't we give him a good reason for his complaints?'

Hans advanced in long strides, followed at a brisk trot by our small party. Our pace tried to mask the exertion and effort applied, trying to give the impression this walking rhythm was something habitual in us.

In this way we passed in front of the so-called Fernán González Tower, located close to the Arlanza river, catching in passing —not an easy task due to our fast walking—, a glimpse of Dona Sancha's house, one of the compulsory visits, which, like almost other visits here, we would be unable to carry out. We limited ourselves instead to seeing its shape retreating behind us. On the right, an arched river bridge and some bare trees seemed to speak of another time, preparing us for the mission that had led us here.

Certainly, we must have appeared to be a curious group that evening, attracting the gazes and interest of visitors and tourists that walked the streets, camera in hand, as well as of the patrons seated at any of the tables of the three bars that occupied the central square.

Unfortunately, I had not had time up till now due to the initial excitement and our rapid pace, to contemplate the image we formed.

Hans was walking in the centre, with the assurance of a commander or a knight from the Middle Ages, according to the simile that one should prefer, his thoughtful figure attentive to Carlos Lafuente's conversation, who occasionally nodded in agreement to some of his numerous comments. Elena stood to the right of the group, wearing a long, exquisite floral dress she had brought for the occasion. She was engaged in animated conversation with Clarissa, who wearing a long skirt and a navy blue top, resembled a woman out of a Norman Rockwell illustration. Trevelyan completed such a picturesque painting with his university rowing cap, giving the impression of having being taken out of an English engraving and looking for the way to return to it.

Hans reminded me that evening of that other literary Hans, the one appearing in Jules Verne's novel *Journey to the Centre of the Earth,* a man of few words who served as a guide and silent companion to Professor Liddenbrock and his nephew while they explored the planet's interior.

This literary association warmed my heart and made me feel as though

I had known this person for a long time.

When I finally caught up with the group among the envy of some female tourists we passed by, our Norwegian attaché was speaking,

'Nothing you may see here is real. The hamlet comes to life during the summer festival, especially on July 24th, St. Christina's Day, as Mr Valverde has undoubtedly informed you. The remainder of the year is, as of now, an empty shell awaiting the occasional visitor, the Norwegian pilgrim coming to honour his princess, with the exception of the months of April and September, when the Norwegian foundation celebrates a music festival with a flea market featuring traditional Norwegian products.'

'Well, it's a real shame that people should leave villages like this for the city,' I said.

I leant on the bridge's parapet. I felt compelled to observe the river, its flow, the live concern that shaped its waters.

A tourist appeared rushing down the incline of a nearby street. She apparently had left her camera in a bar near the arched bridge we had seen minutes before and was on her way to recover it, amid shouts from the other passengers as the bus that had brought her was about to leave.

Inside me —and despite my attempts to maintain a calm front, I had a strong urge to reach as soon as possible the collegiate church and its secrets, to stand before the statue. That figure and that tomb I had seen so many times on the Internet along with the strange and romantic story I heard for the first time in Valladolid, had brought us here. We were also accompanied by some apprehension, the almost childish thrill of hope that reality would not shatter the mental image I had forged inside me. Had we come seeking the truth, data, or just a ghost? As a writer, I could not rule out this final possibility, if only as an excuse to justify many of the things I had recently experienced.

CHAPTER 18

THE COLLEGIATE CHURCH OF SAINTS COSME AND DAMIAN

After crossing a stone cross in the middle of a square, Hans halted. We had spotted the Collegiate Church of St Cosme and St Damián a few steps further down to the left. Then, with a theatrical gesture not devoid of personal pride, he pointed to a bronze statue to our right, within a tiny flower bed green surrounded by chains. A plaque at its foot summarised the well-known story.

'Here is our particular Arlanzón princess.' said Hans, pointing to the statue looming in front of us.

'So this is young Kristina,' I said.

I couldn't help but smile upon seeing the effigy. It was precisely as I had imagined it.

'When was it placed here?' Elena inquired.

'It was erected in 1978. It was a gift from Bergen, the princess's hometown to commemorate the anniversary of her arrival. There is a duplicate statue of her there,' Hans responded.

'It must have been a curious sight,' Arthur said.

'Yes,' Hans answered, a note of pride in his voice, 'Norwegian celebrities and even the municipal Tønsberg band attended.

Clarissa, meanwhile, had approached the statue in silence, saving the ornate chains that encircled the small green in order to touch it. She appeared to be fascinated by its majestic bearing and icy stare that seemed to peer through time, through the ages. The statue's was an endless contemplation of melancholy, affection, a northern gaze. It was the look of a princess who had come to live here, in these Burgos land. Here, she had discovered houses built with a stone of a similar hue to those in her country. Circumstances made her die in this southern world, far from her homeland and natural surroundings, far from Norway's leaden skies. But it was in this other northern region we had met her. Haughty and proud, she wore a small crown on her head and a cape that appeared to rise in the breeze on this cold, wintry day, as befitting a queen.

She stood next to that brilliant and narrow river that flowed beneath her regal bearings, perpetually reminding the occasional visitor of her roots, in eternal homage.

She appeared to be fascinated by its majestic bearing and icy stare.

Statues have always transmitted me a peculiar notion of unreality or, to be more accurate, of hyper-reality, as if they were the ones inhabiting the real world, the genuine reality, while we were in another dimension, on the wrong side of existence. In their endless contemplation, they appear as though time and moments had been magically preserved, frozen in their prime for our benefit. I wish we could do something similar in our lives as we do when, pausing a movie with the remote control, stepping back to better observe the scene and the people in it, would return to examine our own and our interlocutor's faces at leisure!

Yes, statues and old buildings, such as monasteries and cathedrals, are there to remind us that our acts can affect the future and that, as John Donne wrote, "we are all connected under the ocean."

Elena was equally in rapture, gazing at the effigy. I felt a sudden shiver run down my spine.

'I feel the presence of the North in my bones,' I said.

'Around here, we call that cold,' Carlos replied with one of his grimaces. 'It's quite common given the time of year.'

'I cannot dispute that this part of Spain has its fair share of princesses and knights, such as My Cid and others, right? Nothing to do with the place I grew up, I am afraid!'

'Yes, it's true. The Rachelillos, as the locals of Covarrubias are known, are thrilled with the idea,' said Hans.

Hans was the first to enter the collegiate, striding forward. Moments later, after passing beneath the enormous rose-shaped stained-glass window that greeted visitors, we thought we had lost our guide. We saw him then standing in front of us. Next to him was a small man hiding behind one of those counters strategically placed outside any temple entrance. Counters apparently designed with the express purpose of demanding the right of admission. Hans gestured for us to wait while he seemed to be explaining the reasons for our late arrival. His interlocutor moved his arms with a certain nervousness, although we could hear nothing of their words given the distance between us. Finally, at a certain point in the negotiations, the Norwegian turned to our group and with his normal cool demeanour, as if what we had just witnessed had not taken place said,

'Please come this way! A group of tourists has just entered, and the priest is about to deliver a brief lecture. We can freely interact with no problem. They won't complain or tell us anything; they already know me as I come and go every other day with members of the foundation or Norwegian students.' Hans added with a genuine smile. ' It's almost like being invisible.'

Indeed, our small group was not detected, or at least it did not elicit more than a passing glance due of Hans's tall figure, sitting down in silence on one of the church benches next to the group of visitors already present that had paid the fee of three euros per head to be allowed entrance to St Cosme and St Damian's church. The priest was delighted. So many eager listeners in front of him, ready to listen to his words! Today he finally had an audience.

Summer was still months away, and few visitors had arrived thus far. And what about the speech he had meticulously developed and perfected over the years? Would he have to leave it aside, awaiting the holidays after all his creative touch-ups and editing efforts?

'All right, let's get started' the priest began, raising his right arm, in which he held a key ring covered by a leather sheath that he used as a pointer to underline the most important points of his explanation.

'Fernán Gonzalez passed away in 970, but you won't remember that, will you? You were not present, were you? The count's remains were buried in St Pedro de Arlanza monastery —some of you may have seen the ruins upon your arrival in Covarrubias. They were kept there until 1841 when they were transferred here. To my left—a fresh indication of the keychain—you could see his grave and, in front of it, his wife's. As you can see, the upper slabs do not belong to these graves. Look carefully; you can easily notice that because the top slab protrudes a few centimetres over the lower ones.'

He made a pause.

'I'm talking too much, right?' He chuckled with a magisterial air, much like those national school teachers of the 1940s still remembered in the collective unconscious of a nation being diluted by the Internet.

'Isn't that what is expected of us, priests?' he said slyly as he surveyed the audience. 'Fernán González'—he persisted inflexibly —'had the original church built. Abbot Diego Fernández would rebuild it in 1474 on the location of the old temple. You will undoubtedly remember that year. You were there by then, won't you?'—again the irritating sarcastic tone. 'Now, come over here. We're about to enter the cloister. You can take photos and videos there if you want, but, however...' He took another, longer pause, comparable to that of Hamlet in his famous monologue: 'No flash!'

These words were followed by nervous movements among the tourists in search of their cameras and cell phones.

Yes, we had indeed entered the cloister. Over time, a small museum had been formed within the collegiate church. The priest had explained the building had become a site where valuable archaeological remains unearthed in the area had been slowly and haphazardly stored, with no special arrangement. In the first aisle we discovered a magnificent raw marble column made of sigillata stone. Suddenly, the door through which we had entered opened, and the small man with the dry, rough appearance we had seen guarding the entrance, popped his head out:

'Do you have keys to lock?' he asked bluntly.

'Leave them out there on the counter,' the priest retorted, a distinctly angry tone filling the air as a result of having been interrupted in this way as soon as he had begun his speech.

'So you have keys to lock the church yourself then?' The man was adamant.

'I told you to leave them outside. I will close the gates myself,' said again the priest. This time, the tone was firm, almost menacing.

The door closed.

After this interruption he tried to continue his explanation, but before a few more sentences were said, we were astonished to see the cloister's entrance door reopen. This time, it was the head of he guide who had brought the group here. She, with a pitiful expression and hands clasped in supplication, addressed the priest:

'Father, please, at twenty-six, we have so little time, please...' And upon realising she had disrupted the explanation, she vanished quickly like a puppet before receiving the villain's club to the skull.

The priest regarded us with blank eyes.

'Miracles, true miracles. I honestly don't know how to achieve,' he added with a defeated sigh, seeking the audience's compliance, and continuing his presentation in the same deliberate manner with which he had begun. Nothing was going to spoil his great scene, his particular Hamlet monologue he had written with so much care.

'Take a look at these statuettes here, if you please. Until recently, it was believed that this saint belonged to the altarpiece. Someone then realised that the artwork was not of the same quality as the others. Observe that it lacks the same sheen and smoothness as the rest. Now, focus on the triptych if you please. This saint appears twice; there is no reason for two similar figures to be in the same location, do you not agree?'

The remains of the old collegiate church, reused and recycled, could be seen in its irregular masonry walls, where bits of columns and stones formed whimsical designs, the past as always feeding its successors.

We arrived then at an exquisite wooden altarpiece, a triptych.

'Here we have the Virgin Mary and the three Magi. Please observe the black king. What can you perceive in him? In what way do you believe he distinguishes himself from the rest?'

'Well, he's taller' someone said.

'More refined' remarked another.

'Anything else?'

A woman, more daring than the others, spoke up,

'Wow, he's much more attractive!'

There was some pent-up laughter.

'Well, this altarpiece was requested in 1992 by the Vatican pavilion for the Seville Expo, but the Covarrubias people said they would not let it leave the place, and... it didn't!' Again he paused, indulging in the suspense he had created in the crowd. He would need to significantly lengthen the sentences in this section.

When he faced some controversial work, the kind that had turned researchers upside down, he liked to pause and inhale,

'I have an interpretation myself' he said then, still keeping his calculated pause. No more than two seconds, so as not to dull the eager audience.

A little further to the right, within a golden frame he had hardly noticed while focusing on the altarpiece, we could see four pieces of cloth that had been discoloured by time. A little sign at the base identified them as the remains of the garments in which Princess Kristina had been buried.

Our little group approached and read in silence. The parish priest was busy somewhere else describing additional paintings on display, including an additional altarpiece. Apparently this time, the saints had been replaced by a painting that did not correspond to the original or whatever.

I thoroughly examined the fabrics. One of the pieces attracted my attention in particular. It resembled the remainder of a yellow bodice with two black bands at each end, which, even eight centuries later, continued to provide an air of sophistication and a dull sheen to the fabric. The pieces next to it were not as detailed, but they nonetheless demonstrated the greatness, the craftsmanship of an ancient civilisation.

I instantly realised the interest Carlos Lafuente might have in these vestiges. Even with the assistance of her ladies-in-waiting, a woman donned these clothing in the morning eight centuries ago.

She had possibly selected them herself, touching the fabric with her hands, stroking it as only a woman can. Perhaps the last time she did it, she didn't know it would be the last. That thought spanned centuries and caught me up. I perceived my own mortality via hers.

The adventure I had just begun with her was sufficient to remind me that other civilisations had existed before ours. We have made no discoveries. Shakespeare's and Cervantes' works endure precisely because the emotions and passions of men and women who came before us have not changed. Human suffering will continue in the same manner, and occasionally, glory and beauty will emerge alongside it.

'He met her boyfriend over the phone,' the priest said as I emerged from my reverie, his right arm resting on the grave as he regarded the semicircle of visitors gathered around him.

After this contemporary aside, which Carlos clearly found irritating and vulgar judging by a grimace he made, the priest continued with his speech. But I was already uninterested. He appeared to hesitate in the middle, possibly because he was exhausted and could not elaborate too much on his interpretations.

'Then she travelled by boat from Norway to France and from there on horseback.'

He kept playing with the keys he held in his left hand. Had the little man who had dared to poke his head left them? Was it a distinct set than the one used as the initial pointer?

He continued his broken account:

'And on Christmas Eve 1257, they finally arrived at the Royal Monastery of Las Huelgas, and then, well, well...' Here he made an ambiguous gesture, hoping perhaps that the saints he had been mentioning would help him to complete his statement: 'right away...she is married to one of Alfonso X the Wise's brothers. This would later become abbot of this collegiate church, so when she died, he had her interred here.'

He told them a grey legend about the origin of the bell that hung on one of the walls. It was said that the princess rang the bell one night to summon her husband, out hunting, to return to the castle. Clearly, this was a note for tourists.

This had been the least exciting part of our journey. The visitors' interest appeared to wane as the pilgrimage's beat through the interior of the collegiate neared its conclusion. But I did not fail to understand and partly sympathised with the parish priest's position.

After all, he had not chosen to have Princess Kristina's tomb here, nor the large number of Norwegian visitors, no matter how much the Spanish-Norwegian foundation had decorated and embellished it. The purpose of the visit had already been accomplished. There was nothing more to say.

Among all the memories miraculously recovered, preserved, and cared for future generations in this museum, the tourist was primarily searching for the grave of that unknown Viking woman on a kind of quasi-religious altar as if she were the protagonist of a television series.

That must be something the parish priest despised as these visits disturbed the peace of the collegiate church, disdaining and over-looking the rest of hidden treasures. At least the grave could be located as soon as one entered the cloister, allowing him to efficiently handle the visits of the babbling Nordics. They disregarded his explanations, ready to take out the camera as soon as they entered the collegiate and ring the inevitable bell in his very nose, the bell that someone had the great idea to hang in a moment of iconoclastic madness.

I WAS, HOWEVER, AMONG THE PRIVILEGED. YES, BECAUSE I HAD long since fallen behind the group. I had already discovered he princess's grave as we entered the cloister, thanks to the photos I had seen. It was to our right. Except for Clarissa, neither the group nor my companions noticed my action, subjected as they were to the spell of the priest's words. I made urgent hand gestures to Clarissa to conceal my reckless foray. No guided tour would distract me from the reason of our visit. As in any British comedy starring Hugh Grant or Peter Sellers, I scurried towards the coffin with my camera. I would have time later to succumb to the allure of this location's remaining jewels.

I was confronted by an impressive Gothic carved stone tomb with arched openings on top and a frieze of scrolls above.

It was a work of art. No question about that.

On both sides of it were the flags of Castilla and Leon besides those of Spain and Norway.

On a red plaque on the left, we could read the following,

KRISTINA FROM NORWAY
THE PRINCESS WHO CAME FROM THE COLD

AND FOLLOWING THAT, A BRIEF SUMMARY OF HER LIFE.

This wall appeared to be an altar laden with mementos. Next to it was a painting depicting a woman in a long red cape striking a regal pose. On top of the grave, dried flowers had been placed in a ceremonial vessel. They would remain there until the next visit.

I've always enjoyed visiting locations where historical figures or even actors from classic films once stood. This could be viewed as an indirect method of meeting them, sensing them, and growing closer; a false backdoor to experience that reality. But, given the absolute impossibility of coinciding with them, neither in time nor in space, I kept visiting the places where their poor mortal remains were, trying to have that encounter that could not take place in real life, believing ourselves closer to them, in a way.

I was confronted by an impressive Gothic carved stone tomb with arched openings on top and a frieze of scrolls above.

THERE IS, HOWEVER, SOMETHING OUR FLAWED NATURE CAN DO to defend itself against life and, of course, death. And that is chiselling the facts in our mind, fixing them, albeit imperfectly and, thanks to memory, evoke them, recover them, and bring those moments of incomplete happiness back to life. Thus relive a thousand times that kiss, that kind word of the beloved one, that genuine smile, the way wind blew her hair that day.

I was thrilled that I had been able to slip away in those earlier moments and paid the princess my solitary tribute.

Before this stone grave, I felt insignificant and human.

But this had occurred previously. The parish priest was now providing a scientific version to a few historical questions posed by the visitors regarding his private museum. The grave of Kristina was not the end of the journey. And as the doorman had previously reminded him, he had to close early. Perhaps he could enjoy then some *torreznos* at a nearby inn.

'What do you think? Did you find anything interesting?' said Carlos Lafuente.

'Much better than I expected' I replied, still observing my surroundings, wishing to tell him about my recent experience.

Indeed, it was so. I had seen images and read brief descriptions of what I had just discovered: touristic brushstrokes, disjointed annotations, lacking of foundation and authority. It was like seeing Paris, London, or any other great city for the first time and realising that it existed beyond the pages of a book.

The Norwegian flag was very close to the princess's mortal remains. swaying gently as a result of a light breeze. Taking advantage of the fact that no one was looking in my direction, I touched the fabric between my hands. I wished to feel its thickness on her behalf.

It was kind of ironic to think she would never know the chapel she had longed for her entire life, had finally been built.

The bell the priest had previously mentioned was placed to our right, almost concealed by the flag's folds.

'So this is the famous bell?' Carlos said, looking at Hans.

'Yes, at this rate we will need to install another one soon. When people pursue a trend in earnest, they will not stop until breaking it.'

The group of tourists emerged ahead of us, talking to each other, dispersing with alacrity while wondering about the best place to get a beer or French toast given the time of day.

'If you're interested, it would be my pleasure to invite you to a few beers and answer all your questions.' Hans offered 'Are you familiar with the La Serna pub? It is not too far away.'

Elena and Arthur exchanged a smile that passed unnoticed by the others, although not for me, who had been witness to their little joke.

CHAPTER 19

A WALK FOLLOWED BY A REFLECTION

How a stroll can lead to a reflection about brothers and sisters.

The professor and Arthur lagged behind as the group left behind the recently visited church. The former had professed a sudden interest in examining the stone bridge over the Arlanza, which Arthur cleverly saw as a pretext to relight his pipe.

Dark clouds loomed over the horizon. They could smell a pungent musty scent., Trevelyan's scarf began to move in the rising breeze when they reached the bridge.

'People do love hearing about legends and myths. After centuries of varied customs and traditions among civilisations, we are all the same, children of God, as our friend back there would say' the professor said, pointing to the collegiate church and adding 'We, band of brothers.'

'And sisters, professor, please do not overlook the sisters in these politically correct times.'

'My apologies, Trevelyan. Certainly, as brothers and sisters.You're absolutely right there; I apologise for my slip.'

He took a few steps, inhaling the smoke coming out from his pipe, listening to the collegiate bells ringing at that moment as he contemplated the surrounding landscape.

He stopped abruptly. turned around and looked at his pupil.

This took a step back in surprise. The professor's teeth were tightened, his mouth was contorted, his hand glued to the pipe in his immovable hand.

'Is something the matter, professor? Are you all right?'

Lafuente appeared to react then.

'The matter? Yes, yes, I'm fine, Trevelyan,' he replied with a grave expression. 'Listen, I'm going to hang around here for a while smoking my pipe. You are welcome to join the group if you wish. I will come right away. I need to gather my thoughts a bit' —and after saying this, he appeared to change his mind—'No, better still, wait for me in that bar across the street,' he continued, indicating the establishment where the hapless tourist had rushed to retrieve her camera. 'I'll be with you in a jiffy.'

And without waiting for a response from the bewildered Arthur, he stormed out into the winding streets in the direction of the riverbank and a small walkway they had discovered moments earlier.

In front of the little tavern indicated—named with a superb sense of place "The Tower" there was a shady area near a fountain. Arthur waited at one of the tables there for the professor. The place appeared empty at that hour. Eventually, he spotted the professor approaching from a nearby street.

A few minutes after his arrival, two beers had appeared on the table along with two sheets of paper covered in circles.

After completing the much-needed connections between them, the professor eventually he raised his head becoming aware of Trevelyan's presence.

'We made the proper decision coming here, Trevelyan!' he said, 'You know, you were absolutely right!'

'Right? Concerning what? We've just seen Princess Kristina's grave and little at that,' he said, still uneasy about the professor's unusual behaviour.

'Do you remember what you said just a few minutes ago? That remark about not forgetting the female part of my observation? That about brothers and sisters?' While he said this, the professor did not appear to notice he was addressing Arthur on a first-name basis.

'Yes, but I don't see what you mean,' Arthur said, stroking his chin, repeatedly retying his tie around his neck.

'That's precisely the key. We had completely overlooked the feminine aspect of the issue. We have been investigating the mystery surrounding certain scrolls related to a woman, a princess. And precisely I, the author of *Problems of Modern Paleography,* had not noticed it. I hadn't made such a mistake since I was in school! We have been looking for clues in Silos about a supposed copy left "in the care of the brothers" according to the manuscripts. Clearly, we should not have been looking for them in the monastery where they wwere foundd as we had supposed. I'm the only one to blame for that, dear boy.'

Arthur looked at the professor. Then his eyes descended to those papers filled with circles, as if he could find there some explanation to this apparent delirium.

'Arthur, Are you following me? We have misunderstood the context! Take a look at the facsimile we took in Silos,' he added, picking up some photocopies from the black leather folder he had been carrying along during the entire trip. They were those of the *Codex Victorianus written* by the same author. 'Look here, next to this illumination. Notice this "I", the emerald tint of the letter "a"?'

'Yes, of course I see it. We've been through this countless times.'

' Then you will recall the comment made by the copyist at the end of the manuscripts? *"Whoever desires to see another letter will see it; whoever can tell the difference between day and night will have eyes to view God's writing.'*

'Yes of course.'

'Well... therein lays the core issue. The passage makes no mention of Silos' brothers at all. He is constantly mentioning something else. Can't guess what? This here is clearly a female name' he said circling one of the characters on the Xerox in front of him. 'This contrasting colouring in the manuscript is drawing attention to the genre; it is the copyist's way of winking. God, we've been such jerks! The meaning has always been in plain sight. When the original text states "the assistance of a brother or sister is much required," it is actually indicating that the secret is safe "with the sisters".'

Arthur now realised the significance of the professor's words.

There was a strange hush.

'Damn! But how do we know which female religious order the MS may allude to?'

'That answer is all around you right now. I mean Covarrubias,' he said, after observing Arthur's foolish expectation as if expection that the solution would materialise before his eyes. 'Today, while pondering on the tragic destiny of the princess, I stumbled upon the key. I finally understood. Do you recall telling me some time ago that phrase mentioned frequently by Sherlock Holmes? Something along the lines of "When everything reasonable fails to provide an answer, let's consider the unreasonable and no matter how entangled, how far-fetched it may seem, we will find there the solution."'

'Yes, that's right, but I don't see any relation to our case.'

'Well, the exact name of a female religious order is mentioned in the chronicles of Princess Kistina. Precisely, the same order that welcomed her in Burgos on Christmas Eve in that distant year of the Lord 1257, as the good chronicles would say. And now don't tell me the name of a monastery inhabited by nuns of the fair sex doesn't come to mind,' he concluded, observing Trevelyan's face intently.

The professor's eyes sparkled. A smile was crossing his mouth. Arthur laughed, as a thought had been steadily building in his head.

Both men spoke simultaneously:

'The Monastery of Our Lady of Las Huelgas!'

They paid for the beverages without uttering a word and sped up to join the others. At that moment, Carlos Lafuente felt a kind of oppression, He felt restless. An unease that he had sometimes experienced in the midst of an investigation. It was the fear of not finding anything at the end of the journey. A feeling he believed had been banished for good, had reemerged with force.

～

CHAPTER 20
INSIDE PUB "LA SERNA"

Of love letters and rock-and-roll, followed by the howling of wolves.

After leaving the collegiate church, the group crossed the narrow streets of Covarrubias in pursuit of this Norwegian leader who had appeared out of the blue in the heart of Castile-León. They were surprised when they found themselves at the gates of Pub La Serna sooner than expected.

This was indeed a large, secluded and cosy pub, looking more typical of the surrounding buildings than of modern times. The interior was in stark contrast to its rural exterior, which appeared more like a garage or a place where one could store a few tractors and machinery. They noticed upon entering two pool tables and dart boards on the opposite wall as well as some posters advertising upcoming musical events next to a small area reserved for such live performances. Scattered all over that space, there were several instruments and partially installed jacks proving the point.

Twenty minutes later Arthur and the professor arrived. The latter still took an additional ten minutes to finish his pipe.

Elena observed a strange expression on Carlos' face. This, feeling questioned by her gaze, whispered in her ear, 'I'll tell you later,' and directed his gaze to the rest of the table as naturally as if he had been commenting on the outcome of the morning's classes or next term schedule.

There were already some beers on the table distributed among those already present, as well as two teacups for Elena and Arthur.

'Pedro, please put us another round, and make mine the usual this time,' the Norwegian said to the waiter who had come promptly as soon as he saw the arrival of newcomers.

'Sorry, Hans. We don't have *Two Captains* left. I'll get it this afternoon,' he replied, apologetically.

'*Dark Horizon* will do then,' Hans said with some annoyance. 'It's a Norwegian beer,' he explained to those present, after seeing the bewildered expressions on the faces of the visitors, confronted with such an exchange of apparently encrypted codes.

They were surprised when they found themselves at the gates of Pub La Serna

A MAN IN HIS FORTIES WITH A BUSHY BEARD WAS SHOOTINGS darts in the middle of the bar at regular intervals, waiting a few moments between shots before throwing them over the pool tables, deftly avoiding the bodies of the players who seemed accustomed to this unusual procedure. Arthur noticed he seemed to perform a cyclical routine as if he were a Norwegian Rafael Nadal.

He adjusted his glasses first and then, switching hands with the remaining darts in his possession, focusing intently on the game, fully aware of the immense responsibility that had literally fallen into his hands that early afternoon, as the sole entertainer in the pub. Then and only then was he ready to play.

After having a light and quick snack, following after their new friend's repeated insistence in that regard, they talked about the subject that had brought them together.

'Something about what the priest said doesn't agree with what I've read about the princess,' Carlos remarked, once everyone had settled into that cosy corner.

'Yes? What's that?' replied Hans.

'Well, according to your calculations, the princess's journey took about nine and a half months, right? I've read elsewhere that it lasted around two years between one thing and another. Of course, one must have into account the means of transportation at the time. And if she also had to cross England and France...'

'Yes, that's true. There are few other chronicles besides those of Otón de Freising of Norway and Alfonso X. Depending on which reference we use, she could have left Norway at one time or another' said Elena.

The knocking sound of the darts was like a recurring thought. Part of their minds seemed to be unconsciously waiting for the next knock, while the other was fully engaged in the conversation.

'Well, there's one more thing they don't seem to agree on...' Arthur said. He had been observing the evolution of the darts with some amusement while listening to the conversation.

Everyone looked in his direction. He had been sitting quietly his corner for so long, sipping his tea, that he had passed unnoticed.

'Excuse me, Hans,' he said, 'but from what I've read about the case, isn't it true that a worker discovered the grave by chance in 1950 during some maintenance works there? I think he uncovered a wooden urn containing the mummified body in it. Am I right?'

'Yes, yes, that's it,' Hans agreed, astonished that the young man knew that info. 'But the official unveiling did not occur until 1958, when the parish priest of St Damian Collegiate Church discovered a document confirming the suspicions. After that the Norwegian authorities requested verification that the remains were indeed those of the princess. It was in that same year, that a ceremony honouring the "Nordic girl" was organised, with personalities from both nations in attendance.'

'I had also read that when the tomb was opened, a recipe for bad hearing or something to that effect was found next to the body along with some love letters... is that so?'

The raindrops began to tap against the window, adding to the general din. Everyone looked at Hans.

'If so, where are those love letters?" Trevelyan continued. 'In what language were they written? Where were they kept in custody after the opening of the tomb in 1958? Nothing has been heard of them since, has it?'

'Yes, I've also read those articles you mention' said Hans, moving his head 'but there was no love letter. A prayer to the Virgin Mary was actually found though along with that prescription for bad hearing you mentioned, nothing else. I think it was discovered in her hands, but I am not sure. Some jewels, gold embroidery, and precious stones were also found next to the body, indicating her high lineage. She still maintained her blonde hair and pink nails intact.'

'And where is that manuscript now?' Trevelyan insisted, adamant to give up. 'Could it be examined? In what language was it written?'

Clarissa and Ernesto tilted forward, curiosity painted all over their faces.

'Well, I think it was written in Old Norse, but it was tragically lost. It was last spotted in the possession of a pharmacist in Bilbao according to unconfirmed reports.This recipe or remedy, whatever you choose to call it, was reproduced at the time in a sort of medical publication and then...'

Everyone waited in silence for his words.

The young Norwegian, aware of the effect he was causing, gave a smile that wanted to be naïve but that could not hide some embarrassment.

'After that, silence,' Hans finally stated, lowering his head, fully aware his words would be an end to the expectation of his companions.

'Okay!' said Elena 'We have heard so far all that our dashing Norwegian has told us. However, I would like to point something out... If there was a coroner present when the tomb was opened or discovered, there also should have been a notary public. After all, a notarial act had to be drawn up, right?' she said, looking at Hans as if he were about to contradict her.

'Yes, of course, there was one' Hans said again, lowering his head again to look at his pint.

'Well, for the love of it, I'd love to read it,' Carlos said, guessing Elena's thoughts. 'Don't you agree, Ernesto?'

'Definitely, much better than merely listening to a wonderful tale of bells ringing at night for Prince Charming to come and save the princess from peril,' said the novelist, nodding with conviction at such a direct question.

The bartender was pouring mug after mug from the beer tap for a bunch of new customers who appeared be unfamiliar with such beverage. They approached curious, surveying how dispensing and distribution was carried out, how foam crowded and spilled from jars that were consumed before it had the time to spill over the rim and precipitate to the floor.

Professor Lafuente glanced at a sign placed behind Clarissa, announcing the the St. Cosme and St Damian festivities. He hadn't noticed it before.The date was that from the previous year. A talented artist had recreated the village streets with flags hanging from one house to another and,--dancing in the middle of them--, none other than Tintin and Calculus, surrounded by Captain Haddock, appeared among the crowd. Even Castafiore stood on a balcony, adding her unique flair to the the festivities.

Carlos let out a wistful sigh. Even Tintin had arrived there before them, drawn by the fame of the princess!

Ernesto remembered the feeling of familiarity he had experienced upon entering the village. It had reminded him of another hamlet, the one where Pinocchio lived, where Geppetto had given life to a wooden puppet and adopted him as his son. But here, in contrast, a flesh and blood woman had been converted into a statue and remained guarding the collegiate chapel for eternity, asking from each of the passersby where her letters might had gone after so many years.

Elena kept a deep silence. She had positioned herself at the start of the conversation in a cosy corner with a wooden back. From there she could listen closely. The warmth of the cup of green tea in her hands seemed to reinforce her feeling of comfort.

Her position in front of the window mirrored that of her college years, those countless infinite evenings copying notes by the window in her room, a couple of palaeography books by her side. Then as now, cold and wind were kept at bay outside, an unending leaf fall in the garden. Her mother and herself would collect them later.

The raindrops striking the pub windows made her see again the little puddles forming in the porch at home. The leaves her father had collected had been placed in a huge black bag, slowly soaking up.

The tea *à la Proust* had brought all that to mind.

A dart striking the target roused her from her trance. She hoped neither of her table mates had noticed her temporary state of abstraction.

'The princess is buried in Covarrubias, correct?' Elena exclaimed, unsure of what she was actually saying.

'Yeah, certainly,' they all said, with perplexed expressions.

'And she arrived to these lands first, and after marrying her husband in Valladolid, they both travelled to Seville where the court was located, is that correct?'

New nods of heads.

'I wonder, if she died in Seville, regardless of the fact that her husband might be abbot of the collegiate church in Covarrubias, why the heck was this woman buried here? And pardon my French, as the English would say!'

'Now that you mention it, I think that's hardly ever been talked about too often, right?' Trevelyan said with conviction. 'It looks to me as if someone had wished to dispose of her promptly and politely.'

After casting a glance at his table companions, and another one at the noisy group at the bar, Carlos frowned and turned to his colleague,

'Elena, you are the one with the most connections in National Heritage. Do you think you could pull some strings there and see if you can find anything?'

'Of course, You know I'll do my best.'

'Good. I am confident there is one point on which we all agree. This is the 21st century. Do you not find it odd, to say the least, that for such a well-known princess, all paperwork regarding her disappeared in a jiffy as soon as her tomb was uncovered? In other words, we know more about her from ancient chronicles than from the most recent news. All the information related to the tomb discovery and its circumstances, correct? And that was barely some decades ago!'

The volume of the music grew louder. The group of local musicians who until now had been preparing their instruments and electrical connections, began to make itself noticed. Arthur was paying particular attention to the girl playing the synthesiser. This small but nervous girl marked the beat by contorting her left leg with unusual grace. Gradually, the place began to get crowed with young people performing syncopated dance moves. A group of kids behind them were now claiming their space, by quietly pushing, gaining ground, millimetre by millimetre, with a delicate friction that could defined short of pushing in a court of law. Despite this, they were achieving their objective.

Fragments of the tune being performed reached their ears,

"It's possible because it's always possible.

Since rain cannot
Wait for my truth.
It's possible. I believe it is possible.
To be small in my dream and reach the end of my desire."

Those lyrics appeared to the group like a small message of hope, a tiny push of encouragement.

Clarissa was totally immersed in the show, looked at the group of musicians.

Hans did not appear eager to continue discussing a topic that was already tiring him. His jug was empty. He glanced at his watch and rotated the iPhone X encased in gold his right hand.

Feeling a bit awkward and realizing they may have overstayed their welcome, Carlos finished the last of his tea.

'Shall we go?' he said. 'It has stopped raining, but we still have a way to go. We still have to see St Olaf Chapel.'

Therefore, they went their separate ways, leaving the pub to be taken over and run by a new reserve, a new shift of bodies in search of movement.

'Promise to keep me informed of the outcome of your research, okay?' Hans said as he dispensed handshakes and farewells by the side of that same road that had brought them there.

And so, leaving Covarrubias behind, the van gently followed the road in the direction given by the Norwegian.

After having traveled a few kilometres through the mud that had formed as a result of the previous rainfall they arrived at dusk to an small valley. The wind was the only audible sound over the engine.

This place was known as Wolves's Valley, and although none of these animals could be seen they arrived, a strange grey silhouette could be seeing looming in the background of this sheltered area. It seemed to scratch the sky and the few remaining clouds, as if the recent rain had just been a joke. Arthur could not help but be reminded of Mordor, or at least the Dark Tower of Saruman, as he gazed at this structure with its towering dark metal spire, so sombre was this place on this dying evening.

At that moment, on that great, desolate and lonely esplanade, amidst the puddles that surrounded it, the tower resembled a giant sundial with its numbers missing. It gazed dejectedly across the valley, wondering where the North may be while praying to St Olaf.

Next to it, and resembling a whale stranded on a beach, was an incline upon which stood the main building that formed the chapel, built of wood and iron.

The most favourable reviews and comments appearing in the media about this chapel referred to it as an avant-garde work based on the contrast between design and materials. Unfortunately, but kindly, these reviews had avoided discussing that other contrast with the surrounding environment.

'That could be interpreted as a romantic gesture on the part of the government,' Ernesto said.

'What are your thoughts, Trevelyan? Let us not be confused by semantics,' Lafuente said. 'Despite all this nonsense about a tribute to the Norwegian princess, this is nothing more than a multi-purpose meeting space for the Spanish-Nordic enterprises that both embassies want to promote. But, on the other hand, I do not view with a critical eyes those concerts that Hans and the Tourism councillor told us about, those "Nordic Notes", I believe they are called. Anything that serves to connect cultures is certainly valuable.'

'Yes,' said Trevelyan, 'Although viewed in a different light, King Haakon's diplomatic mission paid dividends by forming an alliance with Spain, don't you agree? Despite the fact that the diplomatic mission should have been sadly reduced to...'

The words died in his mouth. Trevelyan felt something awkward that evening.

It was difficult to explain. He couldn't speak of a ghostly presence but he could describe sensations in a manner he had never deciphered, not even to himself. Perhaps the past was not as distant as the books, the methodology, and chronicles wanted him to believe, pertaining instead to the everyday, almost alive in the physical sense of the term.

Half an hour ago as they were leaving the pub, Ernesto had learned that Sergio Leone's film *The Good, the Bad and the Ugly* had been shot in this valley, precisely at Sierra de Hortigüela. Today, at the sight of this chapel, he could easily believe in anything: from the stealthy and silent flight of griffon vultures, hovering over the peaks, announcing the proximity of Covarrubias to Viking explorers swarming to the rescue of a princess kidnapped by those southerners people due to a badly advised king.

The professor surveyed his surroundings.

'Doesn't anyone smell it?' he said.

'Smell? No, I don't smell anything unusual,' Clarissa replied with her typical innocence.

'It's the smell of money. That's what has constructed this chapel. Not the broken promise to the princess. No, it's the wealth that seven hundred thousand annual visits by Norwegian citizens have brought to the village. Let's go now, please,' Lafuente said before returning to the van. 'I want to revise the data pertaining to what Trevelyan said in the pub concerning the letters found along with the princess.'

'Okay, fine by me,' Ernesto said. 'I also need to get my notes in order. It's been an exciting day. Perhaps this is quite normal for all of you. You are used to visiting historical sites and so on, but what do you want? I come from a city where there are very few remnants of the past. And this seems to be quite stimulating.'

None of those present complained that Kristina could not see this chapel stranded in this place. At that moment, Ernesto felt sorry for Kristina. Somehow he had been aware of her closeness since he had first felt that chill at the sight of the statue. Death is merciful to those it claims.

So they stepped out of the valley as shadows, fleeing from what they had seen.

~

CHAPTER 21

THE QUIET CITY

From Ernesto Santos's notes

As we still had a few days free, Clarissa and I decided to visit the tranquil streets of Burgos.

Burgos is not a chilly city, contrary to popular belief. Actually it only comes to life at midnight when the new day had not yet dawned. Its coldness is the coldness of the small hours, when dawn breaks and drives away the dew. New and sluggish, it is the frost awaking life.

Like a pretty lady, the city is only combing her hair and arranging her headdress, waiting for the sun to rise before donning shorts and sallying forth to the terraces. Her beauty is that of a girl sleeping peacefully, her golden hair on the pillow and her clear blue eyes concealed by closed eyelids.

Like Soledad in the well-known Spanish song of the 1970s, Burgos is one of those cities that does not realise how beautiful it is, knowing neither love nor deceit nor vanity. It is not like those cities filled with brand-name stores that eventually take over every historic district. We find in their place a Chinese, italian or kebab restaurant along with their old, silent portals hidden beneath glazed balconies. Yes, one could still hear music emanating from a reckless tavern tucked away in a corner. It's a stale and worn-out rap, danced with jerky movements, yet above and alongside it, the other buildings frown upon it, much like those brothers who disapprove of such improper behaviour, such an ignorant and impolite remark in this place and at this early hour.

A gentle rain begins to fall. I smiled involuntarily. On a day like this, our love was cemented, and such a day reminded me of it again.

Burgos is not a chilly city, contrary to popular belief.

Perhaps rainy days are sad because, like dreams, drops fall from the sky and continue to patter on the ground. Each drop containing a hope, possibly also a memory, a plan, an unmet fantasy. Before breaking it could have housed them all.

Our path was encircled by stones that bloomed peace. From the pedestrian streets, voices and sounds ascended and approached.

The city must learn to protect its beauty, much like that exquisite young lady in her prime who slips discreetly under balconies on her way to a party so as not to attract undue attention. Nature had the ingenuity to assist Burgos with its many fogs and clouds, concealing it beneath snow, making it disappear from view behind a layer of rain. It is our own special Rivendell. If only one had the patience to slow down and listen to its breath, observe its respiration. Topography has retreated its calm, bustling streets for companionship. Outside of this circle of old friends are the contemporary streets and broad avenues.

Modern brands and fashion boutiques attempt to seduce it, but it resists. Opposite the cathedral, on Lain Calvo and La Paloma streets, we can still see souvenir shops though.

A little further, along the street we are in, there is a tiny triangular square where you can see, sitting on a bench, a bronze statue representing a Burgos couple, impervious to the cold. They appear to be watching the passers-by going their different ways.

Las Huelgas Abbey--The cathedral's old sister, located a short distance away, looks dejected and forlorn, although it too has a beautiful square. Clarissa has urged we must visit it before returning home.

Woe betide the passerby when Burgos opens his eyes! He would be doomed, restrained and immobilised in this location.

Only the river moves, slowly, unhurriedly.

CHAPTER 22

THE BLACK LAGOON

Two figures moved in the landscape. Just two distant silhouettes moving through the tall grass.

Behind one of them, skipping through the tall bushes and low forest, a long scarf crawls. The second figure pauses, looks around, and observes again, like a hunting dog sniffing the environment and surrounding world before moving forward.

Lafuente had parked the small Volkswagen on a small esplanade a few minutes before setting foot with his peculiar companion across the fields.

He was now standing in the centre of the path they were descending. A left-hand sign indicated a detour to the Black Lagoon. There it was.

A real place.

All previous poetry and mysticism had been reduced to black text on a white background. Now he only desired to arrive. There would be time later to examine the area in detail, and seek for additional Lepidoptera to add to his collection, that is, as long as Ismael did not show an excessive amount of curiosity in them. "The Black Lagoon," he repeated himself.

The very name conjured ghostly images, legends, macabre and

creepy tales, the sort of stories that are whispered around the hearth on cold winter nights.

Yes, this was indeed a peaceful place. Some lost birds traversed the landscape. Jackdaws? Crows? It was hard to know with certainty, given their remoteness, They were simply dots in the blue sky. He felt as though the scenery was shifting. Too fast. Yes, fleeting. Carlos felt a certain vertigo, both professional and physical. The last few days had been hectic and messy, and he couldn't bear it. He needed to put some order before obtaining permission to visit Las Huelgas Abbey.

Christmas season would serve this function all right. A couple of days would be sufficient. The report could be delayed a little longer. Patricio Noguer and his Renaissance egotism would have to wait.

He had recently returned from Santander, where he had spent a few days visiting his parents and brother, Marcelo. After all, Santander was not that far away. He felt that he had ignored his filial duties in recent months quite enough. Santander in autumn and winter. His very personal Santander. His father, a moderately retired clerk from a dark insurance office, expressed his delight at seeing him with grunts and a few masculine hugs when he opened the door of the house in front of the Sardinero beach.

While children, the two brothers had been under the protective wings of Aunt Engracia, married to a renowned physician who had lived his best moments in the sixties and seventies once he established his private practice in Burgos.

'Look, look at this sextant. Don't you think it marvellous?' His brother had said, 'I discovered it in a Parisian street market. Look! It dates back to 1850 or thereabouts. A true marvel, wouldn't you say?'

And he stared at it once more, caressing its shape before placing it back in its display case alongside three or four others already there, as part of a collection revisited repeatedly.

How changed had he found his brother Marcelo! It was funny how much alike they were in countless ways, despite their age difference of only ten years. While history had been Carlos's devotion,

Marcelo had crossed the pragmatic world of everyday life with the usual modesty of the scholar.

Carlos could not avoid a strange sensation every time he saw his brother on those spaced encounters. He could not avoid recalling the child with brilliant eyes and charming grin. In an obvious display of juvenile masochism, on some occasions he had enjoyed torturing the boy so that he could subsequently comfort and caress him feeling both guilty and protective after that.

Marcelo had been the family's white ray of hope until a mysterious disease dashed all expectations and confined him to that brown wheelchair.

"And don't spend so much time with your books! You know it's bad for your eyes, and don't you forget either to put your "sariana" on when you go out at night!" Thus her mother had told him again and again upon his departure, still not used to that strange compulsion of the men of the house towards books. The so-called "sariana" had been for ages the cause of many jokes between his brother and him. This was the peculiar way his mother referred to that kind of coat— the huntress or Saharan coat.

Neither time nor the dictionary had erased such a peculiar term from her lexicon. Thus, it had become one of those names that, when uttered, conjured up entire scenarios, snippets of life from a distant past, of family meals in front of endless bowls of soup as the family watched the only channel available in the Spain in the 1960s on the small TV set.

On the 17th of December upon his return from Santander, and still with some free time left, and under Trevelyan's insistence, they left Montanilla before daybreak.

'Professor, you *must* see Soria' Arthur said as soon as they were in the car. 'It's essential. And you must not miss Vitoria city either as soon as you have the chance. I used to go there as a child on the weekends to see my uncles.' he said with that precision and insistence of the pressing, the crucial, that urgency that youth creates by itself.

Lafuente had always wanted to visit these cities, both so near to

Burgos although for him, perpetually engrossed in his studies, appearing as distant as if they were on another continent.

There were always books to read, exams to prepare, meeting to attend to. Is that the way how precious time is spent? Lost? Won? He had repeatedly put off the visit in this way, as he had made with so many other tasks. After all, he couldn't just quit his classes just like that, could he? Besides, the new university demanded his complete focus.

The cold, frigid air entered their noses, passing over their faces, surrounding them, making their walk a series of continuous leaps. In that way, they could feel a new impulse of blood throughout their bodies.

Clouds had been accumulating in varying shades of grey, surrounding the sky at horizon level. The lower portion, more bluish-grey, seemed to blend into it, creating the impression of a sea arm that passers-by could navigate to.

Lafuente remembered the last conversation he had had with his Elena, the intensity and anger in her eyes as she spoke, her face in front of him,

"Carlos, you won't believe it! I have inquired everywhere about the notary public who reportedly issued the certificate, also about the worker who accidentally found the grave, and even the innkeeper's name. Ah! Not forgetting the beer brand they served there as well. This was merely an attempt to obtain an answer, any kind of answer! Do you know what I discovered? Absolutely nothing, zero! I felt as though we were bloody Scully and Mulder, instead of a couple of palaeographers. Gosh! This is frustrating!"

And now here they were, near the Black Lagoon. The name seemed to contain in itself a potential drama. An historical thriller.

Part of an intrigue. Of a mystery. What would Trevelyan say now if asked for his views? Would he talk about the fucking significant coincidences again?

He wondered why they had travelled to this location in the first place. Here, of all possible places. Did he require a break from the laboratory and the office? It was highly probable. As he never ceased to explain in class, he occasionally did so to confirm that essays conformed to the exterior world. At that point, he wished he had Trevelyan's discernment to adopt the correct attitude. Sometimes he wondered who was the pupil and who the instructor.

They halted beneath a signpost bearing several inscriptions: Path of the Elderly of the Woods, Three Fountains Rise, Urbion Pike, and, in smaller print, Birth of Rio Duero.

'Well, Trevelyan, we are here as you requested, although I must admit, based on your past recommendations of these days, I had assumed you wanted to show me another Soria. Soria City, I mean.'

'We will have time to see the city another day, which is not without interest,' Trevelyan stated, oblivious to the professor's objections, as he surveyed the desolate landscape.

'Tell me something,' asked the professor, 'Based on these signposts, I assume that the next crossing will lead us to the Seven Dwarfs cottage, right? Oh, no, I apologise, I got confused about the story. Did I mean the Queen of Hearts' Castle then?'

'I realise my insistence in coming here may seem odd to you, but consider it logically for a second! Doesn't everything leave a trace? From a passing car to whatever decision we could make at any given moment, everything influences our actions. Isn't that one of the parapsychological explanations for the queer sounds heard in haunted houses? Certain traumatic events somehow might get embedded in the surroundings. Do you recall that master I took in the United States? I remember in particular a presentation by a Robert Root titled entitled *"To Know Who You Are and Where You Have Been,"* . In it he stated, "We don't just occupy or pass through certain areas throughout our lives; we carry them with us; they live within us!"

'Yes, it makes sense,' responded Lafuente. 'Sometimes, we remember the sights that have left a lasting impression on us. But from there to haunted houses, Trevelyan...'

'OK, so far so good. Now, just continuing with our logical reasoning the converse might also be true, right? If we have been joyful, sad, or uniquely marked by a certain environment or place, is it not possible that at least a portion of us would remain there?'

'As a kind of ghost? Nonsense! It's absurd that a student like yourself, Trevelyan, should speak on those terms! Precisely you, two days after completing a doctoral study that I would have killed to replicate.'

'You have a scientific and logical mind. Do not be carried away by the easy etiquette. Just consider what I've told you! That would certainly explain a number of facts, such as why some people feel the environment speaking to them at specific times and places. It would not be unreasonable to assume that after so many years of coexistence, nature and humanity would have learnt to communicate and comprehend one another, wouldn't you agree? When Wordsworth and Coleridge decided to reside in the Lake District, neither of them felt it odd. Neither did Thoreau when he retired to that secluded paradise of Walden.'

Then, after seeing his mentor's face, he altered the conversation's tone slightly:

'There is something in the popular imagination about this place that intrigues me. From Pedro de Medina in 1548, to a certain Juan José García in 1880, Pío Baroja, and our Antonio Machado in the *Land of Alvar González*, there are several legends that speak of odd things at the bottom of the lagoon.'

Upon noticing the interest he had aroused in the professor, he continued speaking, signalling different spots on the landscape with his arms, as if he wished to conjure up the presence of each thing he mentioned, like a conductor demanding a furious *staccato* from the strings. 'Giant lizards, odd noises, mysterious men traversing its waters, you name it. Pío Baroja even said that a woman lived at the bottom of the lagoon, and that anyone who looked at her perished. Every legend contains some element of reality. In short, many people have spoken here of terrible things happening here,' said Trevelyan, continuing his walk down the hill with little concern, as if the previous words had been delivered by a guide and not by him. After taking a few step, he turned around and said, as if on a final note. 'Let me remind you that this is one of the precise locations where Princess Kristina passed by and where she fell ill with a mysterious ailment that delayed her voyage and her meeting with the king, although some chroniclers fail to mention it!'

After hearing these last words, Carlos looked around him. The trail was flanked by overgrown and sparsely trodden old trees on either side. His imagination, sparked by Ernesto Santos' novel *The Sunset Light*, he had been reading lately, made him imagine briefly the princess and her retinue crossing the space in front of him.

He could see in that picture the lagoon closed by an almost vertical stone wall on its left, and the Sierra de Urbión's trees and forests on its right.

He took a look at the top of the incline. Yes, it was easy to imagine the entourage stopped there, on that little hill. A female figure in the centre of the circle the soldiers had formed before descending. He couldn't see her face though, no matter how hard he tried. Only her long locks neatly tucked behind her ears in a braid. It was enough. She comes ready to face the dazzling lights and sounds of a foreign land.

Trained to survive, with that grit that women of that era, of any age, can find within themselves to resist and adapt. With that power to persevere in the face of adversity since birth. He had always admired women. Like Truffaut and his character Antoine Doinel, he believed they were magical creatures.

He heard a muffled sound. A thud to the left. When he looked he discovered it had been caused by droplets hitting nearby bushes, bursting and spreading over the leaves.

He noticed then they had heard no birds during the past few minutes. A few seconds later, raindrops began to fall on his head.

Upon gazing upward hey noticed that in the interim, a solitary cloud had being moving and covered the entire sky.

The two men lightened their pace, widening their strides, with no regard whatsoever now.

'I think I saw some kind of shelter over there.' Lafuente remarked, 'Let's move, or we'll get drenched. If you want to soak up in the atmosphere in that creepy way of yours, we need only to stay here a while longer under this downpour.'

Trevelyan agreed, the two of them proceeding accordingly, leaping through the bushes as best they could.

When they arrived at the shelter, they took a look back up the slope they had just come down. The automobile was visible at its highest point. Protected by the foliage, it appeared to mock their predicament; two wayward scouts getting lost after leaving the track.

The rain had made its presence known in no uncertain terms. Intense and silent it fell on the leaves and plants without any breeze disturbing it, making a mild rustling sound when hitting its objective.

Arthur laughed 'As long as none of the monsters from the lagoon's bottom arrive, I hope everything will be alright.'

The temperature had dropped suddenly. The rain had certainly come by surprise, that was a fact, and they had no choice but to cope with it with the scarce wardrobe resources they had as well as with the expeditious remedy of rubbing their hands.

'Perhaps others had their first encounter with the impossible here,' the professor mused while they waited.

In a way, he had one of those, too. He had witnessed another theory of this wayward student that fate had placed in his path. This time, however, it wasn't about embracing trees to balance the energy of the universe or searching for flying saucers on lazy summer afternoons, but it was near enough.

'I believed I spotted a dragonfly trying to dodge the rain.' Arthur said, pointing to a half-destroyed structure a few yards away. 'I believe it went on that roof.'

'A dragonfly, eh? Now that you've brought it up, and because I believe we will have to wait here till weather improves, I will tell you an intriguing tale myself.' Lafuente said. 'It took place many years ago in the middle of a warm June afternoon in Santander. The place, the nearby fishing village of Sotileza where I was visiting my friend Isabella.'

And as he began to recount his tale in a drowsy voice perhaps caused by the rhythm of the rain and the repetitive splattering of raindrops falling on the surrounding vegetation, Lafuente relived that distant experience again,

. . .

THAT EVENING THE RED LIGHT OF THE DARKROOM PERMEATED everything. Isabella was developing her photographs.

A song by the Carpenters was coming out of the tiny Telefunken radio placed on a small wooden shelf.

Isabella counted softly dipping her hands into the developer liquid. Although she had a stopwatch and other technological devices for this purpose, she had always preferred the traditional method of counting out loud to do so.

'My father taught me to reveal in this manner, and that's how I like doing it,' she had once confessed.

There, in that dark room, she felt she was in absolute control.

Bathed in that red light that flooded the entire place, with lights and reality outside the door, she believed she could control the world, or at least its appearance. It would stay out as long as she desired. In here she could enlarge or shrink it to the desired dimensions, eliminate flaws, hide unwanted figures.

Only a wall-mounted clock showed a tenuous connection with reality and time, albeit with a significant interpretation of time. This watch measured the time of magic, the emergence of forms, sensations and impressions.

'Can you pass me that paper you have on your right, please?' she said.

I found what she requested as best I could, moving awkwardly in that foreign environment, hitting things here and there in a world that appeared as disturbing as it might seem to a bat in broad daylight.

After introducing the photographic paper into the developer liquid and placing it beneath the plate, she awaited expectantly for the miracle to take place. That miracle, which continually amazed her.

Slowly, incrementally, first in slight grey tones —or what passed through grey tones under those lighting conditions—a familiar, recognisable outline emerged. It swiftly completed its transformation, adding another being to the world, even if this was only on the surface of a blackening piece of paper.

There it was, the result of that morning's work—a splendid dragonfly gliding majestically, even with gallantry through the air. Two sets of wings moved defiantly, gracefully spreading across the paper.

'I saw it yesterday while walking my dog in the open field behind my house. Isn't it splendid?' she remarked, gazing at me with that eternal smile, characteristic in her.

Isabella was a lover of life, of the triumph of nature, light, colour, and brightness over all things, always attentive to the smallest gestures and signs, always ready to embrace a friend, companion, or her loyal dog with a warmth that left no one unmoved.

Now, devoted to her task in that dim room, she appeared to be a different person from the one I had previously known.

There had been an undoubted connection between us in the past: a shared appreciation for the enchantment of life. For me, it was butterflies and history, for her it was photography and medicine.

The now doctor liked to hang up her white coat as soon as she arrived home and forget her responsibilities and the harsh, unjust world of the morning, immerse herself instead in this other alternative reality.

Every time I revisited Isabella years later, that other old friend, the dragonfly greeted me from her frame atop her desk, inevitably bringing to mind that evening spent in Sotileza, listening to the Carpenters on a transistor radio.

CHAPTER 23

THE HOUSE ON ESPOLON WALK

Throughout our lives, we become acquainted with various forms of wind. Thus, we familiarise ourselves with the gentle breeze that caresses our ear tips before gliding over them and launching itself at its next victim. We are well aware of the zephyr and the dreaded gale. We know the confident air that whispers secrets in our ears but stops when we try to listen only to reappear after a few seconds, head bowed, possibly embarrassed for having shared so much.

We certainly know our evening friend, the bierzo, that breeze loved by Burgos people, which arrives just in time to greet us as we leave home, caressing our cheeks. But among all of them, the most dreaded, however, is unquestionably the hurricane gale, a vengeful wind, enraged by the prospect of circling the globe incessantly till kingdom come.

It is a wind that refuses to accept its fate, since it desires to remain in a place when its essence is precisely motion. It is the wind that blows violently over the cemeteries, rattling the leaves in anger so that they could fall and remain quiet on the benches, in silent reverence for the dead. This wind attacks, targeting the very faces of living creatures, jealous of their slower pace, of their earthbound movements.

A distant relative of this, perhaps a descendant of the one that followed Jack London through the Alaskan gorges, has decided this evening to pay a visit to Burgos and specifically, the Espolón Walk.

Unaware of his arrival, Carlos had been peering through the windows of the study for some time. He seems to be considering both the manicured grounds and the music stand placed in front of his house.

Some leaves start to form a circle in the middle of it announcing the approaching dusk and wind.

The professor, remembering the similar temple at the university, speculates that it seems his fate to have one of these buildings around.

Down below, the Espolón Walk conveys that serenity the professor appreciates so much, that calmness that would not be broken until further to his left. There, traffic coming from Mio Cid Square heads over to St Pablo bridge. The small Vena River, that Arlazón apprentice, runs neary, perpetually envious.

Traffic and pedestrians traverse the so-called Via Sacra Cidiana. Unaware of history, they stroll beneath the statues that have been on both sides of the bridge since 1953. And so they pass by without noticing, oblivious to the grandeur of their surroundings. Neither do they notice the lovely street lights made of wrought iron similarly spaced apart.

Despite the wind, though, this portion of the Espolón Walk is still a quiet location.

Lafuente inhales deeply observing the cherished river below, flowing as usual, beside those trees that meet it with their strange forms and dense knots, twisting the sky.

Down below, the Espolón Walk conveys that serenity the professor appreciates so much

A FEW METRES BEYOND MODERN BUILDINGS STRETCH ALONG the Espolón Walk. Inch by inc the old city has been gradually supplanted by nondescript, contemporary buildings. Only some administrative buildings, the cathedral, and nearby St Maria Gate remain of the old city by the riverbank. Many of the original structures have vanished.

In this part of the river, a small sample of them could be between St Maria Gate and the Mio Cid area.

Number 26 of the promenade is completely occupied by the Palace of Culture and Recreation, formerly known as the Union Circle.

However, for the average Burgos resident, it is simply known as "the casino." The institution was established in 1881, as shown by the plaque on the left of the main entrance. The current structure, however, had been built in 1930 as a result of the merger of La Amistad and Café Montañés clubs, both of them descendants in turn of the famous Swiss Café on the same walk.We mentioned before that the building is almost practically occupied by the Union Circle because on its top floor exists an invincible fortress that has steadfastly resisted the sale and subsequent possession by any firm, association, or individual. This is the floor where the professor has its digs.

Here, in this nearly impregnable citadel, like a mediaeval fortress from one of Professor Lafuente's many books, lives the professor.

The building has carried on with these two tenants, stubborn in its position. It has refused to make room for these upstarts in the form of modern premises hosting banks and businesses on their ground floors. From its three rows of towers that complete its silhouette, the building sneers at the street and passersby below who dare to disturb the peace of the place.

There is a justification for this opposition. The Bordallo family, one of the many families involved in the casino's creation, had been respected and held in high regard by the bourgeoisie of the time. The Bordallos had insisted on maintaining this part of the building for their own use, being aware perhaps of the property's potential significance in days to come.

Here they had lived discreetly since then without great ostentation.

Such had been their discretion that few members of the casino knew of the particular arrangement made between society and the family many years ago. Neither the local corporation nor the most prominent members of Burgos society were aware of the significant role the Bordallo family had played all along--particularly, the one of Evaristo Bordallo-- in the design, financing, and final construction of the building.

Don Evaristo had not been a man of gestures, social notes, or public events; letting others receive the spotlights on their faces, their names published in the *Diario de Burgos*.

And in this silent, discreet way, his name dissolved into the mist of history, among those many others that populate the pantheon of altruistic deeds.

The old entrance gate to the building is situated next to the casino windows on the ground floor.

Another pair of paned windows peer out onto the street, wondering if anyone would enter the building that particular day.

It has been a very long time since a guest has crossed the invisible barrier separating the casino and its library from this exclusive and upscale region in order to spend the evening in this high and private area where resides that strange hindrance that refuses to leave.

Over forty years have passed without the sound of children's feet climbing the flight of stairs, without hearing the neighbouring apartment doors closing as their owners left for work in the mornings.

The barren trees on the front esplanade had been quiet witnesses to the departure of those very neighbours when they were forced to leave, disappearing without further notice.

This had been also Uncle Enrique and Aunt Engracia's house, the latter being Evaristo Bordallo's granddaughter. Carlos would go there every other Thursday of his school days, sometimes accompanied by one of his classmate, to receive some cookies or a sweet that the generous woman always provided them with.

'Your little friend wants some too. Is it not? Well, here's another one for you!' she told his friend Fermin, his companion that day. 'Now go both of you to the living room and do your homework before your mother arrives,'

Carlos had inherited the house. That house, where many Christmases had been celebrated in the company of his parents and uncles, He had never considered selling it, despite receiving numerous tempting offers.

All one had to do was ask Aurelio, the doorman next door, to get all the juicy details, the number of calls and visits from prospective buyers, including the misterious and disguised visit of a purported distant relative attempting to determine how much the eccentric owner would sell it for.

This was something he would never, ever do. In a way, the house would die with him. He was fortunate to reside there smoking his pipe in front of the open window, observing the bare trees and river. Behind this building was Plaza Mayor and the Town Hall, the complete heart and centre of the city.

He owed everything to Uncle Enrique and Aunt Engracia, as they had paid for his education in those years when private education cost an arm and a leg.

He owed them a happy childhood, having shared life and games there with his cousins and nephews who had also frequented the house and treated him as one of the family.

Thanks to his aunt, he had enjoyed the harvests of a class that was not his own. Thanks to her, he had developed a longing for knowledge, an appreciation for excellence that he would not have otherwise known. On Christmas Eve, she used to take him by the hand to the nearest bookshop and buy him a pile of books with which to pass the evening.

After his passing, the Union Circle might retain complete ownership of the mansion in case he had no descendency. That had been the deal.

It was here, in this place, in this office, where thoughts and ideas clicked.

The rector could claim anywhere and everywhere that he was the head of one of the first universities in Spain. Still, he knew in his heart of hearts that he would have to settle for the imaginary image of the university depicted in that painting facing his desk.

On the other hand, and thanks to his good relations with both the board of directors and casino members, he was able to use the two hundred square metres of the Union Circle's library, where he might occasionally be spotted.

On evenings like these, Lafuente is more aware of the wind. On days like these, he misses waking up to the sound of swifts and starlings.

He is seated in a green velvet wing chair, accompanied by his perpetual pipe. A mental assessment of the research is taking place in his mind.

While staring at the opposite wall, his mind drifts. He contemplates the half-hung portraits, the grandfather's clock he has retained out of pure affection along with the 1890s microscope placed next to it. A genuine Carl Zeiss. As he later learned, the very model Ramón y

Cajal had used for his experiments. A microscope through which he received in days of yore his first glimpse of a hidden world.

A true gem that brought back countless happy memories of mornings spent along with Uncle Enrique, eating cookies with milk. The slow, mellow voice of Jorge Sepúlveda was playing on the record player. The song was "Looking at the sea front, I dreamed of you" followed by "Santander". A Santander enveloped and caressed by the voice of this hitherto unknown singer. It was hearing for the first time the name of his hometown in the voice of this interpreter with a thick moustache, that nostalgia entered his life for the first time.

He proceeds to recount in his mind the events of the previous days.

The princess's journey, to put it mildly, had been everything but smooth. From the moment she left Bergen, and set out for England, where she spent several months afraid of the pirates. Horseback would then be used for the rest of the journey across France until reaching the county of Barcelona. After a brief respite in Burgos, where she only stayed for one night, she resumed her journey towards Valladolid. A brief stop in the Black Lagoon of Soria as a result of that weird illness that had held her there for several days. And finally her meeting with the king in Valladolid. Simply thinking about it made him dizzy.

A voyage of approximately nine months, one week more, one week less before continuing to Seville. Only to die there a few years later, childless, with all previous promises made to her fading into thin air. One could not help but feel compassion for that woman who had left everything behind only to end her days in a remote land. A land so dissimilar to the far north. A land where she had encountered an unknown language, unusual customs, and oppressive heat.

Of course she spoke Latin, the international language at the time. That certainly was a plus, but...

He put the pipe in his mouth and inhaled.

The much-disputed love letters found in her coffin came to mind along with the conversation they had with Hans in Covarrubias. Was a letter ever placed inside her coffin? There was some uncertainty in that regard. If so, where were they? What had been written on it? Considering the outcome of Elena's inquiries so far, maybe they would never know.

The Huelgas Abbey in Burgos, only a few kilometres from the Montanilla University campus was now the focus of all attention. A short distance from home. The secret--if such a thing existed--, had been jealously guarded around this location for centuries.

At approximately seven o'clock, the gate of number 26 opened to give way to his figure. As soon as he put his feet on the sidewalk, he was pushed back by a burst of wind. That punctual evening wind caught him by surprise. After being startled in this way, he turned to face the wind blowing in his direction. It seemed intent in avoiding the professor leaving the house that evening.

At number 30, just a few metres from home and to his right was the 1907-founded Espolón Bookshop sign in gold lettering on a crimson background. Although his destination today was further beyond he stopped in front of it under the force of custom, unable to pass without stopping at whatever bookshop he happened to come across. That would have been a gross discourtesy to all of his upbringing, to countless evenings drifting in and out of them. Enter he did many times, even if only to smell the printed paper or touch some new pages that seemed to be waiting for him. Today though after a quick glance at the window out of habit, he kept walking and crossed in front of another old Burgos landmark, the Castellano de Grados Pharmacy, with its beautiful wooden arches and glass doors decorated with modernist themes.

His routine would have been different in the distant past when, after leaving home, he would have turned left, directing his steps towards the nearby Ibáñez Confectionery at number 16 for a cup of hot chocolate. Still, the establishment had been unable to withstand the latest recession. been forced to close after enduring in that place more than a century. A modern chocolate shop there has retained the name of Ibanez. The professor remembered the cordial greetings of Severiano, its former owner every time he saw him accompanied by his aunt to buy sweets or some pastries for a special occasion—which used to be any weekend he spent with his uncles. That experience couldn't be replaced so easily.

The oath of fidelity to these memories made him swear eternal hate to this faker who had the nerve to use the holy name.

Not being able to choose this course of action, Lafuente's directed his steps straight to St Maria Gate where a stronger blast of wind forced him to stop. It caught him completely off guard as he attempted to cross the arch. Shortly afterwards he arrived at his destination: a dark alley near Laín Calvo, just off La Paloma St, one of those places bathed in a continuous shade that seemed to have maintained itself in that place by sheer miracle. Its walls and cobblestoned streets were already slipping away, merging into the city background, making itself virtually invisible, undetectable from the rest of the major streets. There he directed himself to a second-hand bookshop.

Many of these bookstores were already disappearing from the face of the Earth. This and Sons of Santiago Rodriguez, one of Europe's oldest bookshops were frequented by the professor. He inclined himself to search for his first edition books using these old resources rather than the official, well stocked channels of the university library itself. There would be time to turn to them should he not find what he was looking for on these walks.

The setting sun was somehow filtering in some impossible way into the passage, thanks to the whim of the arrangement of a dressing-table mirror in a neighbouring house, which, after reflecting its rays through one of its upper windows, transferred the reflection to the glass of a lamppost on the opposite wall. From there, a narrow beam of light finally projected itself into the bookstore's front window, bathing it in golden hues, those tones without which a bookshop would be nothing.

On the other hand, the window's synchronisation with the bookstore's opening hours seemed somewhat peculiar to say the least. A synchronicity that merited additional in-depth research should someone consider it. The light thus projected warmed and enhanced the old woods and wrinkled volumes displayed in the shop windows, forgotten, longing for a curious soul who, upon discovering the beauty concealed inside them, would enter the premises, and swiftly remove them after a brief commercial transaction.

The incipient Christmas decoration that had already taken over the place reminded the professor of the oncoming holidays. He lingered at the window for a while longer. The bitter wind was bearable when he thought about the shelter he would be experiencing inside the premises. He had always been drawn to those tinsel ribbons placed between the books.

A gnome in the left-hand window corner caught his attention. He was carrying what looked like a bag full of toys, and Carlos Lafuente thought for a moment that he had stepped out of one of the many books that had been put there for the comfort and amusement of younger readers.

It was, in short, one of those small bookshops, paradoxically vast in its hidden secrets, where volumes grew and multiplied on the shelves. Books behind books, bookshelves behind bookshelves. One of those places where you could still hear a faint bell ringing in the distance as you entered. When finally doing so he found old Esteban the librarian conversing with a customer. Lafuente closed the door not without some difficulty, braked as it was by a thread of wind that let out a mournful hiss, a wail at the last second, as it was snared by the door.

'I was searching for a copy of *The Three Musketeers*,' the customer was asking the bookseller.

'What version or translation were you looking for? Someone in particular? the owner kept asking, almost in whispers. Age and the accumulation of dust on books had already altered the old man's nature.

After hearing the response, the bookseller quickly made his way to a dark nook, where he pushed aside a ladder that had likely been in that very place for months. After rearranging two rows of books, he finally reached into the stack, pulled out a big volume, and put it in front of his customer's eyes.

'This Bruguera 1968 edition is one of the best. It's not expensive, it's light, and serves its purpose,' the bookseller added, his eyes glowing with a particular light. 'On the other hand, this novel has a special character for me. The Queen of France and future mother of Louis XIV did not marry in our cathedral for nothing, you know.'

'I'll take it' the customer said, convinced of the benefits of the work.

Carlos took advantage of the waiting time by observing his surroundings. There were other customers in the store. Since the bookshop was similar to those old cafes of the early twentieth century, several of them were rummaging through the books or, more likely, reading them from cover to cover. They, aware of their patron's friendliness, had come here to kill time before supper.

When the bookseller saw Carlos Lafuente, he greeted him with a wide grin.

'Good evening, professor! How are you, sir?'

Lafuente made a query in a low voice, trying to avoid being overheard by the rest of customers.

The bookseller nodded quickly and ascended some stairs behind him, panting towards a loft-like room where no one was allowed to enter.

After some time, he returned with a dark-covered book, exquisitely adorned with golden markings on the cover, spine, and edges.

'Here you are! It's uncommon for anyone to request this nowadays. I've had this volume for years,' he said, bending his head like an oriental, recognising in the professor an initiate with whom to share an ancient rite.

And so Lafuente, comforted with the weight of the volume in his hands, reopened the door through which the wind rushed in, both curious and angry at having being left outdoors.

The professor strolled home as the evening dragged on, carrying the book under his left arm in a silent and meditative walk. He was overtaken by a group of four children kicking a ball, whose voices had reached him minutes before they passed him. They appeared to be heading in the same direction, occupying the entire width of the sidewalk with their masterful passes. One of them, a proud Mirandés football team cap wearing fan, shouted,

'Hey Felipe! ', over here, Felipe, pass it on!'

This same walk had been witness to Carlos Lafuente and his friends exercising themselves by the simple means of tossing stones into the river from its walls. Many times, trying to reach the other shore and others, less confessable ones, the figure of some scoundrel from the opposite gang with the silent hope of hitting him square in the shin.

The streets at the back of Aunt Engracia's house had witnessed many of these raids. At that time, still a far cry from the invasion of the big brand store chains, the merchants would stand outdoors in the late evenings, waiting for a customer to enter while enjoying the presence of the passerby and the children's games. These filling the air with loud laughter, minutes before their mothers called them in for dinner. Dinner appeared to be always announced precisely at the most vital moments of the game, namely when they were about to crown Fort Williams, save the princess, or win the World Song Contest. Oh, gosh! How quickly time passes! Other times, he might be playing Captain Lee from the famous series *Voyage to the Bottom of the Sea*, fighting a sea monster that had got inside the submarine Sea View, or David Janssen from *The Fugitive*, about to be caught by the law.

The evening occasionally found them in the vicinity of the Principal Theatre or running up Mint House or Laín Calvo streets, invading the area around St Lorenzo church with their yells. Both the Inside and the Outside Plains –an area which had been used for street markets in mediaeval Burgos--, were crossed at various points by this band of brothers. There was no nook or cranny unknown to them. The entire Burgos centre was nothing but a giant game board for them. His head had always been full of daring notions, of desert islands, of ships crossing the ocean towards geographical points he didn't know how to decipher or much less name. The globe that Santa would bring him the following Christmas was still but a fervent wish. It seemed to him that Emilio Salgari's or Jules Verne's adventures would be taking place near the Captaincy's Palace, a few streets to the north. That sonorous name held a special fascination

for the young man, making him believe that the heroes of his readings had visited this place at some unknown time. The Alonso
Martínez square looked packed to him, not with tourists looking for
the nearby tourist office, but rather with people with a grim and
concentrated gesture more similar to Phileas Fogg than anything
else.

"Always trying to save the princess," he smiled to himself. "Is that
the reason I am so intrigued by those scrolls, by this bizarre story of
Princess Kristina?" A return to childhood. A trip down memory lane.
A sign maybe that he was getting older; there was no doubt about it.

Back at home, he secluded himself once more in his study. There
he sat, staring at the library on the opposite wall, lined with thick
tomes and books that reached up to the ceiling. Documents and
knowledge of bygone eras. The idea that everything could be found
in books had been drilled into him as a child, but now he couldn't find
what he was looking for anywhere. Except for Ismael, curled up and
snoozing in the wing chair, he was alone with his thoughts. After
great work, he had been able to acclimate his pet to these lodgings,
which lacked the lengthy passageways and tunnels of the university.
Ismael had patiently endured being carried away from one location to
another.

He opened the book he had just purchased, *The Abbess of Las
Huelgas* by none other than José María Escrivá de Balaguer, a work
that had been repudiated by the very Opus Dei religious order that
the very Balaguer had founded. Perhaps it had considered he had
overemphasised the role of women in the church when writing it.

He left the window and sat down at his desk. A few seconds later,
the familiar start-up sound of the iMac computer could be heard, and
the screen filled with a steady stream of icy data characters. His
computer was now a window into the past. He checked the information displayed. Yes, according to the *Frisinicus chronicle* and others,
these were the dates with slight variations.

Lafuente took notes, perused, and scoured the Internet and some
other books from the library. The hours passed. The reproductions in
the volume were priceless. The book confirmed him that the

monastery's influence had permeated much of Burgos province, including entire villages and families, up until quite recently.

Entire households.

He could still hear through the window the muffled sounds of the children playing on the pavement below. Children whom the wind could not dissuade, evening after evening. Children battling age, the future, and time by hitting ball against a wall, a closed door, or their own shins if necessary.

Children.

He recognised among the voices that of the devout Mirandés follower he had the doubtful pleasure of meeting in the street an hour before.

He attempted once more to concentrate on the book and notes on his desk.

"... *Departure om England to France...*"

A tremendous hit against the building wall followed by a triumphant shout coming from the street below, proclaimed a fictional team's goal, an unconquerable opponent's defeat, a victory.

"*The time employed in her trip...*"

'That's not fair! I wasn't even looking!' cried an angry voice in the street.

"*The princess.*"

"*Those nine months.*"

The blessed children were screaming like lunatics, straining their voices to outdo the wind that had stolen their ball.

"*Nine months of travel across Europe.*"

"*Princess Kristina.*"

"*May the Brethen continue to guard the sacred mystery of the Flower of the North.*"

'Well, next day, go and play with those scumbags in your street, you idiot! ' A new howl from the outside world.

"*A nine-month journey.*"

"*Practicay a pregnancy.*"

"*Nine months.*"

'Goal this time you fool!'

That bunch of blighters!...

Lafuente chuckled at his abundant creative juices. He had watched a lot of conspiracy and intrigue films lately.

'I mustn't read so much,' he told himself.

Nonetheless, he had to concede that despite his reservations, the theory itself was intriguing. Should something like this ever happened, there wasn't a trace in any chronicle, article, or study about it.

He rose from his seat and took three or four strides across the room, repeatedly running his hand over his chin and hair as he went.

Then, he finally opened Wikipedia and typed "*Huelgas Monastery*" with anger at the search bar. When the result came on the screen, he devoured every word.

That was it!

He read the abbess's name at the time,

Sister Elvira Fernández.

There was once again a trail leading to the abbey.

The princess concealed something.

Certainly, the abbess had enjoyed access to all manner of privileges.

Legal, religious, able to collect tithes and other contributions until the 19th century. Could the abbey have been involved in the princess's secret in some way? Impossible. Berenguela, the king's sister, had been present on that Christmas Eve a long time ago, although, as far as he knew, the real power, the power of the day-today, was held by the abbess, Dona Elvira, a position that was permanent at that time.

The sentence that had initially brought them to Silos appeared now to have an additional meaning.

'*May the Brethen continue to guard...*" This could refer both to the secret itself as to this additional aspect burning in his mind.

He recalled the feeling he had as a child when he and his friends used to stare intently at the windows of a derelict house they believed was haunted until, in their longing, in the suspense thus created, in the fever of their very desire, they finally saw what they feared the most, ghostly figures moving in the darkness of the abandoned house, whitish shadows of uncertain movements passing from room to room.

Was he currently experiencing this? Assuming things or events? His pragmatic and scientific intellect rejected such notions.

Had Aunt Engracia been present that evening and witnessed his expression at that moment, the good woman would have taken out the thermometer without hesitation. He, too, would have been sent to bed with no chocolate cake for dessert.

But Carlos had been left to his own devices, relying on his instincts and a disturbing inner feeling to guide him. The feeling that something was amiss, that there was a crack or a loose stone in the wall that could be pushed open disclosing in this way a hidden passage.

It couldn't be possible.

He was well aware that the princess had never been on her own since she landed in the country. His absurd notion had no basis in reality and could not be supported by any evidence. A concept he did not wish to articulate just yet. She had been accompanied since leaving Bergen by a considerable entourage, which included Loddin Nepur, the king's diplomat, and Bishop Hamar. Her ladies-in-waiting were also around. Furthermore, on that distant Christmas Eve, the monastery nuns had enveloped Kristina beneath the sanctuary's protection.

The safeguarding of the sanctuary.

Surrounded by those saintly women.

"May the Brethen continue to guard."

Could this indeed have been the princess's secret? Some sort of protection?

It was easier to imagine conspiracies, alliances, and counter alliances between neighbouring kingdoms. However, the truth can be frighteningly simple at times.

As simple as a child's cry at night.

Princess Kristina did really have a secret, yes.

It was not, however, a state secret. At least not just that.

When the princess arrived in Spain, she was nine months pregnant.

However, if this were the case, why had it been hidden? Where did she spend her first night in Burgos?

In the Monastery.

As if by magic, everything was becoming more and more obvious.

Or more perplexing.

Once more, the presence of white ghosts appearing outside the windows startled him. He needed confirmation from his colleagues he was not imagining an alternative universe.

Not again.

He donned the heavy coat and stepped out into the street, where a fierce wind had remerged.

Fucking Trevelyan was right again.

~

CHAPTER 24

THE FLOWER VASE

How botany assists in controlling time.

Elena placed the cup on the table and gazed intently at her colleague seated across from her. They were in the professor's study. She had only reached there a few minutes earlier, after battling through a a wind-whipped Burgos enticed by her colleague's call.

She had brought with her a cellophane-wrapped bouquet of triumphant flowers she had just purchased that afternoon from a neighbouring store.

'You told me once that you didn't have any plants here,' she said with a smile as she entered leaving the pot momentarily on the window ledge. 'so I figured this might enhance your view, sort of. Among so many papers and books, it would not be a bad idea if you had some other leaves to look at. I'll see later where it looks better.'

And, removing her coat, Elena discovered a red and black plaid dress with a turndown collar. She crossed her arms and allowed the bow around her waist, and the wide necklace to do all the talking.

In front of her, papers were dropping like torrents, protruding from every nook and cranny of the furniture, out of sync with the neatly arranged books and evenly spaced ornaments.

It was the first time she had dared to venture into Professor Lafuente's sanctuary, and the occasion did not disappoint her discerning intellect.

In milliseconds, she had studied the shelves, the paintings, and the accumulated trinkets. Clearly Carlos had transformed this area into an extension of his other, more diverse and expansive university office.

On a little table by the window a tea service had been carefully prepared. The cup from which Elena had been drinking laid there undisturbed.

She had heard a fantastic tale during the previous half an hour.

'Professor Carlos Lafuente' said she finally, rising from the chair she had been sitting in, her arms crossed over her chest, marching resolutely towards the window overlooking the park. 'Are you aware of what you're saying? Have you heard yourself speaking? You are a history professor at Montanilla University, not at a polytechnic and certainly not at a local institute. Have you ever considered that someone in so large a group coming along the princess would not have notice something like that? Not taking into account the crowds awaiting her in Barcelona, Burgos, Soria, or Valladolid. That woman, for good or bad, was never alone on her travels. Is this so difficult for you to understand? She was the closest thing to a pop artist at the time that we can think of.'

'Yes, I suppose you're right. I must confess, I liked the concept, though. However, you are absolutely right. She was never alone' the professor said, dropping his head and repeating those arguments in monotonous words. 'Besides, why the abbess might have concealed such information? A state secret, no less! A forbidden love also.'

'And don't forget it would also have endangered the union of the two crowns,' Elena said, 'which was precisely what they were attempting to do, right? the very reason for the start and end of the trip? What are you trying to tell me, Carlos, that the princess would have been able return to her homeland as if nothing had happened and inform her father she had failed as both daughter and wife? Do you really want to tell me this? ' she said, slamming the table with her open hand with such force that the vibration was transferred to the pens in the wooden pencil holder in the corner.

The professor looked up at his colleague. He left in silence the cup of tea he had held in his hands for the past few minutes, a cup he had been manipulating all this time without entirely drinking its content. He shifted then his gaze to the window.

Elena was alarmed by the eerie look on the face of her colleague, standing still. She stood up and leaned against the windowpane next to him. Ismael meowed in protest as he saw his corner being invaded, that territory no one had ever occupied before.

'Believe me Elena, I know what I'm talking about.' The professor said, turning around and looking his colleague in the face. Had she always had those green eyes? 'Listen to me, if I'm wrong, if there's nothing there, we've just wasted a little more of our time. However, an inner voice tells me there is here more than meets the eye. We did not discover the manuscripts by chance. Sometimes things do occur for a purpose, a reason for which we have no explanation. If it didn't seem ridiculous, I could even say the manuscripts have found us.'

Carlos wandered from one side of the room to the other, his extended arms matching his misery. Now and then he placed his left hand in his pocket while moving the right one in the air, as if his arguments had a physical presence and he could like a potter of history give them form and consistency.

'Carlos, your status is wonderful; you are a highly regarded professor at this university. Even a novice such as myself can see this. You wish to ruin it all for an idea?'

Elena had seated on the windowsill, cross-legged, observing him. Her tiny feet were dressed in green ankle boots with a crimson bow that matched the colour of the flowers she had brought and that were now placed next to her.

'Take a look at what we have so far' said Carlos at last. 'I'm not asking you to consider anything beyond that. It's a unique opportunity. We have before us an important story. Not just the tale of a Norwegian princess. Not simply the tale of an illegitimate birth, one of many now and then. It goes beyond that. Do you remember what I told you once? What Ernesto said in his Valladolid speech? "We recall what we want in order to explain to ourselves who we were." That was my only wish as an undergraduate, to comprehend...'

Elena nodded. There was something about Carlos's speaking intensity that made it impossible to ignore his ideas.

The professor continued in a calmer tone, 'In science, that's all we have at the beginning, Elena. Just ideas. Until now, I thought we were working on something more substantial. But even the most solid scientific theory, Elena, is founded on a notion, a testable hypothesis. I don't think I need to remind you of that, right? At least not to you.'

And when he said this, the professor's tone sank.

Had Elena observed a certain softness in it, like a countermelody at the back of the main one?

Carlos had once more turned to face the window, so Elena was unable to validate her peculiar sensation or intuition. Had the professor's normal brusqueness been softened by a certain degree of finesse?

Elena stared at the warrior's figurine on the shelf, the spear at the ready, similar to the one in the professor's office in Montanilla. It reminded her of one of her favourite mythological characters, Lancelot Du Lac, head over heels in love with Queen Guinevere.

She recalled again those summer evenings spent with her friends reading Virginia Woolf on a balcony in a far away summer.

.'Oh my gosh! Why not?' she said aloud, suddenly placing the bouquet of flowers in one of the empty vases by the fireplace. 'They will be happier here! This is unquestionably the place, wouldn't you agree?' Elena said briskly. 'And now I must go; I have much to arrange. I have to look up in my agenda for the number of National Heritage. This visit to Huelgas Monastery must be put through its paces!'

Ismael, who had been snoozing in the wing chair, sat up now noticing a change in the room's routine. Evidently, the voices had disturbed his rest. He was now pondering, leaning on his hind legs, the evolution of this visitor who dared to alter the furnishings by placing a vase in "his" window, adding insult to injury.

'Are you going to call them in good faith? You just told me you needed to focus on the next symposia, those awaiting publications....'

'Well, Professor Lafuente, that shouldn't be a problem for two historians like you and me,' Elena remarked, narrowing her eyes as she smiled. 'Keep in mind that we work with history. We have all the time in the world in our hands.'

And then, after giving the plant that finishing touch that only a woman could think of, equivalent to a signature, the personal finish of a well done job, Elena left the office with agility and short but rapid strides, without another word. Carlos watched her passed in front of the assortment of classic books he had arranged on the lowest shelf. It was incredible how a pair of shoes can enhance the movement of a woman's hips. Or perhaps it was the plaid dress's fault.

Carlos tapped the pipe bowl on his desk, spilling in so doing some of the contents across its surface. He was smiling.

It was true. They were going to waste some additional time. His colleague had put it in so many words. They had all the time in the world.

~

CHAPTER 25

UNDER THE CUSTODY OF SISTERS

Of haunted places, of how Arthur strolled through Disneyland, of rockets and castles, with an addition about how cold affects the Administration.

A reckless sun shined brightly in the sky, illuminating the city crossed by wind below.

Arthur was striding down the street toward the arranged meeting point with the professors. To better protect himself from the chilly air that was just starting to rise, he re-adjusted the grey scarf he had purchased the day before, relishing the simple joy of being enveloped in his own warmth breath, with a feeling of comfort. Madrid St had just replaced Plaza Vega St. Nearby was St Augustine Chambers, —the university residence—, where some of his peers, less fortunate than he, would be cramming knowledge into their brains in those few hours prior to the examinations taking place the following day. Or perhaps it was the other way round? Unlike him, they were not enthralled in a tale of intrigue and historical secrets. When he looked ahead, he saw that the Old Lady seemed to have noticed his wanderings. Every time he looked at the cathedral, he was unable to escape the peculiar, dreamy impression of a half-ajar door that seemed to beckoning him to the discovery of another region, another world beyond the everyday, far apart from the one he knew.

He reached the end of the street; there it was, more or less obscured by a city bus crossing his field of vision at that moment:

St Mary's Gate and its two little towers, inviting him, enticingly, to pass under its arch once more, daring to penetrate that secret world he somehow guessed existed beyond. Everything he had studied thus far about inexplicable emotions and concepts had, in some way, a connection to that building and that river.

Despite appearing to have been fixed there forever, they were at the same time constantly shifting, causing him to believe that things were not as they appeared. Why hadn't Professor Lafuente told him that the two crenellated turrets on either side of St. Mary's Gate were in fact two silos containing a few long-range rockets? The outcome of a plan between Alfonso XI and Pope Clement VI while the gate was being built? Certainly those extravagances would have been tolerated in a university professor. But no, Lafuente had told him instead about a princess who had concealed her pregnancy on a lengthy tour to Spain. And he was the one with wild ideas just for reading Theosophy and hoping to witness a flying saucer or two!

The vision of the gate from the street through which he had previously descended, revealed the white stone of St Mary Gate and its six niches at its top in a manner that Arthur Trevelyan had always compared in his mind to the main entrance to Disneyland. Of course, that thought would never leave his mouth, even if someone put him to some kind of torture, but there it was in his mind whenever he travelled that path. With more panache, yes, with more history behind it, more cultural background and the like, yes. All that was fine. But for him, this location had always been magical. For, behind that wonderful gate, the cathedral stood, and next to it was a world he admired. There, street lights with black wrought iron arms could be seen. Underneath them, the core of pedestrian streets forked. There were in the neighbourhood a pair of squares known for centuries as Las Llanas, complete with terraces, numerous bars, restaurants, and inns, a variety of stores of all kinds, and those narrow passages that seemed to go nowhere. He would leave the place after half an hour with the feeling of having travelled hundreds of metres, realising only then he had not moved from the vicinity of the cathedral, as if a strange and powerful magnetism drew all life, commerce, and activity towards it.

Behind the gate, the cathedral towers loomed like those in Sleeping Beauty Castle, possibly anticipating the young man's thoughts. Curious and inquisitive, they seemed to take a foresighted look at what kind of people would pass in front of her that evening, those few, those fortunate few.

Arthur had engaged in numerous discussions with his English friends, contrasting the advantages of living in a region traversed by a tranquil and low-flowing river as opposed to the more populated and active Thames. Neither did he envy those hundreds of students on the Cam keen on rowing towards Grantchester for afternoon pastries and tea.

The wind was penetrating; it pursued the walkers, asking for a moment of their time, pleading with its howl for their attention.

There were few pedestrians on that December afternoon, a colder-than-usual day even by Burgos's standards. Far away remained the mild heat of summer, as did spring and young leaves. Only the wind dared to cross the empty streets again and again. The shops behind the cathedral, particularly those on La Paloma St had shut their doors to protect their merchandise. Customers were calmed by cafeterias at crossroads with coffee and hot chocolate enveloped in friendly conversation. Through many windows, the contained joy of Christmas light spilt out.

The car of Carlos Lafuente was already waiting in the taxi area at the end of Plaza Vega Street. His owner. leaning against it and enjoying his pipe despite the cold.

The professor was seeking cover inside the raised lapels of a long coat he had brought for the occasion. Arthur raised his against the blizzard before entering the vehicle. He heard the cathedral clock strike a quarter past five. Elena sat in the passenger seat, wrapped and encased in a turtleneck sweater and a wool cap. As soon as the automobile doors were shut, the wind appeared to stop, some leaves pursuing it a few metres, infuriated at the disrespect displayed.

'Not a good day to carry valuable documents' Elena said after a few minutes while they stood at a traffic lights.

Completely unaware of the ferocity of the elements, they continued along the N-120 road, oblivious to the gorgeous scene of willows dispersed here and there along the riverbank to their right, their branches furiously swaying. Burgos looked to be silently weeping in their midst behind the closed windows of the car.

Arthur, cuddled against the back window, gave himself permission to let his thoughts run wild. He wondered what reason might the city have to be in such a depressing state. Did it miss anything, anyone?

Professor Lafuente drove left after leaving Island Park to their right, oblivious to the ideas flowing through his student's head. After passing in front of the old King's Hospital, now housing Burgos University's annex buildings, they seemed to have entered another world. The clattering of the car tires on the cobblestones seemed to have risen this slumbering residential neighbourhood from its nap.

The half-moon-shaped street, named after Alfonso VIII, the monastery's first monarch, preserved its original structures, hardly sustained under the influence of the monastery. They were the so called Compass Houses.

They parked in front of the monastery near to Faja de Huelgas Bar.

Several yards to the left of its door they could see a contemporary "no parking" sign in sheer contrast to the monastic dream of the place.

They had arrived to their destination.

They stood in front of that unique stone pile, the Monastery of Our Lady of Huelgas. From the top of a square tower, its bells loomed through semicircular arches.

The three of them walked in perfect formation. It would have been a curious sight to any onlooker. They resembled more a group of jittery freshmen on their first day of class at a top university than researches.

Carlos wearing his heavy coat looked at Elena who was attempting to carry a folder under her right arm and a bag under her left one as efficiently as possible. Arthur kept his iPhone 8 Plus in the right pocket of his suit, ready for any scenario.

The special authorisations had arrived from Madrid the day before bearing the seal from Royal Archives were now kept in the small suitcase Carlos carried in his right hand. Without them they would have been unable to examine the intended codices. Ink over ink in order to inspect older spellings. He had been lucky enough to circumvent the most difficult obstacle due to both his reputation in the academic world and his university contacts but it was Elena's prompt assistance that had guaranteed the necessary permissions.

They entered the Huelgas Trust offices through the same door that led to the souvenir shop and the booth where tickets to visit the monument could be purchased.

They were greeted upon entering by a young woman in blue uniform and long hair. A Christmas tree with sombre ornaments and a nativity scene by her side gave her the appearance of a Santa Claus representative for the occasion. Clearly a member of National Heritage.

The nuns had long ago relinquished their power over the world in exchange for permission to continue living in the monastery.

'Good morning! Are you the Montanilla professors? ' said she extending her hand. 'My name's Remedios Ponciel, from the Huelgas Board. Please follow me; I'll lead you to the administrative offices on the first floor.

They passed the souvenir shop and followed through an adjacent entrance disguised within the wall, unnoticed till then, giving way to a staircase lighted with diffuse light.

'Please, come this way,' repeated her guide after having reaching the threshold and climbing the stairs with a martial dexterity, the result of both training and youth thus allowing the young man to examine her well-formed calves in detail without fear of being caught in this pleasurable task.

They discovered a new world in this upper area inhabited by

National Heritage staff; some spacious offices faced the Inside Compass through wide windows.

Arthur couldn't help but notice that the young woman moved with a professional air, as if the desks and file cabinets they passed were incunabula and the computers, cables, and other office supplies surrounding them were part of National Heritage and, thus, worthy of respect.

Nothing outside the building would have led a visitor to suspect that behind those antique windows were contemporary offices equipped with central heating, computers and Internet.

On a wet and cold day like this, though, the structure resembled more a large lodge where hunters may seek cover while fleeing the storm outside than anything else. A variety of outwear hung on three racks strategically placed across the area supported this initial impression. On the other hand the central heating made people feel comfortable, so visitors had to rapidly remove their clothing and find a place to put them if they didn't want to die of suffocation.

Carlos cast a despondent glance around him. His companions, quicker than he, had already got rid of their coats and had hung them on one of the nearest hooks, threatening in so doing to topple it with their weight. On a final thought, he folded his heavy overcoat over his right arm with some resignation.

The offices filled a significant portion of the first level of the monastery. Modern office supplies harmonised in varied degrees with the surround antique stone. A picture of King Felipe VI that Alfonso VIII wouldn't have expected to find there, hung on a wall, smiling and friendly.

In dealing with ecclesiastical and local authorities, the monastery had never abandoned practicality, as seen by the art books on the shelves, interspersed with volumes on economics and accountancy. Among them, the received light occasionally illuminated a Christmas ball.

This had not been merely a religious retreat centre for royalty and women from the nobility. Another noble blood now occupied it. The Board of Trustees and personnel in charge of its care and upkeep were now an integral part of the institution, exuding the same aura of legitimate authority as the previous proprietors.

The young woman sat behind a table where a screen displayed in crisp tones, the daily realities of the 21st century. The mouse awaiting a click on the screen.

'I believe you wish to inspect some codices in the monastery,' she began, assuming a businesslike tone once more. 'As you might expect, we preserve a precise and comprehensive record of everything stored here, information such as the year each codex entered Huelgas, the monastery or religious order to whom it was leased, etcetera. Well, now my colleague at the second desk will fill out the research form for you, and, once that has been verified, I will call the archives' technician to begin the procedure.'

'Stop standing there and come over here, if you please! You won't expect me to go there, will you?' a shrill rose from the location specified by the young woman, specifically behind a computer display at the opposite end of the workplace.

As they approached, they discovered a little woman concealed behind it. As soon as Arthur noticed the alternative arrangement of her hair, he recalled he had not stored the carpet in his room. The lady was making peremptory signals for them to approach.

'I must fill in your researcher's form first. Please hand over your ID's and the Royal Archives authorization.' she added with the secret hope they should not have it. The woman's motions reminded Elena of the Punch and Judy plays she used to witness at country fairs when she was a youngster.

'Naturally,' remarked Carlos placing his briefcase on the chair facing the clerk's desk.

'Excuse me', replied the woman briskly. 'I told you to show me your identity cards. I made no mention of your leaving your belongings on my chair. This, as you probably have noticed is my workspace.'

Carlos quickly retrieved the culprit and placed it on the table's right side.

'You can't put it there either. As a matter of fact, you're not required to position yourself behind or close to my table. Let me finish my current task first, and I'll be able then to attend you.'

'I beg your pardon, but you urged us to approach, and I assumed....'

'Just because I told you to approach, it doesn't necessarily mean you have to present me any documents until you are required to do so. As you will understand, many people come here every day, and there are various steps to carry out before we are ready to proceed.'

When the paperwork ultimately ended after a time of some anxiety and they turned to leave, Carlos's coat dropped to the ground. Both he and Elena knelt to pick it up.

Remedios Ponciel who had been maintaining a safe distance with the help of the two displays on her desk, stood up and followed them to the door down the hallway.

'The archives technician will arrive tomorrow first thing in the morning. But since you are already here, perhaps you'd be interested in taking a tour of the monastery?' she inquired with a smile that was an attempt to dispel the chill both outside and inside the premises. 'If you will be so kind as to wait for me downstairs for a few minutes, I'll gladly give you a quick tour as soon as I finish a few emails. There's no one around at this hour and I have a few spare minutes.'

Arthur, glancing up at the windows of the offices they had just left, mused that it would be ideal, now that the wind and snow had gone, to spend the remainder of the evening in this manner. A white sheet of snow had draped itself over the fountains and a portion of the interior courtyards.

Every good army must begin a battle with a thorough reconnaissance of the terrain. A visit to the monastery a day prior to locking themselves in the consulting room to confront volumes and codices after such a frosty reception would be a breath of fresh air.

The temperature was not excessively low for December. Burgos was satisfied with those two degrees Celsius. The weather forecast for the evening and the next few days had predicted a three degree drop in temperature which certainly increased the likelihood that people would remain indoors.

They were in the so-called Inside Compass, the inner courtyard. There, despite the chilly weather several tourists were already waiting to be assigned a guide for the standard tourist itinerary.

'It's been a very long time since my previous visit but nothing has changed,' Elena added with a smile, her nose slightly reddening from the cold.

A building wing in the background faced the small group. Between its stone arches there hung some chains enclosing that small internal area. To their right Arthur immediately recognised the Knights' Cloister from the images he had seen in his books.

'This is the place where the knights visiting the monastery left their armour, stables, and other possessions before being allowed to enter it' said their impromptu guide.

Elena was pointing at a fountain a little smaller than the central one. It was placed on a sidewall a few steps away from them. The inscription "Built by order of Abbess Dona Benita Oñate y Samaniego..." was difficult to read on a stone plaque at the top. A slight trickle of water gushed out of it. She instinctively reached out and touched it with her palms, seemingly unconcerned by the freezing water. At that moment Elena looked to Carlos as a mischievous child playing during her teacher's absence from class.

It was as if one of the damsels from Ernesto Santos's historical novels had come to life.

Out of the corner of his eye, the professor detected a slight movement.

Yes, there was a motionless figure behind the fence and near the exist door through with the previous group had departed. Upon becoming aware of their presence the figure took a slight step back. She was a nun. Apparently she had been observing the group of visitors while this was waiting restless for their guide by the central fountain.

Lafuente thought then how boring a nun's life must be: prisoner of routine, condemned to repeating the same walk day after day, the same jobs and chores, unable to view the outside world. Perhaps she was lucky though, not being able to watch the news or cable television. But how many experiences and unfulfilled life opportunities missed as a result!

He offered her a kind grin. So many nuns from his boyhood came back to life in his memory! In his experience, sisters devoted and concerned about children, with a true passion for their job, with immense capacity and devotion to their mission.

Remedios Ponciel exited then the building with quick steps, her blue outfit and nameplate affixed to her lapel standing out against the snowy backdrop.

When Carlos glanced again, the nun was no longer present.

'Due to so much royal tutelage, the monastery many prominent Castilian ladies of the aristocracy entered it as nuns,' Remedios began, not wasting a second, with professional clarity, walking with short and determined steps, adopting the formal air of her profession. 'It also functioned as the royal pantheon as well as a place of the utmost political and military significance. It saw the coronation of several kings. It was here, too, that monarchs ordered knights. As you can see it contains Roman, Gothic, Mudejar, Almohad, and Renaissance elements.' After crossing the Knight's Cloister, she stopped, 'Well, I'm afraid I must leave you here. I assume you'd like to go at your own pace from this point forward. In any case, the guided tours will begin shortly, and you may follow any of the guides if you like.'

And having said this, she left them with the utmost regret on the part of young Arthur.

Once alone, Lafuente surveyed the surroundings. Dona Leonor, the founder's wife, had desired to establish an abbey where women might acquire the same authority as men, in the style of the French Monastery of Fotevrault, to which her mother had retired. Yes, she had succeeded, but only to be defeated at the hands of the most fearsome enemy of all: Time. After the Council of Trent, time, betraying everything, had deprived the monastery of all its rights. "For ever" had been reduced to the weak memory of men.

As Remedios Ponciel had said, the opening hour for visitors was quickly approaching. Soon, groups of five to fifteen individuals would fill the place.

Arthur stumbled, observing the different images, columns, and sarcophagi that comprised the church's chaotic ornamentation.

They passed in this way from cloister to cloister, looking at the numerous capitals, columns, and inscriptions.

Behind them the professional, fatigued, and high-pitched voice of the first guide approaching with the first group could be heard, getting nearer,

'And there we have it, next to her parents in an unadorned tomb, just the place where she desired to be interred... ... Berenguela, queen... She wanted her son to be king, so she handed him the throne immediately. He was the great Fernando III, called the Saint. I assure you, the sisters had resources. That's why the kings asked for them, including Carlos I of Spain and V of Germany. In exchange for their money, Carlos offered them these resting chairs. Velvet, god brocade and natural silk were used in their making. They are not restored—here with an emphasis on her voice—, so one can only assume their quality they must have. You can see behind you the altarpiece of Las Manchas. It's a Renaissance-era walnut wood piece. Depicted in the centre, Santa Maria la Mayor, the patron saint of the city; on the left, the Last Supper by an artist of the Diego de Siloé school. The latter was creator of the Constables' Chapel and the Golden Staircase, both of them can be seen in the cathedral.

To our right we can see Our Lady of Huelgas. Do you recall what I previously explained? "Holgar" meaning "to rest, to relax"; that's how the fields on which the monastery was built were called, and that's why the monastery was named after them. And the graves to the right and left are those of princesses, the one on the left, a daughter of Ferdinand III who wanted to be a nun. Some princesses came with vocations. And when they became nuns and princesses, they were abbesses; abbesses till death.'

Carlos smiled to himself. That was not completely accurate. How many of little yet slanted mistakes were thus transmitted little by little, day by day? The truth was few princesses became abbess, although this has been misunderstood for centuries due to historical mistakes.

A monastery granted in perpetuity to the Cistercian order, in accordance with the relativity of "eternal" that human condition allows. In front of the choir, Queen Eleanor's grave—the mastermind behind the entire scheme—, prompted one to recall this purpose with recalcitrant stubbornness.

If they attempted to outpace that group or, better still, stayed behind enabling them to pass and remain alone to inspect the structure more fully, the accompanying happiness was not long lasting, vanishing from their faces to Arthur's dismay when another group, even more numerous than the first, followed at half hour intervals, accompanied by another guide and another version of events and dates. Arthur regarded the figures and reliefs of the tombs on the vaults above his head with intense concentration, appreciating the fact that photographs were not allowed during visits.

The ever-present tombs situated on each side of the Knights' Porch and in other parts of the building reminded him that this entire structure was a shrine not just to grandeur but also to ashes.

The stone had been worn away, yet each centimetre of deterioration was counterbalanced by an additional layer of history and distant melancholy.

They reached the end of the visit, obviously accompanied by one of the groups. They were at the Rich Clothes Museum where the the Navas de Tolosa flag was displayed along with the real vestments and costumes worn by ancient kings, queens, and knights, preserved in almost mint condition. Napoleonic troops had not taken them along, deeming them useless.

The three visitors spoke in whispers, thinking with some apprehension about all the individuals who had packed these halls and cloisters.

All those presences had remained silent, silent in those tombs scattered throughout the monastery. Shadows among shadows, sheltering others in turn.

'Stepping on historic places like this and realising the names we have studied in books really existed always cause me some wonder.' Trevelyan told the professor. 'I don't believe I'll ever adjust to this.

It's like reading about a city of an unknown country, and then...
Then, visiting it one day by surprise and discovering it has three
dimensions, odours; people stroll there through the streets; ride on
the bus; smoke; play games; go to school...'

It was time to abandon so much historical gloom. Tomorrow they
would come to the visitors' parlour and begin the task that had
brought them there.

~

CHAPTER 26

SISTER AMALIA

How Arthur examined capitals and arches at sunset and had a peculiar vision.

Next day Burgos surprised them with a fresh snowstorm.

A person was already waiting for them at the foot of the stairs they had ascended the day before. It was a tall, middle-aged man with a trimmed goatee that framed his features, making him appear as if one of the ancient nobility who had passed through the monument in times of yore had decided to stretch his legs before returning to the tapestry or painting from whence he had emerged.

Had this good man chosen to wait for them downstairs as a preventive measure? Was he familiar with the hairy lady in charge of accreditations on the first floor? It was hard to tell. Nothing but naturalness emanated from his gestures, demeanour, and motions while he rubbed his hands and stomped to ward off the cold.

'Hello!' he exclaimed, shaking hands in a calm but firm manner through the rabbit fur gloves that radiated heat at their mere touch.

'My name's Marcos San Lúcar, from the Royal Archives. I've been tasked to help you with the manuscripts you're interested in.'

Once inside and after double-checking their credentials once more, he addressed them as if they were a group of tourists about to embark on a tour.

'Good, good, the documentation appears to be in order. I think you already know the regulations, correct? I will summarise them anyway. You may not enter the library itself, but the mother archivist can provide you with any books you may choose to peruse. She will carry them to the parlour for examination. And now, if you follow me, I'll take you to her. I believe she's already awaiting your arrival. She will be your primary point of contact these days. It goes without saying that you should direct any questions or requests for special procedures to me. And please remember that the monument is still inside a Benedictine order.'

'We understand,' Lafuente agreed.

'One further thing,' the technician added in a courteous tone, 'the archivist's mother is the oldest nun living in the monastery, and the poor thing cannot hear very well. Therefore, you will need to talk louder to her. Her character has developed a certain degree of eccentricity as a result of so many years of seclusion without more than a few sporadic visitors like you coming to examine books and codices. Still, she's amazingly fine for her age.'

After guiding them through the Claustrillas, the oldest cloister of the ancient pile, built in the XIII century, the technician took them to a door placed at the end of a long corridor.

Upon crossing it they found themselves in a whitewashed room illuminated with sharp clarity by a modern lamp on the ceiling. A dark oak door walled off the far end of the place. Its Gothic arch gave Arthur the impression it was frowning at them.

The space contained tables for the perusal and reading of books and documents. A few lamps and a crucifix were visible at the back. The tables, made of the same wood as the door, had been arranged facing the wall, possibly with the sinister intent of making the researchers who might visit feel like punished children condemned to repeat their lessons multiple times. On the other hand the situation was ideal to make them feel like copyists and scribes of the Middle Ages, bent over their scrolls for hours.

Above them, a beautiful plaster strip ran from one end of the vaulted ceiling to the other. Along the walls, modern filing cabinets completed the space's furnishings. A window on the far wall overlooked the monastery garden, which could be accessed through a small door.

Carlos surveyed his surroundings with unease.

'Is there something wrong?' murmured Elena, noticing it.

'Not really, just schoolboy stuff. I suppose I had envisioned myself in a dreary, dusty room with wooden bookcases with lots of musty and aged books. Influence of literature and cinema, I suppose.'

'Yes, realism robs life of some of its poetry.'

'An odd place to examine a codex,' Arthur whispered.

'It certainly doesn't invite to spend many hours in it,' replied the professor.

'So the archives are close by?' Elena asked Marcos San Lúcar.

'Yes, certainly. Right behind these walls, so that the mother archivist can easily transport the books and documents.'

The soft tones of a song could be heard in the distance.

'You may stay here. I'll wait outside until till the codices are delivered to you for examination' said San Lúcar, presumably accustomed to this daily task in any part of the Spanish geography.

And saying this, he exited the room.

The mysterious wooden door they had noticed previously at the rear opened at that moment. From it aroused a tiny-looking nun walking with a little waddle, perhaps due to a hip condition, without ceasing in the hum they had heard. The nun was clearly having a hard time walking. She carried a large metal cart that resembled a stretcher upon which two hefty books appeared to be awaiting surgery.

Sister Amalia, for such was the nun who had just entered the room, continued humming under her breath as she jiggled the cart. She had made a game of this chore, something with which to honour

God, they guessed. And because she didn't have a rope nearby and her age didn't allow for too much audacity, she had made this work her hobby. Clearly she had taken St Benedict's motto, *Ora et labora*, seriously to heart.

Upon reaching the centre of the room, she stopped by a small table on which numerous flowerpots had been arranged. Sister Amalia approached slowly and after pattering them grabbed a watering can, ignoring both the people present and the books she had brought along.

'Don't get sick now, huh? I know it's freezing, but nothing will happen to you here. I'll take care of you, my sweets.'

On one of the tables there was a tiny pot decorated with drawings of dragons. A good number of sweets filled it.

'Professor, look at this! Sweets!' Arthur remarked with a smile.

Sister Amalia noticed the interest of the young man.

'Want one? They are tasty, huh?' she said smiling, affably pushing the container towards them. 'I eat them all the time.'

'Thanks but I can't eat sweets.' the professor muttered as he fiddled with the pipe he carried in his right pocket. 'Sugar is not for me, thanks.'

'Don't be shy! You can take as many as you wish. Well, here are some of the books you requested on the form you filled yesterday. You will feel more at ease sitting at that table in the corner over there. That place is warmer than the others. I'm going to see if Sister Otilia has turned on the heating in this room. I won't be late!'

Sister Amalia had indeed resided in the monastery for many years. So much so that she couldn't remember if she ever was asked about the time when, being a lost child in the middle of the civil strife, she was found wandering the streets looking for her parents. She had been tutored and cared for in one of the Huelgas homes in the neighbourhood. Since then she had remained loyal to the place that had provided her with a roof and food. And more than that, faith; the faith to continue believing in the human being, having recovered the joy of living through helping others.

'I hope you find what you're looking for in those books,' Sister Amalia said.

'Really, mother, I'm aware that what we're looking for is somewhat vague. We'd like to see particularly the thirteenth-century codices and letters.' Carlos said opening one of the books in front of them, attempting to replicate the tactics employed in Silos.

'Well, there are quite a few of them. You're going to need a lot of time. If you could tell me something else, maybe I could help you. You see, we have two funds here: that of the monastery itself and another belonging to the King's Hospital, which, as you know, depends on Huelgas, legally and administratively.'

'Well. It's difficult to pin down. We're studying some extant texts that appears to be part of some codex. Our interest is to find to which manuscript it may belong, if possible, by looking at the illuminations and miniatures of similar ones of the same epoch.'

'You will forgive me, but I have committed a sin,' interrupted the nun. 'I did mention that there are many of these documents when I should have told you the figure should be around millions. And mind you! We are talking here only of the files pertaining to the minutes of the chapters celebrated throughout the monastery's history.'

'I understand there was an inventory of all the deeds, censuses, swears, fiefdoms, and related matters referring to the monastery's assets, am I right?'

'I see you know your job, professor. Yes, you mean the "Definitions" that Dona Ana de Austria wrote. She was very punctilious about what she called "making a minute of it all" to avoid taking out the originals from the archives. The particular drawer, file and punctual annotation were noted there. Before that, as you surely know, abbesses were perpetual until that condition was abolished by the bishop of Segovia in 1490. When that happened, I suppose the control over the archive lowered a bit. If we add to that the codices and documents we would be talking then about a very considerable number. And let me tell you, you've been fortunate! The National Heritage people—and here the nun looked over her shoulder to check Marcos San Lúcar was still away in the outer cloister—, don't allow for the books to be seen just like that. They take away the minor distraction that one could have, but in short, these are things of the current times, with all this about computers and things like that! Perhaps it's just that I'm getting old,' she said with the air of having recently entered that stage of life. 'You can believe me if I tell you that not even sweets taste as before,' she continued with a sigh that Elena didn't know if it was related to the changing times or the lost quality of the sweets.

Professor Lafuente had imagined something similar, but he had expected nevertheless a sweetening of reality.

THE THREE HAD BEEN CONSULTING THE WEEK BEFORE THE MOST recent general inventory of the works contained there catalogued by different authors. Therefore, the information given by the nun did not catch them off guard.

What they were looking for was no longer the writing to be collated, the supposed copy kept in the monastery, but any aspect related to the hypothetical secret of the princess herself, i.e. private letters from the abbesses, trades of the time, events, chapters celebrated by the two abbesses holding the baton in the 13th century and beyond.

'Okay, let's start with the first book and see where it all leads up to,' Carlos said with a sigh.

And so, for the next three days, Sister Amalia could see the three of them going over the codices and other documents that she brought along. The patient pattern of work at Silos was repeating itself. The nun was already accustomed to the look of joy or hope on the face of many many researchers upon being presented with an old book. She was used too to seeing their faces and gaze resting on each of the pages, take notes, feeling the slow, dull and almost insensitive tiredness seize their features and gestures while sitting on those benches.

Not even the sporadic crooning of Sister Amalia when bringing a new batch of folios and codices made a dent in that contained silence that reigned in the study room.

Even after the initial filtering, they were carrying out a daunting task with the best of wills.

Arthur was in charge of looking at the digital documents on his laptop quickly, filtering the material examined, according to the copyist's tracing, the epoch and, finally, the subject matter.

Sitting next to the professor, Elena examined the codices and letters in silence.

The precious miniature codices of the monastery were thus exhibited before them. Arthur marvelled at the vegetal themes elaborated and developed in the initials that opened the chapters, at those finials of calligraphic strokes. The tails of dragons and harpies invaded the manuscripts. The stems lengthening and multiplying in volleys that filled all the spaces, united at a broad and symmetrical bouquet at the beginning.

They knew it was a race against time. Silos –in spite of Fray Anselmo-- seemed in hindsight a paradise for researchers, free to loiter, sit, and consult. Here the pressure of time and the power of the omnipresent administration embodied in the technician —who made his presence in the room felt from time to time—was oppressive.

And so the days went by. Time, that material with which their work was built, passed by. They had seen everything: commandments, private letters from the different abbesses, up to two generations after Kristina's, beginning with Dona Elvira Fernández, the one ruling Huelgas when the princess arrived. The minutes of the different chapters held during the following years had not escaped their perusal. But nothing came out of it. Nothing. Had it all been all but an improbable dream?

The third day of their seclusion in that small room came with only the occasional escape to smoke a pipe, have a coffee or simply stretch their legs in any of the cloisters.

'The past resists' Lafuente said aloud.

'The past is never closed until the last book is read, until the last signature is written, until we stop looking and inquiring,' Trevelyan answered mechanically, without noticing the extreme, almost theatrical solemnity of his tone, nor its dramatic air that had made an impression on his companions.

He would have liked to believe those very words, however. Could they be nothing less than a pure rhetorical game, those traps that language uses, playing with our humanity to make existence more bearable? Pure rhetoric, in short?

History was, in fact, a teacher who never put a mark on the work done. Never underlining mistakes, missed or poor results with a red pen. As a result, we are never punished by delaying ourselves on our way home and never told to put more enthusiasm into our tasks.

'I'm going to take a break,' Arthur said, trying to suppress a yawn. 'the sight of the cursor is killing me.'

Thus, the young man left the parlour.

He knew it was cold outside, but he could make good use of it. His head ached. He had been seeing those illuminations too close for a very long time in that dim and diffuse light.

There was parallel to the parlour a narrow passage leading from the new and wide—in relative terms—, St Fernando cloister to a smaller one called Las Claustrillas, the oldest in the monastery, built in the 13th century. It was the so-called passage of Santiago, or more simply "the hallway", as the nuns preferred to call it.

As the young made made his way crossing the semicircular arch leading to this corridor the cold outside slowly woke up his stiff limbs.

In the background to his left, a door closed the way, implanted through the blackness, in that stillness of the evening enveloped in the dim light of the place. It was surrounded by a dark frame, guarded on both sides by dark plates on the walls.

At the end of the long passage, he could also see the door that led to Assumption Chapel.

Arthur had wrapped the scarf around his neck despite its thickness and apparent weight as if he were a tamer of beasts showing a serpent calmly to the public at the local fair.

There was parallel to the parlour a narrow passage leading from the new and
wide—in relative terms—, St Fernando cloister to a smaller one called Las
Claustrillas.

The young man looked absentmindedly at the various columns,
touching them lightly, appreciating their capitals and arches, noticing
that on some of them had an "R" printed on one side—a sign those
arches and chapels had been restored during the fifties and sixties.
He noticed too the precision of the finishing in the oldest ones, the
excellent craftsmanship of the workers of centuries ago.

During such evenings it was simple to feel alone and isolated
from the rest of the world. It was a strange feeling to describe, similar
to be watching a movie, being both aware of his surroundings while
removed from them. He had no idea how long he had been in that
position, focusing solely on the figures, the filigrees of the columns
surrounding him, the tricks performed by the light invading the cloister. Spreading shadows projected themselves into the ground,
forming erratic forms that merged under the influence of the light,
forming a camel in one location, a three-wheeled vehicle in another...

The reflections on the floor appeared to speak in a language of their own.

A movement at the opposite end of the cloister.

Yes, a figure had moved in the eastern part of the Claustrillas. There was there one the old sealed doors that had once provided entry to the church. The motion had roused him from the endless reverie he had fallen into.

It was a woman.

Perhaps one of the nuns that had been kept late outside or did not realise that visiting hours had not yet ended and that she could find a tourist there?

He was struck by the fact that the figure was barely wearing appropriate clothing for the day's frigid conditions, as though she were used to these low temperatures. Moreover, she wasn't even wearing the nun's headgear, the cowl.

Was she perhaps one of the Board of Trustees civil servants seeking pardon for her sins? Possibly the lackadaisical supervisor with brushy hair who had attended them on their first day? He grinned, visualising Mercedes Ponciel's face as a counterbalance to the preceding image.

The figure appeared to be examining one of the columns in a manner similar to Arthur a few minutes ago, although on the opposite side of the cloister. The central stone fountain unfortunately prevented him from seeing her features properly. From what he could see at this distance, she looked like a foreigner.

A surge of cutting and icy wind rose. It was a sharp, icy pang, even for a Burgos native as if the temperature had dropped dramatically in a matter of seconds after wallowing in the snow of the cloister. Arthur bowed his head and fled the place, seeking cover in the cloister beneath one of the stone doors that faced the parlour. The phenomena vanished as abruptly as it had come.

He was again alone in the cloister.

No sign of any person or shadow.

Maybe it had been a false impression caused merely by the

evening lights playing upon him. The Claustrillas, however, appeared to have been fixed on an imprecise time and date.

It did not take a significant excess of imagination for anyone to envision in front of him a figure halted at the back of the cloister, curiously looking at her surroundings with her eyes fixed on the central garden, just as he had imagined seeing animals and vehicles projected upon the ground minutes before.

'It may not be as chilly as I thought. I ran into a girl out there who wasn't wearing a coat,' he said as soon as he entered the consulting room. 'She must have been part of the last group that passed.'

Sister Amalia was handing the professors a box holding some letters. She stopped in her tracks and glanced up at Arthur. She frowned, opened her mouth but abruptly shut it with a sigh. She appeared to have changed her mind, disappearing seconds later through the rear door while shaking her head.

THE FOLLOWING DAY, LAFUENTE WENT ON ONE OF HIS SOLITARY walks. It was as if each internal pilgrimage had to be preceded by an exterior one in a kind of peripatetic reflection. The door connecting the parlour to the garden was undoubtedly a temptation for him. He reflected on the life of nuns living there, many of them locked up here for years, in that world apart, to which the rest of the world had no access.

Two sisters walked past by, their heads bowed, praying in silence possibly in a similar state of mind similar to the one experienced so many evenings in front of his books. Not very different from those times when he allowed himself to get swept away by the landscape, a rowing day on the river or just by music. Yes, the nuns were locked up; that was certain, but only from our peculiar and biassed perspective. That concept stands supreme because it is our own.

Or were we perhaps the ones who had been locked out?

Who would not yearn for such peace here, to live this alternate existence without shocks other tan those nature provides?

Years of soup served at school.

Yes, that was what memory brought him whenever he thought of nuns in general. If religion had a smell to him, it was that of soup. A scent that permeated the steps leading from the yard, ascending to the small dining room.

Was this the aroma of holiness discussed so extensively in the compulsory reading books of his youth? If it was, he had never been conscious of it when punished for speaking in class, kneeling in that corner with two books balanced precariously on his open palms, under the threat of a worse punishment, should one of them fall to the floor. All of this in front of a classroom divided between those who laughed at him and others who avoided his gaze out of sheer embarrassment.

He felt the hidden secrets around the place, the enigmatic corners reminiscent of the various mediaeval corridors in the neighbouring cathedral. Less frequented possibly they slumber calmly without arousing the envy of their possession or the curiosity of the passersby. Perhaps in this way and only in this way, they had been able to survive to the present day.

At the end of the third day, both Arthur and Elena noticed the professor kept lengthy periods of silence.

'What's the matter, Carlos?' said Elena, looking up from some letters written by Abbess Ana de Austria and taking advantage of the fact that the technician from National Heritage had just left the place, remarked, "I've noticed you've been a bit withdrawn and glum for the past several hours.'

'Have you not been amazed by how easily and kindly we have been shown everything? Gosh, they have even provided us with sweets! ' Lafuente replied raising both hands in the air.

'Well, what's wrong with that?' Arthur stepped in. 'Your behaviour borders on paranoia, if you pardon my saying so. You already stated in Silos that things were concealed from us. Now you're whining about the exact opposite. Are you suggesting that

Sister Amalia's kindness is suspicious, too? Or are you maybe implying that the sweets are poisonous? Is that it, professor?'

'Listen carefully and pay close attention. You were supposed to be writing a thesis on this subject, weren't you? A book about the plots of history and so on. Well, these things should not be viewed as relics of the distant past from which we shall never hear again. Intrigues, dear boy, secrets in one way or another, are part of our daily life, the very essence of the human race. If that wasn't clear to you in Silos, it never would be. But, like the scarf that is part of you and the tie that I presume is hidden somewhere under it, all this apparent openness, ease, and good manners indicate something else to me.'

'What else, Carlos? Please make eye contact with me. What do you imply?' Said Elena, a bit tired of this negative attitude.

'Elena, I'm not raving even if it appears that way to you two. I see it perfectly now. When there's nothing to fear, when a secret is well-hidden, it's precisely when we can allow ourselves the luxury of jumping on top of the place where it is buried, with the confidence and audacity of knowing that no one will ever discover it. We will discover nothing here, I assure you. At least if we use the highway that everyone else uses with manicured hedges and tolls.'

'And what do you suggest?' Elena pointed out.

'I'm confident that if we could speak with the abbess, she would be able to provide us with some information or insight. I'm sure what we're looking for is most likely not to be found in the usual places. Something tells me it's here, but not where it should be. The proverbial "needle in the haystack" comes to mind.'

'Carlos! Let your imagination rest for a while and focus a little. You've seen that nuns no longer have any relevance here. They simply keep their mouths shut and go quietly to mass' remarked Elena.

'I will speak first with Marcos San Lúcar. We have nothing to lose,' Carlos said, and without saying a further word, left the room and ascended two at a time the stairs leading to the offices.

Elena and Arthur looked at each other, saying nothing. The latter collapsed into one of the chairs and got busy interlacing his scarf, making elaborate designs that he would need to reverse later.

After a few minutes had passed, Professor Lafuente entered the room again. He had a frown on his face, not uttering a word. It wasn't required. His lively, quick, and dry gestures said it all. He sat down and removed the pipe from his pocket, stowing it again, upon recalling that smoking was prohibited. He jutted out his chin.

'Nothing to do. We're not authorised to speak with the nuns outside the parlour, much less the abbess. It can only be done in rare, extreme circumstances involving very close relatives, about which they simply refused to enlighten me or provide me with more information.'

'It's only comprehensible, Carlos. We'e talking about precious books. Those responsible for its custody are not the nuns but Royal Archives and National Heritage.'

A few minutes later, they exited the parlour making their way to the car.

'You were right, Elena; I mean, how could something be transmitted, especially a secret such as the one I have so happily pulled up from my sleeve?" By means of a letter to the editor? No, you were all right. It was all too fantastic, too incredible. Even so... even so,' he said with a dismissive tone as he smiled at his companions and said: 'Eve so, I have got thanks to our new friend, an appointment for a little chat with Mother Abbess tomorrow. Only for a few minutes, but I think that should be enough.'

And, without saying a further word, Carlos took a few steps forward in the direction of the exit, walking with long strides through the cobblestones of the Inside Compass.

~

BÚRGOS.—PATIO DEL MONAS

...RÍA LA REAL DE LAS HUELGAS.

CHAPTER 27

A LITTLE CHAT WITH MOTHER ABBESS

Accompanied by the sister gatekeeper, they traversed Ladies's Yard. This was a quaint, glazed area encircled by little flowerpots in close proximity to the monastery inn. "Mother Abbess must walk around here many times" thought Arthur.

When they entered the abbess' office, they found her hiding her eyes behind thick glasses made of that paste rarely seen anymore. From that position, clear, deep-set eyes swiftly surveyed the visitors in front of her.

'Good evening! Please receive first my cordial greetings and best wishes. May the Lord guide your steps in your quest to do good in your various activities,' said sister Irene, the Mother Abbess, aptly titled De la Cruz, waving her hand and inviting them to sit down on some tiny chairs facing her desk. 'I'll be delighted to answer your questions, and, should the answer not be in my hands, I will simply tell you and part as friends.' Mother Abbess said smiling as if she had found the solution to a difficult puzzle.

'Thank you, sister. Please excuse us for disturbing you in this manner,' said Lafuente, encouraged by her warm aura. 'As the Royal Archives technician may have informed you, we've spent the entire

week in the parlour examining books and codices in quest of thirteenth-century material, more specifically documents related to
Princess Kristina of Norway's stay in the monastery.'

'To tell you the truth, professor,' she continued in a tone that
suggested censoring, 'you should have asked me straight on your first
day here. Sometimes National Heritage employees take their duties
too seriously. You are well aware that the Cistercian order itself, and
more specifically, we nuns cut no ice in these times. However, as long
as we are allowed to devote ourselves to prayer and worship God, we
can't complain, my son. We can't complain!' she said with a look in
which Arthur could observe a certain sadness. 'There are no special
procedures or hidden books here, anyway', she added after a few
seconds, feeling perhaps that she may have lowered her guard. 'You
must understand that the community restricts the use of books for
any purpose other than our own. After all, these are documents
relating to the monastery's property and privileges'.

'THE CLUE IS HERE. I KNOW.' CARLOS SAID AS SOON AS THEY
left the abbess. 'I've never been so confident about something like this
before. Perhaps you were right with your paranormal theories,
Arthur, or perhaps I'm catching it after visiting so many cloisters, so
many manuscripts...'

He halted and looked from side to side.

'I don't know under what form, but it's here.' he repeated,
removing his pipe from his inside pocket and, without bringing it to
his mouth, signalled their surroundings with his both arms beneath
the weak sun that had dared to defy the clouds.

'If that's the case,' Arthur said with an exasperated sigh, 'it's
evident the guys at National Heritage care more about their facilities
than nuns themselves. Although on the other hand it's only natural.
The institution is housed in the Royal Palace; and, like every self-
respecting administration, it appropriates the power it has borrowed.
Remember Silos!'

'They demonstrate the validity of the saying "against the evil of asking, the virtue of not giving." In our task we are like truth-seeking crusaders, searching for the lost ark.'

'Yes, I have realised that. Mankind appears to be constantly divided between those who zealously want to conceal knowledge, either by hidden symbols in cathedrals, secret codes and so on—sometimes for absolutely trivial reasons--, and those who desire to uncover it just for the sake of it.'

'There you are, Arthur. There you are! Do you remember when, on some occasions, your mother withheld a gift from you or simply refused to discuss something claiming it was inappropriate for children to hear or that she had to discuss it with your father first? It could be something as simple as an overdue electricity bill or a brochure discovered in the mailbox regarding a new carpet for the living room. It didn't matter. You would not stop until discovering what your parents had been talking about in the living room in urgent tones.'

'Yes, it has become clear even to me,' Elena intervened, unwilling to remain a solitary witness to her companions' crossing of theories; 'if, thanks to the concern and desire of the abbess of the time, precautions had been taken to conceal the princess's secret—assuming it had ever existed—, there would have to be at least one notation of that fact, something making the task entrusted to the nuns at the monastery obvious. So much care should have been translated, I mean, reflected in instructions passed down from generation to generation in some way or another. Even more so in a place like Las Huelgas. A codex or some written letters would be the logical means of communication.'

'Yes, that seems like it,' Arthur said with conviction.

'But no, nothing of the sort appears anywhere. Could it be that nuns preferred to rely on word-of-mouth instructions passed from abbess to abbess in order to keep the secret despite the theories so thoroughly and carefully presented? If so, anything, including an unexpected death or an inconvenience preventing her successor from being by the dying side of Mother Abbess, would have ruined everything. It's hard to believe that a person capable of ecclesiastical and civil control over levies, taxes, and the lives of hundreds of people would rely on the frail human memory.'

'However, we cannot rule out this possibility, no matter how absurd or remote it may seem.' Lafuente said.

'Yes, at least we would be certain in that case we have not left any hypothesis unverified,' Elena said with a dejected expression. It's also possible that when manuscripts were catalogued either by National Heritage or an earlier palaeographer, some scattered texts or loose scrolls might have been grouped under the general category "various manuscripts." It's another option to consider.'

'You're right, Elena. Could you take care of it?' Lafuente said to her with a grateful smile. 'Obviously,' continued the professor 'there's also the possibility that the secret lost its stating allure with the passage of time, as happens with love, and that it was simply forgotten, lost.

Carlos took a few more steps, folding his raincoat under his right arm and keeping his eyes on the ground. Should he have raised his head, he would have seen the reflective face of Elena set on him.

'On the other hand,' the professor continued, 'another thing that intrigues me is the possible connection between Silos and this place.' Don't forget that the relationship between religious orders during the Middle Ages was more fluid that it is today. They were the travelling bookshops of the time, loaning each other books and manuscripts for copying, reading, and consultation. I am confident that what we are seeking is in front of us, albeit in a way we have yet to recognise.

IT WAS DEFINITELY TIME TO DEPART.

'I'm sorry you did not find what you were looking for,' said Marcos San Lúcar. 'I'll still be around for a few more hours today, should you need me. My train doesn't depart from Rosa de Lima station until 7:30 pm'

Carlos nodded with a grunt as he shook the technician's hand.

'Sister Amalia has certainly been a sweetheart,' Elena said. 'We have felt well cared after with her around.'

'If I may abuse your kindness,' said Arthur unexpectedly, to the surprise of his companions, 'I wonder if it would be possible for me to finish examining some documents I've been reading. It's more out of sheer curiosity about the monastery's history than anything else.'

'Of course,' San Lúcar replied with an amused expression given the young man's academic zeal. 'I'll notify the archivist mother about that.'

The steely gaze of the bushy-browed, frizzy-haired clerk who had greeted them on their first day remained fixed on the three of them as they were leaving. Carlos was the forerunner, clearly uncomfortable and eager to leave the area immediately.

Trevelyan demurred. He adjusted his tie and scarf with a broad, elegant backwards motion, accompanied by with one of his most emphatic glances at young Remedios. When he was by the Christmas tree, next to the door, he said, looking to the ice-eyed clerk, after resisting the urge to give her a brush with his name engraved on it, given the endearing time of year: 'By the by, my dear, I haven't asked you, but should there be some secret manuscripts containing some exciting clues about the monastery past, you would surely tell us, wouldn't you?'

Upon hearing these words, Carlos definitely quickened his pace, disappearing into the outer corridor.

The fins of the woman moved upward. Her mouth began to open.

"Yeah, I guess not,' replied Trevelyan, vanishing with sudden speed behind the professor, but not before pausing briefly by Remedios' table and winking at her.

'Merry Christmas!' he said.

After leaving the offices, Arthur directed his steps to the documentation room to finish the promised volume. Carlos and Elena walked through the San Fernando cloister on their way to their final cup of coffee in the premises.

. . .

Yes, it was their final day here. They had said their goodbyes, but not quite.

That evening, however, a single lamp remained lit in the consulting room.

A lonely figure was there, bent over a book.

Arthur was perusing codex he had been studying before, an act of 1263.

It was not within the young student's parameters to leave something undone, hard for him to say goodbye to their research here.

A hand landed on his shoulder.

He uttered a little cry that died as soon as he recognised who it was.

Sister Amalia had quietly approached him. The absence of her customary chants had prevented the student from hearing her until she reached him.

Her expression was peculiar. She was staring at Arthur with a grave look he hadn't been used to, except for that strange day after his walk around the Claustrillas cloister.

'I'm sorry, mother. I just wanted to take one last look at this book, 'he said, thinking the mother might be upset to find him still here after having having said goodbye some minutes ago. 'Mr San Lúcar allowed me to examine this codex. He told me he would tell you, and since it was still on the table, I had assumed he did.'

'No, my son, calm down. Take your time. It's not about that. So much has been written about the monastery, such a long and unfortunate history. I believe all known information has been published and then some. There are practically no documents left in the monastery to study, except for the chronicles, but those, of course, you will have already seen.'

She looked then at the book the young man had been examining until now.

'I see that you value art. I could not help noticing you all this week looking at the many illuminations of the codices. You've been particularly interested in books related to the place's art and architecture. So allow me to suggest both you and your colleagues to attend Vespers Mass. Only twenty minutes before it begins. I am confident that Gregorian chant will enrapture and calm you. At the very least it will relax and soothe your souls. I can't let a single day pass without hearing it after a day of work devoted to God. No, don't look at me like that; I'm aware the professor isn't a practising Catholic; even so, he can still honour God. And ask me no more, because if you can't figure it out on your own, you're not quite as bright as I thought you were young man. And now, take this with you and join your friends.'

And with these words she placed a handful of sweets in the hand of a stupefied Arthur as if he had been a schoolboy waiting for the school doors to open and the cook sister had rewarded him for the wait.

In this state, he stood up and made a move to kiss the nun on the cheek.

'But what are you doing? Let go of trifles, young man!' exclaimed the nun, trying to sound serious.

'I just wanted to wish you a Merry Christmas,' he said quickly handing over the codex he had been examining. The mother librarian placed it gently on the cart, wrapping it in a cloth she had prepared for that purpose.

The nun had already vanished through the same back door from which she had emerged the first day they arrived at the monastery, as if she were a mysterious fairy out of a Cistercian tale.

After removing his protective gloves, he walked towards the door. He heard the sister's voice again,

'Young man!'

She was at the door, still holding the cart.

'Merry Christmas to you too! May God dwell in your heart. I know light shines on you. I have observed some of it in your professor, but it's you who will understand the truth. The truth no one else can perceive.'

'Likewise, mother,' Arthur murmured, lighting up his face,

already wholly stunned. It was evident that the woman was too old to continue working in this capacity—'Merry Christmas!' and, putting on his scarf, he left the place.

The nun was still smiling behind him as she switched off the lights of the room.

CHAPTER 28

SINGING A CAPELLA

It was almost six p.m.

Vespers mass was about to begin in a few minutes.

The figures of Lafuente and Elena entered the church following Arthur's.

The first thing Elena did upon entering was to look up at the ceiling.

She had learned during her college years that the raison d'être of churches and cathedrals' high ceilings was that of eliciting an echo effect, to make the choir's voices bounce off the high vaults, return that sound, multiply the voices, imbuing them with strength and symbolism, thus making it look like descending from Heaven.

And so it had been from Notre-Dame to Chartres, passing through Vienna, Burgos, and hundreds of other places of devotion, making it appear that angels themselves spoke, that God was showing himself before the congregation, and that the Bible's scripture became true in the sense that God, if not flesh, had become voice and had descended to dwell among us.

"All emanating from mere human voice." thought Elena. The Word multiplied, transmitting His message daily to the nuns. The sensation was skin-deep.

As soon as the mass began, Elena closed her eyes, overcome with emotion. The voices reverberated off of the headboard and the transept. So very long ago, she had abandoned the naive faith of her childhood, possessed and kidnapped by reason, doubt, and a thousand other things that took hold of her adolescence. But now, feeling the music, everything was suspended; doubt, reason, thought, logic, all abandoned to the deepest of feelings, the same emotion that had caused her to linger for hours before a beautiful Constable painting.

She felt a warm substance dripping down her face. She quickly took a handkerchief from her purse.

She looked askance at Professor Lafuente, hoping he had not noticed.

However, she found out her colleague to be in a similar state to hers: rapt, his eyes closed, perhaps his mind riding over the notes. So was Arthur: looking around, eyes and mouth wide open, so her brief emotional rapture had passed unnoticed.

The analytical mind of the professor was already seeking for an explanation for these sensations. Yes. The music appeared to progress while remaining still; implying there was no progression. The listener thus induced into a trance-like state in which time stood still and hours may pass while being rocked by the notes, conveying calmness, placidity, and serenity. And Gregorian chant, possibly the sole true chant, only increased the emotions produced by the religious ceremony.

'Quite an experience, wasn't it, Elena?' said Carlos after leaving the chapel and found themselves at the Inside Compass.

'Very thrilling. That's the truth. Magic in plain daylight.' Arthur exclaimed.

'No, magic, no. A miracle!' Elena said without looking at her companions, her eyes fixed on the lofty tower and high walls in front of them. 'Every time one of these throats dares to open its mouth and sing, a miracle from the past is repeated a thousand times over. The thing is, we observe this on a day-to-day basis, so it doesn't surprise us much. It's a phenomenon similar to electricity and so many, many other things that we take for granted. Ultimately, chant is nothing but a low-cost means of communication to convey a message through the centuries.'

Carlos regarded her colleague with awe. She would occasionally surprise him with one of these musings. He cleared his throat and rummaged in his right pocket, where he had placed his pipe half an hour earlier. The task seemed to resist him because it took him about a minute to find it.

As soon as he had it in his hands, he inquired 'Do you remember the bar we saw in front of the monastery gates on our first day here?' The place where we parked the first day? We could make use of it after this experience. Don't you agree?'

And so the three of them traversed the arch beneath the keep towards the Compas' dwellings which bravely faced the monastery.

A CUP OF COFFEE WAS ALREADY IN LAFUENTE'S HANDS. HE GAVE it a few twists and placed it on his right side, watching the spoon turning in a motion that had long lost all purpose, as if this were a strange object that should not be there.

'Do you remember Elena, what I told you about steganography a few days back? Something like, 'It could be possible that the key could be in front of us the entire time, only we could not see it.'

Elena nodded.

'What you just said at the conclusion of the mass about music rang a bell in my mind.'

'You mean that bit about it being like magic?' Elena said with a puzzled smile.

Arthur observed the professors's ball game, trying to follow Lafuente's mental thread as he had been used to doing so many times.

'No, no, the other thing... that part about music being an affordable mode of communication used for generations to transmit a message.'

'Oh, yes, I suppose it was one of those artistic metaphors that occasionally occur to me.' she remarked, feeling her cheeks reddening.

The professor paused for a long time. 'I've been wondering. Couldn't music have been the common thread, the thread that carried the message about Princess Kristina?' he finally said. 'Think about it for a moment. Until now we've been searching for a codex where, in plain Castilian or at least in universal Latin, we would find, explained to us as if in a textbook, that Kristina arrived to Spain while pregnant, with all the minutiae, details and implications for both her and her unborn child. Nonetheless, we never imagined for a moment they could be using an encoding method to transmit such information.'

'An encrypted message?' said Arthur. 'In the choral music? I'm afraid I don't get it... and what the hell is steganography? Based on your tone, I fear it's something to be added to the schedule at some point this term. Am I wrong?'

'It could be, it could be,' Carlos replied with a smile. 'Deep down, it's a quite basic thing, Arthur. You see, someone realised that human mind has always being extremely lazy. Hence, the value of word games, why from the most remote antiquity, along with crosswords and puzzles in more contemporary times, they attempt to fight against that laxity. Hence the "looking for Wally" and similar games. The underlying principle of steganography is straightforward, Arthur. It's based on placing information in front of the person seeking it, although hiding it amid similar items, similar bits of info. As a student, you will be familiar with the iconic stone frog that adorns the exterior of Salamanca's Escuelas Mayores. In one of the most recent restorations, someone came up with the idea of "updating" it, so to speak, by placing an astronaut among the monks, demons, angels, and other mischievous figurines that populate it.'

'Yes, I see where you want to go.'

'But, as in these two examples, once we are given the clue of where and how to look, nothing could return the object to its hiding place again. Do you follow me, boy? '

'Blimey! Something like putting a pearl among a bunch of tiny white pebbles, right? No matter how bright it might be, it would be difficult to find because we would need to know it's there before beginning the search. Nobody would consider observing each one of them individually, would they? We prefer to know that our efforts are proportional to the results we obtain. Or in plain words, it's worth the while.'

'Exactly! And what we have here, both in the manuscript and in the music, may be a similar case. This is an obvious steganographic code, but we don't know yet how to decipher it. Think about it! We've been searching for written texts until now. And I ask myself. What work contains the majority of liturgical music from the 12th century to the present? Yes, my friends, there is such a work! One of the oldest musical codices in the world, if not the oldest, a record of all religious music sung from antiquity until today: The musical Codex.'

'And where is that codex kept?' asked Arthur.

'That's precisely the irony, Arthur. Look around you! We are precisely in the place where it has been kept since the Middle Ages. It has never left this site. It has always been here. Not in any museum, mansion, estate, public building or anything like that. In the same place where it was written.'

The professor looked around him. From the tavern windows, it appeared as if the monastery walls, and with them, the fountain, the old towers, the courtyard, the Knights' Cloister, and the entire area surrounding Compas Square, were listening. There were no tourists at that hour, nor last-minute guides going outside to smoke. No one.

"A message concealed from view," thought Arthur "practically hovering in the air around them, in the air expelled by the nuns' daily chant, perpetuating that heritage, that legacy and duty."

The secret, the secrets of past times, of which all or almost all had been forgotten, might be contained in music.

At that moment, except for their western and contemporary attire, they might have been in ancient times, waiting perhaps for Queen Eleanor and her maids to enter through the door leading to the chapel.

Arthur reacted quickly.

'Well, it's quite simple then. I know it's late today, but we can return tomorrow to see it.'

'It's useless, Arthur. You should be aware that things do not function that way. The Royal Archives technician will have left by now, remember? He had to catch a train. In addition, Royal Archives must grant permission for every document to be examined. In other words, we must renew our plea again. This is still Spain, and its bureaucracy has a long history that I hope to share with you one day. And being near Christmas is going to delay it even more.'

The professor remained motionless, as he studied with great interest the cobblestones in the Outside Compass, the row of houses lined up in front of him, and the no-parking sign next to the bar, as if the latter were a priceless piece belonging to the monastery.

The Codex was not to be found in Paris, London, Berlin, Brussels, or any other lost corner of Europe. Instead, it was in the same city where he had lived and worked for more than twenty years.

And what could be a more timeless medium than music? It stands the test of time like no other. The music sung day after day in the choir reminding the sisters who had been in the know, apart from the abbess herself, of the birth of that being!

But now, with the monastery doors closed, and the Royal Archives technician on his way back to Madrid, the professor could not help but exhale a sigh of disappointment, as he contemplated this delay, albeit with newfound optimism.

They were beside the car. Trevelyan lingered, looking at the place where they had spent so many hours in the last few days, as they had made at Silos before. The feelings were very similar. He introduced his right hand into his coat to pick up his gloves when he felt something inside. Some sweets left from those Sister Amalia had given him. Another kind of food for the soul?

He recalled the advise of the archivist nun to attend Vespers Mass.

He shook his head and entered the vehicle.

After starting the car and making it advance a few metres, the professor halted it at the Outside Compass. It was a farewell to Huelgas Monastery for now.

They took in the massive square tower, the thick and sturdy walls, and the towering buttresses that supported them. Carlos thought of the number of kings, queens and nobility who had lived within its walls for over eight centuries.

'You're here waiting, right?' he said between clenched teeth. 'We will meet again soon, my friend' he said as he turned the ignition key to the on position.

On the drive back, nobody spoke; everyone was completely engrossed in their own thoughts.

But that evening, it looked as if dawn had appeared already and the sun had been in the wrong place.

CHAPTER 29

A DISAGREEMENT AND TWO ENCOUNTERS

Of reddish hues, disappearances, and unexpected visits.

Arthur went down to the common room, hoping to read the newspaper before going to the river for some training.

'There is little time left for the regatta, Arthur chappie! Have you changed your nappies yet? They have told me those boys at Burgos University are ready to wreck havoc on you!' Meseguer yelled from his corner as soon as the student entered the common room.

Arthur, busy in his search for his usual corner or a similar one, was not paying any attention to the broadcast on the TV set. television show. He then heard some words that made him forget his pursuit of a perfect place.

He had heard the phrase "Huelgas Monastery."

He raised his head. On the telly the anchorwoman gave way to the image of a female professor speaking. He paid attention. Her face looked somewhat familiar. A text at the bottom identified her as a Burgos University professor, but it was her warm, close, and smiling face that inspired instant trust, as if she were one of his professors or a friend of mother's.

The journalist inquired, 'We are aware that you have published a book specifically dedicated to this subject. Please, tell us more about it.'

They were discussing mediaeval stained glass. It seemed the interviewee was a specialist in the field. Professor Abad, the journalist explained, had established herself as a true expert in that field as well as on the study of the Camino de Santiago. All that followed by the publication of several works and the garnering of some awards.

'I have only found the so-called Burgos Red here in the Huelgas Monastery and Burgos Cathedral.' she stated.

'And what kind of red might that be? What is so special about this hue in the Burgos cathedral stained-glass windows?' The interviewer went on, visibly surprised by the qualifier.

'Mind you! I don't want to imply that it is exclusive to Burgos,' the professor clarified, still smiling, 'although this is the only place in Europe where I have encountered it. I have made multiple visits to see cathedrals such as Chartres, Notre-Dame, and others, as I am particularly interested in the technique employed to get the quality found in many of those glasses.'

' "Burgos Red."' the anchorwoman repeated with a smile, 'I do like the name. I cannot dispute that it is euphonic. And in this age of branding and corporate identity, a claim of this nature does not hurt, does it?'

Yes, Arthur knew what she was talking about. He had experienced something similar during his recent visits to Silos and Huelgas monasteries. Namely, the intimate recollection under the spectral and multicoloured light of the tall windows; the silence that had accompanied him at the time, inviting him to prayer and meditation.

'Could we thus be talking about a language of colours?' continued the anchorwoman.

'Undoubtedly,' enthused the professor. 'It has existed in all cultures; a language closely associated with religion, reappearing in the stained-glass windows of Gothic cathedrals during the Middle Ages.'

The genuineness of Professor Abad, that handkerchief hanging around her neck so naturally, and her close smile on that April morning, contrasting with her resolute, precise, and plain phrases. Each of them sounded like raindrops falling, hitting the glass; a call of attention to consciousness. "Something crucial" thought Arthur.

LAFUENTE ENTERED HIS UNIVERSITY OFFICE THAT MORNING deep in thought when, on opening the door, Ismael run out, tripping over his legs. After petting him in an attempt to calm the cat down, he closed the door behind him, his mind still rearranging the latest events. He mechanically tucked the security key away in his shirt pocket.

It was then he became aware of the new state of affairs.

It wasn't only that Ismael had began meowing long before the door was opened. No, the first thing that drew his attention was that one of the volumes he liked to keep on the side table, a small book on European butterflies, had been removed from its usual place and put on one of the shelves.

Somebody had been here.

'Who the hell?' he said aloud.

It dawned on him. His work area was organised and tidy. Yes, but perhaps a little *too* tidy, not the way he typically left it after setting the pencils and pens inside the small wooden container on the desk right side.

There were no papers on the table's surface. No book was in it.

He dashed across the room to the table in the far corner.

The little chest of rotted wood sat on top of it, its lid open revealing an empty space.

The manuscripts were no longer inside.

· · ·

THE RECTOR WAS BLOCKING WITH HIS BACK THE LITTLE LIGHT that was attempting to penetrate through the window at that hour in his office. Thick red curtains flanked his silhouette on either side.This was both the place and gesture he had calculated would emphasise his position of power the most in moments like this, a position as calculated as the false neoclassical temple in the university campus and the gardens design.

He quietly looked at the lanky professor in front of him before speaking with deliberate calm.

'Why aren't the manuscripts on your desk, Professor Lafuente?' he said advancing towards the centre of the room, lighting a cigarette, cleverly taking advantage of this action to avoid the professor's eyes. 'Simply because they did nothing there. Royal Archives informed me yesterday afternoon. It appears you have requested a new permission to examine another codex guarded at the Huelgas monastery, isn't that so?' His voice seemed to emanate mysteriously from between his tightly clinched jaws, as if he were a ventriloquist. 'The three days granted to you were not enough?' And here, he made an ineffective attempt at sarcasm that failed from start.

Patricio Noguer stood in front of the window again, this time with his back to the professor, seeming enamoured with the newly rebuilt campus, as well as with the bend of the river visible from there. Some boys were rowing a little further on in anticipation of the upcoming race. Among them he could see the figure of Alfonso Trevelyan encouraging his companions. Or was he Alberto? All those names seemed the same to him. Other youths stationed closer to the main building were dragging a canoe amidst raucous laughter from the shed where it had been stored. They had no choice but to win that race. Blast it all!

Lafuente, still unable to comprehend the rector's words, responded: 'Yes, that's true. Still I don't know why they have not informed me first. I gave them the direct number of my department so they could send me their response, as they did last time.'

The rector retreated his gaze. His face was red. The maroon tie he wore that day seem to heighten the effect.

'They did respond, but this time they did it to the right person, though, me! In addition, I believe someone must act responsibly in such a case, don't you think? Professor Lafuente, there is something at this university that you still do not get.' And here he emphasised his words further 'I must authorise any particular research. At least I must be grateful that both National Heritage and Royal Archives had the good sense to call me and inform me of these circumstances. I told you only two week ago we were running out of time. That it was essential to prepare the report so the manuscripts could be returned to their owner in the event that incontrovertible proof could not be obtained to declare them a national heritage asset. On top of that, Count Dabrowski has threatened us with civil actions if we don't return the documents within a month. And in the meantime...what were you doing, dear professor? Well, certainly sprinting around the peninsula's monasteries while pretending to be Indiana Jones, to be sure! Moreover, not happy enough with this, you have persuaded another colleague from this university and one of your students to join you on that crazy adventure you insist on calling research and that I, for want of a better term, refer to as insanity, complete insanity! I am very sorry, but since you were too busy putting pressure on the same people who commissioned us to prepare a report instead of doing it yourself, I have delegated the task to Professor Manuel Tordesillas. In fact, I'm certain he must already have begun it as instructed initially, swiftly and meticulously. Therefore, we shall conclude and resolve this matter to the satisfaction of all parties.'

Another thoughtful pause, conscious of the effect his words were having on Lafuente. He took pleasure in this sensation as he inhaled and savoured the cigar he had taken from the carved wooden box, under the watchful eye of the mahout engraved into it.

'That and that alone was our sole mission.' he continued 'You've placed me in a difficult situation before Royal Archives, professor, pressing them simply to support your theory! In addition, they have received a formal complaint from Count Dabrowski himself. Under the circumstances, I will be gladly ensure that any complaint brought to my attention reaches the right ears.'

Carlos Lafuente's eyes were drawn to the Burgos picture at the rector's table as he listened in disbelief. It seemed like it was the first time he had seen it. This alteration of reality to accommodate personal ends suddenly provoked a sudden feeling of revulsion in him. To construct a riverbed where none existed? Change the terrain's course? From an artistic point of view, he could comprehend it; yet, this work, a commission created in this manner...

'Excuse me, Mr. Noguer, but the hypothesis on which we have been working...'

'I beg your pardon; I did not hear you very clearly. Did you just say the word hypothesis again?' Patricio Noguer interrupted abruptly while seated in front of his interlocutor, tapping his fingers on the table in a tense beat. The rector's anger was hardly concealed. While maintaining his index finger in front of Lafuente, he brusquely pushed away a book in his path. 'I've already told you, and I'll say it again. This entire story about Princess Kristina so skilfully crafted by you, this entire—.' And here he glanced out the window, biting his lower lip, looking for the precise, deciding qualifier that his condition as the visible leader of the institution deserved, 'It's a sheer construction of castles in the air. This is in no way scientific, Lafuente, and don't misjudge me. You've performed admirable at this university during these past years in the teaching field. You've carried out courses with brilliance and skill, yet your research and theories are too eccentric, too out of the way. Since you arrived from Valladolid, you have become a very different person, if you allow me to say so.'

'But Mr Noguer, we are talking here about authentic documents. I merely request the opportunity to inspect the extant musical codex at the monastery, a genuine document. I'm certain that if it has survived there for over eight centuries, there may be something in it to corroborate my suspicions.'

Patricio Noguer was standing near the wooden globe. He leaned forward, like Atlas taking an impulse before putting it on his shoulders.

'I will summarise the current condition of your hypothesis for your benefit. You're telling me that during the height of the Middle

Ages, a foreign woman arrived and gave birth to a bastard child shortly before meeting her future husband? And not only that, but—please tell me how—no one in her entire entourage discovered it! Moreover, the princess spent the entire night of Christmas Eve in a Cistercian monastery, and no one was the wiser. Believe me; I have no idea where all of this came from!' He marked each point with his fingers like a teacher presenting his arguments in front of a class for the pupils' benefit. 'Perhaps it all begun when you met that novelist at Valladolid so eager about—what was the word you employed?' He pondered for a while. 'Oh, yes, "Significant coincidences" endorsed by none other than Dr Jung! Come on, man! Are you serious? In any case, and without getting into the heart of the matter, we don't deal with social psychology in this faculty, right? Leave that to the UBU people, if you please.'

Here, he took a little pause before continuing:

'Additionally, the foundation has also demanded an explanation. Your path of study threatens the newly authorised monies for university expansion.'

'But this is a new field. A university that does not support innovative ways of thinking is fundamentally flawed, fails at its core. Frankly, I fail to comprehend your refusal to examine one document, one final document.'

'You are oblivious to the fact that your field is palaeography, the interpretation of codices, manuscripts, and chronicles, not the pursuit of innovative ideas, however picturesque they may seem. Please leave this post to the literature teachers. On the other hand, I do not believe that your association with a more or less well-known novelist in your research should be taken seriously as support for your purported claims.' Here, he spat out the word without concealment or deception. 'Let's examine the situation with calm. This time, you may call it a hypothesis if you want. How do you suggest it could have taken place, especially since none other than Dona Berenguela herself was present during the whole stay of the princess, the very sister of King Alfonso X, the king with whom Princess Kristina was meant to bond? I also know history. I've done my lessons. Everyone was gathered there in anticipation of a young and gorgeous virgin princess. And you intend to tell me that among all that multitude of escorts, soldiers, priests, and ambassadors, the pregnancy and subsequent birth were concealed? Yes, the machinations for the Germanic throne, the dominance over Europe at the period, the struggle against the infidels, and all of these other events are fascinating. However, you are attempting to reduce all that more to modern reality show-worthy gossip than to actual events. And upon what does it rest? In writings, citations, or historical accounts? No, gentlemen, no, our renowned professor at the prestigious Montanilla University has pulled out of the hat an intuition based on a text fragment in order to assert the existence of a gigantic conspiracy. No, not even a complete and compiled codex, no. You imply nothing less than all the women in her retinue, along with the Huelgas Abbey nuns and, of course, the abbess in charge had decided to safeguard the birth of a baby!'

'Mr Noguer, it's not quite like that,' Lafuente intervened, uneasy at being portrayed in such a light. 'The manuscripts we've been examining include references to a real, hidden secret, unless we are forced to accept the evidence of a joke made by the copyist. Furthermore, it wouldn't be just any baby. It could have been the descendant who could have thwarted the union of the kingdoms Haakon IV and Alfonso X were trying so hard to forge. In addition, finding out about its birth would have ended her beloved father's project, something which never would have entered into Kristina's head. And later, already in Seville, knowing she would not be the promised queen but the perpetual infanta, not knowing what had might have happened to her offspring in the far north of Spain, it's not so far-fetched to think she would have allowed herself to be overcome by despair and bitterness. For all practical purposes it was the same as if her baby were in Norway itself!'

Patricio Noguer was staring at Lafuente as though he had just become aware of his presence. The professor, encouraged by the silence, thinking his message had reached his interlocutor, continued,

'Moreover, the hypothesis we've been working on, the work we've done so far point unequivocally to...'

'Allow me a precision, professor,' the rector interrupted sharply, 'and please don't be upset by what I'm about to say. This is the second time you refer to it as a hypothesis. If you refer to the story you previously mentioned, then you have none. What you have is a screenplay, or an idea for a novel if you like, but not a hypothesis. At this stage in your career, you should be aware that hypotheses are only legitimate as statements inside a scientific process. You know: hypothesis, theses, and synthesis, all of them supported by objective evidence. In history, as in any other field, our own views and judgments are not such. They are merely "opinions." And in your case, more of a comic strip, something unscientific. I will say this one last time. Should the Mogueroles foundation, the source of this university as you keep forgetting, discover these chimaeras, this pursuit of wisps it would leave the university without a euro. I can assure you, professor, that if this ever occurs, you will be forced to seek employment elsewhere. I'd like to remind you that I've worked very hard to make the idea of the regatta with other universities finally taken form. I have a meeting with the Foundation Board next week. I don't intend to let everything go to Hell for a misinterpretation of our academic duty, of your academic responsibility, professor! So please don't waste my time, and forget about all that nonsense! And let your friend write novels about it if he so wishes.'

And, without further ado, he stood up, concluding the meeting and making a movement to the globe that, should it have been inhabited, would have caused its occupants to leap into the air.

Carlos Lafuente realised that he had spoken too much at the worst possible time, right at the end.

THAT EVENING, AFTER RETURNING HOME AND PLACING ISMAEL'S case on the floor, Lafuente sat by the window. To his right was a glass of scotch and ice, a drink that, deep down, he detested, but that, precisely for that reason, helped him meditate, the ice melting within the glass.

Sounds were experienced with complete clarity at that hour. The distant horn of an automobile. An isolated cry from a mother calling for her child. The clock, ticking away the seconds behind him. He had never noticed before that continuous, repetitive sound, that tiny object in his study that apparently had always been there, immersed as he was in his studies and books, conversing with his students in his tutorials, or engrossed in his own thoughts.

At a different time, these noises would have calmed him, but not today.

Today instead they reminded him of the inevitable passage of time, the countless tasks and efforts they had undertaken over the past few months, how foolish he now felt. He had got lost at some point. Throughout the journey it seemed he had left aside thousands of dreams, of all kinds.

'Well, I suppose that's what "growing older" implies,' he replied, sipping scotch from the glass.

But something inside him told him this was not totally accurate. This misnamed "research" was merely the tip of the iceberg; perhaps he had to give up following the will of a wisp, yes, look around him again, redraw the map of his life and consider where he was headed once more.

As Scarlett O'Hara did, this would occur at a later date. He was now fatigued and disoriented.

He questioned the source of his sudden professional fervour, this desire to uncover the hidden truth in the manuscripts, that thirst for knowledge. Wasn't he happy enough with his usual research, set at his own pace, as did other university researchers? His works on the use of wood in the Middle Ages now appeared faded to him. Had he become exhausted by his scientific pursuits? Absolutely not! Precisely that same thirst had brought him here to this no-man's-land.

Worst of all, he had dragged two individuals with him. If he ever believed in anything resembling friendship, it was with Elena and Arthur over the past few weeks. And now, he had been forced to leave the research aside.

They had chased a mirage, carried away by the hope of being hailed as the discoverer of Princess Kristina's secret. Who was he kidding? Perhaps he only had sought to escape from himself during this time. But life was not a film that ended well.

Nor a book we can close if the plot is not to our liking.

He peered long and hard at the opposite wall. Elena had once told him, what was time for someone whose job was to rummage through it?

He was roused from his trance by an unusual sound. Ismael leaped to the ground and began to meow, an evident sign that he was requesting food, already tired of the lethargy into which his master seemed to have fallen.

"But if I have just put you some ten minutes ago! What happens to you today? Well, at least someone wants to eat something."

It was around six o'clock in the afternoon. A week had passed.

Carlos was looking at the figure sitting in the armchair opposite him.

Arthur seemed to have matured since their last encounter. He no longer resembled that student he had accompanied to the deanery's offices that afternoon to assist him with scholarship formalities. He wasn't either the shy boy who hardly dared raise his hand in class before expounding any theory. In fact, a part of him admired this new persona that stood before him.

The light coming from the room's huge windows on the east wall illuminated the golden edges of the volumes in the bookshelf.

Lafuente felt like a different man, too. He was quiet, staring at the garden in front of the window.

'Excuse me, professor,' Arthur remarked, 'but I believe there's something I need to understand. I have followed your teaching for years. Your comments, observation skills, and intellectual acuity are beyond doubt, not just for me but also for this academic world in which we are. But, if I may say so, there is something you have over-looked in this research, something that we should all consider.'

The professor, about to lit his pipe, paused and regarded his pupil with bewilderment. The young man's gaze was different now, self-assured, his eyes gleaming as he spoke.

'It's not just merely a matter of literature,' he said, upon noticing the professor's silence, 'nor of beautiful metaphors. At the dawn of environmentalism the American biologist Barry Compose set the first law of ecology: "Everything is connected to everything else."

'I don't know if I grasp what you mean, Arthur,' Carlos said. 'I have told you that there's nothing to do. I acknowledge that I erred in my approach. I got swept away. That's all. But please continue with that law if you feel so inclined.'

'Think, feel inside you all we've done so far but don't stay only in the facts, think about the emotions! feel in your guts the disconnected thoughts we've had, the messages not heard, whispered from the unconscious, giving us hints we were oblivious to.'

'And what's the second law of that man so intelligent?'

'"Everything goes somewhere", and before you ask, I am going to tell you the third one: Nature knows what to do. Oh, and the fourth and last, as a bonus, is "there is no such thing as a free lunch anyplace in the world,"' he finished with a smile. 'Professor, I try to follow the scientific methods you taught me, but when science runs out of arguments, when there's nowhere else to look to, when science runs out of arguments, you know what I do? I rely on my instincts.'

Trevelyan leaned forward in his chair and said, 'Please don't stop now.'

The young man rose to his feet and began fidgeting with his tie as he did so. He walked over to the nearest window and peered outside. Fragmented and distant laughter came floating across the air. After having confirmed its origin, the student turned to his mentor once more.

'Remember that a university is more than just a campus or its location by a river or other. Not even for the views your office may have. Nothing to do of course with the existence or absence of bloody regattas. Well, everyone knows how important rowing is to me, but I'd cheerfully leave that Blue behind if I could discover the truth concealed in the musical Codex!'

The professor's gaze remained fixed on him, saying not a word. Arthur was strolling in front of the bookcase, pausing occasionally to emphasise a point while placing his left arm behind his jacket and raising his right for emphasis, as if the student were a carbon copy of Lafuente in the classroom.

'Professor, consider what I have said, but don't simply do it in your head. Allow your heart to play its part, too. Feel it in your guts, and you will realise we have a long way to go. You told me once you not only learn to be humble in this profession but also to be respectful, remember? Because I have vivid memories of it. Where is your conception of respect now, Professor Lafuente? In this scenario, the reverence due not only to history proper but to your own methods as well. Where is the person who not only taught me to be patient but to face the daily frustrations that palaeographic research, history, and science in general bring along? You have a duty to fulfil; that of reminding us of who and what we have been, of our past selves. Your role is vital. Consider this carefully, and once you have, tell me I was wrong and that everything you taught me was a lie. That the purpose of my studies was all sheer bullshit.'

'Wait, Arthur, that's not the case; I did not intend...'

The door had slammed shut.

Arthur had left.

The professor glanced around the room. He appeared to be examining the library and windows.

Carlos Lafuente was alone, alone in that library, surrounded by the impressive collection of volumes he had amassed over the years, since in his youth he had felt the itch and curiosity of reading. In this library he had created a space for meditation, just as he had done in his own office. A meditation he had long desired. Now, it appeared empty and cold.

Now he finally understood that strange feeling he had perceived while entering his empty classroom in the evenings when, devoid it of students, not even the beauty and fragrance of the gardens wafting through the windows could distract him from this absence. It was all too perfect—an empty shell devoid of soul.

Had he forgotten to give life to that being to whom he had been creating daily throughout school hours?

A piece of the puzzle had been missing, and it had been one of his students that had brought it to his attention.

The room was getting darker. As it did every day, the evening came crashing in through the window. What was it about this day that made it stand out from the rest making it special and unique? Why couldn't he recall how he had got to that chair in the first place? He had no recollection of even lighting his pipe. In this way the minutes ticked by, he clock atop the library continued to strike the hours silently, used to do so in this workplace.

The fire was fading out in the hearth. The cat, requiring warmth and possibly some more food, brushed against his legs for a few minutes, eventually perching on the table, placing himself between the keyboard and the screen. No one pushed him away this time. This time he curled up quietly in a deliberate movement, certain of being close to that source of light that captivated him every single day.

The pipe was consuming itself in silence.

On the table behind Professor Lafuente, the old wooden box in which the manuscripts had been, lay opened and forgotten.

However, his visits had not ended that day.

A few hours later, after completing his daily stroll and returning to his office, he heard a soft knock on the door.

'May I come in, Carlos?' A familiar voice said, opening it.

Elena's slender figure entered the room, clutching a folder under her left arm.

The professor's desk was as usual during the past few months, clean, neat, and uncluttered. Pencils and pens appeared gathered and put in their proper place. There was no open book in sight.

Elena was surprised to find her colleague sitting in the wingback chair that Arthur had occupied hours before, mechanically petting the kitten on his lap, the heart clearly visible on the cat's side.

After a brief exchange of pleasantries, Elena took immediate control of the situation, directing herself with determined gestures to the coffee machine in the small inner tower.

A coffee service appeared a few minutes later on the table. Everything about it, from the carefully selected porcelain Japanese tea service, that had been stored in a small cabinet near the fireplace, to the spoons and sugar bowl betrayed the female hand in its preparation. Elena extended a cup to Carlos who took it with a mechanical motion.

Elena sipped her coffee slowly, following the pattern on the carpet with her eyes.

'This time, it appears the rector has made his intentions clear.' she said looking directly at Carlos.

'Yes, it looks like it' Carlos said laconically.

'Shit, this is the last one!' Elena exclaimed as she shook the pack of cigarettes and lifted the last one greedily to her lips. 'Sometimes I must seek refuge in fiction to find examples of smokers. This is not what it used to be. Authentic researchers should be heavy smokers, like in detective novels. Those were indeed the days!'

Elena's comment drew a smile in the professor's concentrated face.

'Yeah, with the entire computer screen covered in smoke, huh?' he replied.

Elena looked at her colleague closely.

'Carlos, as you know, history is a science, although it appears only some of my classmates and myself believe this nowadays. I am exhausted from arguing with those who disagree in the seeming absence of scientific procedures to establish theories and from listening to those who claim it's impossible to conduct experiments to demonstrate what you wish to prove. Since the human being is the subject of our study, it's impossible to prescribe laws, as variables are subject to change. Nonetheless, we must adhere to a technique, certain criteria, and the comparison of data. We are aware of this, Carlos, but I also assumed you had an adventurous spirit inside, correct?'

'With my current income, I can't afford that luxury. This is not like one of our friend Ernesto's historical novels that you adore, you know?'

'Stop such nonsense. Carlos, the answer is waiting for you if you're brave enough to look beyond the obvious. The text on the poster is large and easy to read. As a palaeographer, you just need to comprehend the language being spoken. You understand that, don't you?'

They would not leave him alone that evening. Perhaps these two had practised their different statements before approaching him, thought Lafuente.

'I have spent some time reviewing our work in recent days.' said Elena 'The words "the care of the child" "let us take care of the child," "left the child in the care of the holy women," have been practically parading before us the entire time, describing what was occurring. During this time however we have not understood the message, perhaps influenced by custom, Christian iconography, our culture or what the hell.'

At this moment Elena crushed the cigarette she was holding by pressing it firmly on the ashtray that resembled the hilt of a Spanish colonial sword, 'but our forefathers did know what we were going to try. They anticipated that we would not see the forest because the trees obscured it. It's not a symbolic message, divine, heavenly, or whatever you like to call it, Carlos.'

At that instant, she rose from her chair, carrying her coffee cup with her.

'Here they were not discussing the Son of God but a real child! Review your notes. Just go over your notes one more time and prove to me that you are capable of facing the truth! I misunderstood you otherwise. The depiction of a woman riding the monster in the Codex that you saw at Silos was merely another copyist attempt to translate the realm of desire into visual terms as perceived by the religion of the day, the encroachment on the intellect by common passions. And one more point Carlos: you are a historian and a good palaeographer at that, but our task is not to merely account for history, documenting the past. That would be fine for a high school teacher. Our objective is to provide an account as accurate as possible of what actually occurred and to convey its relative significance for generations to come. If we forget this, we will fall pray to the arguments of those who claim history is irrelevant. That only present is to be taken into account. Have the present and we would be doomed to repeat the past.'

Now it was Carlos's turn to see his colleague move from one end to the other of the workplace.

He squinted at her, his expression conveying the untranslated question: *"Et tu, Brute?"* (— 'You too, Brutus?) He had been wounded. She had reached some part of the target, although Elena never knew which circle of it had been struck. However, unlike Arthur, Elena did not go to the window. Instead, she proceeded to arrange some of the figures on the mantelpiece scattering them on the shelves, pausing briefly in front of the butterfly painting hanging there.

She remained in front of it for a long period of time before speaking.

'You should know by now that answers produce further questions,' she continued, 'If you still haven't realised that after all these years of experience, it's best to find something else for your time and energy to focus on instead. This is our destiny. This is where we're headed. The perpetual dilemma of a life spent in constant uncertainty.'

There was a pause. The professor shook his head.

Without looking up, Elena removed the coffee set off the table and placed the tray in the little turret. She turned, ready to leave.

'You told me once you wanted to see your brother again, didn't you? Returning to Santander and perhaps visiting Soria, right? Indeed, do that. Do it! Take a week or two off! I am able to review the examinations that you have yet to grade. Find some quiet nook if you wish. I merely request that you don't give up. Please, Carlos, not yet.'

She gazed into his eyes for a long time.

'Not yet. Can you promise me at least that?'

Finally, after a few seconds that appeared to stretch out in time, like that Arlanzón river which they could only guess from this window, the professor eventually raised his head.

'I promise, Elena.'

The door quietly closed behind his colleague's figure. Carlos maintained his gaze upon it for several seconds.

THERE ARE TIMES WHEN THE WEATHER CONTRIBUTES TO THE expression of particular feelings. Especially on rainy days, when the heart lies fully open, listening to the joyful patter of the raindrops on the glass, their monotonous sound filling the moments of solitude.

Like music, rain induces a unique state of trance. Overcoats, coats, scarves, and hats wait in the corner until the end of the evening.

Images emerge to consciousness, half-formed ideas shape under the influence of the environment. In such evenings, one can remember those minor sensations, those details previously unnoticed, such as a glove in the inside pocket of a coat or a forgotten cup on a shelf, both of them below the threshold of consciousness. These are moments in tune with the melancholic, which we only remember in those moments of our lives when we are on the same wavelength.

Perhaps it should awaken a long memory, the vivid recollection of an afternoon spent on the balcony at home, shouting with delight at the first raindrops, gazing at distant lightning, and marvelling at the miracle of rain. Or perhaps we remember walking to school on the first day of term in our band-new and spotless uniform, dragging a huge wallet. And yes, there is also time for love, time to recall those dreams of yesterday, those faces that, although far back in time, will remain in our memory as alive as the first day, emerging at times like these.

On days like this, it is easy to find Professor Lafuente seated at a table in The Bier restaurant, his eyes fastened to one of those thick, opaque, tinted glass windows that allow the view of the vague silhouettes of passersby outside while preventing at the same time any view of this inner world from the outside.

Under that ceiling carved with gusto, under these metal lamps, the parquet floor of the room stands out. A framed engraving of a vintage steam engine hangs behind the professor. Next to this lithograph, a barbel tries to swim while linked to a wooden board that has been nailed to the wall, looking shocked by the potential speed of this hellish contraption, displayed near a sign that reads "Blended Whiskeys."

Thankfully, Carlos has a book and some papers in front of him.

By virtue of frequenting this place his presence has long ago ceased to be visible to the employees of the premises. But, like the barbel dangling from the board, like those other paintings, lamps, and coloured glass that fill the central bar, like the lights that swing from its metal supports, he is part of the furnishings.

He is a note more there, a recognised stamp of colour, required by the occasional student who may enter the premises.

Although the place becomes noisy at some times of the day, it is here, at this moment, between three and four in the afternoon, when the sun is falling on the tables, that the professor prefers to seek that unique state of abstraction, surrounded by everyday sounds. From there he requests beers, daily menus, and the recurrent offer of desserts. And it is there, amidst the din of everyday life, that his inner inspiration keeps him connected to the real world.

CHAPTER 30

THROUGH THE LANDS OF CASTILE

Of riverside strolls along the Duero river, poetry,
and the proper method for smoking a pipe.

The road stretched before of him, empty. A car or two traversed the Soria plain occasionally.

"Soria wants a future," said the graffiti he had read that morning in the town hall square as he sallied forth to wander the city after having left his suitcase at Vitorina, the pension on Paseo Florida, the main thoroughfare.

He found the motto repeated in many other places in the city. Unlike the wording, though, the visitor yearned for the past, something to cling on to. How did all this begin? How did he come to be here, in search of who knows what? Why had he paid attention to some out-of- the-blue remarks, taken off the beaten path from nowhere? He might have been sitting comfortably in his office, going through his butterfly collection, seeing Ismael squatting in front of the fireplace, as was his custom at this time of day.

Yes, he could have easily spent one more evening engrossed in his books, with the certainty that gives the knowledge kept and guarded between their pages.

He was instead in the middle of a plain with a few brief notes and dates he had been jotting down here and there, which certainly did not appear to be of much importance to anyone.

After emptying his pipe thoroughly, he returned to the car. He cast a peek at the rear seat.

There was the book that Trevelyan had lent him,

Lands of Castile, by Machado.

'Please read it, professor. I know you are not given to poetry, but if you go to Soria, promise me that at least you will give it try' his student had asked him with his usual enthusiasm that afternoon as he extracted a book from one of the many huge pockets of his coat and handed it over, perhaps as an apologetic gesture after his reprimand days earlier: 'You certainly will love it.'

He recalled having unwillingly nodded. Now he had another duty to perform.

Perhaps his father had been correct that afternoon as the two of them sat on the old, slashed-up wooden bench in front of home. He had said then that reading history was not a future.

Perhaps he had been right.

Perhaps he ought to have devoted himself to something else, biology? Should he have continued drawing those endless species categorisation trees, memorising those Latin names that rang so true for him? Yes, he recalled some of those details with a sour grin: the order of passerines, commonly referred to as birds... And yes, the finches, such as the goldfinch that always swung in the cage behind him in those days. What a lark it was for him back then to parade around in front of his peers reciting those thunderous titles on the tip of his tongue! How much he enjoyed sketching and writing them, copying the classifications, genera, and species in his notebook!

He could have roamed the mountains like he was doing now, but in that case, it would have been for a definite reason, as an official follower of some endangered wolf species, a second Rodriguez de la Fuente. Maybe.

Or perhaps he simply was allowing himself to become disheartened, something he was prone to on days like this.

The mountains, the slopes, the roads, the people walking along the sides of the road, all reminded him that these areas had been crossed again and again since time immemorial, since the very fog began to cover them. Perhaps even the very fog did not exist yet. He was in Castile, the same land that El Cid, Machado, Fernán Gómez, and hundreds of other men had inhabited. All of them probably wrong in their respective dreams. Maybe they had the same internal doubts as him. Perhaps some of them even stopped by the side of one of these roads, perhaps sharing his internal reservations and contemplated abandoning everything. History however also reveals something else. This had been a land of tenacious men and women, with grit and character. Of that character it was no longer trendy to advocate, the kind that justifies many of our actions. Trevelyan often emphasised that one must immerse oneself in the places visited and communicate with them at your own pace.

Yes. History tells us about those who passed through here, about their accomplishments. It tells us, in its unique vernacular, of those who travelled through here. Of those that us that kept fighting—the only thing remaining at the end of the day.

The ancients knew a great deal about this, allowing the weapons to rest prior to the next battle.

Soria. Isolated and distant. Those words might as easily have been written by the poet Garcia Lorca. This emotion was particularly strong on a day like this.

He continued his wanderings through Soria, allowing his feet to carry him until he reached the lower part of town and that natural border that was the Duero river.

A little further away to his left were the ruins of the primitive cloister of St Juan de Duero monastery, which flaunted its eclectic mix of styles in the open air.

Facing the opposite mountain, a group of tourists was surrounding a guide wearing tortoiseshell glasses and sports shoes to match his bellicose suit.

'This is the so-called Mount of the Spirits,' the guide said, with relish at seeing poorly disguised fear in the faces of the tourists who surrounded him, uttering nervous laughter. 'Other of my companions used to come here, genuflect, and recite ceremonial phrases to summon the Earth's energies, things like that.'

Gosh! Had the cage of beasts come loose? He'd had enough of Trevelyan's nonsense to hear it again in a different form. What would be next?

He surveyed the surrounding hills. Here, or close by stood the border between Soria and the old kingdom of Navarre, swords ready, nerves on edge.

He continued his stroll, passing St. Polo's church a little further, on that pleasant evening that flowed like the river. There was just the right amount of breeze, rustling the elms and creating a lovely, constant whisper that caressed the ears of passersby.

He sat on a lonely bench. From that vantage point he could hear the voice of the guide with tortoiseshell glasses.

The group had caught up with him. His words came to him in a murmur. He was standing on a low wall of the bridge below St Saturio Chapel, which could be seen on the hilltop. There, with no blush, the guide took a book from his pocket and declaimed Machado in the best possible place, next to the Duero.

The elms seemed flattered.

Carlos noticed that the volume he was holding in his hands showed all the signs of extensive use, the result of repeated inquiries, of sneaky glances inside.

Guides possess mall hearts, after all.

'I have seen the golden poplars again,
poplars by the Duero riverbank,
between St Polo and St Saturio,
behind the old walls of Soria,
barbacana en route to Aragon,
in Castilian land.'

After reading these words, perhaps a little afraid of having revealed too much of himself over that low wall, the guide quickly stuffed the book back into his coat pocket, as if it had been another guide who had uttered those verses instead of him.

As he listened, Carlos recalled he still had the book Trevelyan had lent him in his pocket.

He took it and examined the cover.

A typical old book, one of those that is a pleasure to hold in one's hands, to smell the paper over and over again, and to examine the characters and shape of the letters, the printing date, the colour of its faded pages, all those tasks in sum that are done with a book prior to reading it.

Perhaps this was a way of delaying pleasure, of putting off facing its many secrets, similar to how our parents prepared us for bedtime stories. The preparation itself was already a party—the dim light of the room, his mother's face blurred by darkness, and that sense of confidence about to be unveiled. All those images had come back to him when he opened this small book of poems.

He had read that many believers opened the Bible at random and that, laying their eyes on the first verse that caught their eye, they could find there the answer to their problems. If this was good enough with the Bible, then, oh, profane thought! It could work equally well with any novel or, in this case, a collection of poetry.

So, thinking no more about it, and after one last glance at St Saturio church on the heights, as if awaiting its approval, he randomly opened the book and read,

'The soul of the poet
orients itself towards mystery.
Only he can
Look at what is far away
Inside the soul, it is cloudy
And the sun's magic wrapped-'

Not entirely convinced, he tried another random page, a second chance,

'In our souls, everything exists.
By mysterious hand, the world is governed.
Incomprehensible, mute,
Nothing do we know of our souls.'

Well, it hadn't been bad this time, not bad at all. Yes, possibly the poem was right. This mysterious metaphor reminded him too much of the bloody manuscripts they had been working on. he attempted to dismiss the thought. He had come here to forget it. And that's what he intended to do, by Jove!

On the other hand, these verses, like good horoscopes, were composed of half-truths equally applicable to anyone, depending on the reader's state of mind. A brilliant way to hook readers. Creating an aura of mystery so you don't have to explain yourself. On the other hand, though, hadn't he experienced certain familiarity with the described emotion? Hadn't the words been accurate, like arrows hitting the target fully?

The group of tourists was now walking away, following their guide at a brisk pace, the poetic interlude now over.

The bus was waiting. Life was waiting. The dizzying pace of a planned trip. You must see things, more things. There is no end in sight. There was so much to see.

Here there were no shops here.

Lafuente remained seated on that solitary bench alongside the Duero. He could perceive the landscape, hear the flow of the river. It brought to mind his evening strolls in Montanilla or those in front of home. Here, however, it appeared to have a distinct voice. The sound produced by the leaves of the poplars rustling in the wind.

The sound of a thrush, a distracted bird flying over the water and vanishing behind the opposite shoreline bluffs, Among them, linnets and greenfinches reminded him of his dreams as a budding ornithologist.

He saw then a red-backed shriek on the opposite shore, ascending towards St Saturio.

He took out his pipe. He smiled looking at it. How could anyone claim that smoking was unhealthy? Yes, all that could certainly be true in the case of the hurried smoker who urgently consumes a cigarette and discards it before returning to work while the tobacco is still lit. His pipe instead brought him serenity. It was a gateway, a door to reflection, an alternate way of perceiving reality. The entire procedure of opening his tobacco bag, smelling it--similar to the scent of a freshly opened book--, mixing it, and gently placing a small amount in the bowls of his pipe. The entire protocol involving an infinite number of sensations. To crush the mixture afterwards and then, oh! just prior to lighting it, bring the string lighter in at just the precise angle! Yes, all that liturgy plunged him into a trance he had learned to recognise, if not to name. The almost promiscuous and forbidden caresses imprinted on the base of the bowl as the pipe rests in the mouth, the masculinity of the fingers' correct posture as they encircle it, and, finally, the ultimate decision to inspire by the nozzle.

*At that moment, he saw a red-backed shriek on the opposite
shore, ascending towards St. Saturio*

Yes, Machado had left without writing the ultimate poem describing a good pipe by the Duero banks, while the oriole and the finch made their voices heard.

He surveyed his surroundings. Only one man was sitting on a bench in the distance, absorbed in the landscape, apparently oblivious to his presence. He was the only person visible in that Soria that was sadly emptying itself. The evening had somehow been frozen in an early 20th-century picture. Perhaps, Lafuente thought, if he waited a little longer, he might see Antonio Machado and his beloved wife appear walking arm in arm along the promenade, coming from the nearby hermitage of St Polo. How easily did our ancestors attain satisfaction!

In this crazy time in which we cross the world, seas, and cities at incredible speed, going to thousands of places at once, and eating every day in a different restaurant in a mad rush to dislodge the opposite through our experiences, we have forgotten the pleasure of a simple daily walk, the joy of lazy evenings with the loved one while visiting familiar places and greeting someone here and there.

The man on the bench continued staring at the river.

After some minutes passed, he stood up and, with what appeared to be a regretful sigh, took a cane that had been resting against the bench, ready to return to the town centre. Due to the manner in which he walked, now to the right of the road, now to the left, the urban area appeared to be miles away rather than just a few hundred meters. He resembled a hidden watercourse beneath the path, that, running parallel to the river were in search of the main course.

The man stopped by his side. His absent gaze and straightforward, kind eyes fell almost unintentionally on him, then on the bench, and finally on the book resting in the professor's left hand.

The apparent weariness on his face vanished abruptly, and a smile appeared on it. The rocking ceased.

'I see you're reading Machado' he stated with conviction. 'Not that I am surprised, mind you. Many do it here, like that guide a few minutes ago. What has caught my attention is that you are taking your time doing it.'

'Yes, well, I suppose I do enjoy the place. It's quiet here,' Lafuente said, searching for words, waking up from his particular reverie.

The old man appeared to be in search of friendly conversation.

'Yes, yes, that's fine. One must seek out for the feeling in the surroundings, in the trees that border the Duero, in the poplars themselves. There's more here than meets the eye, you know. I can tell from your face that you were meditating. It's what this location has. It captivates us in various ways. I would be unable to put it into words. For some, it's the sounds of the leaves; for others, the colours, the water flow, I don't know what. The important thing is to remain trapped in some manner.'

He looked back at the river for a few seconds without speaking, as if he had heard his name being called. He nodded twice then, and striking the ground with his cane, sat down on the opposite end of the bench in the most natural way imaginable. His staff had a curious silver handle in the shape of a lion; the wood was covered in whimsical figures all over. It was evident it had been carved with care, a remnant of a craft already in decline.

'And tell me, how long do you intend to remain in Soria?' he said 'I conclude, based on your appearance and the fact that I've never seen you around here, that you are a forastero, as we used to say here.'

'No, no, I'm leaving tomorrow as a matter of fact. I am just passing through on my way to Burgos from Santander. The truth is one of my students recommended me this visit' he concluded in a low voice, by way of apology.

'Ah! So you're a professor? Perhaps in some institute?'

'No, no, actually from Montanilla University in Burgos. I teach history.'

'History? Oh, quite fascinating, quite fascinating. I'm certain you must have read many surprising things. I am sure.'

The man stared straight ahead as he drew small circles in the sand with his cane, pressing it to the ground with both hands.

'A History professor! Oh my goodness! How much I wished I had studied myself! Yes, all of those things! How much I would have enjoyed it!' And he continued to shake his head as if a secret spring within it had broken, unable to stop the motion. After a few seconds, he pointed his cane towards the nearby river, a malicious and bright wink on his face.

'I also know some history, you know? In this location, for example, you can hear the past speaking to you. It keeps telling you things. Perhaps they don't seem important. Things such as the dry leaves piling up under the tree next to the church, the cry of a baby on his first outing with his parents, the chickens that have just laid another egg. Things like that, you just have to stop and listen.'

'Yours is a nice cane' Lafuente said without thinking, hypnotised by the man's movements on the ground.

'It belonged to my father' he replied with a proud gesture as he looked at it, swinging it in the air for a few moments as if to attest to its flawless workmanship and sturdiness. 'When I sit here, on this restored bench, I feel as though no time has passed. Here is where he and I sat many days. Obviously, this bench did not exist then, only a rock. But it makes no difference. I only need to stay a few minutes, and I always sense his presence at a particular time of day. Always. It's as if, somehow, something of him had remained here. Can you see that hill in the distance?' he said pointing to a slight incline in front of the St Saturio-facing bridge. 'We used to fly kites there once spring arrived. You know something?' he asked, his expression suddenly changing, shaking his head. 'No, no, you wouldn't possibly believe me. I'm just a crazy old man by the river on a weekday morning, watching the world go by. But hold on a second!'

Lafuente looked with curiosity as the man extracted a wallet fully crossed by rubber bands all over its surface, preventing its contents from leaking out. Finally and with great care, he extracted from it a photograph wrapped in thin folded paper. It was old and dingy, with a distinct early-twentieth-century sepia hue. A photograph of some solemn looking schoolboys and their teacher posing at the entrance of the old Jesuitas school in Soria. The man pointed at the teacher in the centre of the photograph.

'Do you recognise him? It's Machado himself when he taught at this school here,' he said, looking at Lafuente as if to encourage him to disagree. 'He stayed here for five years. And this... this one right here...' he said, pointing to the figure of a child, smaller than the rest, standing closer to the teacher than the others, as if seeking shelter: 'This was my father. As you can see, a lot of water has passed under the bridge since then. Tell me' he said abruptly and with a sense of urgency. 'In which pension do you reside?'

'I'm at Vitorina in Paseo Florida. Why do you ask?' Carlos asked, smiling despite himself.

'I believe I have something at home that might be of some interest to a professor like you, something that has been in my family for many years, somewhat related to what I've just described. And now, if you'll excuse me, I still have a pleasant ride home on these legs. Sorry if I have bothered you with my thoughts. Have a nice day, sir!'

And with these hasty farewells, the mysterious old man arose from the bench with the same surprising speed and dexterity with which he had got there, bound for St Polo with that peculiar swing that made his body resemble a pendulum.

A slight breeze rose again.

It was the professor's last day in Soria. The lightweight suitcase had already been loaded into the car. He had also consumed his second cup of coffee in the town hall square, having left behind on his way there the statue of Machado patiently allowing to be photographed with whoever occupied the opposite bench.

As he regarded the town hall's clock and the old wrought-iron bell, Lafuente recalled the events of the previous day, specially the strange little man he had met by the river, as well as his promise to bring him some mementos before leaving the city.

He shook his head with a thoughtful smile.

Certainly, the man had lived a long and **possibly** difficult life.

Such a life that people like him, raised in a wealthy family in distant Santander and later in Aunt Engracia's home, could only comprehend through books.

At that moment he noticed him approaching, walking down the street with the same distinctive sway that had captivated him the day before.

'Good morning, sir' the man greeted the professor upon recognising him, looking at him with clear eyes, stopping the cane and breaking in doing so the hypnotic rhythm it produced. 'I'm glad I found you. I was en route to your boarding house to see if you had already departed. I am glad you didn't'

'Good morning!' Lafuente answered with a smile. 'Can I get you a cup of coffee? I have just finished my breakfast.'

'No, no, thank you very much' he swiftly responded. 'At my age, I only have one around six in the morning and nothing else until eleven. One gets used to carrying on with that.'

He seemed rushed and a little cut off. Perhaps he regretted his long lengthy speech from the day before, or perhaps he was simply exhausted from walking up the street slope up to the square.

'I hope your stay has been profitable' he said after a few silent minutes, which the two men employed gazing intently at the clock face in the square as if it were an incredible rarity. Two women crossed the square greeting them in a friendly manner.

After a few minutes of discussing the current affairs of the square and its historical development, the man stood up and, with a determined expression on his face, took a letter from the inside pocket of his jacket.

'You see, maybe I bored you yesterday with all my babbling. What do you want?' He shrugged. 'Possibly I've lost my measure in conversation, but I could tell you were a man of letters, a well-read man, as my father used to say, and that's why, after consulting with my wife, I've decided to give you this. It's a small thing, but it means a great deal to me. My daughter made a copy and we all agreed to give it to you. It's the last letter written by my father. It has always been sort of a testament to me. He speaks in it about his school days, all that I told you about, and such. Perhaps you could put it to good use at that university of yours. We Sorians have our hearts in the proper place.'

The protests and attempts to refuse such a gift by the professor were futile.

The letter was now in his briefcase, along with a stack of folios and notes complied over the last few days.

· · ·

ARTHUR HADN'T BEEN IDLE DURING THIS TIME, EITHER.

The new term had began three weeks ago. With the upcoming regatta and first exams, he attempted to keep himself occupied and not worry about the unfortunate interruption in their research.

Princess Kristina's world appeared to be out of his field of vision for the time being.

After studying in his room and training for an hour on the Oxford fixed-bench rowing machine, he went downstairs to the common room to unwind in the company of his friends and colleagues.

'I'll see you later,' he said before leaving his room, tapping the poster in front of his study table that displayed the photographs of the "forty-year-old" Cracknell and the Spaniard Pérez, both representing Oxford in the 2019 race against Cambridge. They served as his inspiration in the months leading up to the race with the UBU.

Six students were already present, six students lounging around, sitting in the armchairs that surrounded the room, their legs capriciously dangling over the side, facing the well-stocked library in front of the fireplace. Some were reading; others leafed through newspapers, played chess, or chatted quietly.

Meseguer approached Arthur as soon as he saw him enter, and, after giving the book the latter had brought with him a contemptuous glance, he turned to face the others. Meseguer, who sat two benches behind him in class, was unable to overcome his envy of this newcomer who after only one year here, having moved from Santander, had quickly become the focus of professors' and female students' expectations due to his outstanding academic performance. But what he found most intolerable was the lightness, apparent indifference and lack of interest in these questions by young Trevelyan. So, as the only manifest way of showing his aggressiveness, Meseguer had decided to address Trevelyan with the nickname *Laudy,* a clear reference to his high marks. Unfortunately, however, the sobriquet had been adopted by the rest of students with a clear positive connotation, thus thwarting his initial intentions.

'Wow! *The Mystery of Cathedrals!* he said, reading the title on the cover as soon as Arthur entered the common room. 'Have you guys noticed what our *Laudy* reads for leisure? What can be mysterious about a cathedral, old chap? The location where hosts are kept? Some sort of special blend of wine for the Eucharist?' he asked, twisting one corner of his mouth.

Arthur took the book from Meseguer's hands without a word, maintaining his gaze.

Fulcanelli, that mysterious author, whom he hadn't had time to read in full, captivated him. He had given him a new perspective.

After a few moments, Pedro Santillana entered the room, placed a few books on the table and approached him. Also a newcomer, studying medicine and enthralled like him by the experience that this university represented. Both of them had exchanged many discussions in this same place. It wasn't long before Claudia Cocaro followed suit, accompanied by Azhira, a Pakistani girl. Arthur considered Claudia his biggest confidante due to the fact that she also studied palaeography.

She had come recently from Argentina and combined her interest in history with literature and drawing. These were Arthur's closest friends in this world of privilege.

'And why does this author seem so special to you?' inquired Pedro picking up the book and flipping through it with natural curiosity.

Arthur, sensing the self-confident smiles of Meseguer and his partner Redondo at the back of the room, explained,

'You see, according to the author, Gothic cathedrals conceal messages within their design and architecture. Churches would be a very complete, comprehensive and diverse encyclopaedia of all mediaeval knowledge. Stone effigies serving as educators and initiators.'

'And how could that knowledge transmitted? I mean, without putting it in writing?'

Claudia and Azhira leaned forward, their curiosity aroused.

'As you know, during the Middle Ages, books were reserved for a selected few. In fact, the very word "gothic" comes from "slang", meaning a particular language used by individuals interested to communicate their thoughts without being understood by others. So, just think about that hidden knowledge, the possible secrets written in that magical book, hanging on the walls of our cathedrals. Teachers without voice, as Fulcanelli himself used to call them' Trevelyan concluded, aware of the effect caused.

'Aren't you going to take notes with your Montblanc, Laudy?' interrupted Meseguer from his corner, jealous of the attention Arthur was receiving. 'Aren't you going to show us if it's longer than ours? My father told me it stinks because it leaks ink when you least expect it. It will leave your fingers so full of ink that not even a shoe shiner would be able to remove it.'

Meseguer's father was the external reference he used for everything his intellect was incapable of doing on its own. Not in vain, his influence and money had made his stay at the university possible.

Pedro had opened the book to the first page.

Canseliet's 1925 preface stood out on the page.

'Let's see,' he said, reading the prologue in a quiet voice. "You have truly received God's gift" someone says in a letter to the author. I would like to know what these guys mean when they refer to "God's gift", some paranormal ability, perhaps?' he smiled then, regarding his friend as if he were reading a Marvel comic.

'I have no idea' Arthur said, putting the book down for a moment.

Pedro was one of the few friends he had made in college, despite his outgoing nature. One of the few people to whom he could express his concerns. 'The expression has become a mixed bag over the years to mean in general terms, either something good that God gives you, or a unique ability that opens up fresh paths without apparent effort.'

'Like superpowers, right?' his friend Claudia asked with a chuckle.

'The key to the major arcanum consists simply of a colour, manifested to the artisan from the first job' Pedro continued reading, and here he stopped, looking at his friend.

'What colour could it possibly be?' said he, relentless in his questioning.

'That's the good thing; he never mentioned it to my knowledge' Arthur replied. 'It's most strongly implied in alchemy treatises. All of these texts contain but hints. Something the initiate must discover for himself. I guess it's intentionally inaccurate, just like the colour of your car.'

'Too deep for me' said his friend as he glanced at the more prosaic *Burgos Daily* that lay on the table. On its front page the result of the Copa del Rey match between Mirandes' football club and the opposing team was announced with great fanfare: 3–0. Spectacular. Now that was truly magical!

The wall clock at the top of the stairs leading to the study struck twelve. The room's lights gradually dimmed as each student turned off those next to their seat.

This was not the only book that had piqued young Trevelyan lately.

What would his classmates in the common room have thought if they had known he had been reading some of the great Einstein's essays only the week before?

His relativity theory applied to time showed that neither past nor future existed, only a timeline on which everything coexisted.

It was all a matter of tuning the right channel to receive the broadcast.

Arthur turned off his light with a smile that was more of a wink to himself than anything else.

CHAPTER 31

A BUTTERFLY RETURNS HOME

It was already late when Carlos Lafuente left Montanilla University. Dark clouds were slowly forming in the sky.

Once he arrived to Burgos, he ate hastily at the Ducal Inn in Plaza Mayor, restraining himself from eating at the La Mayor Brewery or the more international Sibuya Sushi instead. After bidding farewell to Mariana, her kind owner, he walked home and locked himself in his ivory tower.

After donning his robe, he sat at his preferred location for meditation, the library window. There, her restless mind reflected on the past few days' events. In his abstraction, he did not realise he was still wearing his gloves.

His attention was drawn to the small book resting on the side table.

Lands of Castille.

He had to give it back to Trevelyan as soon as he saw him again.

The recent trip to the lands of Soria was on his mind. How distant summer appeared now!

Trevelyan certainly would certainly have enjoyed everything about the poplars, the flow of the stream, all that stuff.

Had the trees indeed spoken to Machado? Had they revealed

their secrets to him? Had the poet some unique ability that had enabled him to effortlessly tune into nature, sense its pulse, impressions, hear its messages for mankind?

How little we understand the natural world and the language of trees!

Viewed only as a beautiful addition to our environment.

These significant coincidences, or what the hell we might call them, did they intend to convey a message? Was there a secret force in the universe about which we know nothing? Was Laudy ultimately right with his theories? As a historian, he could not omit many things simply because there were no explanation for them.

Were poets psychics who could communicate with the dark and mysterious side of things? If such was the case, then Machado was undoubtedly one of the many trainees and initiates.

The old elm had desired to communicate with the poet, offering him optimism.

In contrast, he... He knew nothing.

Nothing for sure.

Merely that he was alone this evening.

Although not entirely. His mind overwhelmed him, pursuing novel concepts. methods of action.

He looked at the falling-asleep city through the window, cradled by the Arlanzón. He let the hours go by. The clock on the mantelpiece ticked the quarters, relentlessly, uncompromising, second after second for yet another hour.

He could hear thunder in the distance.

Carlos raised his head and gazed at the exquisitely framed butterfly specimen placed to the left of the window, the crown jewel of the collection that occupied an entire room.

The beautiful specimen, --a *Diaetheria anna* or butterfly 88 for the rest of us, named so due to the numbers appearing on its wings--, stood out with its brilliant colours against the ochre background of the professor's office.

He looked at his hands and realised he was still wearing his gloves, removING them while observing the butterfly as one would a recently completed painting, marvelling at its finishing, preparation, and framing.

Crisp, straightforward, its taxonomy clearly established by science as a result of a historical consensus, the result of congresses in natural sciences. Why couldn't history be that straightforward? Why couldn't the cultural movements, events, and motivations that preceded them have a similarly obvious cause? Consider the butterfly: classified, specific, like the name of a hummingbird. Its habitat, its behaviour, all clear, framed and fixed against a neutral green background for posterity.

He had always understood that this lament was merely an outlet for his rage.

For had the study of history been as straightforward as he claimed, he never would have devoted his life to it, as it was his insatiable curiosity and thirst for knowledge that complemented his other collector's appetite. The certainty that there would always be gaps in the world, shadows where the scientist's lantern would never reach, drove him to devour more and more books, fighting against time, against his own mortality, in an effort to compensate for his profound discontent.

With his gaze still fixed on the butterfly, he picked up a worn leather-bound journal that hung near it. As he began to read, distant echoes rang inside his head, reaching his consciousness.

'"Are you sure we're on the right track? I see nothing but banana trees everywhere. For all I care, we might as well be in fucking Santa Rosa.'

'Yeah, yeah, please continue with the damn machete. There must be a path around here. That's what that man at the canteen told us.'

'I'm not very convinced by his indications, you know. He appeared more interested in selling us brandy than putting us on the right direction.'

Brazil, July 17, 1977—Somewhere in the jungle.

A sticky, oppressive climate. We feel damp on all sides. It simultaneously enters and exits our bodies in an endless process.

We are approximately forty kilometres away from Cuachibamba, the closest town where we stocked up on provisions three days prior to entering the jungle. Just now we've crossed the Urua River. Our position is 55° west longitude and 8° 30' 40" degrees south latitude, or so it was the last time I checked our sextant and stopwatch.

Those gadgets and a faulty compass are our only means of survival.

However, the compass is not really awful if we take care of striking it repeatedly now and then against the trunks of the trees we pass through in order to help it remember where north is. Aside from that, we rely on a few cans of food and our canteens filled with water from the scarce streams we can find.

We've been in this place for nine days. Our equivalent of the long tour. Other colleagues have gone on a spree to Paris, Las Vegas,

London, or Thailand. In contrast, we had decided to enter the Brazilian jungle in mid-August. Felipe and Alvaro are far more tolerant of heat and mosquito bites than I am. Tobias just walked away, saying nothing. Even his thick clothing cannot shield him from their bites.

I had read about this butterfly in specialised books many years ago. It would be fantastic to obtain an specimen.

We have tried a variety of creams and ointments, including those got from a local piercing-eyed shaman, we found in a hut that threatened to fall on us at any moment.

"With this, bites will disappear for years. It's an old recipe passed from my ancestors!" he had said with a composed expression.

Fifty dollars had changed hands in exchange for such a prodigious formula. Fifty dollars that would escape into the jungle en route to a gambling den in the nearest village.

The three of us would soon utter curses far worse than any shouts or incantations the would-be shaman could have uttered.

'I believe we should pause and take a break. I'm exhausted,' Felipe said.

'Didn't you say this was the area where it is usually seen?' I replied.

'Yes, but I don't know what's wrong. You can't find one for love or money.'

'Could you please restrain from discussing payments of any kind,' Alvaro pleaded.

We finally halted in a clearing. In the distance, the mountains appeared obscured by the dense vegetation.

'If we leave the thicket, I think we'd be better able to determine our position,' I said, observing the dense undergrowth surrounding us.

It didn't take us long to build a campfire shortly afterwards. Felipe and Alvaro inspected with a gourmet's eye the most desirable cans in our backpacks, attempting to distinguish between those that had been dented by blows from those whose exterior were rusted.

While we were engaged in these activities, I felt a strong urge to urinate, so I moved away slightly. I had spotted an intriguing tree a few metres ahead and I assumed that this would be the objective of my short-term cultural mission.

As I stood concentrating beneath the tree, I surveyed my surroundings. A ring of varying shades and intensities of green encircled me in hues that seemed to reflect the plethora of animal species hidden among the foliage. A red dot appeared to float suddenly near my eyes. I turned my head to the right in pursuit of that action. Three more emerged from the same place. Three spots moving together.

Three butterflies Three magnificent specimens.

'Felipe! Alvaro! Come! They are here! They are here!'

In a mad dash to capture one, we had to quickly remove the

butterfly net and make a blocking move around the tree, each of us trying our best.

Upon spotting one of these red floating spots close to me, I veered away with what I believed to be skill. Nonetheless, I was so excited that I had been unable to see the small ditch at my feet or prevent my left foot from falling in. I landed backwards in a small stream that would eventually feed the Urua a few kilometres away, still holding the net tightly in my right hand.

'Are you okay, Carlos? Have you been injured?' asked Felipe as he ran towards me, asking that question invariably uttered when we are pretty confident that our interlocutor is mortally wounded.

'Yes, yes, I'm fine' I replied, feeling more offended in my self-esteem than anything else. 'I have nothing broken, but let's follow them. Let's go!'

There we were, three figures jumping with butterfly nets and straw hats.

'You've got it! You've got it!' I was startled by Tobias's screams as he appeared from behind a heap of lush vegetation, all his har tousled forward, pointing to the net I was holding.

I looked at the net. I had never released my grip. Indeed, a coloured shape was moving within it.

I had captured the specimen by accident at the precise moment of my fall.

We placed it with more care than to food itself into one of the jars we had stored for this purpose, for fear it would break.

That had been the story.

He put the agenda back in its place.

That specimen was now displayed in front of him. A time-frozen adventure.

There was a photograph of his old friends in another corner. Felipe had a grey beard even then. Felipe, who would foolishly die years later by the shoulder of a county road after having stopped his car to photograph birds in a nearby wetland, A careless driver killed him in a matter of seconds. He had survived typhus and malaria in

Brazil only to perish between Torrevieja and Santa Pola one April morning.

April. The cruellest month, according to T. S. Eliot.

A bright day with pleasant weather. To the left of the photograph was good old Alvaro. He had had better luck. He recalled his enthusiasm when discussing his plans of forming a musical group to challenge the establishment.

He regarded the butterfly and recalled the peculiar sensation of holding it for the first time. Those peculiar shapes on its wings looking like number sixty-eight or sixty-nine drawn on them, depending on the case. Nature had designed those delicate wings.

Yes, the search and effort in that suffocating heat had been worthwhile.

His friends had been there. They had fought together, both with each other and against misfortune.

This and much more was contained within that display case.

He realised what he had been seeking all along was merely to recapture the passion and illusion of yesterday. And the manuscripts had triggered that.

He had feared among other things seeking and not finding, disorder, the futility of life and love. He had learned to seek refuge in his ivory castle, his office, with closed things and theories that he only had to explain.

It was easier to live that way. more comfortable. Funkier, but more secure. He was afraid to feel. Seeing his students' curiosity gave him some hope; he could live vicariously through them, specially through Trevelyan. He could launch them into an exploration that for him had become dangerous, inconsistent, full of fear and possibilities.

The world had not yet taught Carlos enough. He longed for someone to speak to him with the illusion of an impossible spring; of the timid Edelweiss flower bursting from the snow, triumphant, continuing to seek the unexpected in the ordinary.

All that squeezed into that moment, in that night, behind that moon already obscured by clouds.

There was no breeze today; no birds to distract him; nothing to break the silence; only the flow of water and the soft, dark glow between the city lights reflected in its waters, under the glances of passers-by, of late-night lovers who threw a flower, a glance, or a hope into the river to see how it was carried across its surface.

All the legends he knew about the Arlanzón came back to him now, that past and experienced symbology of recent months, the significant coincidences associated with that perennial, unavoidable watercourse.

The Arlanzón River had relinquished his inheritance. His seclusion had taken its toll on the professor. How much water had flowed, and how many misfortunes and happinesses had occurred along its banks!

Carlos's had been a unique privilege. He had a special bond with that river. He had watched his flow and it in return had witnessed the birth of his interest, his academic development, and his adolescent wanderings in front of the same path that now extended beneath his balcony. With the experience and perspective only years can provide, it had patiently waited with a kind and understanding gesture to receive a call of recognition one day, as a frustrated lover hopes

to see the admiring gaze returned, or a father the call of a far-off son.

A call that was about to occur.

'Good night, old river' he said.

His figure was in front of the window. The vase of freshly cut flowers was on its right side. He looked at it.

He was not alone.

No, not tonight.

CHAPTER 32

THE SCHOOL TEACHER

Of raging waves, memories concealed in old letters, and evening strolls, all accompanied by a consideration on the importance of French and spelling classes.

November was ending.

The warmth of wood enveloped everything in the room.

First term had ended. A period in which he had been involved in the correction of the first exams that were now heaped up on his desk, covered with notes and pen marks, not counting the tutorials, Arthur's visits, and teas consumed in Elena's company in front of the window.

He was grateful for the crackling sound of the fireplace, lit after considerable effort with frigid hands.

He walked to the north side of the room and faced the large window there.

On the other wall hung his second favourite piece of art. A marine that appeared to drag in its waves everyone who had the audacity to gaze upon it.

He could look at it for hours. Just waves and sea. Just blue, infinite shades of it.

He stood motionless in front of it, pipe in hand.

He had often attempted to determine why he was so drawn to this painting. The wildness of the subject? Loneliness, the force of nature? That it contained no human figure?

Perhaps it was its simple beauty. To be sure, the exquisite sensation of feeling helpless before something we cannot control.

That painting had always hung in Aunt Engracia's living room for as long as he could remember. Now it was part of his life.

When he looked at it, he felt like he could enter into it, listen to the waves, feel the breeze, allowing for that feeling of tranquility that inspired introspection. To contemplate the meaning of life and existence. On seeing it, he could remember a distant childhood that used to turn hostile to memory. He recalled the kind words of Aunt Engracia when, in the company of Uncle Enrique, contemplated the painting:

"Your uncle purchased it at an auction in London," she said one day upon observing his rapt attention. Multiple times, he had approached the frame to verify the title and name of the painter: "*Wuthering Storm*" —Richard

Wilson, 1756–.

This piece, along with a Renaissance Madonna that Dr Bordallo had also acquired that very summer, had been hiding in this room behind a nine-digit security code in an abandoned mansion that almost no one had inhabited or visited until he inherited it.

Was this the fate of all discoveries? To be forgotten in dusty rooms?

The picture also awakened in him a peculiar sense of time. When he stood before it, it seemed as if time itself had stopped. Only the urge of life, which was almost like an instinct, drew him back to the world.

And through beauty, everything once again made sense. Everything restarted once more.

How accurate was the English poet Keats when he stated,

"Beauty is Truth, and Truth is Beauty, that is all that we need to know!"

He realised he had left some scattered documents on the bureau.

He took a small key and opened the top drawer.

At the bottom of it his fingers found what looked like and envelope.

A manila coloured envelope.

He remembered what it was.

It was the letter that curious little man had handed him in Soria after that stroll along the Duero.

With the recent exams and enquiries still fresh in his mind, he had put off its reading until he had completely forgotten about it. One envelope lost among the many items he stored in those drawers beside old photographs, travel brochures, and keepsakes from his travels.

He settled into his favourite chair, and lit his pipe. The cat had made a nest at his feet. The only source of light was the bulb on the side table by the armchair.

A gloomy Arlanzón and some late-night pedestrians could be seen from the window.

He opened the letter with the utmost expertise and slow movements, as if it were a codex itself. He observed the yellow marks which denoted the passage of time. The stamps were nearly erased, and the date on the postmark, May 29, 1955, was nearly undetectable.

The calligraphy was exquisite, the tight handwriting showing it had been written slowly and with care. Each letter evidence of an age when such writing was both a virtue and an art:

In Soria on the 24th of May, 1955.

I have realised my son I am an old man now.

But above all, I have realised I have not talked with you as much as should. I would have liked —and I think this feeling is common to all parents —to have been a better father. Sometimes however the appropriate words come to mind late, when the moment has passed.

Getting old is merely the accumulation of regrets, not just moments.

So I apologise here, son, for those moments, for those silences I did not fill with explanations, for that phrase left unsaid.

But I think that here, now, at this moment, I can correct something if I speak to you from the sincerity of my heart.

Had to sum up a lesson of everything I lived in my time. If I had to save something that the damned civil war had not reaped, it would be the generosity and kindness I met with.

And yes, among all of them, my teacher stands out.

My French teacher was a good and kind man. Some have spoken highly of him, and some even claim to have known him.

Years later he would become a great poet of worldwide renown.

For me and my classmates, he was simply our French teacher.

Professor Machado.

The French teacher.

My friend Alberto and I would sometimes see him walking with his wife in the evenings, to a place next to the church, leaning against the upper wall overlooking the river.

I will never forget his silhouette next to his wife's wheelchair, silently gazing into the stream. Occasionally, he crouched next to her and then, placing his hand on her shoulder and exerting a slight amount of pressure, whispered a few words into her ear, before resuming his previous attitude.

It is not uncommon today to see people coming to visit the current Antonio Machado Institute, and see the classroom where he taught. For these people, these visitors, this space is a symbol, almost a place of worship. For me, however, it will always be my old class, a part of me, of my memories, of my impressions of those distant years, despite the renovations the building has undergone over time.

At that time, drawing, calligraphy, singing, work, and physical education were scheduled to be done in the afternoon, leaving the most arduous efforts of language and mathematics for the mornings.

My mind burns with the recollection of the ink stains on my tiny hands sweating on the desk, notched this under hundreds of previous students' fingerprints; notches that only stopped by the presence of the inkwell itself and the slot intended to place the pencils and fountain pen.

What a daunting task was it then to fill the pen on those first attempts!

What gratification felt when, with my hands completely blue from my exertions, I was able to make lines appear, to take form at the pen's tip! How many visits to the toilet and scoldings from my mother when I arrived home, my uniform in such a terrible condition! Under his care, letters, lines, and phrases began to connect themselves, to make sense. Little by little, French was gradually detaching itself from the tip of my pen and reflecting, elusively, in a manner I could not entirely comprehend, on the paper.

I often found myself gazing out the window, observing flies landing on the glass, accompanied by that sound that both irritated and fascinated me.

'Carmelo...' a soft voice by my side, a hand resting on my shoulder.

'My explanations must be very dull; please pardon me'

His voice was warm, friendly. There was no sign of irony, double meaning or rebuke on his face; only concern, as he felt that something was escaping him in his teaching. He wanted to know what it could be, in view of my lack of attention in class.

Every morning, after greeting the class, he would place on the table the only textbook we used at the time. After opening it, he stared out of the window at an unidentified point among the rooftops of Soria that could be seen from there.

Thus, thanks to his influence, I began to focus on my handwriting, to maintain the line, pay attention the formation of each letter within the lines on the graph paper. I remember the comparisons made with another classmate as if we were competing for a master's degree. We discussed the different advantages of using one type or another of graph paper or pen. How many comparisons of the qualities, textures and final finish!

A school inspector's intermittent visits would be the lone exception to this schedule.

Many years after graduating and moving away from that school, I would see my teacher again in every kind word received. I will never forget his reassuring pat on the back as he corrected my booklet, full of poorly constructed French sentences.

'Keep it up, Carmelo. You're doing great. Keep it up. *'Ca c'est tres bien.'*

Simply put, he was a decent human being. And with that, I stay.

All of Soria's good citizens felt his pain when his young wife fell ill.

I'll never forget the expressions on the faces of the grocer or the watchman as the young couple walked past them on their daily evening stroll towards the river in a fight against time.

There was as I said before, a spot on that wall, not farm from the church Don Antonio liked to frequent.

From that vantage point, his hand constantly resting on the back of poor Eleanor's wheelchair, they both observed the river, the poplars, and the setting sun.

Once, when going out to play soccer with my friends, we sprinted right into the middle of the square without noticing them. Our ball slammed into the church wall, with a noice that reverberated all over the square.

Upon noticing them we hurriedly picked up the ball and went away in silence down the street. There was no need to say anything.

Those, in short, were years marked by the simplicity of my beliefs and my sincere and straightforward tastes, which may seem strange to you. My first experience with kindness, love, and unselfish dedication came from my good French teacher. I recall that with affection, sweetness, and anguish.

Then, you know, that person became something different, historical.

From those classroom windows, I had observed the city's growth alongside me.

Today, I see with a melancholic air and a peculiar mix of emotions, people visiting the place, that classroom. Perhaps I, the sole living members of my class of yore, keep in secret the echoes of the conversations and experiences that took place there.

I can't tell you many more things. I have searched in my memory for something to leave you, something which could help you, son, but I don't want to leave you with empty words. Whenever I think about my teacher and his wife, I always picture them standing close to the river, gazing into the distance. I suppose that we felt others' lives like our own then, or perhaps, as I said previously, I have grown older and feel compassion for even the stone I have just kicked. Nevertheless, if getting older implies becoming more sensitive or connected to others, then old age is welcome. I do not wish to rely on second-hand truths expressed by others, on something I have not experienced myself. I can only tell you that human goodness is the greatest thing we have inside us. That is something worth looking for. Be therefore a good man no matter how simple and admonishing this may seem to you".

IN THAT FARAWAY EVENING, OBLIVIOUS TO THE TRIBULATIONS that were passing through the minds of the children who had witnessed their presence in that square, careless about any concern other than driving the chair in his hands, the teacher had directed the small wheels of it towards the courtyard. The scorching cobblestones welcomed the brief shade cast by the vehicle's surface.

There was no one there at that hour. Moving the chair in this manner became a pleasurable task. To move it, advance, and feel like he was heading somewhere, that both had a destination and a purpose.

Even if it was only that small wall over the Duero river.

Yes, it was nice, that little breath of peace, of tranquility, the two of them gazing at the hill in front of them.

Without a word, he reached out and put his hand on Leonor's arm.

He put a little pressure on it, gently, as with all mis moves over the past few days. It was his way of reminding her he was there.

She acknowledged his presence by placing her right palm on his arm before returning her gaze to the distant countryside.

The bouncing of a ball filled the empty square with sound, but neither of them paid any attention to it, for both had already made in their world the space they needed.

A thrush strutted on the opposite bank.

They could remain there for several minutes. As a matter of fact, so they did before returning home, passing in front of the church once more.

Waters were flowing strongly that day.

It was the power of nature, manifested in the resistance of the poplars. Antonio remembered the one he had found a few days ago, its dead, parched trunk. A green shoot on the tree's side, however, heralded new life on the tree.

He would have to write something about that.

About these blue days and this sun from childhood.

About the resilience of nature, about life.

Before it was too late.

Carlos left the letter on the windowsill. The Christmas lights of the city flooded through the glass and bounced off the mirrors in his office, casting a rainbow on his face. Now, contemplating the Espolón Walk, it appeared as other eyes would be seeing it, that this was the first time.

CHAPTER 33
A NEW BEGINNING

The doorbell rang.

It was Elena.

After exchanging pleasantries and expressing a passing interest in the professor's classes, she remarked, 'I haven't brought up the topic in a long time since our last talk. I'm well aware of the fact that we are unable to proceed with the research, at least not in the manner that you had intended.

'Of course not. Yo know that perfectly well.'

'That's exactly what I told my Deusto colleague.'

Elena, a talented historian and palaeographer, halted at this point, delaying information and stimulating the interlocutor's curiosity by adopting the practise of time management and information delaying. A strategy that has been utilised by humans since the beginning of time.

'What for?' said Lafuente after a brief pause.

'Apparently he seems to be eager to lend me a hand in whatever investigation I may be working in.'

The room felt silent again while Elena held between her lips the unlit cigarette she had just removed from her purse, while eagerly searching in it for the lighter.

'An investigation?' said a befuddled Carlos without understanding, dropping line, hook and sinker into the net so skilfully laid by his partner.

'Well, both of us know there are certain steps in the Kristina inquiry that we can't pursue, right?' she repeated, again lowering her head, concentrated on lighting the cigarette.

'Yes, I have understood that thus far, but still, I have not yet prepared my resumes to send them if that is what you mean.'

'Merely that I sympathise with you, Carlos. Just imagine, I can see why you decided to abandon the research before leaving for your vacation. Yet, here we are, still unable to take a final look at the musical Codex and any such documents that may be housed in Huelgas Monastery. And to think on the other hand, that they might be readily available to any other researcher from any other university in the globe, seems a bit unfair, don't you think? Perhaps some of them are already in possession of that much needed authorisation'

Even the most inwardly oriented palaeographer would have been able to pick up on Elena's sarcastic undertones.

'Are you playing tricks on me, Elena? Is this some kind of Lewis Carroll riddle you have up your sleeve?'

'No, no. You may rest assured that's not the case. Let's pretend for a moment that a history professor at a Spanish university, motivated by pure professional fervour —completely professional, of course, mind you—and desiring to assist a colleague in need, would like to do her a favour by requesting authorisation on her behalf. What would you say to that?'

'Please stop kidding me and explain what this is all about!'

Elena jumped up from her seat and dashed to the tiny turret and began to handle the coffee machine, always at the ready.

'Do you want a cup of coffee? I believe I have earned some today. My last lecture wasn't one of my best,' she replied, inhaling the cigarette smoke with particular relish. 'Whatever of what sceptics may say, a Winston smoked in the early afternoon is a veritable rush of energy.'

Then, without further ado, she sat down and calmly prepared the coffee pot, her languid actions heightening Carlos's annoyance.

'For God's sake, Elena, could you please stop messing around with those cups of coffee and explain what you mean? When you put on those dramatic airs, it really gets on my nerves.'

'It's nothing, I simply thought that perhaps my old friend, Nicolás Pedrosa, with whom I shared a bench in college and who used to throw glances at me, perhaps driven by tender impulses not very academic or intellectual, would be able to do me a favour. Founded on those quaint sentiments which, being antiquated, are, well... historical.'

Carlos's face was a poem. He was completely confused by the trail of the conversation.

'Do I understand right?' he said, volunteering.

'There is ancient Chinese proverb that says: *"Never give up, for the last key is often the one that unlocks the door".'* she added cryptically with a malicious smile as she removed an object from her bag.

An envelope.

An official seal and the words "University of Deusto, Faculty of History" were prominently displayed on one of the corners.

'Challenge your knowledge of Latin with these lines from Seneca: *"Ignoranti quem portum petat quilibet Ventus suus est"*? Or, in fine Burgos dialect: "The one who does not know to which port he is bound, any wind will do him good." In case you were paying attention, you might have noticed that I made some minor changes to the quoted material.'

The professor stood up and took several steps around the room.

He studied Elena as if for the first time, then the window, and the marina in the distance as if they were the set for an opera began without him noticing it..

The picture now made sense. He realised why he'd been always drawn to that marina. The never-ending battle between waves and the shore. Once and again, despite knowing they would never reach it.

There was a knock at the door.

'It's open!' the professor said in an absent voice.

It was Arthur. Arthur, indeed, his eyes radiant, his scarf positioned at an impossible angle. It appeared as if the poor boy had attempted to strangle himself at his digs before descending.

'I've been told a local tour is being organised. 'Am I right?' he said, sniffing the smell of coffee that filled the room. 'Only a spoonful of sugar for me, please' Elena nodded with a knowing wink in response to his smile.

A slight grimace appeared on the professor's face. Hell of a boy!

'Yes, you're not mistaken,' he finally said, his face brimming with a grin. 'It's impossible for me to fight you both at the same time. Just you wait musical Codex!'

~

CHAPTER 34

ARTHUR DRINKS A BEER

Ramblings and music at sunset.

A flock of swifts crossed the sky flying westward. They suddenly changed their flight and headed instead towards the horizon line, having received apparently a signal from their leader, as if they had spotted there something of the utmost significance that had escaped the observation of mere mortals.

Some lost leaves attempted to imitate them, rising slightly in the air before falling, defeated, to the ground after a few turns.

"The poetry of every day, that's what can be seen from this window" thought Arthur.

He was with his pals in the "Eloisa" pub, one of his regular watering holes on the very Espolón Walk, quite close to Plaza Mayor. He needed a bit of relaxation.

There had been far too many unexpected developments for one day.

The bar's lively thump at that hour was a welcome sound. The same din every day, the incessant chatter of innumerable voices, of countless minds telling different stories, one on top of the other, shuffling hypotheses about lived and future life, at war over how to best load the dishwasher or brew a cup of coffee, in that eternal struggle of wills that is existence.

In front of him, the certainty of that mug of beer, its foam creating rings on the table as it clung to the sides of the glass. He lazily glanced at the folder he had placed next to the window, away from prying eyes. At long last, Evaristo had given him his notes for review. Evaristo —the lucky rock owner of that van that had led the group from Burgos en route to Covarrubias in quest of Kristina's tomb. Evaristo, the companion of many holidays and evenings spent rowing on the Arlanzón. Of walks in and out of the Lyda Antiquarian bookshop in quest of books with varied levels of dust covering them. Both of them liked to compare the scents of their pages, the colour of their covers, and so on. They shared the theory that you could determine the content of a book based entirely on its odour as well as by the amount and quality of the dust that covered it.

He adjusted his collar. He felt comfortable in that chair by the window, between the two flowerpots placed harmoniously there by the bar's owner, Veronica.

He looked outside again. The elderly lady who used to walk her two tiny dogs every day was passing now by the window, on time as always, the collar of her coat turned up, occasionally smiling at a familiar face, living her cheerful routine.

Oh! The realities of an autumn afternoon mark an expectation, ushering those familiar sounds that signal the end of the day, mark an expectation, paving the way for the beginning of a new daily narrative. What a lovely sensation he felt as as he abandoned the necessity for rapid action, the prompt solution to a problem, allowing instead his mind to roam near the warmth of the pub's fireplace!

Verónica greeted him from the bar. She had known the young student since he arrived to Burgos and was used to his ways. Arthur allowed his thoughts to wander, joining each other out of pure inertia, out of habit.

A girl in a turtleneck was playing darts. A wool sweater. A cardigan. It had a decidedly Scottish air to it. The Highlands. He wold have to travel some day across those barren slopes with melodious names. it was weird to think they were part of old Europe. Names like Portree or Dunvegan, Clay or Fort Williams looked to him like coming from the Far East.

It's funny how essential hair is to a woman's beauty. Should this young woman have her hair pulled back back, would she present a different aspect, another identity? Would we be seeing a different side of this young lady? For a world based on symbols, this was the sole requirement. Another appearance, another sign, another identity. Other way to be perceived. Perception was everything.

He made an attempt to get nothing but blankness in his mind. These days had been really exhausting. He couldn't theorise anymore. He didn't want to give any thought to anything other than the beer in his hand and the presence of his pals Claudia and Pedro. Claudia was in the midst of describing her recent trip to Germany,

'Well, there we were, lugging those huge suitcases across the streets of Munich without a clue. You wouldn't have found us in a worse situation. I only had one of them left, and on top of that, its wheels were shattered. Therefore, I was compelled to carry it through the underground and the streets, walking as best I could, carrying its weight. God, how I came to hate it!'

After finishing her story, Claudia picked up the guitar that had been resting silently by her side and began singing with the same seeming ease as if she were holding in her hands one of those cups of coffee her companions were enjoying. She did it with the same attitude as if doing so were the logical, natural step after relating such a story.

Arthur had heard snippets of this song before, but never the whole thing,

According to legend, in a tree
A little Guarani Indian was perched.
Startled by a cry from his mother,
lost support and fell to his death.
And that between the maternal arms.
By a strange spell, he became a chogüí bird.
Chogüí, chogüí, chogüí, chogüí, It kept singing, looking here,
    looking there,
Crying and flying, he went away.
Chogüí, chogüí, chogüí, chogüí,
How beautiful is, how beautiful was
losing itself in the Guaraní sky...

That vocal delivery, paired with that song, seemed to infuse the evening with the appropriate enchantment and nostalgia. It was the same tone that would make more than a man to fall in love with the singer in days ahead.

Arthur had the unsettling sensation of being trapped by an unfamiliar emotion. Faceless, expressionless yet, but there it was.

Like many others before and after him, Trevelyan had fallen under the song's charm.

Like so many other ballads he had heard, it would make him to look deep inside himself, with the feeling of having lost something he was not yet aware of, becoming an integral part of his life from that point on.

His friend's guitar made him feel like he was floating in a sea of human suffering, accompanied by a sense of inner loss.

Once Claudia finished singing and set the guitar aside, Arthur wished the song had lasted a bit longer. Just a tiny bit longer. Perhaps then he would have been able to identify or pinned down the emotion he was experiencing. However, much like the small Indian in the lyrics, it also had vanished.

'Well, finding accommodation was another story altogether' Claudia continued after this brief *intermezzo*, putting the guitar aside

as if the conversation had not stopped and this were the logical consequence. 'It was absolute mayhem in the underground. All those
German names! Wherever you went, it seemed like you were always
following the same maze of corridors lined with stores advertising
their wares.'

He was listening with an absent smile. Yes, he repeated himself;
it was good not having to think about anything in particular, making
any decisions once the task of ordering a specific variety of beer was
completed.

A Paulaner would suffice for today.

Arthur peered out the window. There were no passersby at that
time.

Outside, the window's light was shifting. The orange tones had
gone from solid to more marked ones, filtering through the glass
panes, through the bevelled glass, falling on the table, creating
shadows where none had existed before, thus creating strange drawings on it, making the shadow of the jug, of the computer and his pen
resemble dragons, ships sailing on the open sea...

His focus returned to the jug in front of him, where the light's
journey through the beer and foam were leaving a whimsical patter
on the table.

Those forms wandering aimlessly across the tablecloth reminded
Arthur of ships searching for a destination, an unidentified crew on
board, possibly awaiting accreditation, a doubtful past behind them.

That light made him think of those endless horizons of Charlie
Chaplin's films towards which the trump inexorably sailed at the end
of his movies. Or that other horizon, that orange-hued one against
which a cowboy rides in countless westerns. The allure of the horizon
and the setting sun. There 's something captivating about it. It always
has been like that throughout human history.

He stared at the jug intently.

That shadow cast over the table.

Those strangely beautiful, yet eerie shapes.

As Truffaut stated, humans have always been intrigued by images projected on a wall, even before the birth of cinema and the magic lantern. And even before that, the *camera oscura,* until reaching the ultimate stage of our journey, seeing flames dancing on the walls of a cave in prehistoric times.

CHAPTER 35

A SWEET FAREWELL

Where it is shown that God helps early risers or how the early bird catches the worm.

Carlos approached Arthur with an air of intrigue that evening. The student was closely examining a book about mediaeval crystal glass.

'There's something I need to tell you before we go back to Our Lady of Huelgas, Arthur' said the professor in a hushed voice.

The student, caught in the consultation of the volume in his hands, stared at him, thrilled.

'I've had time to think over the events of last months, you know. So much to consider' added the professor in a serious, almost solemn tone. Almost fumbling over his words, he stated, 'I swear I won't laugh at your significant coincidences again. Never in a million years did I think I'd say this, but recent events have convinced me that a unique energy may be permeating and linking us all. I would never have believed it if I'd heard myself speak like this in the past. Nevertheless, I have not asserted their existence; I've only admitted the possibility.'

While this was going on, Elena was studying the scattered notes on the table and casting periodic glances at both student and teacher from that vantage point.

The thought that she might have overheard the exchange made Carlos glance at her warily. Being re-assured this was not the case he went on:

'I want you to do me a favour in this research of ours.'

'What is it, professor? I'm getting a little piqued off now.'

'It's elementary. Should you have any of those insights, any sudden epiphany whatever it is, follow it through to its logical conclusion. Don't fight what I believe to be the natural direction of your subconscious.'

'I will promise if it puts your mind at peace.' replied Arthur, used to his mentor's quirks. 'Fulcanelli writes: "There is no chance, no coincidence, or fortuitous relationship down here.", which is food for thought if you need it.'

The three of them resuming focus on their task at hand. After a few minutes, Trevelyan's voice was heard again over the papers, accompanied by a countenance that sought to be as thoughtful and innocent as his age allowed.

'Professor?'

'Yes, Arthur? What is it now?'

'Before our visit to the monastery, I watched on TV a professor from Burgos University raving about its spectacular stained-glass windows. Her name was "Abbot". Could this count as just another significant coincidence?' he replied with a an innocent-appearing smile.

DECEMBER 15TH, 20...

As he left home that evening, Carlos Lafuente noticed the weather beginning to show signs of change. Fog was creeping up the riverbanks, enclosing the Arlanzón. It was difficult to see the sky due to that grey hue that enveloped everything, resembling a long strip of colour applied to a canvas prior to be painted.

Was actually 5:00 p.m., or had the hour vanished into another time, another dimension?

'Carlos, over here!'

The voice had come from his left, at the end of the road. Elena's Opel Crossland X was easy to spot, parked on the corner, next to a coffee shop on the other side of the river. He could see Arthur's head bobbing around in the passenger seat.

After greeting them and getting into the car, Carlos kept silent the whole ride. Nobody seemed particularly interested in making small talk.

Once again they retraced the same route. The car made a left turn onto a street that led directly to the Compass houses. They chose to park this time in a sport at the front of a row of them, near a bar with the name "Teresa" painted on its front.

It appeared as though the mist had tinted the light in the streets a bluish-grey hue that insisted on creeping over their feet, crawling up to their waists.

The surprise lay around the corner.

Compass St seemed to have suddenly vanished. They turned around. Only the cafeteria sign could be seen behind them. Their destiny had disappeared, engulfed by mist. The houses on the right could hardly be guessed.

The old monastery had been transformed into a strange, fascinating, intriguing, and foreboding place. It appeared to be filled with tens of thousands of secrets, of infinite nooks to investigate, giving the sense that the souls and ghosts of its ancient occupants, as well as the figures lying in it, were getting ready to make their way across the damp and lonely passageways that evening.

Arthur peered at the tower, rubbing his hands through his leather gloves, sticking his nose through the scarf. The steeple ripped open the greyish, moist shape that seemed to envelope everything. In such an evening, the placement of the two upper arches atop the lower one looked like a silent cry of panic. He pictured himself climbing the spiral staircase he knew was there, and the mere image gave him the creeps.

The huge jackets and thick coats they wore did little to ward off the chill that seemed to seep through every layer of their attire, as if some magical force was at work.

Elena stomped her feet on the ground.

'Oh, my God, I just can't get my cold feet and legs to warm up! Get moving, would you!'

'I'm afraid the interior won't be any warmer on such a day,' replied the professor.

With the exception of the previously mentioned tavern, all the passersbyes and residents seemed to have vanished. A couple of automobiles sat idly in the the deserted street, their lights off and grey, resembling out-of-place sconces, as if they were apologising for being there at that time and location, reminding them they were still in the twenty-first century.

Their noses were assaulted by the sharp, distinctive scent of wet stone. They kept trying to find the old placards on the walls to make sure they were heading in the right direction. Gates were thus rediscovered by these brave and daring explorers from a world that had vanished. Were they in the Huelgas Monastery they were familiar with, or some other place lost in the sands of time? Evidently their senses had deceived them. The dense fog covered the landscape. This phenomenon had swallowed up the outer lawn, the thick walls, the royal gate, the lofty tower with its battlements, all.

A parked car started its engine, turning on its lights at the precise moment they were only but a few metres from it, giving the impression that it had emerged from nowhere. They were drawn by the warm orange glow emanating from inside the premises, beckoning them to enter and seek refuge from the outside world. For a brief second, it seemed as though the professor was wavering. It was tempting to imagine himself indoors, quietly smoking a pipe, perhaps sipping a cup of hot coffee with milk should a smoking area not be available, while watching the regulars play darts or debate the relative merits of Real Madrid and Barça, as it had been done for decades.

Elena, holding under her right arm the safety-conduct she had acquired for this purpose, said, 'Come on, don't linger; I remind you that the technician from Royal Archives is waiting for us.'

Thus, the professor had little choice but to scrap the entire concept altogether. Instead, they'd have to traverse the monastery's dank walls and be confronted once more with statues, chilly stone tombs, and an unfathomable riddle.

The three of them exchanged dubious glances.

Carlos was the first to move forward. Passing silently beneath the tall tower where the chaplains had been locked up for disobeying the abbesses' commands, he continued on his way.

Once they reached the Inside Compass, the tall form of a man in a raincoat seemed to stand out from that environment, glowing in that white aura, in that cloud that covered everything. His silhouette was hardly discernible in the darkened environment in which he moved, making him looked like an angel who had been waiting for a new soul to guide at that point in the journey. A faint glow emanating from his mouth indicated that he was smoking a cigarette. Light, in the end. On such an evening, even birds remained silent.

The absence of sounds made the metallic-sounding footsteps of the man outside the offices all the more noticeable. When he reached the opposite end, he retraced his steps.

'Good evening! I was waiting for you,' a deep voice stated, cutting through the mist as if they had been spoken from another world, once he guessed their presence. 'I appreciate you punctuality.'

'Was there a Plan B?' Elena replied. 'I would have preferred to walk a bit in the park, but the weather had other plans.'

The man pouted his lips in a manner that could indicate either appreciation or disapproval of Elena's wit. He threw out the stub of his cigarette to the floor. They could then see his features in the faint light that emanated from the half-open door. They had hoped to meet the previous technician, but the figure before them could not be more different. The combination of his pale, dry face, his closed eyes, and thin lips, as well as the gloomy surroundings, made the visitors take a step back.

'If you don't mind, let's walk straight to the study room,' the man stated dryly, perhaps out of habit, without seeming to notice the effect his words had on the newcomers, giving his leather gloves a slight tug to ensure his fingers were properly positioned within. 'From what I've been told, I believe you already have a solid grasp of the place.'

After following him inside, the door that had revealed the crimson, warm light within the building slammed shut with a piercing sound, leaving that grey world behind for the moment.

The mist had awaited their arrival, ready to engulf everything.

WHEN THEY ENTERED THE CONSULTATION ROOM, THEY DID NOT see anyone there. The place seemed to be empty.

Someone had turned on the lights a few minutes before.

Strangeness permeated the entire site, from the brightness and colour of the walls to the excessive light that bounced off the contemporary filing cabinets positioned on either sides.

'The archivist mother will come presently. I've just called for her,' the man stated in a businesslike manner as he placed carefully a leather suitcase on the table. They nodded in silence and waited to hear sister Amalia's familiar humming.

Elena was struck by the distinctive chrome clasp on the suitcase, bearing the letters "C.R." in large characters.

Arthur, possibly influenced by the Latin class he had attended that morning, spent the few minutes they waited in the room wondering if the initials could be those of "Christianus Rex," and if the man who carried them was indeed his messenger.

In due time, a nun appeared through the room's back door. A set of round glasses sat hesitantly on her crooked nose, reluctant to ride it. She looked around her, beginning with the lamp on a nearby side table, as if it were a miracle that it should be lit. The nun looked up from the floor and across the room to the opposite wall before returning her gaze to the folks in front of her with a sense of inevitable disappointment.

'Isn't here Sister Amalia, the archivist?' Elena asked, catching the nun's attention.

'I am Sister Marcela, the new archivist here. Sister Amalia passed into God's mercy just a few weeks ago.' The nun crossed herself and whispered in an acerbic tone: 'God bless her!'

Seeing the shock on the visitor's face, she continued her explanation. It was clear from her tone and body language that this fell outside the bounds of her duties.

'In a short time, she began to weaken. She started off coughing a little bit in the evenings, but it quickly expanded during the rest of her waking hours. Food was carried to her cell, where she remained. A few days later, she was no longer with us.'

Arthur remained silent, scanning the visitor's room as if in quest of an answer. He hadn't noticed until that moment that the group of plants wasn't in their usual spot. Nor was there any sight of the ceramic dish full of sweets.

Sister Amalia couldn't have departed in that way. Her words echoed in his head even now. He felt as though a conversation had abruptly been cut short since he last saw her. Something had been left unsaid. Questions to be posed. Yes, they were indeed in the same sober room the'd been in before, but the fog outside seemed to have completely altered it. Today, neither Remedios Ponciel, the affable administrative advisor, nor Marcos San Lúcar, the former Royal Archives technician were present. Youth was quickly leaving Arthur. He could literally feel it ebbing away from him.

'I need to go out for a bit' Arthur said, and Elena thought she had heard a particular quiver in his voice. Once outside, he looked up at the pointed arch of Santiago Pass, the tiny passageway that led to the Claustrillas, that place where he thought he had seen the figure of a young woman traversing its arches.

He surveyed this place full of peace and secrets. He reflected on the pleasant evenings and walks he had taken there, the friendly glances he had received from of the elderly nun whenever he encountered her in his walks. And that final, peculiar farewell! He appreciated the mist on his face and the crisp, clean air. It seemed as though he were living in a world full with ghosts. That evening, all possibilities appeared to be real. Perhaps their attempts to unravel the monastery's mysteries had earned them the wrath of the monastery's resident ghosts. Had been the professor right when he said that it might be better to just leave the past alone, with all of its mysteries and untold tales?

Memories surfaced of his past evening strolls around these now empty cloisters. Images of him contemplating the columns and door tympanums patiently worked, oblivious to the sinister shadows that winked at him from compromising corners.

His return to the consulting room was met with silence, for which he was grateful. At that that moment, the professor was having a conversation with the out-of-beyond man.

'I just say that sometimes it takes perseverance to achieve something' Lafuente was saying.

'You're probably right and best of luck with that, of course. Although I don't believe that to be the case, you know' replied the man who had not yet finished putting his leather gloves. 'As far as I know, just two permissions to access the physical codices of the archive have been granted in the past eleven years. But you, from what I have seen in your file, have already being here twice in two months' he said with a certain sarcasm.

After a few tense minutes, the mother archivist returned.

Aware that all eyes were on her, she pushed the now-familiar rolling table containing a large book, placing it carefully in front of them.

The visitors, who had already put on their gloves in the meanwhile, approached with reverence to examine its contents.

There it was... The object of their investigations: a large volume roughly 260 by 180 mm in size. Bound in wood, one centimetre thick and covered in fabric.

The musical Codex of Las Huelgas

A large red "B" on the pentagram was the first thing that attracted

Arthur's notice when the professor opened it with reverence and silence under the technician's cautious eye. The ancient notation was surrounded by symbols that resembled little insects tempted by its coppery colour. The initials' reddish and blue tones revealed to the visitors a beauty that left them speechless.

'This is, my friends, the representation of the so-called *Ars Antigua*, the music of antiquity made up of motets, conduits, organum, and sequences,' the professor said in a low voice. 'The only surviving compilation of ancient music that has survived in its original location for over seven centuries.' He lifted his head from the object of his silent examination and cast his gaze from Elena to Arthur. 'All here in nineteen parchment parts.'

When this conversation was taking place, the technician kept a close eye on them, looking at their figures hunched over the codex, the papers, and the forms, constantly hoping to find any loophole that would justify putting a halt to the whole procedure.

Unaware of this concern, the professor examined and compared each pages of the original codex to the facsimile reproductions they held in their hands.

Yes, there was again the marginal Annotation that appeared on some folios,

17): "*Johannes Roderici fecit me*" (18), — Johannes Roderici made me and "*cantat me sin miedo que Johan rodrigues me enmendi*" —sing me without fear that Johan Rodriguez corrects me—, with a slight alteration in the spelling name in the second sentence.

'Nothing less than the equivalent of our contemporary errata! A warning that, should anything go wrong with the composition or the codex, the copyist, making good use of his outstanding craftsmanship, would immediately correct the mess upon being notified of the fact so that everything could move forward.' he said, a grin on his face as he pondered this thought.

Unwillingly, Arthur turned his head to glance at the technician standing nearby. He could find in him no trace of the kindness and warmth shown by his predecessor. This man was indeed a perpetual shadow, as chilly and grey like the mist from which he risen from.

Luckily, after a few frigid minutes, the dreary passage of minutes seemed to be making a dent in his humanity. Tired of the routine examination of the visitors, he must have believed he had already given ample proof both of his competence and professional dedication, for, after observing that the professors and the student were using the gloves and the codex correctly, and concluding he did not need to provide excessive oversight, he relaxed. Grabbing a western novel from one of the inside pockets of his raincoat, he headed towards one of the available seats.

"As long as they don't touch the manuscript too much, everything will be fine," he thought to himself. "What strange people do come to examine the books lately! I will have to speak to Royal Archives about it. You can't just allow anybody", and he proceeded to give a rogue glove a gentle tug as he opened the novel, ready to face an inevitable gunfight in Main St.

'This aspiring mobster from 1930s Hollywood is really getting on my nerves' Arthur said quietly to Elena.

Elena couldn't help but smile in response as she watched the pages with interest. After several hours of scrutinising the codex, Lafuente finally got up and, after looking at his notes, rubbed his eyes, tired of fixing them on the text and the tiny characters.

'I see nothing relevant here' he said in a low, almost whispering voice, biting his upper lip, adding after a few seconds, a little louder this time, 'not this time either.'

'We had no choice, you know. But we had to try,' Elena stated, putting a hand on his shoulder. 'At least, what you claimed about the music was plausible.'

'You see nothing significant either, do you? This is sheer madness. Perhaps we should examine a different manuscript. Despite this, I have a hunch that the answer is here, someplace in Huelgas. I felt it the first time we came.

When the technician heard the professor's new tone, he raised his head; he should have had to demand silence should he persist in it.

'Nothing,' Carlos said 'As far as I can see there are no discrepancies between this document and the facsimile copy. I have carefully examined the characters and the musical notation colouring for any indication of difference, but to no avail. They were right. The original and the Higinio Angles copy are the same.'

'Damn these National Heritage people! In the end, they were right, and everything we've done is useless' Elena whispered.

'There has to be something. Oh my God! There has to be something we've missed.'

'Don't despair, professor. We have at least tried as Elena pointed out', Arthur said, approaching the two of them. 'This time, we certainly tried. But that sentence, that phrase regarding light in the Montanilla manuscript— "at the hour of prima from light shall come light" ... There's nothing here to clarify it either, is there? Not a single clue. It's strange; the totality of the evidence we have found guides us here. But nothing in the entire codex refers, not even distantly, to that phrase or any of the others appearing in the manuscripts.'

The technician sighed as he retrieved the documents he had prepared to finalise the proceedings.

Elena paused for a moment before marking the box next to "consultation carried out" written next to her name on the form. When she was done, she handed it back to the silent man who folded it with deliberate and professional motions, stowing it in the bag he always carried around with ill-concealed satisfaction.

After closing it, he pulled out a handkerchief and rubbed the metal clasps until they had the desired level of brilliance he liked them to offer.

'Well, that's all then. If there is anything else you may require, please do not hesitate to contact us,' he said with a polite cough. A small puff of frigid air emanated from his mouth as he said this.

But his gaze showed hope that this circumstance would not recur in the near or far future.

The man in the raincoat walked away from the cloister much like and MI5 official after a quick debriefing with his superior.

The archivist nun looked askance at him, before putting on her specs and making her way towards the door that led to the archive, the codex on the tray.

Only the three friends remained in that place, surrounded by the sleek, modern filing cabinets.

Nobody ventured to speak to end the day.

Except by the faint illumination from some candles in the room, only the dim light penetrating through the stained-glass windows and the nearby cloister remained.

'By the way,' said the nun, turning to the professor and the young man, 'I nearly forgot, 'Does anyone of you go by the name of Arthur?'

When Arthur gasped, betraying his identity, the archivist approached him with confidence and a bowed head.

'A few days before her passing, Mother Amalia requested that, should you come here again, I was to show you one of the monastery's ancient writings for your perusal. She told me you might find some interest in the same as a kind of curiosity.'

'The truth is that in light of today's developments...' Lafuente said, eager for the visit to end.

'Wait a sec, professor, if you don't mind. I would very much like to see that book, sister' Arthur exclaimed, feeling his heart rate increase.'

How had Sister Amalia anticipated their return to the abbey?

'This is incredible!' Elena said, looking from one to the other. 'They offer us a manuscript without even asking for it.'

For what seemed like an age, the three of them stood silently waiting.

'Please come this way!' said the archivist mother, appearing again and making a sign with her right hand.

They were on the verge of doing so when the nun's gesture stopped them in their tracks.

'No! Sister Amalia specified quite plainly that only Arthur should pass,' she added, looking at the young man in a tone that admitted no reply, 'please proceed to the parlour next door.'

Arthur complied and followed the archivist nun into a smaller chamber.

It was impossible to make out anything in the room at first glance.

There was a table in the corner opposite the entrance and, placed next to it, he noticed a curious book covered in dark skin and protected by a sheet of paper. A lonely lamp was its only companion. Its shadows had initially prevented him from seeing the book. On top of it was a little, circular object that he could not identify due to the near-total darkness of the place.

A small square-shaped object.

A sweet.

He opened the package. The title of the volume brought a grin to the face of young man, *Codex Arturicus*. The late Sister Amalia's prank on him from beyond the dead was not lost on him.

He observed the wrapping protecting the book. It wasn't a regular paper, to say the least. There were some carefully calligraphed characters inscribed on the brown paper.

Arthur could barely distinguish them in the dim light.

He drew the lamp closer to him. He could read then the text written on the small piece of paper.

Just five words.

"Quis davit capiti meo aquam."

And a little further down, on the bottom line,

"Let there be light."

Nothing more.

That reference to light again.

What had Sister Amalia meant?

He felt like Professor Lafuente, lost in a sea of possibilities, clues, and dead ends that closed as soon as he stepped through the doors that led to them.

As he walked to meet his friends, he thought back on the elderly nun's parting words to him.

"There's something in you that shines. I've seen it in the professor as well, but you're the one who will understand the truth. The truth that no one else can perceive."

Sitting in the consulting room, he looked up at the white ceiling with its central stripe, pondering the laborious work it represented, the hours of work that went into creating the intricate pattern of lines and arabesques that adorned it.

Exactly the right allegory for their current predicament.

How was that other phrase in the initial manuscripts? Yes, it was one of his favourite phrases: "Whoever wants to see a different letter in God will see it". He loved the uncomplicated poetry, the sense of destiny and of predestination and, of course, of adventure that seemed to permeate it, hidden behind the door. Did this have anything to do with the remarks of the mother archivist?

'The truth is, Sister Amalia' he murmured to himself, 'is that should I be chosen for something, it will surely be to have the biggest headache in history.'

∾

CHAPTER 36

ARTHUR GETS SLEEPY

How dozing off can sometimes reawaken the yearning for conversation and social life.

Two shafts of light entered Professor Lafuente's study through the partially closed windows. Skewed, like two flashlights searching for an interesting book to read, investigating slowly and carefully, first the shelves, and then, after carefully perusing them, daring to fall onto the table and floor.

The carpet was appreciative of the interest provided by these sun rays which only visited it a few minutes per day.

Arthur was snoozing in the velvet upholstered armchair placed next to the motley bookcase, his favourite, taking advantage of the absence of the professor, being exhausted after a long day of document scanning and filing. That armchair would be his undoing someday.

His awakening coincided with that mystical violet hour, that enchanted time in which appearances can be deceiving. He blinked his eyes around, still not sure where he was. No, these were not his digs to be sure—there were no posters or a paddle on the wall facing his bed.

The old inkwell on the desk appeared, pierced by light to be holding liquid fire, an alchemic fire.

The paintings peered warily about the room making sure no one was sneaking into the study at that time to take a book without permission. In another picture, the clad marquis occupying the bottom left corner behind the bureau, and the couple of peasants standing next to it with a cart by the river shared the same attentive disposition.

Arthur stared in awe at the floating specks of dust that stretched, weightless in those rays of sunlight. These rays had betrayed their relentless movement by searching the floor, the furniture, and the books. Dust was nothing more than time materialised. More than any other factor, dust exemplified the passage of time wearing down and eventually destroying everything.

Pierced by the evening light.

The light moved with balletic grace. At times, it appeared to repent and climb back up, as if to deceive the spectator, before eventually falling, over the Ortega y Gasset books, the globe on the windowsill, and the spear-wielding warrior, with the same treatment, without distinctions for any of these objects.

Arthur noticed a few specks of the same dust particles had began to settle upon his black shoes.

The library, the old black chairs, the porcelain dogs, and the countless books that surrounded him seemed different.

"What has changed?" his rational mind wondered, mulling over the situation, attempting to resist an overwhelming sense of unease.

The ray of sunshine.

The light falling on the window sill and from there to the carpet, illuminating it.

Before him, a cloud of dust drifted. Illuminated. Revealed in its darkness and silence. Invisible until that very moment.

He remembered something that had been striving to emerge from

his mind's deepest dependencies. Up till now. That Latin phrase they
had first read in the Silos manuscripts,

"At the time of prima, from light will come light"

The sentence never went away from his head.

He felt he was on the verge of something. Then, barely able to
finish evolving that thought, he rose to his feet, overcome by a weird
anxiety and eagerness. He needed to find professor Lafuente and
Elena right away. Where would they be at that time?

He recalled they had mentioned something about going for a
walk near the Greek temple.

Indeed, there they were, idling away the time before their
evening classes. They had stopped by the stunning monopter next to
a massive clump of the professor's favourite plant, the strikingly
colourful Japanese bamboo, (also known as Nandina), with its distinct
scarlet tones and green hues. A plant that defiantly held out against
the frost. The leafless willows appeared envious, their branches
swaying in dialogue with the wind, chatting about the event.

'Professor! Professor!' Arthur shouted as he advanced, his scarf
flapping in the air in danger of being lost. 'Professor, do you recall
what you told me a few days ago? Regarding trusting my gut?'

'Yes, certainly. What of it? You don't tell me you have come
running here just to tell us that.'

'The moment has come. I've got one of those damn things.'

'And what's the matter this time?' Lafuente answered, attempting
once more to follow the ins and outs of Arthur's mind.

'I think it's best not to break the magic by explaining it. It would
ruing the mystery, if such it is. I still have my doubts, anyway.
However, we need to take another look at the Musical Codex.'

Lafuente raised his gaze to make sure the sky wasn't falling on
their heads.

'But we have seen the damned thing thoroughly, Arthur, inside
and out if you please! We have compared it to the existing facsimile.
Haven't we? Even that folio the archivist mother left you. So what do
you want to do? Return to the monastery for the umpteenth time to

examine the red tape? I'm not interested, thanks very much. I would rather enter a convent myself.'

'It's true, professor. We've seen it. but not in the right way. The way it must be seen.'

'And how else is it to be seen? Upside down?'

'You grant us access to the codex once more, and I will prove it to you.'

'Royal Archives will not be pleased about it. They will not permit us to view the codex again, whether for love or money. Our recent acquaintance in the grey raincoat made it quite plain before joining the rest of the men in black.'

'Don't forget to mention the gloves he was wearing,' Elena pointed out solicitously, following the sly tone of her friend.

'Yes, everything you say it's true,' said Arthur. 'We can't accomplish anything through the official channels, but perhaps we could have access using other channels.'

'What other channels are there? Entering under the cover of darkness at night, you mean?'

'Professor, please lay off the irony. It doesn't fit you. The nuns, as everyone knows have full access to the archives and can look over any files they see necessary for managing the remaining assets in their care, correct?'

'They cannot bypass the rules, Arthur! Not for you, nor for anybody else. That is undeniable. Damn the day I urged you to trust your instincts!'

However, something about the young man's demeanour and the intensity with which he had spoken made it difficult for the professor to refuse his plea.

'Well, let me know should you get anything fresh,' Arthur finally said, taking his request for granted and running away with his knapsack on his back. 'I must go now to the inn at the abbey.'

'The Abbey Inn? What have you missed there?' the professor called out after him.

'Let's say it's part of the investigation.' said Arthur, turning slightly as he went. 'One of those things every researcher must pursue to the end.' And after saying this, he rounded the corner and was no longer in sight.

'Is everybody going to speak to me in riddles the whole day? It serves me right for having discussed steganography!' said a confused Lafuente.

Arthur was again at Huelgas Monastery. This time inside the Huelgas Inn itself.

He was awaiting the arrival of Sister Carmen, the mother caretaker. He had read about her special calling, how she had joined the monastic order of her own free will, leaving behind her life as a mother and grandmother.

While he waited, he approached the church. As he did so, he could once again hear choir chanting emanating from within those walls. He felt as though he had returned to his old school again, his teacher about to emerge from a concealed nook to review his latest exams. These stones and musical notes spoke to him, especially of the past. They grew, rose, and rotated in the chapel's roof. Professor Lafuente was right. Thanks to the marvel of musical notation, the very same notes that someone had written centuries before were now being reproduced. He listened to the nuns' choir sing the ancient hymn from the benches intended for visitors and residents of the inn. From this vantage point, this bench was like a kind of telescope that would allow to look into the past.

'Good evening, young man! How may I be of assistance?' asked Sister Carmen with energy as she entered the dining area of the inn where Arthur was having a white coffee. She appeared to be on the verge of moving all the chairs aside and setting them face down on the tables in preparation for sweeping and scrubbing the entire room.

'Good evening, sister Carmen. We spoke on the phone last week, remember?'

'Oh, the young investigator, huh?' The mother beamed. 'How is everything going?'

'Well, sister, not very well. You see, I don't want to abuse your trust, but...'

'Wait, please!' said Sister Carmen, interrupting him with a kind gesture. 'Before you ask me any questions, you must understand that we cannot breach our closure rule and that we have several limitations.'

'Don't fret. I understand. By the by, I read that you entered the monastery after becoming a widow. Is that right?'

'Yes, that's true' the nun replied with a big smile in response to the candour with which the question had been asked. 'After my husband passed away, I entered the old monastery. I've been blessed with children and grandchildren. I can claim I have lived a joyful life. Believe me. I had been to Huelgas many times before with my family'—she looked around her with a grateful look, 'but nothing could have prepared me for the fact that I would end my days here, devoted to others and carrying out a duty that gives me great pleasure.'

Arthur smiled. By observing the woman's motions and the manner in which Sister Carmen organised the breakfast tables and chairs while conversing, he knew without words that such was the case.

'On occasion, my kids and grandkids come to see me. Every time this occurs, they ask whether I have reconsidered my position, whether I have changed my mind, if I've become "reasonable", I suppose' said she, laughing and gazing out the window,' as if the outside world were that wise! Don't you think so? And then, after staying with me or spending a week or two on vacation at the inn, they leave with another opinion. Closer to Christ, I guess. Closer to their inner peace for those who are not believers.'

'Mother, how well acquainted were you with Sister Amalia?' Arthur pointed bravely.

'Sister Amalia and I cultivated a small garden at the abbey. One used to finish in the evening what the other left unfinished in the morning. That is if she was not telling jokes or eating those disgusting sweets that she ate at all hours.'

She looked up at the sky accusingly, crossed her arms, and said, 'Now I'm afraid I'll have to do it all by myself.'

'Well, I would like to ask you a very simple thing. And that is, could you persuade Mother Abbess to let us view the archives once more? I'm aware you have an excellent relationship with her. We would like at least to have the chance to speak with her in private.'

'Oh, goodness me! Good relationships between us are not subjected to the use or achievement of personal goals. You ought to know that. Mother Abbess has been extremely busy and in poor health as of late. As you are already aware the National Heritage staff are currently in charge of all matters pertaining to the monastery archives.'

'I apologise if I appeared to you a bit daring. Allow me to explain myself. Sister Amalia left me a somewhat peculiar message to the care of the current archivist mother. I have a vague notion of what it could represent, but I need to consult with the abbess first. As the monastery head, I guess she may know or have an inkling of what Sister Amalia wanted to tell me.'

'Did you say a message? May I look at it?' Sister Carmen said with genuine curiosity.

'Yes, I don't see why not' said Arthur carefully extracting from his blazer the note containing the bizarre message.

'You're right, boy' she said after reading it, a bewildered expression on her face. For a split second, the woman's face seemed to cycle through a spectrum of emotions, gradually darkening and lighting as if under the influence of a faulty light bulb that randomly and partially would illuminate the items underneath as it blinked. 'You must certainly speak with Mother Abbess. However, I shall not reveal her what I've read on this piece of paper. You will be able to inform her on your own. Listen, I know what I'm saying. Is this your phone number? I'll try to talk to her when she leaves the refectory. If she agrees to receive you, I'll call you!'

The sister hurried along the back hall, waving her hands to either side, leaving a confused Arthur at the inn's entrance.

The tolling of the bells could be heard coming from the tower. The same sound as centuries ago? Probably not; More likely the ancient bells had been replaced by some recording or other. Simpler to use and control.

Arthur had somewhat neglected his attire while talking to the nun. His cherished scarf hung unevenly over the front of his jumper, but he wasted no time fixing it this time.

This time, he knew what to do.

CHAPTER 37

A TALK IN THE GARDEN

Carlos Lafuente and Mother Abbess take a stroll
through St Ferdinand's Cloister.

It was the morning after Laudy's visit, and Carlos had come to see Mother Abbess. He was alone. Following his directions, his companions had been kept waiting in front of Teresa Bar, where they had parked previously.

He had to do this by himself, just like one of the characters in those films he liked so much.

He was uncertain about his purpose in being there. What did he plan to tell Mother Abbess? That one of his postgraduate students had an insight that he hadn't dared to develop? Indeed, he couldn't say that, but the alternative wasn't any better either. Because the truth was, he had never as lost as he was now.

'Don't forget to tell her what I mentioned, Professor' had been Arthur's last words.

Carlos had been waiting a long time in that parlour, already so familiar to him, when a little nun approached.

'Please follow me, sir. Mother Abbess is waiting for you.'

Mother Abbess leaned back in her office chair and surveyed in detail the person in front of her through her thick glasses, as if the professor had proposed entering the monastery as a novice rather than requesting specific information about documents stored in it. Not in vain. This was the second time she had him in her office.

Behind her lay a few books on a tiny shelf. A bright, full-colour cookbook by the famed chef Karlos Arguinano, lay unexpectedly, next to an old, covered Bible, trying to pass unnoticed. They shared shelf space with the writings of St Teresa. A bit further to its right, he noticed several tapes bearing the famous chef's name on their side, stacked atop an ancient Panasonic VHS player.

'What can I say?' she asked, noticing the professor's gaze on these objects. 'One has to go with the times; that is true. Although in my particular case, it takes as long for things to enter our life as it does for them to go. I know, of course, that maybe other devices, other inventions, might suit my interests better than this one, but I'm not the kind to change overnight, that much is certain.'

Before continuing, Sister Irene seemed to recall Sister Carmen's words and the purpose of this visit.

'What exactly are you looking for this time, professor?' she asked after this introduction. 'Keep in mind that I have only agreed to meet you just at Sister Carmen's request. She is an example to us all. She has done a great deal for this community. I thought I already told you everything I had to say last time.'

Carlos stared directly at the abbess before speaking:

'I am aware that you have discretionary access to the monastery's archives relating to the properties it still retains for its logical private use. We would like to examine the Musical Codex again' and at this point he closed his eyes for a brief moment. 'The people at Royal Archives have denied our doing so. However, we believe there may be something in there that we were unable to notice with the naked eye in the examination we carried out' he said, barely containing the urge to close his eyes as he used to do as a child to avoid seeing his interlocutor's reaction.

'I'm surprised by your asking so professor. As you just stated, access is for our exclusive use only. I cannot grant access to any material in the archives without express authorisation of National Heritage or Royal Archives. Should any of the stored documents in it get damaged or misused as a result it would be a tremendous responsibility for us. Particularly, and please do not take office, Professor, the Musical Codex should not be handled lightly. I believe you have already had many opportunities to examine it.'

Mother Abbess glanced seriously at her interlocutor before continuing:

'Moreover, there is one thing I would like to clarify for you. The purpose of the walls surrounding convents and this monastery in particular is not to isolate us from the outside world, as is commonly believed or thought by the world at large. Instead, they were built so that this very world would not enter them. I trust that you, as a university professor, can appreciate the subtle difference. We are the ones who choose what part of that world we want to enter here. God gave us free will to choose the life we wanted to live, among other things. This may be perceived by others as irresponsibility or laziness. Still, from our perspective, the burden of our responsibilities is already boundless. Believe me. Life itself is full of secret designs.'

Unable to contain his excitement any longer, Carlos stood up from his seat.

'Secrets! Secrets!' he yelled 'Ever since I started looking into this, I've found nothing but indirect references. Of all kinds! Well done, medium and rare! From the peculiar way of watering the monastery's plants to a recipe dating from mediaeval times, everything is mysterious, secretive, unfathomable, esoteric! I would go so far as to say that the original motivation for many of them remaining hidden has been lost to history. Nobody remembers what was kept that way anymore, and even if they do, what was the purpose of preserving them in the first place!'

The abbess looked at this man, who seemed to have gone mad.

'Sorry, mother, but've been subjected under a lot of stress lately,' Lafuente stated, as he looked at the floor, realising his untimely departure. He took a few mechanical and indecisive steps that took him away from the chair he had been sitting in. Then, he returned to his interlocutor, his long arms dangling from his sides.

'What I don't understand is your concern for an old legend, for an uncorroborated theory' the abbess replied, partly recovered.

'I won't be a great believer, that's the truth' Lafuente said, waving his left arm like he used to do in class. 'Possibly, I never have been. But I think I once was. And do you know something? As I understood it then, I do not believe that faith should belong to a single group of people, entrusted to a select few. What I remember most about those years is mainly the references to the goodness of man and the ethical responsibility of the human race, that kind of thing. They talked to me about something different. I believe that in this case, we should be more concerned about the memory and suffering of that lonely, forgotten, and frightened young woman who arrived in Spain with her sincere desire—and I don't think it was nothing related at all in this politically correct world of ours, to the construction or not of a chapel to St Olaf or St Ataulfo or the latter's mother, may God forgive me!'

The abbess remained mute. She seemed tired already of this man, who had disrupted both her daily routine and her morning walk. A man who gesticulated and spoke loudly in her office! Still, she perceived something in his tone, infused with conviction and fervour, that left her magnetised drawn to his words and the movement of his arms.

'Come with me,' she said after a moment's hesitation. 'I must carry some things to the administration building. If you don't mind, we might continue our conversation as we walk through the galleries. I believe a little walk will be beneficial for both of us.'

'We should care more,' the professor said once they had left the office and passed under the Knights' Arch, 'why she wanted such a chapel built. I believe the underlying reason was that she realised she had sinned and failed her father in the duty he had entrusted her with. But not just him, if my reasoning is sound! She had left the man she loved behind her, in her native Norway in order to fulfil a diplomatic mission of sorts. The same kind of sacrifice that years, centuries later, the current empress of Japan, Masako Owada, had to make by marrying Prince Haito against her will as a descendent of the Shogun dynasty. But there's more. If what I think is right, if my theory is accurate, the princess also left under the monastery's care, what she most wanted, a newborn baby. You know it, I know it too. I had that certainty again today as soon as I entered here, as soon as I heard the choir singing, the voices rising and falling from the chapel's vaults. And you are aware of it as well! What are we going to do now? What are we going to do with that knowledge? That's my doubt. That's my question. But what difference does it make now? We already have St. Olaf's Chapel... the brotherhood among the peoples, and all that. Why worry, sister? Why bother? The monastery is already part of sacred history, art, the human and the divine. There is nothing more to do. The ancients did it all, didn't they?'

'Please, professor, don't blaspheme, I beg you.'

'Excuse me, sister. I've had a bad day. A poor year, I could say. That's all. I was going to say a terrible life as well, but I admit there, that would be overdoing it a little bit, even for an agnostic.'

Carlos realised that their conversation had lead them to one end of St Ferdinand's Cloister. A dark made of dark wood in the background seemed to symbolise everything the monastery had been hiding within. How cruel, however, was the light filtering through the upper arches! It projected itself on the floor, on the pointed ceiling, giving the whole complex a magical aura! Was the building, on the one hand, tempting him, discouraging him from accessing one of his most well held secrets, while, on the other hand, inciting him to keep hope? He remembered the typical phrase any practising believer would typically say to him at that moment: that God was testing him. 'Fuck it!' thought Lafuente, following the sceptical answer of our present time.

'Well, professor, I am truly sorry, but we must part ways here. I am sorry I could not have been of greater assistance to you.' said the abbess, ending the conversation as they reached the opposite end of the cloister.

'Mother, I beg you, hold on for a sec, if you please!' Carlos said as he remembered the scrap of paper Arthur had handed him earlier but which he had forgotten about in the thick of the conversation.

'Yes, my son? What is the matter now?'

'Does the phrase *"At the hour of prima, from light, will come light"* ring a bell?' said the professor as he handed over the small piece of paper.

Carlos had the impression that a cloud, a veil, or a curtain had passed over Sister Ines's face, but if it did, it must have been extremely brief because when he paid closer attention, Sister Ines's gaze was as vacant as it had been previously. The nun lowered her head in response, shaking it, and heading towards the dark wooden door at the back.

Carlos Lafuente retraced his steps, watching how the tips of his shoes hit the pavement. One step after the other. Something mechanical, concrete, and predictable, about which any speculation was vain and superfluous.

As he crossed the Claustrillas, ready to retreat towards the exit, he heard a curious sound behind him.

It was a queer one, similar to a tinkerbell.

Intrigued, he turned his head.

He was surprised to see a nun coming briskly in his direction.

It was Mother Abbess. The noise he had heard had been produced by the rosary she carried in her left hand, not unlike that other sisters in God would have used in a college, when intent upon calling the attention of a reprobate student who had skipped class. It dawned on him that what he had taken to be a weird sound was nothing more than the method the holy mother had found to get someone's attention without raising her voice too much.

Carlos stopped short.

'Wait, I have a question for you before you leave,' she said as he caught up with him.

'Whatever you say, mother.'

'Why do you care so much about Princess Kristina—and that story about an alleged offspring?'

'Mother ...' the professor began, ready to argue once more about the historical benefits of knowing the truth and the responsibility he felt as a historian and scientist. However, just as he was on the verge of opening his mouth, he appeared to change his mind. 'Look, I believe that woman suffered. She endured great suffering for that child she was carrying in her womb. Neither you nor I can do anything but guess how much. But something had to make the abbess of that time long past be moved by her. I am only guessing, of course, but she had to break her oath, the protocol of the order, and everything that were regarded as holy at the time. I believe that we all owe them some respect. Don't you think that everyone of us should compensate in some way for the wrongs done by history to our ancestors? We know nothing about her. True, but who actually knows anything about other people? We couldn't do anything for her since neither you nor I existed then. However, here we are, you and me, aren't we? In most cases, we can do little to avoid the suffering of others, but we can do a certain type of justice, if not divine, God forbid! historical, at least. I do believe we are united to her through time, through history. Perhaps if we knew more about what happened, we would be able to pay some kind of tribute by taking some sort of action. Say it's my discipline if you want to, or what the hell, but I do not believe history should be nothing more than water filtered through the past.'

And at this point he halted, unwilling to continue, overcome by his own words and astonished by his own rhetoric. The burden of history seemed to fall heavily upon him at that moment.

The abbess remained silent. She extended her hand and touched the professor's arm. He looked at her.

The nun had a curious expression on her face. It had something unique on it. Something that hadn't been there before.

'Come with me.' she said.

Mother Abbess was sitting in her office once more. The Christ statuette on the table cast a shadow that seemed to envelop her. The nun's eyes, those light green eyes now that she was not wearing spectacles, appeared livelier than ever, as she looked from one of her interlocutors to the other, seemingly looking for the right words.

Elena and Arthur were also there, sitting silently on either side of the professor, after having waited expectantly for an hour the result of the conversation with the abbess.

Arthur, in particular, felt something momentous was about to take place, and he held his breath fiddling nervously with his scarf, knotting and untying it.

'Since I accepted the abbess position, I have always known that there was more to my duties than what I had been taught—something else I would discover one day. Please don't ask me what it was right now. I wouldn't know what to answer, but it certainly wasn't like in films or books. Not a single bird sang to me from a tree branch or anything like that. Not even a little bush in the garden from which a voice would emerge. Living within these walls steeped in history has a peculiar effect, as you can imagine. We sisters know by keeping silence among these walls to interpret it as if it were a dialogue, rich in sounds and nuances. After countless hours walking through the cloisters, we learn to decipher the inscriptions on its walls and the now-closed, ancient doors leading to the church. Sister Amalia must have made a particular reading of this young student of yours to give him that note, that's for certain,' she added, staring at Arthur with interest.

She leaned back in the high-backed chair and gazed at the crucifix to her left for a time.

After this little pause, the abbess resumed her tale:

'Long ago, when I was praying one evening in the St. Domingo cloister after my daily walk and shortly after assuming office, one of the older sisters approached me. A sister who was already in the community when I arrived as a novice. They all held her in high regard as a holy woman who had lived practically her entire life within these walls. As we gazed at the garden fountain, she spoke to me for the first time about the monastery's secret with the utmost simplicity, as if she were discussing the condition of the garden or the monthly account balance. I shall never forget the exact location in front of us, precisely between these two columns. She never referred to it in any other way: "The secret of the monastery" and, perhaps—

should a sister be especially witty and daring—, as "the secret of the
north." One morning, the morning of your first arrival, she came to
me after leaving the consulting room and informed me, in a tense
tone, and with a trembling I had never seen in her before, that the
time had for the monastery to open up. To open up in the most intimate of the senses. The burden that had been carried in silence for
centuries—continually fearing that it might be forgotten as yet
another legend among the stories in the great tapestry of human
drama—should be lifted.'

'That's excellent, but it doesn't get us any closer to the solution,'
Arthur remarked, cutting off the abbess mid-confession.

Elena was going to say something, but Carlos raised his left hand.

'Sorry Elena, but if the boy has an intuition, it's better that he
should pursue it. Please go on, Arthur!

'Excuse me, mother,' Arthur continued. This reverend's mother
was Sister Amalia. Am I right?'

"Yes, that's right, you guessed correctly.' she said, smiling broadly
at Arthur.

'And did you believe her?' Now it was up to the professor to
interrupt...

'In a nutshell, no, not at all. Not at first, anyway. Age had taken
its toll on Sister Amalia, and her oddities were well known. It is one
thing to read about God's miracles and another is to contemplate
being near one. As a novice, one learns not to desire the role of leader,
but rather to be a member of the group and contribute to everyday
tasks. For generations, the secret had been passed down from abbess
to abbess, and maybe to a second, trusted sister should the abbess
become ill or pass away before passing on the necessary instructions.
Then, as you know, we experienced the invasion of Napoleonic
forces, the Mendizábal seizure, the Carlist War, and the Civil War,
all within a short span of time considering the monastery's long
history. And of course, to top it all off, the devastating fact for this
community, as you know, was that, beginning with the Council of
Trent, the "forever" powers the abbey had possessed since its foundation were irretrievably lost. Not to mention that, under Pius IX, t the

abbesses' privileged authority was eliminated. What I learned then was nothing more than a legend. There was no evidence supporting this. At least not until you showed me this afternoon that scrap of paper, professor, until I saw this young man's face.'

'And that was...?'

'The only thing I was able to determine with any certainty is that there was some kind of hidden message written in some unknown key in the musical codex, as you suspected, but the manner in which it should have been read was somehow lost along the way. I suppose that, as time passed, Dona María Dolores de Agüero, the abbess who commissioned Johannes Rodrigues, or Roderick, to make the Codex in 1325, may have feared that the word-of-mouth approach employed thus far was insufficient to assure its transfer as time passed. Therefore, over time, I assume they began to believe it was one of those bizarre, senseless mediaeval tales,' said the mother abbess, with a gesture of frustration that someone less informed than them would have failed to detect. 'We liked to refer to the so-called secret as a divine gift, the kind of gift mentioned so frequently in the Bible and sacred books, but which occurs infrequently in real life. As such, the only thing I can tell you, professor, is that, as you said, the Codex contains something. Still, on what part of it is to be found, what it consists of, where it is hidden, what it comprises, and how it should be read, I cannot tell you, except that it is related in one way or another to the offspring of Princess Kristina.'

'You stated as much, Mother Abbess. Only it's not just a matter of how to read it,' Arthur said unexpectedly, standing up.

Everyone looked at him with surprise, except the abbess, who was already accustomed to people abruptly rising from their seats.

'I daresay it's more a question of where and when to read it,' Arthur said.

Carlos and Elena leaned their bodies forward unconsciously, full of curiosity. The professor's eyes had widened, and his eyebrows were raised, as if he was witnessing the movement of one of the statues in the old pile or the very Queen Eleanor herself emerging from her coffin.

Mother Abbess leaned in close, too.

'Don't you see it? We must see it in the right place!' the student continued, turning to the professor with a triumphant smile. 'Yesterday, I figured out the how, and I believe I now know where that place should be, professor. I think I know the right place.'

'The right place?' Lafuente said.

'Can't you guess, professor?' Arthur said, looking at his watch.

A quarter to five.

He looked at Mother Abbess now.

'Sister, the stained-glass windows that are preserved in the chapter house haven't been in that place all these centuries, have they?'

'No, son, they were not installed in the chapter house until 1965.'

'That is all! According to what I have learned, they were placed there for reasons that were never revealed. Oh, one more detail that might seem irrelevant: what is the date today?'

'Nineteen, why?'

'Just as I guessed, allow me a moment, please,' muttered Arthur, looking at his watch.

A quarter to five.

He opened the notebook he had on his knees and, after consulting his mobile, raised his head with a particular glitter in his eyes.

There was no time to lose.

'We must all of us be early risers on the 21st and be in the Monastery's Chapter house by 8:00 a.m. And of course, '—he said here, looking at the abbess with an enigmatic smile—,' bring the Codex and a small table or lectern to support it. We should move soon. Do you think it would be possible?'

In the hush that followed Arthur's words, one could have heard heels click into place, standing at attention. Yet, none of those present dared to challenge the reasoning or intentions of the young man Sister Amalia had her eye on one day.

Soon, there was going to be light.

ELENA'S SMILE

CHAPTER 38

THE LIGHT OF SAINT JOHN

In the Prime hour from light will come light

It was Monday, December 21st.

The hour, seven o'clock a.m.

They were in the chapter house.

"Of course" said Arthur to himself with a nervous smile.

The chapter house was a vast, almost empty space they had crossed numerous times before and paid only cursory attention to, filled as it usually was always with tour groups in pursuit of a guide.

Now, amid the solitude and stillness, after having crossed the flared access door with pointed arches carved with saw teeth, the stained-glass windows seemed to speak in their own voice. The four columns that distributed that space endowed the place with solemnity, making it look like a stage.

There were only five people present at that early hour. They were three researchers accompanied by Mother Abbess and the archivist mother.

The stained-glass windows seemed to contemplate the scene from the top—elegant figures above the divine and the human. A bit lower down, the portraits of the abbesses, Dona Ana de Austria and

Dona Antonia Jacinta de Navarra, also regarded the scene with solemnity, especially the first of the two.

The knowledge that some of the nuns shown in those paintings were buried beneath their feet made a strange impression on them.

At that early hour, the light was still weak and grey.

The vault ribs above branched out from their ring-shaped bases. "Corbels," Arthur remember the name automatically, congratulating himself on his knowledge in matters of art.

On a wooden platform facing the chairs in the centre, the nuns had placed a small table. On this and following Arthur's instructions the Musical Codex had been carefully placed, opened to a specific page.

Arthur observed the amazing stained-glass windows, sleeping, shining even at this darkened hour. A hazy light was gathering insensibly behind them. Had he been wrong in his intuition?

He checked his watch. If everything turned out as expected, barely a few minutes remained for something to occur—only a few minutes.

The Codex had been placed in front of the chair allocated for Mother Abbess when, in ancient times, this had presided over chapters in that very chamber. The present one did not lose a single movement or preparations of the young man who was moving to and fro with assurance about the room, as if he should have been rehearsing the moment quite in advance.

He was observing the tapestries that lined both ends of the room. The central columns resembled a canopy supporting the ceiling.

"From light, will come light," Arthur repeated to himself over and over. This must be the place. He felt it that way. But the *precise* location?

'Mother, I've read that the *Armariolum,* the space where the reading and meditation books used to be stored had been here somewhere, right?'

The look of the abbess towards one of the walls, was answer enough. He retraced his steps, looking again at the pictures of the abbesses placed atop the chairs, presiding over the room. The four images seemed to look at him from above, resembling an end-of-term jury as he read his thesis. Would the moment be like this in his own case? He felt, looking at that kind of holy throne, a sort of calm growing inside him, doubts dissipating. 'You know it, don't you, reverend mothers?' Arthur said in a low, almost respectful tone. Anne of Austria seemed especially complicit under that light and at that hour.

Arthur looked at his watch once again. It was seventeen minutes past seven.

The Prima Hour.

He recalled popular imagination used to refer to this part of the day as "the magic hour."

Another confirmation of his theory?

Finally, with extreme slowness, a cluster of light seemed to charge itself behind the red area of the stained glass, filling it, overflowing it.

Arthur's gaze shifted then to the one presiding over the central space. Within it, the figure of St John stood out from the rest. A cloud of light was already behind the reddish halo around his head. The figure's eyes seemed to look backwards, trying to ascertain its origin. The young man lowered his gaze toward the portraits of the abbesses, all of them now secret and silent partners in the secret. For a second, he thought they were smiling.

Arthur remained still, uncertain, looking forward, letting his gaze rest on the chairs, or at least on the spot where most of the abbesses would have sat long ago, one after the other, celebrating the chapters of the order, administering lands, property, tithes, ecclesiastical and civil laws. Presiding as monarchs over this small kingdom.

Had he erred in his estimation of the time? Was this, after all, the right place? And ultimately, was his theory one more insanity of his?

A sudden thought entered his head.

"Johann will fix it."

So fast, he had no time to analyse it.

'Mother, professor, Elena, please help me to place the Codex under the St John window, right where I am, quickly!'

Excited by the young man's words, raising no questions, the book and the lectern where promptly placed where he had instructed.

After doing this, all of them looked up. They had the impression the figure of St John had been waiting for that very moment. More likely, it was the light above his head who did for, at that very moment, like a focused wake, it passed through the miraculous red crown of holiness, falling on the chapter house floor and over the place the Codex was, falling relentlessly on its open pages, resembling a divine ray revealing the truth.

Arthur approached with hesitant steps. He walked toward the Codex. Carlos and Elena stood respectfully one step behind him, all their faith put in their young companion. They both craved for and feared what the book might contain. Maybe nothing. Maybe another failure.

Arthur was standing before the Codex. Silent as if the sun beam had transformed him in a salt statue.

His companions exchanged glances.

'Arthur,' the professor remarked in a shaky voice, not daring to approach. 'Is there anything?'

He did not appear to have been heard by the student, hunched over the Codex, his eyes narrowed, apparently reading something.

Unable to contain their curiosity any longer, Elena and Carlos mooed forward. Mother Abbess followed suit.

There, next to one of the large illuminated red letters that had first drawn the young man's attention the first time he put his eyes on the Codex, stood a phrase in pale characters.

They recognised the familiar heading of the dispatches issued by the Huelgas Abbess since ancient times,

"We Dona ... by the grace of God and of the Holy Apostolic See, Abbess of the Royal Monastery of Las Huelgas, near the city of Burgos, Order of the Cistercian,"

The sentence was followed by a long list of titles that strained the eyes and patience of the reader.

They proceeded reading that lengthy protocolary phrase, turning frantically the page in search of the following lines.

There it was, a little further down,

"I command that the offspring of Princess Kristina, born in this Nativity, be protected and raised in a family with local roots, at The Golden Mount, and under the watchful eye of the Lord and the guardianship of this cloister. Amen"

Nothing more.

He reread it.

It couldn't be true.

Finally.

After months and months of research.

Only a brief paragraph summarising the entire search.

Just a few letters, a few words, yet so loaded with meaning!

Here they were. In full view of the world: the instructions clearLy indicated as Trevelyan had said and Lafuente had pointed out with his steganography theory.

After the first seconds of shock, Elena took photographs of the newly discovered text in order to document the discovery. The professor, his hand still quivering, dared to turn a few more pages of the Codex among the silence of those around him.

The light that continued falling on the Codex was creating subtle brown outlines between the lines closest to the opening capital letter. Then, like in Isabela's developing room—the professor's friend of yestersummer—, the silhouettes became more pronounced, more defined, joining one another, showing at first only an ant-like line of spots, only to reveal their full profile a few seconds later.

Another text appeared on the page, written in a different letter, only by a short phrase:

"The Virgin Mary, sits in her temple, purified by the sun."

An hour later and after having left Mother Abbess in a state of total stress and the Codex in a safe place, the three of them sat at a table in Teresa's tavern. This group differed significantly from the one that had formed in that very place long ago. The cheerful faces, beer mugs, and the glass of wine in Elena's hand were a stark contrast to that day.

'Do you know Arthur?' said Lafuente with a grin. 'There's further coincidence or symbolism that none of us noticed, despite its constant presence. Even a poor apprentice in the field like myself couldn't avoid spotting it.'

'In front of us?'

'Well, to put it more simply, one of us is the symbol itself. Do you recall I told you I had a certain feeling about you? Well, the time has come to say it.' the professor stated, adopting a mysterious air. 'That symbol is you, Arthur. Yes, don't make faces. In the distant Middle Ages, it was another Arthur who draw the sword from the rock. Call it a mythical or symbolic name load if you like, but if I've learnt anything from this, it's that neither you nor I, nor anybody else, will ever have absolute knowledge of the unseen forces that move the universe. However, we can at least learn to respect them. And perhaps they in return, will shed a little light.'

Here, he paused deliberately for dramatic effect.

'Perhaps' Lafuente remarked with a wink.

The three chuckled at the professor's joke. Carlos was exultant, looking at his notes repeatedly.

After a few seconds of reflection, it was Arthur's turn to break the silence, laughing. He was making vain attempts to control it, but all he could do was wave his hand, signalling his friends to wait. Perhaps he thought it would end soon, but the laughter continued, showing no trace of stopping any time soon.

'Arthur, what happens? Please say anything; you're worrying us. Try and have some water,' Elena said in alarm.

'I'm fine; I'm really fine. I feel better now,' Arthur said, taking a deep breath. 'I've just realised the irony of the whole thing. It was not only the professor's prank, no. For a moment, I have contemplated our grupo from afar. And suddenly, everything I've done in preparation for my thesis, everything we've been doing up to this point, took on the character of a revelation, like one of Ernesto's much-discussed epiphanies.'

'I think you have put too much pressure on this boy to complete his thesis on time.' said Elena.

'I solemnly swear I have no idea what he's talking about.'

'Well, it's only that I've realised the episode has far deeper symbolic importance than I originally thought.' Arthur said. 'Wait a minute, when did the princess arrived to Burgos?'

' You know that perfectly well. In December 1257.'

'Yes, of course, but what day was it?'

'Well, on Christmas Eve, you know, when she and her entourage spent the night in Huelgas. Are you dumb or something?'

'And what precisely is commemorated on Christmas Eve, Professor? What is celebrated? The Nativity of Jesus —but boil it down to something simpler in symbolic terms: a child's birth!'

'Wow, that's really creative thinking!'

'Take some distance, Professor. Take some distance as you always say!' Here he adopted a solemn demeanour, moving his right arm as if an invisible pipe were in it, imitating his mentor actions in class. 'Let's take a step back and look at the symbols before us. It's as simple as all that. Here now, in the twenty-first century, two professors and a graduate student come to this very place looking for signs of that child in a kind of postmodern "adoration" of that historical fact. It's funny, isn't it? We would be the modern equivalent of the Three Magi, and I, due to my status as an apprentice of the profession, would be the "black" king in the pejorative term previously employed without scorn. If we allow ourselves the freedom to consider Montanilla— located to the east of Burgos and the monastery itself—, we could even say that three Magi followed a star, or in our case, a light, all the way from the East in quest of a newborn child.'

The young man showed his fellow explorers a page from his notebook on which he had carefully written a sentence:

'*The sign that led the Magi to the cave of Bethlehem placed itself, before disappearing, on the Saviour's head, enveloping him with a brilliant halo."*

'And we know that sign' continued Arthur, 'the so-called star of Bethlehem, which appeared to the ancients, results in our more scientific times from the conjunction of Saturn and Jupiter. And now, after eight hundred years, coinciding with the Burgos Cathedral's eighth centennial, we shall once again be able to see it by night. But, of course, Elena this is pure chance as is the fact that your name in Greek should mean "Torch of light!" Did you know that?'

'On the other hand' said Elena, smiling at the observation and trying to enter into the conversation, 'all churches as you know have an invariable orientation, established so that both the faithful and the profane, when entering the temple from the West and proceeding directly to the sanctuary, would face the sunrise, the East, and Palestine, the cradle of Christianity. In that way, the attendants would emerge from the darkness and move towards the light.'

Yes.

It had a literal meaning. It referred to a child.

A child entrusted in the care of a local family with deep roots.

THE FOLLOWING DAY FOUND THE SAME GROUP SEATED IN Professor Lafuente's office.

Elena sat in the much sought-after green armchair while the professor occupied his desk. This presented a pitiful appearance, crossed and dotted from side to side by pages full of annotations, diagrams, and circles. Arthur leaned against the little window and the faux-medieval tower adjacent to the spiral staircase, which concealed in its shadows the much-coveted coffee machine and tea set. Ismael's waited eagerly at the young man's feet to reclaim it as soon as he would leave the spot.

'Well, my dear boy,' Carlos began 'now that everything is over, or at least the intrigue and everything that brought us to this point, why don't you shed some light for us as well? How did the idea come to you? How did you discovered the text was written in some sort of invisible ink? And most of all, the concept of the red light? The stained glass windows in the chapter house? And particularly, how did you know the specific page to examine? As much as I read my notes, I am unable to learn anything from them.'

'A few days ago you talked about secrets in plain sight that, however, could not be seen by the naked eye. That prompted me to believe that the copyist might have used some kind of invisible ink,' Arthur said, fully aware of the interest he had aroused and knowing this was the moment to explain himself as if he were presenting his thesis. 'It's a well-known fact that in ancient times there were a number of people using similar techniques to prevent knowledge from falling into the wrong hands. A week ago when I heard Professor Pilar Alonso on the telly, and knew about her research on the distinctive "Burgos Red" of the stained glass windows, which exist only in Huelgas and the cathedral, it made me wonder what function this different consistency of glass could serve, what could be the reason for its difference. You told me once a story about your doctor friend and that darkroom in Santander. And lastly in *The Mystery of the Cathedrals*, Fulcanelli mentions: "The key to the major arcane consists simply of a colour, manifested to the artisan from the first work," all knowledge condensed into a colour...

Then I pondered if that colour may have been the red one. On the other hand, this identical hue is the main protagonist in the illuminated initials and stained glass windows! And finally, my friends,' Trevelyan added, leaning forward and pushing up with his feet to underline his speech withdraw the curtains, 'the diva, the star of the show in its own right: the sun. The sun, appearing on the winter equinox, would be the one revealing the message to everyone— although hiding it from prying eyes. A message written with an special ink; created with a secret ingredient that the copyist elaborated jointly or in partnership with the glassmakers, with the same dexterity with which those goldsmiths and masons built the temple in such a way that "forced" the sun to fall on it. With the help of the alchemists of the time? Perhaps. The concept is not so far-fetched. You just have to connect the dots to find the figure hidden in the children's book. To discover the hidden drawing. And regarding the "when"... The monastic hour of Prima, now in disuse, was for the ancients the hour of revelation, very different from the early risers in Silos,' he said, looking at the professor with some reproach. 'It is related to the departure of the sun, with awakening, birth, and resurrection. A moment of joy for the new day that begins.'

Arthur hurried to the window, pointing to the landscape outside as if he were a conjurer, showing the place where the beams of that very fell to the floor, the creator of the miracle they had witnessed the previous morning, gathering his things before retiring to rest.

'Do you remember the expression that the very forest obscures our view of the trees? Well, this concrete tree has been directly in front of us the entire time, yet we failed to notice it!'

And with a theatrical gesture, he pointed to the image of a child that appeared on one of the open parchments that lay on the table.

'And regarding the page... it has no merit whatsoever. That piece of paper Sister Amalia left me along with the book, clearly a wink. On the paper were the words: *"Quis dabit capiti meo aquam...."*

"...Et oculist meis fontem!" Elena went on, recognising the psalm.

'"Who will give me water to my head and fountains of tears for my eyes as I mourn day and night for my sins?" Arthur recited triumphantly on the run. 'Of the 32 *conductus* in the work, fifteen are for a single voice. Only six of these appear in Las Huelgas Codex. I have woven them even finer: among them are four funerary hymns — or *planctus*, dedicated in principle to notable characters. However, it is only in one of them, —only in one mind you, that the recipient is unknown, and that is: *"Quis dabit capiti meo"*. Who could be that relevant figure whose importance did not prevent the name from fading into obscurity? Perhaps Princess Kristina? There's no better way to conceal a stolen sheep than to put it in an enclosure with a hundred other sheep. But here, here in this Codex, we are talking at all times about an actual child, an infant. Nothing is easier for Catholicism than to conceal the events. Clear as rain to talk about a newborn and its care without raising suspicions, don't you think? At one point, all the parts of the puzzle fitted together in my subconscious, one after the other, without my realising it'. It was now Arthur's turn to shift from one side of the office to the other, a moment Ismael took advantage of to install himself definitively in the small window the young man had left vacant. 'What we had been searching for, the text or instructions left in the monastery, had been both in plain sight and concealed, and, of course, Sister Amalia's cryptic note served as confirmation we were on the right track. It displayed nothing less than the Codex page and song in question. But how to find the key to read it?'

At this point, Arthur paused, exhausted by his constant movement around the table.

'It was then that I put all the pieces together: the capitular letters illuminated with that magnificent red tone, Professor Abad's televised talk regarding Huelgas stained glass windows, and the hidden reference in the manuscripts discovered in Silos: "*At the hour of Prima, from light will come light*"; the mention of Priest Don Alberto's recent television appearance in which he described a strange phenomenon induced by particular light effects observed in St. Nicolas Church and San Juan de Ortega monastery, both in the province of Burgos. All of this without mentioning an experience I had a few days ago right here as I was dozing off in the armchair' he continued, growing red following this confession. 'And last of all, the words of that guide mentioning that the stained glass windows had been relocated in 1965 and installed in the chapter house. Everything was too fantastic. There were far too many coincidences for them not to indicate something or point in a particular direction. Every wild question I asked myself, every hypothesis, had an even more incredible explanation. It was a crazy intuition. Logic told me there was no way invisible ink based on lemon or other natural chemicals could have survived for eight centuries and made it to the present day, but my gut told me otherwise.

A few years after the Codex was compiled, there appeared in it a funeral song called "*O moniales met Burgensis*" attributed to González de Agüero, the abbess who commissioned its collection.' for those who want to spin or do mathematical calculations.

'Of course' said Elena, who had kept silent for fear of interrupting the explanation, 'the words "*Cantat me sin miedo que Johannes Rodrigues me enmendi*" appearing in various parts of the Codex could be translated as: "write what you want, and I'll take care to encode it properly."

'If it's not that, it's the closest thing I can think of,' said Arthur, 'apart from the fact that light originated precisely through St John—or "Johannes" in Latin.'

'That's true, but now that you mention it, why did you make us move the Codex at the very last minute? What led you to believe it would be visible through that precise window?'

'I'm surprised you didn't come up with that answer yourselves. It was the easiest part. I just remembered my religion classes. It was all about shedding light in every way, right? Please recall that according to the Gospel, St. John the Evangelist is the light that shines in the darkness, the light that the world did not know, and that the saint was preceded by John the Baptist, the messenger sent by Providence.'

'However,' the professor remarked with a neutral tone in his voice, 'those descendants under the monastery tutelage were lost amid all the others subjected to the Huelgas patronage. Yes, a foster family, you are right there, but just one more family, one more child who would be asking for bread among the hundreds that the abbey must have protected by then. Now we reach the second part. I'm sorry to break the excitement of the moment, but, as in any puzzle game, every answer raises new questions.'

'And that question is...' Elena said.

'What course shall we take now? Or to put it in other words, in which family did the nuns place the princess's offspring? The Mother Abbess then could have placed the infant in the care of a local family with old genealogy in exchange for specific privileges or ecclesiastical gifts, and under the threat of excommunication if the truth were exposed. Nothing simpler than that. The hardest part would come later, much later. That would be to devise with the help of the alchemists and artisan glassmakers building part of the cathedral the orchestration of that silent conspiracy. A curious thing the mediaeval mind, if you think about it!'

WHEN HIS COMPANIONS LEFT, AND JUST THE STAINS ON Ismael's back remained as the only witnesses in the room, the professor was immersed in thought. It was hard to believe all this had been orchestrated to conceal an illegitimate birth by an unknown princess who had travelled to Spain for an uncertain wedding. Was there something else Alfonso X knew? Was the princess involved in any other mission involving the famous "dome of the world" intended to enthrone the king of Castile as the emperor of Europe?

The many technical resources and knowledge employed to hide the secret stood in stark contrast to those available at the time. Several people had worked together, coordinated their efforts to create this piece of Swiss machinery, making sure that it would accurately and reliably keep time for hundreds of years.

The Cabala, the hermetic work containing secrets one within the other, surfaced—like a gigantic matryoshka—, as a possible necessary collaborator. A universe of references relating to everything. Arthur was right. He saw it now.

CHAPTER 39

NEW YEAR'S EVE

A steganographic example

Carlos and Elena were standing by the large window at the Espolón Walk flat, looking at the river down below. The clock had just struck 11:00 p.m.

It was December 31st.

It had been indeed a hectic week. Fascinating.

Arthur had gone to rest half an hour earlier to celebrate New Year's Eve with his buddies.wholly exhausted yet bubbling with enthusiasm.

'I've been always fascinated by that butterfly hanging there. ' Elena said suddenly as she stood in front of the butterfly after abruptly rising from her chair. 'How did you get it?' It was the first time Carlos had seen her do something like this. He was aware she had not been particularly fond of lepidoptera of any kind. This sudden interest caught him by surprise. He coughed slightly, looked down, and then back up at Elena.

'It is a queer story of youth. It's been a long time since then.'

'No, please, if you don't mind, I'm all ears. I would like to hear a story that has nothing to do with a more or less remote antiquity. I don't think my mind could take any more for today.'

'Well... if you really want to know it all began in Brazil in 1985...' Carlos began, his eyes locked on the frame in front of them.

And so, for a few minutes their minds left the office and immersed themselves in the wonders and beauty of a butterfly that had resisted capture, a butterfly that now occupied a prominent place in that office, framed over the great fireplace.

Elena remained silent throughout all the narrative, leaning slightly forward, taking an occasional drag on her cigarette now and then, that puff recognised among smokers that denotes a higher level of mental concentration. She showed her interest with slight head nods, her hands outstretched in front of her, one on top of the other, the spitting image of interest.

When Carlos finished his narration, Elena sat back on the couch, her emerald eyes speaking for themselves. Her expression had changed.

'You want to know about my significant experience?' she said after a lengthy pause. 'I hadn't heard the term that much until you first brought it up at that dinner in Montanilla. For over fourteen years, I had a little dog. A lively, mischievous, barking little creature who regularly ran away from home, leaping into the garden and chasing any person, cat, or dog who dared to cross the threshold of my tiny bungalow. My friends, less compassionate, affectionately referred to him as "little rascal." His name was Scotty. He witnessed my misery during the final years of a failed marriage. Scotty stayed with me, faithful to the end.'

Elena's gaze was lost in the void for an instant. In those few seconds, she was seeing her pet once more. Perhaps she also saw herself, the two of them together on the balcony, looking out onto the street after the one who had been her husband left the house that very evening.

'Scotty died during the night. It took me entirely by surprise. I had to attend a course in Vitoria the next day. I had already purchased the train tickets. Printed and saved. My friends and colleagues who were traveling with me told me it would be better if I cancelled the trip, arguing that the course was not so relevant or urgent after all, things like that, but I declined their advice. I had to go. I was unable to stay at home alone at that moment without my beloved Scotty. Not only that, I had to make a full stop in my life. Create a mourning space if you will. I'd have time later on my return to sort out his clothes, food bowl, and other things. So, after talking to my friends, I made up my mind and, opening my laptop in a state of sleepwalking, intended to write on my Facebook profile. The blinking cursor waited in front of me. I felt as though I had something to say to that small creature who had been with me for so many years, through my greatest and worst times. Witness, if you will, to a period in my life. It's easy to slide into a hurried sentimentality while speaking in this manner, but not when recalling the precise times and experiences I had shared with Scotty. I owed that being a bit of poetry, don't you think? And before I knew what I was doing, my hands were moving over the keyboard and I wrote "I am certain you are not dead. I know you will be in the air, floating around, barking at your own pace, helping butterflies fly," Corny but effective. A tribute to a tiny hero, these brief remarks, seemingly trivial and commonplace words helped me feel better and more at ease. I closed the laptop, my eyes filled with tears. I still dared to eat a morsel for dinner, lie down on the bed, and close my eyes.

However, I did not fall asleep until very late, not until I had mulled over in my mind numerous times the pain that remained within me, refusing to depart. The following day, I prepared the washing machine with the garments that had gathered in the basket during the previous few days. I hadn't been in the appropriate frame of mind to consider doing the dishes, sweeping, or replacing the coffee filter till then. I opened the washing machine with mechanical movements, still half asleep, while coffee was brewing on the stove.

I dragged the laundry basket toward me mechanically, like I had done countless times before.

When I opened it, though, a big red butterfly emerged. It

lingered, close to my face for several seconds before flying over my bungalow's garden wall.

Now you know why I didn't want to see your butterflies, why I cut you off when you were trying to tell me about your passion' Elena finished, lifting her head, which she had kept down for the past few minutes and looked at Carlos in the face. 'I suppose that was my way of protecting myself, not wanting to talk about that past again.'

Next to the flowerpot she had prepared a few weeks prior, Elena became silent.

Professor Lafuente remained mute after hearing his colleague's words. The moonlight—illuminating Elena's shoulders from above—provided a luminous highlight to her silhouette against the window. She raised her arms, releasing the ponytail she had previously secured as usual to work with some comfort.

It was a quick and natural movement. Her hair fell or, instead, seemed to drop off her shoulders. Carlos Lafuente loved to watch it sway as she walked alongside him on similar occasions, forming different shapes and patterns in the space as she did so.

He drew in a full breath. Air seemed to be lacking in his lungs. Carlos noticed a hidden, late, and deep secret within himself.

'You know' he said before paying attention to his words, 'you look great beneath the moon.'

Elena didn't answer. He couldn't see her face in that semi-darkness, in that tiny space beside the window. Just the moonlight falling across her shoulders and hair from above. Had her hair being always so silky, or was it the result of an optical effect caused by the angle at which she received light from the window? It didn't matter.

The clock struck a quarter to twelve.

'Fuck! I had entirely forgotten!' Elena remarked smacking her forehead. 'Carlos, it's New Year's Eve! —quickly, run! I left a bottle on the table behind you. Hurry! We are still on time to celebrate.'

Lafuente unfamiliar with the new arrangement of objects in his library, did as he was told and scanned the entire space. Indeed, Elena—always at the ready for detail—had prepared on the indicated table a small tray on which a bottle, two glasses, and the mandatory grapes lay at the ready.

The shape of the glasses had definitely been made with care. The craftsman had carved the glass in the right places, with clear, precise lines that aligned with the curvature angle.

The glazier's work, moulded using the technique of blown glass, had concretised from an imprecise shape, a figure caressed by fire. This was also a tribute to light, to the way it is employed to enhance the design of the glass itself, allowing us, in a split second, when exhibited, to see a brief flash of light emanate from a spot we had not foreseen, surprising the eye and causing astonishment at the beauty thus perceived.

And underneath everything, supporting the whole, the base, much like the trunk of a tree supports and makes its upper part stand out, highlighting its branches.

It was surprising to realise how that set of glasses had remained in that cupboard for months, while he had been searching for written truths, while all the time this beauty had been at his fingertips, unnoticed.

Yes. It was New Year's Eve.

Rays of moonlight were falling on the glasses.

'Happy New Year, Elena!' Carlos said, offering a toast.

'Happy New Year, Carlos.'

The glasses smashed against one another. A slight, frail, delicate sound.

The two figures were silhouetted against the window in the moonlight. They both stared into each other's eyes for a while. Carlos thought that maybe he had done something foolish. Again. As usual.

'I'd best fetch another bottle,' he said. 'I believe there is not much champagne remaining in my glass.'

When he was rising from the chair, he felt Elena's firm but gentle touch on his forearm.

'There is still enough,' she said, laying her hands on his lapels and gazing at him with eyes emerging from the shadows where they had been concealed, illuminated by the lamp in the corner of the tower where they were both standing.

Carlos, forgetting all theory, plan, or strategy, wrapped his arms around the slim waist of that woman he had just discovered that night, and, drawing her towards him, kissed her in front of the window, gently at first, like a caress, beneath the large framed butterfly, his hands exploring new territories, a world he had forgotten existed.

CHAPTER 40

SQUIRRELS IN ISLAND PARK

From Carlos Lafuente's notes

Sometimes I have seen squirrels in Island Park.

Between seven and eight a.m. specially they tend to gather in small groups on its less travelled paths, when the morning air is still enlivened by dew, when the last dream is still glued to the heart.

The squirrels, calm and methodical at that hour, advance in modest leaps, tiny brown dots on the grass, still damp, shiny and fresh.

Some groups of walkers, used to this behaviour, patiently await this moment, taking slow steps, holding nuts or almonds in their palms to entice them to come closer.

In the farthest area of the park, near Island Palace, the trees group together, making a perfect hiding place to conceal the small rodents' adventures.

In one of these groups you may discover the raised palmetto, the cypress, the white and Boolean poplar keeping company with the yew, the weeping willow, and their cousin, the weeping elm, with the park's insistence towards melancholy, perhaps adhering to the spirit of its creation as a Romantic walk many years ago.

Before the municipal cleaning staff takes possession of a park and mothers with stubborn strollers would occupy its trails, the early morning can be a time of extraordinary tranquilly.

Before that, though, far before that, though, squirrels had already begun their daily exploration of the various ruins scattered throughout its extension.

Indeed, they do. Coming from the Commander's Arches, they conquer and save for posterity the Romanesque portal of the vanished Church of Our Lady of the Plain and the colonial-style fountain formerly located in the cloister of the now-forgotten monastery of St Pedro de Arlanza.

They have gone to great lengths to conceal acorns and other fruits among the crevices of the stone, oblivious to the magnitude and effort of the constructors.

There, these hidden treasures, protected by the atmosphere of the place, would wait, —like other provisions hidden in less significant places, a few centimetres below the park's entire expanse— the joyful moment, the future time when they would be unearthed and enjoyed by the small colony.

However, those tiny creatures that leap from branch to branch using their long tails don't know about that moment yet. Neither are them aware of the existence of this open-air museum.

Elena and I arrived there on New Year's Day.

I desired to show her my favourite corner.

I had specifically chosen this location from amid the park's vast floral diversity. We were standing close to the *Cercis siliquastrum*, sometimes known as the "tree of love."

Upon our arrival Elena digs into her coat pockets and extracts a few acorns, having been informed beforehand of the event we were going to see.

Nothing seemed to happen for several seconds, then we notice a flicker in the bushes before us.

'Look, look, they're squirrels!' Elena says, in a voice full of suppressed emotion, as though she were a schoolgirl on a school outing.

Certainly they were. A quick movement from our left, stops for a few seconds in front of us, and then veers off to the right, in the same jerky manner in which it came.

What first appears to be a brown and fluffy patch surging across the park's ground is actually two squirrels chasing each other. The patch ascends a tree, wiggles around in the branches, and then drops back down the trunk in a circling motion before climbing another tree a little distance away to repeat the entire process. The eye barely has time to recognise the shapes and tails that propel them. They appear anxious about some special event that has nothing to do with our presence there.

Meanwhile, a tiny specimen has made its appearance, straddling one of the metal fences that protected the flowerbeds and bushes, only to stand motionless in front of Elena.

Another one emerges from the shadows and, casting a wary eye at the woman in front of it and then at me with a certain degree of mistrust, seems to ponder our presence there, evaluate the degree of trust we should deserve.

I hope within myself that they would remember this solitary stroller from so many mornings with the *Burgos Daily* tucked under my arm, the occasional book, crossing the park and seating under the willows' shade, for the better part of an hour immersed in that peculiar occupation, without disturbing the peace of the place.

Elena gives me a thoughtful look before crouching cautiously in front of the two squirrels, as if she had been used to do so on a regular basis.

The second of them, perhaps more nimble and assured than the first—or perhaps just hungrier—, crosses in front of his comrade, reaching the palm that is extended in front of him.

While the experience may not have been as momentous as, say, the Northwest Pass nor the opening of a new frontier, that moment was to me just as culminating as any of the historical milestones I had been teaching about in the past.

At that moment, Elena, crouching with her grey coat lapels lifted and unconscious of anything as the tiny animal nibbled on her palm, seemed to merge with the park, become a part of it.

Undoubtedly, the park has its own rhythm, its own soul. To properly enjoy the experience, we must merge our own dimension to it. It's us who must let the park enter inside us. Only then will we see it as Elena and I did on those mornings. On those evenings.

It was not until years later that, more familiar with Elena's favourite painters, I could recognise that identical sunset light in the paintings of Claude Lorrain, in that plume of treetops outlined against an otherworldly glow that seemed to emanate from another universe, in those ruins conveniently positioned so that the right ray of sunlight would fall on them, bounce off their surface, finally hitting the faces of the people wandering there, frozen in time so that they could savour that moment over and over again.

The early dawn hours bring with it a fresh perspective to the park. As the hours pass, the rhythm is different, just as the walker's gait changes too. It appears the environment has seduced everybody at this time.

Yes, I had previously visited Island Park, but this time with Elena was the time I discovered it.

∼

CHAPTER 41

A BURGOS WALK

After the recent visit to the park Lafuente felt the time had come to take a proper stroll through Burgos after one year spent in his study. Time to roam beneath the weeping willows, feel the rain pouring and the cool breeze on his face.

On that frigid winter afternoon, as he wandered through the deserted streets and observed the old-fashioned shops, he had the overwhelming impression that time had stopped.

He walked with slow steps, his eyes filled of dreams, in a state of inner peace. In these moments, he felt closer than ever to Elena.

He leaned on the parapet of the bridge and looking at the Arlanzon down there took a deep breath of fresh air. The river, unconscious of his gaze kept flowing at its own beat, as it had done for all these years, centuries, millennia.

The Arlanzón River.

It was funny to consider he had lived all his life near it, without ever suspecting it might exist, be contemplated in this way. But it was now, inexplicably, when its memory assailed him: the longing, the sensation of seeing it again through other eyes; the knowledge that she had also traversed these places, jumping and throwing her laughter into the air, like that group of girls who had just passed him on the street sidewalk with no purpose other than to enjoy the afternoon.

He left behind the Espolón Walk, the former railway station, and the avenue that has remained following its demolition. That was the final stage of his trek before stopping for a much needed cup of coffee.

He could no longer live without this new Burgos. He needed to remember the union of these two feelings. Nothing could separate that experience from inside him now, the impression of living and witnessing the city where Elena had grown up.

He had been wrong his whole life. Now, in his adult years, he had discovered the city he had not perceived till now. He was amazed to discover that it had been waiting for him, patiently, without reproach. It had always been there, like a pilgrim travelling to Compostela, awaiting his journey to the north. This, though, was a peaceful, fuss-free pilgrimage. A journey made in silent solitude.

He focused on one of those cosy cafes with amber lighting inside that seemed to speak of leisurely moments and where the time spent sipping coffee and eating a pastry with Elena seemed not to pass at all.

He saw the expansive gardens, bike pathways, and enclosed balconies and gates.

Burgos and the professor talked through them, sharing their tiny secrets.

But the wonder, the miracle, if you will, had been the fact of being able to walk the places and feel the smells and sights associated with her.

And if there was neither fog or rain while he wandered its streets, he would return again and again, searching for it, remembering her among the streets, always pursuing a dream.

~

PART II
FOLLOWING THE CLUE
IN SEARCH OF ANSWERS

There is a cry in the breeze. It's a silent one.
It comes from the Arlanzón.
It comes from Seville.
It is the lament for a lost child in the labyrinths of time,
beyond the fog
Beyond summer rain,
In a one-way trip beyond the unthinkable.

CHAPTER 42

IN SEARCH OF EL DORADO

Regarding aircrafts, roads, and the game of the geese.

January 20th. Before going to the university that afternoon, Carlos Lafuente approached the nearby Espolón bookshop. He took a brief glance as usual at the window. His attention was drawn to its lower part. There, a sober but striking cover book featured a sombre yet aesthetically pleasing design showing the solitary figure of a woman in the middle of nature against backdrop of greyish, hazy mountains.

The perfumed Institute, read the title. He noticed the author. Ernesto Santos.

Wow! This must be one of the projects he was preparing when they met in Valladolid. A poster advertising the book's upcoming publication was placed in the corner.

The sky began now to fill the afternoon with ominous dark clouds, signalling the impending storm. The campus that had been previously gleaming in all its splendour, gave off that distinct smell of newly cut grass. The statues and the river seemed to watch the scene serenely despite the inclement weather.

In the professor's office, two figures were waiting for him under the golden-spined books. A vase of flowers had been placed above the fireplace, and one of the figures was carefully arranging them.

Having completed the task with meticulous care, placed it back on the window sill.

The woman who had committed this deed looked at the garden below.

There appeared the elongated figure of Carlos Lafuente approaching, deep in thought, pipe in hand, illuminated by the ashen light that dominated the sky. He didn't seem to notice the increasing storm clouds or their erratic movement.

As he made his way among the statues, he could have been mistaken for one of them: a gorgeous knight from the Middle Ages, polishing and repairing his armour before heading back into battle.

Elena turned to Arthur, who had been sitting in the green armchair behind her with a thick book in his hands, and mumbled, 'He's still there.'

Arthur was trying to red without losing sight of the spectacle in front of him. This prompted a grin from the young man. He could not help but notice the appreciable change in his two friends. Who could have predicted the feeling he had scarcely noticed in Valladolid would have led to this?

'I don't know' Elena said with a frown as she continued looking down. 'I thought he'd be happier now that we've done with the Codex, but it seems his thoughts haven't slowed down.

'It's true. He should definitely get some rest,' suggested Arthur.

'These last few days have been exhausting for all of us. I've just missed two midterm parties, something that has never occurred to me before.'

Another hour passed before Carlos finally entered the office. He appeared surprised at discovering them there, even though he had summoned his two companions the day before.

'¡Sorry! Just out for a walk. I didn't realise you were already here' he apologised as he hung up his jacket.

'Wow! And me thinking you were on your way to the Chicago Symposium on the *History of the Seminoles and their impact on modern agriculture,*' Elena said, with an irony that passed unnoticed to the professor, still lost in his thoughts.

Lafuente sat at his desk and went for the black leather folder holding the crucial data from the preceding months.

'Well, as far as the MS's is concerned, it's all over, that's for sure,' Elena added with a broad smile, turning back at the garden and rearranging the hydrangeas in the porcelain vase she had neglected in her previous floral care, in an effort to engage her colleague in some light conversation.

Carlos nodded absentmindedly as he arranged the pencils on his table employing the unusual procedure of removing them from the cup they had been in and putting them back again.

'Is anything the matter?' Elena said, walking up to the desk, sitting in a corner and looking at the professor with a questioning look.

Lafuente was inspecting some papers in front of him. He paused at the question and looked at the bookshelves as if the inquiry had come from far away. He flipped three or four further pages before repeating the procedure.

'As far as I know, all that remains is to seal the file and issue the damned report that our respected rector demanded in such an earnest way' Elena persisted taking her brown-ribboned leather purse from the chair in front of the desk and taking out a cigarette from it.

'Unfortunately, being the manuscripts authentic and rightfully belonging to Silos or at least Huelgas the present owner won't be able to auction off the manuscripts, will he?' Poor Dabrowski. Deep down in my heart, I really do feel bad for him. On the other hand, I also feel some pity for the unfortunate Manuel Tordesillas. His report was spotless; he did a fantastic job. Now he may use it to keep the flies away from his office.

'Thankfully, that is not a concern of mine' said Lafuente. In any event, Patricio Noguer has only acknowledged the authenticity of the

Silos manuscripts, nothing more. To him, the Codex's unseen writing was only a religious symbol of some kind!'

That had indeed been the case when Carlos Iafuente, still buzzing as a result of the finding under the stained-glass light, was faced with the solid and stoic figure of the rector standing behind his desk, blocking the garden view like a statue on a plinth.

'I'm delighted for you, Professor,' he had told him that day, after all the evidence had been laid out for him in the presence of a taciturn Elena. 'Despite the fact that you've defied me by using your peculiar tactics to reexamine that Codex. I trust now the two of you will find time now to return to your academic duties. Don't you agree?'

Lafuente's eyes traced the pattern on the carpet, bringing back memories, his own thoughts far removed from this office, the tea tray, the vase of flowers, and the sight of the weeping willow branches brushing against the window panes.

'I's no longer about the research now, is it?' said Elena, breaking the ice after such a long period of silence, swinging her right leg and making the most of her commanding position at the table.

Now that she knew she could cause earthquakes with her legs, the only thing left to do was to fully employ all her weapons.

'No, I suppose not. We have done what we were supposed to do, I hope' Carlos said. The soft perfume Elena wore that morning was reaching him.

'What is it then, Carlos? What is it?'

Still, a few seconds passed while the professor kept his head bowed.

'It's the butterfly again, right?' Elena asked at last.

Carlos's head sprang up as if he were a youngster caught with a chocolate bar in his pocket, only acknowledging the truth when the stain shows through his jeans.

'Yes, I suppose so' he said as he put the last pencil into the wooden cup.

He stood up, eager to take the pipe that had waited obediently on the side table, always at the ready for daily research. Taking advantage of the fact Elena was close by, he reached across his desk and gently pet her shoulder and hand.

'I recognise its absurdity. It sounds stupid even to me. I'm also aware that I have completed a more or less detailed report that I will be able to submit at future symposiums or international conferences, to be hailed while we pat each other on the back. I have received the rector's grudging approval, if the flurry of comments made in the dining hall last evening may be read that way. Eight centuries have passed since those instructions were entrusted to the nuns at Las Huelgas. Perhaps it's time to move on to something else.'

'Yes, time flies when you're having fun' Arthur grinned, but his remark was stopped off by the severity and solemnity on his mentor's face.

Lafuente was staring at the wall opposite the large bookcase.

A map of the Iberian Peninsula hung there. On it the old kingdoms returned to life on a daily basis. Looking at it, it was easy to envision riders traversing it on their way to or from a fight, conveying vital message from one kingdom to another, searching for potential treaties.

'Even so, I've been considering something' said the professor as he continued to stare ahead.

'Yes, Carlos?'

'That infant left in the care of the Cistercian nuns...'

A new look from Lafuente at the garden and the papers on the table.

'That infant...?' Elena repeated, trying to get the words out of his mouth and feeling like the prompter at the university theatricals.

'I wonder if that family, despite the passing of centuries, the vagaries of history, plagues, wars, branches vanishing into thin air, a low life expectancy, and anything else you can think of may not have reached our time in one way or another. What would happen if, like Ariadne, the appropriate strings pulled we went in quest of that family? Take it as an intellectual game, as a kind of Scrabble or Cluedo, as an obsession if you like. It seems crazy, but so is catching a butterfly in the deep of the jungle, climbing a mountain that offers resistance, or painting the ephemeral hues of fog or rain for a painter. Of course I am quite certain that the university would not endorse such a venture. It's something I would have to accomplish alone in one way or another. Having come here, I am unable to stop myself.'

'Well, Arthur must, among other things, attend a special course at Ludwig-Maximilians University in Munich, right, Arthur? Regrettably, there are still those who refuse to abandon the mundane physical world. It's remarkable, isn't it? Occasionally, though, it occurs,' Elena said with a face wanting to be stern, distorted by the corners of her lips bent on smiling.

'Yeah, well, it's a consequence of what I did regarding that Napoleon stuff and such, remember?' Arthur said looking from one to the other. 'I wanted to add my own insights to my final degree assignment, but I'll certainly will find time enough.'

That seemed to pull the professor out of his earlier mental thread. He stood up and walked across the room to shake hands with Arthur.

'What wonderful news! Congratulations! I'm so pleased for you, Arthur! You will be a man of success and an outstanding professor!' He stared then at the books strewn about his office, at the large library that had offered him so much solace over the years, until his gaze eventually landed on Elena's face, who was staring at him, with half-closed eyes.

'He's an excellent student, Elena' said Carlos Lafuente in an lower tone upon realising his excess of expressiveness.

'Believe me, You can do much worse than getting a *cum laude*, trust me' said Arthur. 'Cum laude or not, I still get popcorn burned in the microwave.'

By the way, where do you have that butterfly hunting manual?' said Elena, getting up swiftly from the table she had been seating on and retrieving her fountain pen from her jacket, changing the subject when she noticed the young man's cheeks were puffing out of proportion. Carlos Lafuente smiled broadly as he looked from one to the other.

'We are all indeed slaves to our passions,' he continued, 'but I am extremely lucky in this regard. Even if I am my own prisoner, I have the most ideal housemates a person could hope for.' he said, resting his hand on Elena's waist 'Thank you!'

Lafuente reached for his leather folder and, with a swift motion, unzipped it revealing inside his new acquisition at the Espolón bookstore, which he displayed before his companions. A detailed map of Burgos province.

'May I introduce you to the map of the territory?' said Lafuente with a somewhat theatrical air that caught both Arthur and Elena by surprise.

A map, similar to the metaphorical one that had appeared months before at the Valladolid dinner.

'Who said something about coffee? I don't think it would feel bad at this hour. God knows that I would give my last penny on it!' Carlos said, clapping his hands and surprising those present by assuming a heroic stance reminiscent of the local version of Errol Flynn.

Elena and Arthur laughed at the idea. Arthur had certainly discovered a new Lafuente in the last few days, and he knew Elena had been the cause.

The professor unfolded the map entirely. A tangle of small names appeared on it. Mountains, rivers, and settlements.

Arthur recognised a certain resemblance in what they were witnessing.

'Doesn't this map ring any bells?' Lafuente said, noticing it.

'Well, It looks like a treasure map,' said the student, observing the shape and distribution of the towns, feeling a kind of adventurous spirit reborn in him.

'Yes, it's right!' Elena said, examining it closely.

'That's how I suggest you view it from now on. Forget about orthodoxy for the time being. Imagine for a moment we are reading a suspense thriller in which we would like to discover the identity of the murderer. That would be the closest way to understand my idea. Look!' Carlos said, pointing to some colour-coded trails on the map, 'There are tracks, yes, but also roads that lead nowhere and clearly marked highways. It would seem like a Cluedo or Goose game, as we can always go back to the starting square an infinite number of times.

With that spirit of play and persistence, I believe the investigation should be conducted.'

'As true adventurers, tremble, Jim Hawkins, tremble!' exclaimed Arthur, more versed than the others in Stevenson's work.

"Any thoughts? Any ideas? Anything that should stimulate the imagination is valuable to me. But first, please hear me out, both of you! I want you to review everything we've learned up to this point, and specially in your case, Arthur, everything I have ever taught you, in case something has sunk into that head of yours busy with esoteric theories. Think for a moment about other players who might have passed through here and played this game, moving from one location to another.

They built bonfires, hunted game, and farmed the land. Marks and inscriptions attest to their presence and activity. Many of these locations' names may have been altered so drastically by time and language that they now refer to completely different things. We must read through them. But the game is still the same. The rules have not changed either. Only we, the new players, are now facing it. If we take a Sherlock-like approach, we should be able to reconstruct the previous movements of the players by analysing the state of the game as it stands now. Are you staying with me?'

'It would never have occurred to me to examine history from that perspective. But I suppose you are right, professor,' said Trevelyan, shaking his head.

'Yes,' Lafuente concluded after examining the map. Thousands of souls have traversed these harsh and practically barren landscapes, these desolate and almost uninhabited wastelands.

Were the souls of yesterday still there, as Trevelyan believed?, he thought. Were they out at a neighbour's house planning to return in the late afternoon for a hot dinner? Would they bring with them a thousand new anecdotes, fresh laughter, new cries and grief?

The solitary cottages in these settlements had been as vulnerable to the winter wind as the fields that encircled them. Like those towns surrounded by furrows, tens of millions of crops would be doomed to failure. Others would give rise to seedlings that would eventually develop, produce offspring, building a small forest as time passed, even a grove. However, as strangers to the hands and eyes of the scribe, they would ultimately be lost to history.

More fortunate travellers on the way to the settlement would see the royal scribe searching, inquiring of other hamlets, recording whatever he observed along the way. Families would then become a part of the nation's royal census, obtaining immortality through the relative longevity of records.

The vast majority of these people had lived their whole lives in these fields, leaving no mark of their presence on the flat, neutral items that were the ink and parchment used by the notary, the lawyer, and the parish priest recording their passage through life and death. Without that parchment first, paper later, their names would be nothing more than an echo in the town's elders' memories. Something to talk about, from more and further back each time. Like the old tombstone—if by any chance they could count on a pantheon—something to be remembered by future generations. In less affluent cases, the ancient stones would deteriorate and wear away, erasing all traces of names and dates on them, maybe housing the remains of a newborn baby died just months after birth, leaving behind just the tears of his parents until they, too, faded from the scene.

The land would be undisturbed except by the fallen leaves and the feet of nearby tourists.

For commoners, however, just the common burial in the parish remained. Nameless. with no date. Without identity. One more shadow, one more leaf blown away by the wind during the storm, travelling from one place to another over the far hill, not knowing its destination.

Arthur, Carlos, and Elena had left the library's golden gloom behind.

They were in the university grounds, on those paths where it was common to find any of them taking walks on any given day.

Scattered along that path and lined up on either side, there were some copies of those Neo Greek sculptures that were invading the periphery of the campus little by little.

As soon as he lit his pipe and inhaled the first puff, the professor's arms snapped into action. He held the pipe in his right hand and drew an arc in the air with it, as if he were defining the landscape around him.

'It's not enough to look for any mount or hill in the northern portion of the Burgos province' he began, 'but The Mount. The Mount chosen by the monastery, and —if I my hunch is true—, we are moving along the way a brilliant mind devised this secret, this concealing manoeuvre. We must continue to think along these lines, regardless of whether the initial design originated from the scribe, the abbess, or a group of individuals.

We will never know that. Well! Let's think like them then! We know they would be looking for a family with local ties. Perhaps a nobleman or, failing that, a person in a position of authority whose surname would be likely to be perpetuated or have some guarantee of doing due to the ownership of lands and titles.

'Yeah! As far as the monastery is concerned, we know they had control over land and titles until quite recently,' Arthur said.

They heard a quick pitter-patter of rain on the nearby windowpanes.

It had began to rain hard. A persistent, mild drizzle. They sprinted towards the main building.

A NEW PHASE BEGAN THAT A RAINY AFTERNOON. IT HAD TO BE so. That's how all table games begin, with rain beating against a window. Then, later, much later there is always the urge to continue and complete the play despite exhaustion and cold dinner waiting in the kitchen.

After the three of them had taken cover in the office's warmth, Arthur looked at the map again. Like a checkers player, intent only on the next move, attempting to traverse the board's labyrinthine passages to the opposite side.

'A town in the north, in the hills... in the mountains...' He repeated in a hushed voice, unaware that he was actually pronouncing the words.

"Where to hide the golden seed," Elena continued, like someone reciting an incantation after having read that paragraph hundreds of times.

'Make a list of the different places!' said the professor. 'It's pointless the three would have our eyes glued to the same spot of the map like fools, reading and rereading the names over and over again. It's a waste of time. One of them might easily be overlooked. Could it be Tordesilla del Monte?' he said, paying no attention to his rumbling. He continued in this way, reading the long string of village names that appeared before him: Las Alfuacas, Muño, Arlanzón, Jarros, Losa, Rodilla, Quintanilla Sobresierra, Montorio, Carrion, Deseñas. Villamayor de Los Montes...

He let himself to be carried away by the lilting rhythm of the names, a counterpoint to the patter of rain on the parapet.

The professor fell silent.

He grabbed the map of Huelgas from the adjacent bureau, gave it a cursory examination, and set it on the table next to the provincial map. His fingers were already tracing a groove on the drawing, as if he hadn't entirely noticed the perfectly formed lines.

He went back over the names in the final column.

Elena said nothin, frowning as she continued to examine the map.

'Elena?' Are you thinking the same?' asked Carlos, taken aback by her silence.

His question got no immediate answer.

His colleague had adopted the same solitary demeanour as her companions during the last days, confining herself to a sign requesting silence before writing on her laptop.

The light, that revealing light that had provided the key that early morning in Huelgas was entering the professor's study through the window positioned behind him, having made its way through the rain, producing a curious effect on his appearance.

'Gold is the word!' Elena finally said, with a cry.

The two sort of jumped in response to the exclamation.

'It's gold! Gold is the word!' Elena kept repeating.

Her voice had reached the professor's consciousness slowly, with a rhythm of its own, like the echo of a train, whistling after having left the station for a brief stop.

'OK, Let's put ourselves in the mind of the Mother Abbess of that time,' Elena said, 'the nuns were trying to hide a golden secret; those are the exact words in the Codex, right? So it's gold—or rather light what we should be looking for. A golden place on a mountain!'

They crouched once more over the map they had been scrutinising all the evening. It was filled with minor villages, most of which had been hamlets in the thirteenth century.

Finally, upon seeing a name, Elena stood and grinned. She approached the table.

'I believe I can be of assistance here,' she said cryptically as she removed her reading glasses from their case.

Elena was pointing north of Burgos to a little hamlet.

Montorio.

'Do you not find anything odd about the name? Is there nothing here that has piqued your interest in light of what I have said? I think this is the one!' Elena said with a jubilant grin. 'I attempted not to become bogged down by the concept, but my eyes kept returning once and again to this area. I used to stay with my uncles in it during the summer months. I guess familiarity causes us to stop perceiving what is in front of us. I guess I did not want to impose my subjective view on this.'

Carlos did a quick check on his computer.

Three or four keystrokes on Google's search page. Several seconds of waiting.

'You know? You may be correct, Elena. Here it is: Montorio... In ancient times, just a sleepy settlement. It was established via the donation of several properties in San Adrian and San Miguel, both depopulated lands in the municipality of Montorio, already known as Monte Aureo at the time—carried out on May 6th, 968... Mount

Aureo— Golden Mountain. The golden seed contained in the moun-tain. Doesn't this sound familiar to you?'

Elena and Arthur approached the map.

Carlos had in his hand a book he had taken from the library. A compilation of historical facsimiles.

'Yes, it makes some sense. Besides, the location is relatively close to Burgos, but if I'm not mistaken—and here he paused to pick up one of last week's notebooks—. 'No, I'm afraid it's a closed-end once more. Unfortunately, that area was not under the jurisdictional, civil, or ecclesiastical sovereignty of Las Huelgas.'

'However, what about this other next to Montorio?' Elena continued tenaciously, pointing with her pencil to a village close by on the map: "Quintanilla Sobresierra"—. 'Look! It also contains the suffix "mountain" or "crest" and is only a few kilometres away from the previous one. Quintanilla Sobresierra, or in other words, "on the mountain," makes it clear beyond any shadow of a doubt, this is the place we are looking for. We've been blind as bats.

'Moreover, it reads here that this last settlement was under the civil and religious authority of the monastery,' Lafuente stated, his nose still buried in the book.

It was not a mountain, indeed. It was a village.

'There is now only one minor issue' Lafuente continued.

'Please, professor, don't tell me' Arthur said in a plaintive voice, immersed in the reading of another volume. 'I don't really want to know if I could handle it. If only I could have had a beer earlier...'

After carefully placing his pipe on the table, Carlos climbed the library ladder and spent some time moving books on top of it before descending.

'Look at this codex' the professor exclaimed gleefully, as he exhib-ited a carefully bound facsimile. *The Calf of Cardeña* makes special mention of the hamlet we've just found. Notice this! In 1077, the priest Gundisalvo donated to Sisebuto, the abbot of San Pedro de Cardeña, all the properties he owned in Monte Aureo—the Golden Mount.'

Was this the butterfly at last?

'One final note, professor!' Arthur exclaimed, 'let's imagine for a while that this is the place... Why did you previously advise us to focus on the northern region of the province? Why did you believe the place could be found there and not anywhere else? In fact, "mount" appears as a suffix in a number of locations.'

'You were the one who gave me the idea. Remember your many remarks on about that fellow Fulcanelli on our trip to Soria? Moreover, Elena mentioned something the other day about the orientation of religious temples in the sense they used to be built so that the congregation would be facing east when entering from the west. In light of this and our awe-inspiring encounter with the lighting effects at Huelgas, I began to question whether the stained-glass windows in the chapter house were not there for a hidden purpose as well. Remember that no one knows, or at least there is no record anywhere of the true reasons behind the 1965 relocation. Nevertheless, you must acknowledge that the chapter house was the commanding centre of monastic life, the place where decisions were taken. Where on that distant Christmas day of 1257, or at most a few days later, the decision was made to send the "golden seed" to a host family?'

'I still don't get it. We have already talked about the kings' symbols and such, but the name of the village itself...?'

'The town simply is located at the same cardinal point where the sun's rays impact the chapter house.'

And with a remarkable mastery of the dramatic, Professor Lafuente folded and put the map away in one of his desk drawers, marking the end of the day.

'Now comes the challenging part' he continued.

'The challenging part?'

'Yes,' he said, producing a bag of chopped tobacco out of his pocket. 'Let's hope this new mix is to my liking. It arrived from England today. Honest to God, I can't wait to give it a try. "Duke ofQueensbury," he read, pronouncing the name with careful slowness and precision. 'The name at least piqued my curiosity.'

This was another stage. They had certainly travelled much. And every time, at every moment, they had thought they knew what they needed, but once the initial satisfaction wore off, the restlessness that knowledge brings appeared. The same restlessness about which his professor had warned him about. The restlessness of wanting to know more, of searching for the complete truth which always seemed to escape through seemingly closed doors.

The pipe was eventually lighted, and after extinguishing the match with a flick of the wrist, Professor Lafuente turned to look at the two of them, enjoying both the flavour of the tobacco blend and the idea that was becoming crystal plain in his mind.

'The Golden Mount' he whispered in a low voice.

The others nodded in the twilight.

The sound of the rain kept rattling in the background like a faded soundtrack, setting the rhythm of the evening.

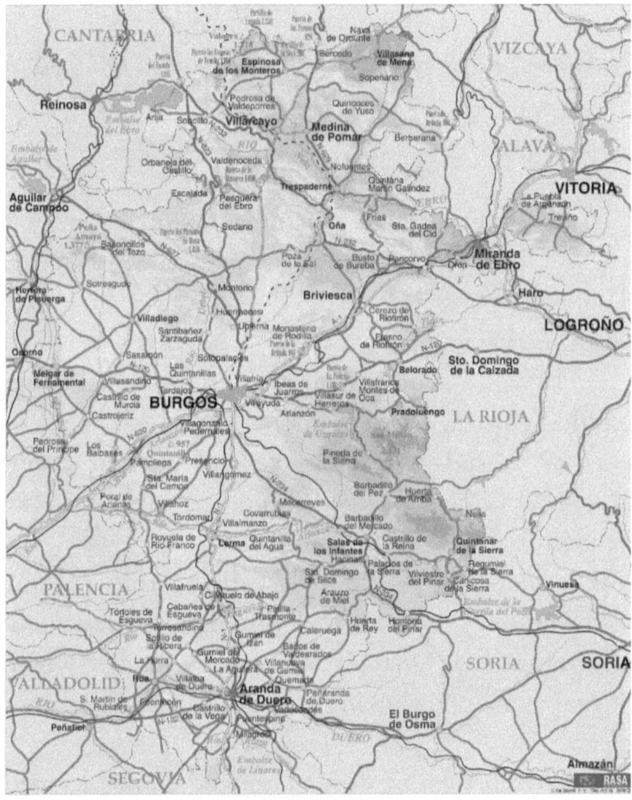

It looks like a treasure map!

CHAPTER 43

THE RETURN OF THE NOVELIST

How a chronicler fulfils up his obligations to History.

From Ernesto Santos's notes
Burgos, January 23, 20...

'Ernesto? Is that you?

The voice sounded frantic and low on the telephone. I couldn't distinguish it at first.

'Who is it?' I said—the damn lack of cellular coverage, that neither 4G nor 5G could solved, hindered my brain from determining the identity of the mysterious caller.

'Carlos? Is that you?' I said at last discovering as a linguist the solution to the mystery in that dry tone, in those short sentences.

It was him, indeed. Our adventurous researcher whom we had seen last a year ago while walking through Covarrubias in search of a Nordic legacy.

After a few exchanges of words I noticed Carlos seemed eager to tell me something. It was evident that the reason for the call had not been just to tell me about the bright day they were enjoying in Burgos. Knowing how sparse my friend was in words, I suspected there was another objective.

'Are you planning to come here any time soon?' he inquired after a few seconds, tired of stringing together what was essentially a meaningless chat.

After reviewing my agenda, I discovered I could book one of my next signing to take place in Burgos. I then looked at Clarissa, who, guessing the tone of the conversation, was nodding her head, encouraging me to take this little getaway.

'See you then!' said Carlos briefly after I confirmed my attendance and agreed to meet as soon as I arrived at Burgos.

The ping in my ear roused me from the trance I had gone into, comparable to the proverbial hen on the chalk line.

HE HADN'T SEEN HIS FRIEND FOR QUITE SOME TIME. ERNESTO was now seated in the green velvet armchair in front of him. From the window his automobile could be seen parked across the river.

Given the rush hour, that had been really a huge stroke of luck. The professor smiled, his back leaning against the curtain, his eyes fixed on the river but without neglecting the attention due to his friend.

'And now let's go to Montanilla!' he said before Ernesto could respond, grabbing his jackets and heading for the door 'There is something in my office that you must see.'

'SO YOU ARE GOING TO PRESENT YOUR BOOK AT CAJA DUERO you say,' Carlos said, after entering his university office and receiving Ismael's greetings. 'They sure will treat you well. There are some some really nice folks there. Most of them involved with publishing on provincial or regional topics.' He took a glance through the window before continuing. 'By the way, do you know who will be there for certain? You'll be glad to meet Clemente

Nasera. That man with that queer moustache who dined with us in Valladolid'

'Really?' said Ernesto tossing his head back in laughter. 'Quite a character out of a nineteenth-century novel, I must say,' He then made his way to where Carlos was standing, looking the two of them at the river below. 'This place is just wonderful!' he said. 'I'll be honest with you: working here won't do much for my writing. This view of the trees and gardens is so relaxing to me! I would be letting my thoughts carry me away, just sitting and staring out the window, letting the hours tick by. And talking of work, what happened to the manuscripts you were researching on Princess Kristine?'

Carlos provided him with a concise summary of the current state of affairs. Map after map of the area began to appear on the desk as he recounted the recent happenings at Las Huelgas monastery.

Ernesto reacted with excitement and some disbelief. How could he have known that going to Covarrubias would lead to this?

'The plot sounds like a novel' he said. 'On the other hand, I find it highly improbable that you could be able to track down the family who took in the baby.'

'Maybe you are right. However, Elena and Arthur have done an amazing work, and with some extra intuition, we've come up with a hypothesis that seems to hold water. Let's say we are now in an investigative lull.'

The conversation was cut off by a knock at the door. Shortly after, the slim form of Elena emerged from behind it, carrying a folder in one hand and a pencil in the other.

'Well, well! Here is the novel author who pledges to revitalise the historical fiction of the current century! Or would Nobel be more appropriate? How are you, Ernesto?' she asked before planting a couple of kisses on his cheek. 'Have you been brought up to speed by our resident professor? Tell me about Clarissa. Is it true she did not come along?'

'No, actually she was unable to make it this time.' Ernesto said, 'She was very remorseful; she really was.'

'Let's say you've caught us both in the midst of debriefing,' said Lafuente, unable to hide his smile as he looked at his colleague.

'After all this, I would not be astonished by anything' stated the aforementioned. 'Is it now when you're going to tell me you're aliens from outer space?'

'Well, as I always say, practical things should come first' Elena remarked. 'Obviously, new ideas must be assimilated. This is like going to the National Gallery of Art in London for the first time. As you enter one of the main wings to the left from the hallway, you'll be able to see there a painting showing the execution of Lady Jane Grey's I had to sit myself on a bench and stare at that painting for a good twenty minutes before I could move on to the next room, such impression it had on me.'

'*Touché*! I had forgotten about your tremendous enthusiasm for the arts.' Ernesto said.

'And in your case' said Elena, giving Carlos a kiss before heading to the concealed coffee machine in the corner, since she had made the professor's office her second home 'when confronted with the impossible and the coincidence, there is always that phrase I read in one of my first books, *Twenty Thousand Leagues Under The Sea*, when Professor Aronnax, confronted with the wonders of the seas and the prodigy represented by the submarine Nautilus, pronounces the phrase, "and yet, it moves." Well, in any case, I see I have distracted you long enough with this literary evocation in order to get to the coffee pot without your noticing. So much for the men of science; you're both at my mercy now.'

'Wow, I've missed a lot of stuff while I've been trapped in my ivory tower!' said Ernesto, perplexed by his friends' recent expressions of affection 'I realise that I enrol myself again in creative writing courses. Truth always wins out in the end, Has this being going on for long?'

THE MAN THREW AWAY THE CIGARETTE HE HAD LIT ONLY moments before out of pure stress.

He was running behind schedule on his delivery route. He still had to make an extra trip to Montanilla University plus four more deliveries in Burgos. Indeed, this morning was something special.

He abruptly opened the two rear doors of the van and manipulated the elevator with one hand in order to unload the to-be delivered boxes, demonstrating in so doing the expertise that comes with over five years of experience performing this duty. He meticulously examined the unreadable handwritten note.

He wished to confirm the department's moniker.

Yes, it was quite clear. It was the palaeography office of that lovely female professor. He felt it would not do to get lost again and be forced to retrace his steps through the maze of corridors, elevators and doors leading nowhere that he knew by experience were an essential part of Montanilla University.

'UNFORTUNATELY, THE RESEARCH HAS NOT GIVEN, SHALL WE say, more noteworthy finds since the discovery of the buried text in the Codex, but that appears to be the norm in our field' Elena said as they made their way to her office. 'There are advances, yes, but not striking ones; this is not, contrary to popular belief, the Ark of the Covenant or anything like that.'

She unlocked the door. The morning light appeared to illuminate the cart and oxen in the Constable painting.

'See you in about an hour, guys. Please give me some time to get my lessons ready, and Ernest, please keep in mind that even though we are talking about the last eight centuries and not ancient Rome, there is still vital information missing. Besides, we are talking about something that, with the exception of a bunch of nuns, many people would prefer to keep under wraps.'

She closed the door behind her. Ernesto —who had been gazing intently at the painting—, found himself looking at the door name-plate at eye level.

"Elena Serna Serna-Paleography Dpt."

He winced.

Serna. Such a nice surname.

THE CONVERSATION HAD PLANTED NEW SEEDS OF UNCERTAINTY in Carlos Lafuente's mind. Like the squirrels he had seen in the park, a thousand thoughts were running amok in his head, settling in front of his eyes, gliding, as if skating on roller skates to the right side of his mind before disappearing. Fleeting. Fast. To be caught in the present moment or to be doomed to perish.

'That information has remained somehow in the place through the centuries, like the one in the Codex' Carlos was saying to a thoughtful Ernest as they walked down the corridor, more to affirm his thoughts than out of a genuine need to communicate. 'I feel it is so. And like the Codex, it must be something clear and invisible at the same time.'

Ernesto shared with his friend Carlos the frustration of having found the answer to the princess's riddle only to get bogged down in yet another line of inquiry.

As I write, my right hand begins to hurt. I hope that writing these brief paragraphs may help the pain go away by making the muscles exercise in a kind of way. All because of a momentary confusion. When Carlos and I left Elena's office this morning and walked along in silence, both of us concentrated on our thoughts. I have only myself to blame, as my thinking is perpetually foggy. It has been ingrained in my nature for years every time I come across anything that stimulates my curiosity.

I did not see the delivery guy. Simply, I did not see him coming.

The collision was violent. I felt a sudden pain in my left side, followed by a loud boom. There were two sounds actually. On the one hand, there was the din produced by the pile of boxes tumbling to the ground, the second created by a myriad of little and muffled sounds as the boxes opened, scattering their content along the corridor.

My fall to the ground generated a third, slower, more deliberate, and louder noise, followed by severe pain. The last thing I needed was a box falling on my head. I was able to barely halt it with my right arm, thank goodness.

Carlos had moved out of the direction of the storm, raising his right arm, but he could no longer halt or avoid anything.

I had been the lucky recipient of all the boxes on my body.

The delivery man was still there, clutching the wheelbarrow, trying to process what had just happened. Holding in his right hand the delivery note and pen. The notebook rattled on top of one of the stacks of boxes. He had been staring at it with such exquisite concentration that he had failed to notice the two men standing in front of him.

He had just wanted to mark the delivery as completed before he actually did it so that he could leave the place sooner.

Unfortunately, he would not be lucky that day.

'I'm very sorry, sir. I didn't see you coming. Are you okay?' he managed to say in a weak voice.

Carlos bent down to check my status, seeing I was not replying.

'What's the matter?' sounded the voice of Elena as she opened the door at the end of the corridor, startled by the commotion. Seeing both of us on the floor, she rushed over and, after verifying that Carlos had escaped unharmed and that I was showing an abject spectacle, forming a peculiar pattern on the corridor floor, asked, 'Are you okay, Ernesto?'

I was given space to sit upright.

'Yes, yes, I'm OK' I muttered as I slowly stood up.

The floor seemed lined within a twenty-foot radius entirely with small business cards and various other office supplies. It seemed as if ten puzzle boxes had been opened and thrown into the air in a kind of carnival to create this effect in the corridor. The fact that they had been printed on light paper had obviously aided in this diaspora.

The four of us squatted collecting and organising silently the cards, placing them as best we could within the boxes.

Rows and rows of them in front of our eyes, covering the surrounding ground. It reminded me of those cutouts I used to make as a child when bored and tired of playing, I employed the time by cutting out the comics I was reading, stamping out the recognisable figures of the protagonists with whom I would later elaborate a story, outside the everyday boundaries of the comic I might reading at that moment.

With the habit that gives a life dedicated to reading every material subjected to my daily attention, from those signs pointing the way to the toilets, traffic ones, directions, pricing tags, product lists, ingredients in supermarkets, and a long etcetera, I couldn't help but to read those business cards over and over again, despite the fact that I already knew their content. And so, like in a hypnotic trance, I read their surface time and again: name, address, title, phone number, and email address.

"Elena Serna Serna-Paleography Dpt." Elena Serna-Serna. Serna

Serna Elena...

The name extended all over the place.

Serna.

The delivery man had, meanwhile, got up, red in the face after having collected the last box. It was uncertain whether this was due to shame at the recent adventure, or out of the effort of card collecting against the clock.

He smiled, embarrassed, with a face that revealed a strong desire to dig a hole and disappear in it as an ultimate refuge.

'Err, could you sign me here, please? I It's a shipment from Castilla Graphics,' he finally told Elena, displaying his tattered Samsung G7 smartphone, which, despite containing an astonishing amount of apps, had been of little use in preventing the catastrophe.

'Yes, I guessed that so far.' Elena said with a grimace of disgust as she pointed the pen at the stacked boxes on the side table.

After this transaction, the delivery man hurried away, embarrassed and partly glad his delivery work had not been interrupted excessively.

Shortly after, Carlos and I were walking towards the parking lot.

It had been a long morning, with adventure included.

As I left the building, though, that feeling of emptiness, of unfinished work, of a looming task I had been unable to shake since receiving Carlos Lafuente's call returned.

Through a peculiar process of mimesis, I had made his research my own.

What had initially had appeared so simple, what we all believed possible, so excited in our search, had been nothing more than a mirage.

I was at least excused as a writer from building castles in the air. Castles! Given the nature of our investigation and the identity of the firm responsible for printing the cards in question, it was hard to imagine a more apt metaphor! I felt somewhat guilty for having infected my friends, especially Carlos, with that picturesque illusion at our initial meeting. I had forced him to leave his ivory tower in quest of a mirage. He had put his soul under the sun, made a deal with the devil for nothing.

This, however, was not a novel. It was real life.

A deep-rooted family, Carlos had told me.

And he pretended to find the traces of a Castilian surname eight centuries later. With just one clue, the clue that had appeared in the Musical Codex? I felt like an asshole for ever entertaining the idea. I wanted to apologise to Carlos for the part I had played in urging him to embark on this adventure when we met in Valladolid. For all the wasted time, for having made him believe in ghosts. And Arthur was going to be just as upset as I was, even though he had feelings similar to mine.

I turned to Carlos and said, 'I wanted to tell you...' Just then my hand suddenly felt something solid in the inside pocket of my jacket. To the touch, it felt like a hard, rectangular object.

Yes, It was one of those damn business cards. Goodness knows how it had ended there after the catastrophe.

"Elena Serna Serna."

It was the third time in a row that I had read it.

I recalled what Elena had told me about its origin:

'It is an extremely common surname in Montorio. More than seventy-five percent of the population has this name. And not only there, but in nearby towns as well. We are all family in one degree or another.'

I remained motionless, staring at the tree in front of me, facing the sun-gilded pool. On that brisk morning, I could hear distant shouts coming from the nearby river, where a group of students were training. Verve and energy in the voice of their captain:

'Come on, come on, come on! I want to see the shade of that bloody blue in the oars!'

I recalled what Carlos said when describing me the recent discovery:

"*According to the Codex, the surname must be a popular one with extensive local roots.*"

Extensive local roots.

Seen everywhere.

Like that stack of cards scattered across the hallway in front of me.

Serna.

Elena's last name.

Serna.

Could this be the elusive patronymic? The lost family? Could it have been there, right under our very noses the whole time?

Such a lot of nonsense. A typical phenomenon produced in any population with low mobility. It happens everywhere.

But what if it wasn't like that?

What if it were true?

There was no risk in trying.

I was standing next to two statues on the west side of the history faculty. They represented a pair of nymphs, their arms raised, covering their faces, apparently amazed and frightened by what they had seen.

That's how I felt myself.

How was that about meaningful coincidences, dear Jung?

Yes, Ernesto felt restless. The idea of that surname had aroused his curiosity, or rather his imagination, always ready to take as valid or at least worthy of study any hypothesis, no matter how far-fetched it seemed. One had to be realistic. This small group of people had achieved in Burgos what an army of officials could not have achieved in several years of research. He had always liked to see the flame of emotion, of an idea, shine on a person's face. If this illusion portrayed itself on the faces of his closest friends, all the more reason to keep his criticism or doubts to himself.

CHAPTER 44

THE SURNAME SERNA

How a surname may captivate the soul and transport us back in time.

Tossing aside the papers on his desk, Carlos Lafuente looked up. Thick tomes of genealogy and local history were stacked on the side table. In stark contrast to them, his friend Ernesto had left a couple of Elena's business cards on the desk after giving a lengthy and eloquent speech before leaving Burgos.

"Serna."

The surname had undoubtedly been "De la Serna" in times of yore. Lafuente froze. It had indeed endured the ravages of time for millennia.

"De la Serna."

"On the Sierra."

"In the mount."

Was Ernesto right?

Had the Serna family provided a home for the defenceless creature educated by the nuns at the nearby monastery?

In a prominent place on his desk lay a study by a UBU professor on the *Cardeña Calf* — that facsimile he had held in his hands just days earlier when they learned about Montorio for the first time. One could read on it that the surname was known as early as the thirteenth century. The author had also had the surname Serna, but that was just one of those awful coincidences.

'Was it also insignificant that the name of the former Silos abbot had been "Serna?' Ernesto had stated. 'That this very abbot sought to revive the ancient surname "De la Serna? and that under his direction, Gregorian chant became popular on CDs and recordings?'

Probably.

It was the sole piece of evidence they had. What could prevent them to follow it a little longer?

He was envious of the intellect of that far ancestor who had concocted such a secret and limpid key, all those obscure references that now appeared clear as light. Well, the metaphor was not inadequate. To reach the light, they had to go places first.

THE TEA SERVICE WAS NEATLY SET UP AND ARRANGED ON THE tray. But the professor let it cool as he kept writing and highlighting furiously. Elena and Arthur were taking little sips, observing him in silence.

'Thus, the Serna trail might come from a family already existing in the north of the Burgos province, close to the Masa plain,' Lafuente emphasised, underlining some text. 'A clan making its home among the region's peaks and valleys. Serna, Sierra...mount. Just the "mount" we needed, the hill mentioned in the Codex again! You see? The surname pointed not only to the household providing lodging, but also the location itself. Don't you see? The copyist reveals both in a single stroke. Think about what he said, will you? *Master Johannes will correct your singing in no time, so have faith.*" He fixed it all right! What better protection than preserving the surname? After all, keeping the name in the family was the best defence. What better way to grab people's attention than wrap everything with a mystical air that even Templars and Rosicrucians would find impressive! Dan Brown himself would bash his head against the wall for such a revelation.'

'Calling myself Serna Serna makes me feel somewhat special' said Elena.

Carlos proceeded, oblivious to Elena's words, 'The family name may have been lost hundreds of times over the years, leaving no trace of the original line, but even so, it's still the only clue we have. Nothing more; no further writings, no books, no legends. So, why not take a moment to think about it? If we solely traced male ancestry, we'd be safe in the knowledge that the surname would be passed down down the generations; however, if a woman were to inherit the surname, its very rapid spread—which was peculiar even then, mind you!—would be an excellent asset in protecting it from being lost if she ever got married. It would help to ensure that its family tree would continue to exist for future generations.'

Carlos looked up, picking up a volume from the floor and placing it on a shelf next to the Encyclopaedia Espasa.

'La Serna, on the other hand, was a term formerly used to designate the majestic reserve or *terra indominicana*, the extension of fields directly exploited by the lord, also called "King's Sernas," the service rendered to him cultivating his land or helping him gather the fruit.' To gauge the reception of his remarks, he paused dramatically. 'You asked me recently if it could have been other the home of the family responsible for "the golden seed." I told you Arthur that such a possibility existed.' he said, pointing to the towns of Montorio and Quintanilla on the map. 'At this point, two parameters intersect. Both the reference to a golden mountain and the surname De la Serna have convinced me we have arrived at our destination.'

He noticed that Elena and Arthur were silent as if they had suddenly lost their ability to speak.

'Elena,' Carlos said, looking at her with a smile. 'In my opinion, we should be making a trip to that village of yours. What do you think?'

'I love you too, darling,' she replied, sticking her tongue out.

.   .   .

Lafuente was at home, looking at the marina, at the sea framed by the picture in front of him. Those waves always on the point of breaking, yet never actually doing so. An eternal Damocles sword, suspended there by the painter.

They would be departing for Montorio the following day. Something different for a change. Carlos was in dire need of a move, neither his large office at the university nor the campus itself provided him with space enough these days.

He took a piece of paper and jotted down the original thoughts that had been passing through his mind.

The Serna surname.

The Silos abbot who had supported the recording and popularisation of religious music.

The monks of the same monastery who, for the second time, "found" a manuscript there; the musical Codex in this case, misplaced or lost amid the existing manuscripts at Las Huelgas Abbey.

Monsignor de Balaguer writing a book about Las Huelgas Abbess and her prerogatives, a book barely mentioned later by the Opus Dei organisation, despite being the first work by the future saint upon after completing his studies and that, according to some, had been his PhD dissertation.

Had been the Opus part of this gigantic concealment as Arthur had pointed out? Was there a connection between the organisation and the Cistercian Order? Had the monks of Silos been a kind of guardian angel before the confiscation, supporting the work carried out by the nuns at Huelgas?

Too many questions and hypotheses. He would never know the whole truth.

Religion had indeed served as a repository for knowledge in the past. It seemed fair to assume that it would be entrusted with something major.

CHAPTER 45
ARRIVING TO MONTORIO

*How our heroes searched for a great surname at the smallest point on
the map*

From Carlos Lafuente's notes
Friday, February 25th, 20...

We have arrived in Montorio. I have stepped on those streets and claimed their actual existence and identity. The national highway cuts through it like a blade. We kept looking to the left, almost expecting to see a group of conquerors coming from the west, over the horizon, a raised pavilion displaying proudly its coat of arms and name as it moves through the empty space between the houses, lonely at this time of day.

We hear in its place a distant rattle that turns in a few moments into a mechanical noise that jogs over the asphalt. A mild buzz initially. We quickly recognise the cause. One tractor, exhausted from ploughing the fields in a daily struggle, more prosaic than in the past, but no less necessary, comes over the bend. A lone tractor, hobbling towards our small group, indicating in the bright green of its paint its recent acquisition.

As it passes in front of us, it leaves in the air a mixture of the scents of the countryside, difficult to classify, made of a mixture of cereals, sunflower corn, and many, many potatoes.

Its driver, startled by the sudden apparition of so many people at this time in the afternoon, raises his left hand by way of greeting. He surely comes from the nearby cooperative, which is notably responsible for the potato growth in this area.

Indeed, as Elena had indicated, Montorio is a small town comprised of a handful of neighbours, a group of houses clustered and crammed together. As cramped as the relationship between its inhabitants. A more dramatic imagination than mine would expect to hear the notes in the air of a western soundtrack heralding the midday shooting.

'I haven't been here for ages, and mind you in spite of it being only a few kilometres from Burgos,' Elena says, gazing around with a guilty tone in her voice as if we had stepped off a spaceship in recognition of the place before taking the first exploratory steps.

Of course, I had seen pictures of the place before coming, prompted by curiosity, by that wild desire new technologies arouse in us; the passion, the belief that we can know a place before actually arriving to it. Alas! I am well aware now of the absurdity of such a longing, of such phantasies of the soul. There is no substitute for the kinaesthetic experience of moving through a location, smelling its odours, hearing its sounds, and touching its walls, monuments, and even park seats.

I try to get immersed in the place.

I examine my surroundings before crossing the street. I don't expect to see New York's Fifth Avenue traffic, but this tranquilly can almost be touched.

This is, after all, the place we have been searching for. At least that's what we think. Nothing less than the "Golden Mount" mentioned in the Codex! And that certainly is something to consider.

'What are we doing here besides admiring the length of the main street and the population density?' Elena says.

'I'm just trying to get an idea of the place, nothing more. You know, a sense of place, as Arthur would say. After all, I need to feel it's a natural site, and not merely an annotation in a manuscript. After so much academic research, don't you think a dash of realism would be welcome?'

'Oh, well, if it's just that, I think it's great. Please let me know when you are done, since I have spotted a little bar farther down and would be glad to eat a salami sandwich there.'

We are in Bar Montorio, near Calle Burgos. We have eaten a couple of sandwiches. It appeared as though every villager was assembled there i.e. five people. Lunch is enlivened by the sound of glasses and *carajillos* served to the beat of a television set that reels off the results of the most recent matches. Once our repast is finished, Elena removes her napkin and pushes it aside with a gesture that admits no reply.

'I think the best thing to do now, if I may say so unless you are trying again to continue with your sense of place, is go and talk to the people at the Montorio Association.'

The association "Golden Mount" is pretty near to where we are. But what location is not quite close by here?

Elena has inquired once more what's the purpose in coming here. Without a specific clue, no reason other than her surname and that identity with the place Arthur talks about every so often.

I suppose a portion of his life's vision has lingered with me by now. The professor-student relationship holds much of the Stockholm syndrome, I suppose. I'll have to think about this calmly. It could be the subject of a study, something to throw in a lecture at one of those tedious symposia or congresses one has to fill up with whatever goes through your head to justify attendance, hotel expenditures, and the succulent dinner or lunch taking place afterwards.

Yes, Elena wants us to see the local association.

20 Félix Rodríguez De Lafuente St turns out to be an isolated

building to our right, seen in the distance, a zebra crossing conveniently placed in front of it.

On the opposite side of the street—or more really, the highway, considering the dispersed housing development surrounding it—, a cluster of brownstone veteran houses of the population do rise, listening quietly, their doors closed; some saplings on drip irrigation stand guard outside. Their chimneys silent at that time of day.

At this point, the nearby smell of the crops is felt with greater intensity.

The silence of our footsteps upon the gravel rouses me from my slumber, caused by the lack of sound at that time of day. Some birds dare to sing and fly without looking to either side of the road before crossing it.

The building itself has a driveway to its left, which, along with the shape of its arched windows, easily distinguishable in the distance, makes it look like a rural McDonald's incorporated somehow into the geography of the population in mimesis with the environment.

We arrive in front of the building, I raise my head and notice the ornate sign over the white entrance door. The letters "Golden Mount Association" appear there, gleaming, and under them, a throng of roughly twenty figures hold hands in the sign. The image beneath this white lantern might represent the actual number of residents at any particular point of the year.

A green seat is squeezed against the windows, so that the elderly can take a break after negotiating the zebra crossing and freshen up before entering the association with their best faces.

Honorio Serna—the surname cannot be any other—, has been president of the Golden Mount Association for a few years. This, along with a few similar others, shows the concern of its inhabitants to take part in the daily life of that little corner lost in the north of the Burgos province.

Honorio is a friendly man with broad gestures and leisurely movement in his gait. When he sees us, he spreads a huge smile, pleased with our inquiries and the interest his village has aroused in the world at large. In his vision of things, he seems to believe we come from some television programme, some reality show that has picked the town as its subject. I try in vain to convince him otherwise, by showing him university documents, accreditations, and other minimal texts to justify our presence there, but to no avail. For him, Elena is simply the exiled neighbour who has triumphantly returned from the adjacent metropolis as a university professor after having survived the local potato crop. A modern Cinderella.

He drags his feet as he moves with the assurance of one used to walking without haste. With the confidence of a person who is certain of naked truths, that pushing them higher off the ground will not hasten the arrival of the future. As naked as those kicks got in the shin during lengthy soccer matches in his youth as he roamed the village streets.

He invites us to go inside the place. There, a group of three or four ladies look at us with long, inquisitive stares that many customs inspectors would love to emulate in order to perform their duties with the utmost accuracy and discretion.

Those looks, however, do not prevent a kind smile from appearing when we greet them, nor the nod of the head as a sign of recognition. After that, they will continue describing the elaboration of that particular recipe to prepare Burgos black pudding in thin slices, or tell you that Julian, Bernarda's son, the one living behind the church, near to Migueleta's house, is once again walking in the evenings with Remedios.

After that, we sat down in front of a tiny table that Honorio proudly called his desk.

On a tiny shelf behind him are numerous books on the region, the majority of them about local celebrations and Montorio itself.

Elena gives me a sidelong glance as if to say:

"We are in Princess Kristina's land; behave yourself."

Yes, she may be right. After the darkness, the secrets of the past few months, and the quest of dark arcana, keys, numerology, etc., the ethereal purity of light... an open field day.

'Don't tell me you're looking after a noble's offspring!' says

Honorio, once we are seated, glancing at the open door behind us, 'we did not think it appropriate to give more information in the village until your arrival in order to have something more solid, more credible. Never have been nobles of any type in Montorio, you know' he says with a wink, turning his attention back to us. 'The village always had a special dislike to them, since a certain baron of a neighbouring village levied a series of taxes in times of old.'

'Oh, I see. I suppose people started then to look for stones to throw at him.' I pointed out with a smile that I immediately restrained, considering that the expression may not have been one of the best.

'Years later,' says Honorio, seeming not to mind my ramblings, 'the new abbot of Silos, Father Serna, desired to adopt himself the old surname "De la Serna." Believe it or not, it caused some stir among the population. Following the example you have just offered, they began to look for stones within reach. Did you know he was born here? Fortunately, blood did not reach the river, as the saying goes. The abbot took a step back and used the more subdued Serna once more for daily use, keeping the other one for the most secret of intimacies.'

At this moment, he seems to recall Elena's presence; his smile spreads again all over his face.

'And you, let yourself be seen more around town! Since you went to the capital, we barely ever see you!' he reproaches her 'Not even for the pilgrimage!'

'What kind of pilgrimage is that?' Arthur asks. 'Excuse me, but coming from Bilbao, I haven't had time to familiarise myself with the local customs.'

'Well, it's a pilgrimage that takes place on September 24 opening the local festival in honour of the Patroness. We go from here to the hermitage of Las Mercedes, which is midway between Montorio and the neighbouring town of Quintanilla. After that we have supper at the sports centre here. It was once performed outdoors under an ancient oak tree near the hermitage.' he says with a smile. 'If you're going to Quintanilla, the people there will tell you other things. They are fond of enlisting themselves for it!'

THE PRIEST SEEMS TO HAVE BEEN WAITING FOR US. BEHIND HIM, upon one of the walls of the St John's parish church, a cross is displayed. It is rather unusual for him to have two professors come all the way from Montanilla University in Burgos in order to share their expertise, their knowledge, their anecdotes, and stories that the limited time of the daily sermon does not allow him to bring out. The few times he has tried, the elder women of the village offered him grim stares and murmured condemnation, which they would later pour into the porridge pot, ultimately coming out at the local tavern through the mouths of their husbands who faced and advised him to abandon the notion.

He is well aware of his surroundings formed by ignorant and hostile people. Still, he is confident his oratory abilities would eventually win back the wayward flock. So long as they don't suggest he wire the entire stretch of Mediavilla Street, where the temple stands, with Wi-Fi, as some bold young people did recently.

"Anything you need from the parish archive is at your disposal,' he says, swaying slightly, pleased to see so much interest in the parish on a single day.

'I THINK YOU WILL FIND IT INTERESTING TO MEET ONE OF OUR older neighbours and collaborators,' Honorio says as we leave the parish. 'She is in fact, one of the association's founding members.'

'That would be great.'

'Her name is Ana Mari. She has published a book on her childhood spent on the streets of the village. But of course you know that writing could also be done only by those without a degree.'

Without a doubt, Ana Mari is one of the more seasoned members of the Montorio team. She has become a benchmark. Such is the case that no party plan or change of decoration or position of the chairs inside the association can be made without consulting her beforehand.

Her residence is only a few metres away, on the same Félix Rodriguez de la Fuente St. Stunning in its whiteness, this building is one of a row of dwellings not far from the bar where we'd had lunch. Its location at that point on the street would have been the perfect place to pay a hypothetical toll on her front steps before continuing the march to the Santiago Walk, running parallel to the town's major route heading north.

'Come inside, if you please! Could I get you a cup of coffee? Honorio told me that you were conducting some kind of research for the University of Burgos, right? ' said the woman after having been introduced.

'Well, not exactly. As a matter of fact, we are from Montanilla University,' I say, clearing my throat.

'Ah, well, sure, I have heard of that university' The old familiar gesture of doubt crosses Ana Mari's forehead quickly as she swiftly serves the coffee she has prepared with incredible celerity. 'Here, too, you'll find tales of thrill and adventure. And you know, our gatherings are still major events. For millennia, two separate pilgrimages have met at this site.'

'You've probably met many people with the Serna surname besides your own family, I guess,' I say with a smile in an effort to draw her attention to the topic that has brought us here.

'That's right, but I am sure Honorio has already told you that,' she replies, giving him a knowing glance. 'It's easy to say when someone is from a few blocks away—pardon my exaggerating a bit—, depending on the number of Sernas they carry in their last name. There are many Sernas too in the next town, Quintanilla. Those, even having a smaller population, bear their small share of blame. You want to know something? My husband was born there himself, but his parents were each from two different towns. So, as you see, the two villages have been forced to communicate with one another. I met him during tone of those pilgrimages.' The woman smiles at the memory. 'But that was a long time ago!' she says, sipping her coffee, taking the matter for granted and cementing in my mind the certainty that Ana Mari is one of those strong northern women with grit who have endured her lot and refuse to accept any more of the cake that life has already put on her plate. No more, no less.

We bid farewell as the sun sets, when its crimson hues call us to that final goodbye seen in so many films, where there is no one on the street, and just a horse, or, in this case, a car on duty, waiting for visitors to depart.

'Please come again when you finish that book or whatever,' Ana says as a parting message from the house door.

CHAPTER 46

THE GAME BOARD

On the parallels between bobbin-making and reverse genealogy, or a
lesson in heritage and lineage.

'It's ludicrous, professor.' Arthur replied, leaning back in his chair and pushing away from him the papers he had been holding up to that moment. 'No one has done a reverse genealogy extending as far back as the one you suggest. It's crazy! And it's me who tells you that. Arthur, your student, remember? The one who believes in flying saucers, ghosts, apparitions, and cabalistic symbols. We'd be in a much better position if we had some kind of lead, a noose to pull, so to speak. The only certain method to discover this lineage would be to track the forebears through the numerous parish records. Pulling the laces. Everything else is pure fiction. And you claim the opposite!'

'No one has to remind me that genealogical research is conducted from the bottom up' Lafuente responded. 'No one save a few some topsy-turvy Montanilla academics would like to flip the equation.

Continue the quest in such a manner. I realise the perspective is crazy, but isn't it wonderfully so?'

Here, the professor hesitated. Elena thought for a moment, he would perform a pirouette on himself like Chaplin's Trump.

'Yes, I know that's the usual procedure,' Lafuente continued. 'Yes, it's scientific too. But don't tell me is the sane thing to do. Maybe we don't have a bond following your literary metaphor. It's true; perhaps we don't count on that, but we have strands. With them and a little patience, we could gather a number of them and form something resembling a small cord, don't you think?'

'Carlos, it amazes me that you might be using such metaphors when you can't even tie your shoes'—Elena intervened with a chuckle —, 'yet, without going so far, I agree that a situation like this transcends decades like butter on bread; and my apologies for the narrow-minded metaphor —my turn. However, we do have an edge in this situation. I would put all my teenage marbles in the same bag that the surname has not left the area in generations. Moreover, that the original family did not move from here. So I suppose I agree with you on that Carlos.'

'Unless, and this seems quite possible,' Arthur insisted 'that they emigrated to America or any other country between the eighteenth and nineteenth century in quest of a better life.'

'Even so' Lafuente argued, 'the trail could be easily followed. Although scarce, there are remnants of the family name in remote areas of the world. All you have to do is read *The Sernas of the World,* by Louis F. Serna. Yes, yes, don't pull faces. I have been informing myself well.'

'And how do you suggest to start, professor?'

'Since both Montorio and Quintanilla are tiny settlements, I believe we should alter our tactics and launch a more aggressive assault.'

'Radical?' Elena said in a particularly alarmed tone, not quite accustomed to Carlos' rapid logic. 'What do you mean by that?'

'Taking into account emigration and relocation as Arthur so

rightly pointed out would make the study of the lineage of both settlements a huge undertaking, one that would take a long time and could even be pointless.'

'Most likely.'

'However, if we believe...' said Carlos starting one of his usual walks, 'If we believe that by following the trail started by the first registry of the family to whom the abbess initially entrusted the infant, we could....'

'So sorry to interrupt you, sir, but as a competent historian, you should be aware that there were no parochial books or registers before 1563 or so, depending on the location. Besides, everyone was buried in the greatest of anonymity in a common grave!'

'Except for the wealthy, Arthur! Except for the wealthy families who could afford a chapel or burial place near the altar and who, in their own wills, would make provisos to be registered in the parish in order to perpetuate their name, remember? Anyway, you have pushed yourself ahead of my thinking. My friends, before both of you interrupted me in the way you usually do, I was about to suggest that, by integrating both methodologies, we might be able to discover a place where our research should converge. That place would be the time, the family, and the person. Don't you agree?'

'And then' said Elena, catching the professor's idea and rising from her chair, 'if the monastery entrusted the care of the forbidden fruit of the princess to the Serna family—or however our particular Child Jesus was referred to at the time—, there should be an explicit mention of the fact somewhere in addition to the one hidden in the Codex.'

'Now you see my point, Elena,' Lafuente replied with a smile that made him look younger. 'I resist the notion that the abbesses did not sign letters, orders, contracts, exemptions or any other sort of civil or ecclesiastical document that mentioned the name of this family, or at least, with more frequency than others.

Arthur stood up and took his scarf that had been resting on the back of the green armchair and began the ritual of tying it around his neck, saying: 'That also signifies something else as I understand it, and with the agility that has come to characterise me recently, I am leaving you both. Business calls!'

'Business calls, Arthur?' said the professor. Elena looked also at the young man with inquisitive eyes. 'What do you mean?'

'Blimey! Obviously that I'm going to meet our old acquaintance the abbess so that she can start perusing through her papers! Don't you remember she told us she would be at our disposal? And please don't tell me you didn't notice how she reacted to my drooping eyes! Gosh! I believe many of those manuscripts have not been leafed over so frequently as they have been in the past few weeks!

And with these words, Arthur disappeared through the door before any of the professors could say anything else.

'Well, my dear professor,' said Elena, once the student had left the office, 'now that our chief assistant has began the investigations on his own, what are you and I left to do? How would you suggest we go about researching the ancestry of two villages, no matter how small they are? And it goes without saying that even if the combined population of Montorio and Quintanilla does not exceed 214 individuals, I doubt the rector would be eager to fund this sort of scholarly endeavour. You also emphasised the need to broaden the search to other localities, which means even more work.'

'Yes, Elena. I had already considered that. As for the answer to your question, believe me when I say I've struggled to find it. I think I can answer your query now. I have an unusual old acquaintance—a bit eccentric, to be honest—, whom I haven't seen in years pursued herself a career as a private eye. The time has come for me to start looking through my old agendas to see if I can dig out her contact information. Besides, I still have part of the money Aunt Engracia left me to use as funding. I can't think of a more just method to put it to use, as it was her express wish in her will. '

'Wow, we've moved on from the Da Vinci Code to 007 *a la* Spanish!'

Elena meant it as a joke, but she already knew pretty well that the task ahead was going to be incredibly huge.

• • •

'I discovered these documents in the monastery's archives,' Arthur remarked as he placed a folder holding several photocopies, letters, scrolls, and copies of wills on the table. A separate page with a long list of documentation was also put along with the rest.

And then, during the next few minutes, Arthur recounted to his friends the conversation he had had that afternoon with Mother Abbess,

'More than once,' she had began as she strolled through the monastery grounds with that strange young man with old eyes, beneath a sun that refused to set, 'I had wondered if the mission this congregation had undertaken could be put through its paces at some point in the future. When I was not praying in the cloister or planting and nurturing my small vegetable plot, evenings were my time for daily walks. When I halted in front of the Stations of the Cross figures in the tiny gallery in that direction, next to the Claustrillas,' she said, pointing to a specific point in front of them. 'I felt as though the monastery was trying to tell me something. I considered my predecessors, all the women who had worshipped, prayed, and served God within these walls before me. At one point, He appeared to have abandoned us, leaving us in the dark. In that frame of mind, I wandered about here, seeing the scenery that surrounded us on a daily basis, the fruits we harvested from the orchard, and I realised that an outsider looking in at this situation would likely find it laughable.

Such nonsense.

To the world, after all, in the grand scheme of things, it was only the fleeting visit of a girl to Spain, and a foreigner at that.'

While she was speaking in this vein, they had reached her office, which she entered without pausing her speech.

Once she sat at her desk, she opened one of the drawers of an old bureau hidden in a corner and seemed to look for something in it.

'But for this community, it meant much more. The only thing I could find was this letter written by the abbess at the time,' she said, gently placing on the table a document wrapped in plastic.

'Since the founding of the monastery the original files were secured in a box under four keys,' Sister Ines continued. 'One of them was always in the abbess's possession, the others were kept by three nuns chosen and appointed by her.' At this point, she read from the parchment in front of her in a low voice: "The girl with blond eyes is gone. She has left behind a seed impossible to erase. May God forgive her and have her in her glory. Let us pray for her! Let us pray for the world that received her and her secret. Let's pray for all of us. I have left everything I know in my prayers, in my singing to God.'

When she finished reading, she placed the letter away with care and waited a few seconds before proceeding in a hushed tone:

'We sisters talk a lot about the joy of God and in God and so do the chaplains in their daily sermons.' Arthur realised he was not the only recipient of that information. Before him, the abbess seemed to be releasing herself from a heavy burden, from a constant and secret duty almost as an act of confession. 'But the joy of God is nothing mystical, dull. It is a part of us all, of our way of life, such as when, bending down in the garden after our daily walks to pick up a ripe radish or a tomato, when we see the results of our work after having finished the daily hours of study, reading, and homework. You, as scholars, know about this. On the way is the prize, am I right? It has always been in the hands of the Mother Abbess to interpret and explain as best she can the dark passages that reading the sacred texts entails but I was unable to solve the portion that was my lot.'

Arthur realised what the nun was referring to.

The hymn to God.

The musical Codex, naturally.

'I had a problem with this dark passage. Like our harvest and the trees you can see both outside and at the nearby King's Hospital, I began to think that many of them, already centenarians, were without a doubt the offspring of those first trees and plants initially planted and cultivated here, in this garden, still bearing fruit after so many centuries. We only had the certainty that the Codex hid some instructions, but we had forgotten how to decipher them. The chain eventually snapped. And so, with each ray of light that fell on the wall before me as I was walked meditating before the different cloister columns, I seemed to hear the answer, but I could neither read nor comprehend it But, as you already know, the answer was, of course, the very light.'

'I HAVE INVESTIGATED THE ROYAL PALACE ARCHIVES' SAID Arthur the next morning as soon as he entered Carlos Lafuente's office 'Particularly everything pertaining to Princess Kristina's stay at the Burgos monastery on Christmas Eve 1257, as well as any information regarding the Serna surname at the time.'

'Well? What about it?' Lafuente said.

'Their servers hold no information related to any of them. Does this imply that neither the princess came to the monastery or that the De la Serna surname never existed? We know that's not true, right? My perusal of the archives only proves that no document mentions the fact, which is not the same. Similarly, the inability to see electricity does not imply that it doesn't exist. And we know from other chronicles of her presence in Spain, we know she is buried in Covarrubias, despite the fact that the above-mentioned dossier does not mention it! And you only have to look around to get confirmation the Serna surname exists,' he said, looking at Elena with a wink.

'Where do you intend to go?' Lafuente said.

'That the absence of written documentation doesn't prove something does not exist.'

Professor Lafuente was paying close attention to his student's words.

'Sometimes, I think that to continue with our current study,' the latter continued 'it would be wiser to hire a devotee of crossword puzzles than a palaeographer or a historian. Yes, we would need to be one of those phenomenal guys that fill up the crosswords at breakneck speed in the dentist's waiting room.'

'In what sense?'

'This is essentially the same as finding in the newspaper crosswords a suitable word horizontally or vertically and then realising it doesn't fit the others four squares below, right?'

'In reference to the map of the province, Arthur remarked, 'Remember I said the first day you showed it to us it seemed like a treasure map to me?'

On Lafuente's desk multiple pages had been scribbled all over with studs, smears, rising and falling lines with no apparent sense. 'And what are those figures? Any new mathematical formulas of yours?'

"I admit it seems that way.' Carlos said, picking up one of the pieces of paper, 'and following with your example of a map, this would be the genealogy we are pursuing. These would be the roads connecting our contemporary cities, see? Look, before now, there were the so-called royal ways, lanes and stone paths, did they? Then came the regional roads, the toll system, the national roads, motor-ways and speedways. What's the result of having used these modern and fast roads for years? Well, to begin with, we have forgotten the first ones! Grass and time have grubbed up the paving stones and left only the ruts.'

'I see where you're headed; the civil and parish registers created after 1840 would be the equivalent of our modern toll highways.'

'Right, from there, you see, it would be relatively easy to track a family, thanks to the wedding, birth, death, and other lesser-known registries. And do you know what happened to a lot of these registries after the first Civil Registry Law was passed and remained in effect until 1870? Nothing dramatic, nothing chilling, unless you count the simple abandonment or destruction due to political reasons, public revolts or the like. And at this point you may be wondering, how does one go back and follow the tracks? Well, thanks to the Council of Trent, which considered the entire population remaining in the peninsula after the expulsion of Moors and Jews around 1550 to be Christian in theory, parish records became mandatory. *Voilà!* It seems like they've finally started building the national highway!'

'But how do you intend to know or track a surname from the thirteenth until the sixteenth centuries, —when the first parish records outside of the private chapels you mentioned the other day could be found?'

'I mentioned that registries were compulsory beginning in 1550, depending on population and implementation, but previous to that, they existed occasionally due to the initiative of a parish, mayor, or notary public. Around 1315, certain churches, albeit a small number decided to retain these records independently. These would be our rural roadways.We still have a long way to go, and I am well conscious of that. The route from Kristina's coming to Spain to the first register was thin and short, but the most arduous and torturous. That would effectively be the weedy road, now forgotten. And to continue my metaphor, since I'm at it, the best tools would be a pair of excellent machetes, in the shape of private letters concealed in monasteries, wills, marriages, contracts, or any other hidden documents. The pillage of Napoleon's troops and the expropriation of Mendizábal, as well as the Carlist wars and following natural calamities, did not significantly help to improve the situation. To cap it all off, in this drama-loving Spain, which had not yet emerged from its internal instability, Civil War erupted to complete the process of rupture, the uprooting and forgetfulness of its history. Consequently, the abandonment and loss would be nearly complete.'

The professor had infected those present with his enthusiasm. Arthur and Elena were fascinated at the way he expressed himself, at the dancer-like steps of the professor as he moved from the window to the library, then to the desk, and back to the window to start all over again.

'We must adopt a different approach while working with descending genealogy in order to trace the conceivable thread of that automobile crisscrossing the highways of time, becoming hopelessly lost, until finally discovering the route that would lead us to the present.'

'That faces us with a problem. Professor, should we follow your beautiful metaphor and all that.'

"What is it? Didn't my explanation seem clear to you?'

'It's only that we should at least consider the possibility that the driver may not have the funds to pay the toll and had decided instead to use a national route.'

CHAPTER 47

ELVIRA

How a tiny detective carries out her work in the Burgos parishes.

'Do you both recall that I told you about an old acquaintance of mine, a detective? I've found out she set a humble office a few years ago. So small, in fact, that she has to share the premises with a real estate agency,' the professor remarked as he sipped his much-needed coffee that morning. 'I believe she might be the ideal person to assist us with our research.'

From Arthur Trevelyan's notes

Today's afternoon will certainly go down in history.

We were assembled in the professor's office as we had been doing the past days. Having all the documents in one location is logistically convenient, quite practical. When I walked in, I was ready for yet another day of theoretical discussions and more book perusing, but as I later discovered, I was grossly mistaken.

Several weeks had passed since the professor had spoke to us about the detective without bringing the subject up again. The three of us were reviewing family trees when we heard a soft and nervous knock on the office door.

'My friends,' said the professor, looking at us with an enigmatic air, 'I think you are going to have the pleasure now of meeting our new research attaché.'

And before any of us could respond or utter a word, the door was flung open and a little figure sallied forth, springing into the room, carrying a bulky backpack.

'Elena, Arthur, may I introduce you to Elvira Redondo of the Redondo Detective Agency?'

Elvira certainly was not the image of the detective I had created in my mind. Until now when I had read or heard the word, I pictured a classic detective out of old paperbacks, someone like Marlowe or Sam Spade or even more modern classics like Mike Spillane; Elvira was nothing of the sort. The figure that walked through the door was barely five feet off the ground and possessed long, straight hair and a pair of eyes lost behind thick glasses. My attention was drawn to her extreme thinness and her quick, jerky movements. She seemed ready in search of a new scent and, should she detect it, to leap and dash after her prey, abandoning the interlocutor in the middle of a sentence.

After making this unexpected introduction, the professor turned to me with a triumphant air and said:

'We can no longer neglect our teaching commitments for more than a few hours per day, and you, Arthur, must catch up on your studies, thesis, and rowing practise. May I remind you that you must defend it within a month and that time is running out? Elvira will be responsible for the fieldwork, of searching and following the parish registers meticulously both online and personally in those cases where she cannot do it otherwise, which will, unfortunately, be most of them. We, apart from some sporadic incursion, will take care of interpreting the data collected in this way. Well, but we can discuss the specifics after tea. Would you like some Elvira?' said the professor, to whom the detective's antics and restless movements in her chair didn't seem to make a dent, as if she were just another specimen in his Lepidoptera collection.

'Hello, yes, this... I'll have some tea. Yes, yes positively, although... I believe... Yes, absolutely! Well, I'll put this over here,' she remarked attempting several simultaneous moves and deciding finally to place the hefty backpack she had carried with her on the table next to Carlos' desk, much to the consternation of the latter.

'I have inside the devices I use to investigate, you know: microphones, recorders, cameras, all that kind of thing. I can't leave it in the car, there's too much son of a bitch out there,' she said apologetically pointing to the window, looking from one side to the other while accepting the cup of tea Elena had offered her, with the same air of threatening to drop it and dash out to take a note, use the restroom, or making double sure the doors to her car —an Opel Kadett of uncertain colour due to the mud and dirt covering it— were properly closed.

To be sure, this was the picturesque specimen of the deduction world we had in front of us. My interest in her was equal parts curiosity and mirth. The formerly gloomy and dreary afternoon was improving minute by minute.

A conventional flashlight —Elvira did not trust cell phones for such a purpose, preferring instead gadgets that had been designed to accomplish one thing, and one thing only—, was in Elvira's palm as she closed the door of the ancient Opel. She immediately placed it on her knapsack, but not before having checked its contents as usual. Her equipment included a microphone, some little gadgets, and a pair of bulky headphones.

Though she was in no particular rush, she walked with quick steps, as was her custom. It was a habit she had picked up in her youth when she had to run countless errands for a family of five brothers.

She was standing in front of a new house in the town of the village she had just arrived to. What role would she be playing today?, Insurance agent, mobile phone or alarm system saleswoman, or the old classic Jehovah's Witness? Depending on who she thought could be home, she instantly assumed a new identity. By doing so, she avoided arousing suspicions, being able to gain entry and learn more about the family, such as the names of the parents, grandparents, siblings, etc.

She would have time later to compare the information she had gathered this way with the records she found in the various parishes she visited, such as the death and baptism books as well as the so called brotherhoods and Tazmias books, which recorded the annual collection of tithes, first fruits and their distribution, the Apeos books, with the inventory of church assets, the Hospital book—for passers-by —, the Matrícula books, where those who confessed and took communion annually on Easter could be found, the Factory books that registered the annual accounts of the Church and finally, those of the local hermitages, if any.

Yes. The little detective was busy at work.

She discovered several things on her travels that she would have preferred not to know.

Parish register after parish register, beginning with those of Montorio and Quintanilla, as they had agreed, to continue later with those of any nearby towns where the surname Serna should have left a trace.

The goal always the same.

The outcome also identical.

No progress.

At some moments in the day she missed the usual infidelity cases to justify a divorce, those of financial suspicions of a partner too friendly with the company's safe, following a debtor until finding out his or her address, always hidden the detective behind corners or seated over the roofs, with an occasional slip in the latter circumstance. All of this gave her work a certain degree of interest; the amount of difficulty offered her something to face instead of the dryness of old churches and the faces full of suspicion of people she encounter day after day. She felt like a thief, an invader of the privacy of the families she visited.

Families of all kinds, but mostly friendly families, who opened their doors to her with a smile.

She especially remembered the face of a lady as thin as a little bird, who had welcomed her into her small apartment; a room with tables and chairs acquired around the late sixties, placed on a worn floor, stepped on millions of times, but which the careful hand of its owner had polished. A home poorly decorated, but that the care and attention of this woman had somehow embellish with the effort what the current account could not amend. The woman told her about the husband who had left her, kindly leaving her with the mortgage debt that she now had to face as guarantor of the loan. Just a few days ago she had received a visit from the judicial commission to carry out the seizure procedure on the house.

The lived years crowded into the eyes of the woman, struggling to come out and flood over her wrinkled cheeks. Behind her eyelashes lied a world of shattered playthings and abandoned dreams. And yet, there she was in front of her, forcing a gentle smile on a face that no longer recalled the shadow of a laugh or a happy moment.

'No, thanks.' Elvira had said politely when the woman offered her something to drink, her eyes fixed on the floor to avoid meeting the look of desperation in her interlocutor's eyes while she was busy promptly putting away her bags and papers.

ELVIRA COULD SEE STORKS WAKING UP AS SHE CLIMBED ONTO the rooftops. She caused pigeons to take flight from barns that had not been trodden on in years, in a Castilian landscape that had stayed untouched for ages.

Indeed, as the professor had told Arthur days earlier, burials had taken place in churches until 1805, making it relatively easy for Elvira to locate certain families in this way. However, the thousands who were born and died without leaving a trace, as Lafuente had also stated, not having made any transaction or purchase, dictated a will, disobeyed the orders of the local king or governor, broken any commandment, or been a party to a lawsuit, had been forgotten.

"These university folks are crazy," the detective told herself whenever she phoned the university for fresh directions or specify a sign or piece of information she had just discovered. "They should leave the dead alone."

'Boy, pour me a cold beer if you please,' Elvira asked as she entered the bar of the third village where she had stopped that day. It was the lovely town of Oña. She had discovered this bar next to the monastery. Three or four men smoking in the doorway looked at her in silence.

A woman alone in an old Opel Kadett, a huge knapsack at her back, was not something you saw every day. If to this vision was added that the car appeared to have been used for a dump and stuffed with papers in the rear seat, it helped to raise the interest of the parishioners on multiple additional levels. To finish off the occasion, Elvira had had the foresight to park the car in the only tacitly forbidden place in the square, to wit, right in front of the town's central fountain, thus adding showiness and a splash of colour to the scene.

'Hey you, gorgeous,' she said in a blunt tone to a boy who jumped at being addressed as such by this strange foreigner, just as he was ready to leave with a can of Heineken to enjoy a game of bowling with his mates. 'Is the church any closer?'

❧

CHAPTER 48

THE CHESTNUTS'S DREAM

How places daydream about the past during rainy weather.

It drizzled that evening.

There was no way to see Arthur's hands safely tucked in the pockets of his grey raincoat. On its back the logo of the canoeing team—a burgundy shield with the St Maria Gate in its centre and a white background.

It was not surprising that it began to rain as professor and student wandered that evening through the streets of the Old Town before making their way back to the comfortable mansion on Espolón Walk.

They took deep whiffs taking in the strong ozone odour that pervaded everything.

'On days like this, one feels as though time doesn't pass,' the young man said as they crossed Entremercados St 'Don't you agree? Consider that store, for example. It must have been there for centuries, right?'

Lafuente followed the pointing hand to the identified store and nodded.

'Not as much as one would like, Arthur. You see, that building on the corner beside the store you mention was originally the location of

Campo Stores. Some years later, Cylsa, the department store, took its place. And now, now after barely sixty years, it's merely a memory. Even the telephone store next door was once a traditional business. Oh, well!'

His gaze brightened. He had a thought.

'Would you like to see something really ancient? Something hidden and mysterious? Some things become clearer in the rain' he said, smiling maliciously. It was his time to enjoy the pleasure of the paradox reflected on his pupil's bewildered face. One of the unspeakable pleasures of being a professor was the satisfaction of indulging himself in the gradual release of knowledge, producing an intellectual tingle both in the one issuing it forth and the one receiving it.

'What do you mean?'

'Just follow me!'

After saying this, and without giving Arthur any chance to react, Carlos strode down Fernán Gonzalez St, leaving behind the always-visible cathedral.

They finally reached Chestnuts Square. This was a place Arthur knew pretty well due to to his regular late-night forays with his pals. It was empty at that hour, except for the two of them sheltering under their umbrellas, surrounded by the five chestnut trees that owned the area. The freshly fallen leaves at their feet received the flowing water as a blessing before dying. They had been conceived in it, and they passed away with it.

In one of the square corners, the nearby steps were almost invisible, buried under the fallen leaves. Only a few modern hardwood benches played the discordant tune with the square ancestral feel.

From the notes of Carlos Lafuente

Arthur and I have gone for a walk today. The boy has been silent most of the time. I believe some portion of his mind is probably speculating on ideas and theories that I do not dare to ask, much less challenge. However, when we passed Entremercados St while strolling through the old town, a curious notion occurred to me. The rain was heavier now. Perhaps rain attracts some of us because it forces us to focus on the here and now by stimulating all of our senses at once.

Its sound, both constant and diverse, the sight of seemingly identical raindrops falling on the tiles; the dampness engulfing us; and the scent of ozone filling the air, rising from the soaked ground all contribute to this immersive experience. Perhaps it's just the warm soil breathing a sigh of relief, though. And when we touch the occasional guard railing, the bark of a tree saturated with rain, or the handle of the complicit umbrella transmitting the coolness of the metal, we experience that watery feeling in our bones.

'We have already arrived. Stay here a moment, if you please,' I told him.

We were in Chesnuts Square.

'I'm sorry, professor, but I don't get it. There is nothing in this place. The pubs are closed. Yes, the trees here are lovely and all that, but...'

The robust roots of the chestnut trees seemed to appreciate this rain-scattered compliment. A few droplets fell from the tree's leaves splattered over the young man.

'As you always say, do not make snap judgments. Close your eyes and give it a try to get one of those ESP perceptions that you keep telling me about all the time. That's it! Do you feel anything? Something springs to mind? Any echo that time might have left in the environment? Anything? Please don't argue with me; I have my reasons. Please give me the benefit of your time for just a second.'

Arthur obliged. He closed his eyes beneath the umbrella, on which tiny drops were falling.

The surrounding old houses were our silent accomplices. They knew the secret very well. Its foundations also knew and kept quiet about it. The street lights had lighted part of it at some point, but now, turned off at this twilight hour, they seemed to hide, awaiting for our words.

'Well, I feel a lot of humidity to begin with,' said Arthur, his eyes still closed. 'Besides that, silence, just silence. Similar to the one we found in the monastery. I guess that is to be expected considering the weather and place, of course.'

'You are not misguided there for a mystery actually lies beneath our feet, here below. You see, below us there is a crypt and in it lies buried the oldest dome in all of Burgos. Following Fernán González's direct command, the first San Llorente church was erected on this site. It was discovered and photographed in 1966 for the final time, before being covered again. Quite a peculiar year that, if you ask me. Especially when we consider that the monastery's stained-glass windows were relocated to their current location around that period.'

The surrounding old houses were our silent accomplices.

'Yes, I remember some repairs have been underway recently,' Arthur said, recalling how tough the access to the entertainment venues had been at the time.

'Yes, the original church is mentioned in the *Gothic Calf of Cardeña* manuscript. Pedro Gutiérrez, the architect in charge at the time of its discovery, hid the remains again, in an attempt to preserve them in case their recovery could be reconsidered at a later time.'

The building I had shown Arthur moments before stood in front of us. The headquarters of a political party coexisting with modern homes and numerous cocktail bars, such as "New La Miel" and "Jabato," which we had just passed.

'Once there was an underground passage allowing access to the crypt. The entrance was under that building adjoining the square over there. Unfortunately, the corridor became obstructed during its construction,' I explained. 'This area is full of them, you see. I come here frequently to remind myself that eleven centuries are not readily forgotten by a few quick, daily experiences, by a few moments. Moved by routine, we have got used to not paying any attention at all to our surroundings.'

'You're right, that is, as long as it's not over the weekend when this place is packed with drunk and rowdy patrons.'

'Yes, the fact that we should place cocktail bars on the site is not enough to supplant the place, to forget the past. And now, here comes the symbolic fact that will come in handy when you eventually undertake the writing of that book you have inside you. According to many neighbours, when those ruins buried beneath concrete and cement were found, a canon of the cathedral took notice. In 1966, he personally visited the crypt. And this man, like that other who was raised out of the darkness of death, was also called Lazarus. Down there, he found an inscription: a funeral plaque that read, "Gonzalo Ruiz de Compludo and his wife, Elvira. Those names mean nothing to us now, but they were the parents of Francisco de Vitoria, the "Father" of International Law, as contested now by Burgos and Vitoria. Unfortunately, that corridor no longer exists, and there is no means to access the mysterious crypt.'

'Amazing! To be honest, I did not know this story at all!'

'The vault is still down there, though. Silent. Bearing the weight of the entire city that came upon it later. Yes, it is both present and invisible. Every so often, we must listen to the city, its events and locations, in the same way that we do to rain. With our five senses. The city demands it. As I said before when we started our walk, some things are better explained under the rain.'

And so, with the rain still falling, I patted Arthur on the back of his soggy raincoat and left the chestnut trees to sing their song in peace.

The secret would remain with them.

CHAPTER 49

MEDITATIONS

*"O Sole Mio", or the relativity of time followed from
a view from St Michael's Hill.*

The professor had placed a record on the fake vintage-looking record player placed by the window. Then, after gently placing its cover on the side, he carefully lowered the pickup onto its black surface, and waited a few seconds to hear the initial sizzling coming out of the speaker. Out of it emerged the notes of "O Sole Mio" in the voice of a young tenor who had just been discovered on a television show.

At the first notes, Elena immediately closed her eyes. She broke out into a broad grin.

'You said before it was only a matter of time before we discovered a clue, right?' said Arthur, looking at the professor, standing by the record player.

Lafuente whirled around, still framed by the aria, bewildered at Trevelyan's query.

'Professor, could you please walk over here slowly?'

Without understanding what his student wanted from him, Carlos complied by crossing the library to where Arthur was.

'Did you notice what you have accomplished with this gesture, moving from the window to where you are now standing?'

'Just follow your indications, that is, walk.'

'You have done more than that, something else entirely. I did not fully appreciate the significance of the equations and formulas we performed in chemistry and mathematics classes. All that about dividing mass by time and the like. You have just traversed more than space; you have embarked, if I may so put it, you have also taken a short trip through time.'

'Hey, my boy, I don't get what you're saying. Too complicated for me to fully grasp at this late hour.'

'What I mean is that the professor Lafuente who heard my plea is no more, remained in the past.' Arthur clarified, 'The person who followed my early instructions so precisely no longer exists save in my mind, as a snapshot in my retina, if you will. Even as I speak, my words continue to echo through the ages. Our acts, repeated throughout our lives, fluctuate and pass through us, causing us to forget this elementary truth. And memory is another factor that diminishes its effect. In the current instance, the memory I carry of you standing there initially, by the window, listening to me.'

'Arthur, you appeared to have just finished reading *Alice in Wonderland* or *Jabberwocky* by Lewis Carroll.' Elena smiled, looking from one to the other.

Arthur turned to her and remarked, 'You've hit the nail on the head. Stories are but a means of understanding the extraordinary, the wonders of the everyday.'

'So you're saying, in the case that occupies us...'

'Yes, the princess's chronology would be existing concurrently with ours. Although, in human terms, her time has passed, the line remains there, existing in perpetuity. You see, it's like the effect of this very melody resonating within us. Music, the art that plays with time, is a good example. I believe I owe you this professor after our recent visit to Chestnuts Square.' Arthur concluded, lifting his coffee cup to his lips with a carefree gesture.

From Professor Lafuente's notes

Friday, April 23rd, 2021

9:00 p.m.

Just like the aria playing on the record player made me tremble inside, creating responses I didn't know were there, those notes rising in the air... that's how I felt, holding my breath, feeling there was some reason for Arthur's impromptu dissertation.

For a moment after he finished talking I felt something. It was almost a second, one of those seconds woven into the fabric of time. I felt the presence of the past at our side, right there, in this same library. I felt that what we had been searching for was not an ancient and forgotten truth relating to people that no longer existed, but rather something strangely alive, I don't know how to explain it. Half an hour later, I was still there listening, concentrated, still hearing the voice and presence of that distant person in a corner of that library where the three of us were seated.

After closing the agenda, the professor tried to get some shut-eye, but no amount of tossing and turning, adjusting his position, or repositioning his pillow produced the desired result. After a while of pointless trying, exhausted by his futile efforts, he stood and sat by the window, staring out at the the still night outside, at the silent city that, like him, could not sleep.

A light snow had begun to fall.

Burgos Winter.

There was snow on the sidewalk below. Snow at the building's main gate and far away too, over the bridge.

He hadn't seen a snowfall this severe since 2007.

Forty inches thick it had been then. He recalled it vividly. He pictured himself studying in his room, pausing every few minutes and lifting his head, looking out of the window to check if the magic was still there, beyond the window.

.   .   .

From yet another vantage point, someone else pondered the city below.

Looking down on the snow-covered trees from the terrace of Patricio Noguer's mansion built on top of St Michael's Hill, one might think they were crushed stars, their tiny points radiating outwards. Burgos Castle could be seen in the distance to his left.

The home loomed behind him, its lights on, ready for action.

He enjoyed the feeling of seeing the house in moments like these when only his wife and he would be the silent wanderers of its many corridors and stairs, quietly exploring its numerous rooms and levels. He hated the idea of walking into a dark room and fumbling around for the dreaded light switch. There was, of course, the possibility of home automation in the present day, but this idea did not appear in his worldview. In any case today there was a reason for this illumination display for today he was throwing a party to which the most well-known politicians and business leaders in Burgos would be expected to attend.

He had worked hard and deserved this reward. To be able to have this exquisite house built in a nearly inaccessible part of the city, with the castle remains as its only visible neighbours.

Undoubtedly, he had battled the city for a thousand and one municipal permissions to accomplish it. Indeed, this was his success. Throughout the years, he had cultivated certain friendships and connections. He was without question a self-made man, a product of his own efforts. The university was not enough for him. No, he had to prove to the rest of the world that this was not another of his delusional fantasies.

The madman, the wacko, was without a shadow of a doubt, that professor Carlos Lafuente and that stupid student who was about to lose both his studies and the race against the other university in the coming months, not to speak about that Elena Serna that followed him like a hot bitch.

He returned indoors.

His body passed beneath the half-circle arch constructed of wood with weird plant patterns so intertwined that it was difficult to discern what its original shape was.

Upon entering the library, his first order of business was to peruse the mail on his desk next to the large neo-Gothic fireplace that warmed the expansive space. Several copies of Greek statuary could be viewed in the estate's grounds via its windows. They, along with the other reproductions on the Montanilla campus, enthralled him.

He glanced over the mail, quickly discarding some of it.

Invitations to countless conferences, congresses abroad and event without number. Again, it was a matter of moving in the right social groups and not beating around the bush chasing chimaeras. That was the key.

'That idiot!' he mumbled, a part of his mind still trapped in the previous thought.

He turned back and closed the library door before heading to the small parlour, where his wife awaited the arrival of the first guests with bourgeois patience. She was deep in one of those French authors' complex novels that curiously continue to have a peculiar hold on women's minds.

Half an hour later, after the lights in the foyer were turned on, the crystal lattice of the gigantic chandelier on the central staircase would dominate the scene. Each guest who entered the mansion and bowed to the host,--who appeared to be guarded by the long row of pictures hanging along the staircase leading to the upper floor--, would be granted a small taste of the estate's dazzling splendour.

Don Patricio Noguer had stepped down from the balcony with such dignity and composure that he failed to notice the alteration to the outer setting. He had undoubtedly stood on that balcony and taken in the sights, gazing upward at the sky and surrounding scenery. He believed he had purchased the sky, just like he had the statues and the university temple, but the moment he shut the door of the terrace, snow started to fall again.

∼

CHAPTER 50

TRAVEL TO QUINTANILLA

*How fabric and a few drops of oil aid in the pursuit of logical
deduction in addition to influencing real estate sales.*

It was quarter to six in the afternoon. Arthur sat in front of the window in the Palaeography office, like he had done countless times before. He appeared to be waiting for something fresh to happen that day. This could be the time. He had been cheering up his companions these last days while within he shifted in doubt.

There was a hesitant knock at the door, followed by four additional ones, almost without pause. There could be no uncertainty regarding the visitor's identity.

The door was flung open, and there was none other than Elvira, carrying her backpack, her arms overflowing with folios, and a cell phone she appeared to have been using up until the moment she knocked.

'Hello, how are you doing? How are things going? How did the day treat you? Yes? Yes, Yes, I'll call you later' she said, speaking this time to the person on the phone. 'Should something arrive, please send it to me via mail.' Then she turned to Arthur and said : 'All right then, jolly good! Amazing, isn't that amazing? The professor has not yet arrived, has he? Excellent, yes, yes. Superb, unquestionably!'

Underneath this deluge of words and while the detective was arranging her belongings on the table, Arthur used his recently gained knowledge of cartography to quickly study the detective's jumper and deduce the origin, consistency, and history of the numerous spots he could see on the detective's jumper. Her clothing, including the ever-present denim jacket, appeared to be the same as the one she wore when she first stepped foot in this workplace more than a week ago.

A patch near her left breast exhibited chocolate-like characteristics. On the other hand, the front of her jumper displayed distinct spots that, similar to cities with different histories, showed clear indications of being ketchup, oil, and other substances that would have to be investigated with a certain reluctance. A palaeographer could even decipher characters in them. At their sight, the young man wondered if the woman slept at all or even had any time during the day to exercise even the most basic of personal care routines.

His concerns regarding her diet were quickly put to rest as soon as he saw her take a little packet wrapped in aluminium foil out of her backpack. It turned out to be a colossal tuna and mayonnaise sandwich.

Elvira continued to put morsels into her mouth with her right hand into her mouth as she stuffed the left one into the back pocket of her pants. Arthur became alarmed when a large glob of mayonnaise threatened to slide off the sandwich.

'Elvira, please be careful.'

'You should read these papers. They will be of great interest to you. You'll see, you'll see...'

Too late. Currently, the detective's jumper had a more topographically complex drop.

From the notes of Carlos Lafuente.

Friday, April 23rd.

I've grown used to reviewing the documentation in the evenings, when the light is dimmer. I believe everything can be seen more clearly at that hour. Even my ideas tend to be more exact after doing other duties, at least in my unique mental process. Since ten o'clock at night, a weird peace washed over me. Outside, the city is quiet and peaceful, and it's as if time itself had stopped, just like it did years ago when I was a student listening to my old transistor radio. tuning radio stations from different nations attentively listening to the distant voice of the speaker.

Elvira has arrived exhausted today, stumbling into the office, muttering incoherently, carrying that musty archive odour with her leaving some notes on my desk before scurrying out of the door, her hair falling over her face. There is just too much on this woman's plate. She is running out.

Weary as I am, though, I must press on. Even if I don't know how, I will find a way to make it happen. Because it's in everyone's best interest, not just mine, but also for Elena and Arthur's sake.

We are moving on.

I have tried to summarise the events and information we have thus far, including dates and family names. No, I don't think any of us are completely off base here, I think. We've been able to track the path up to the early 18th century with a certain degree of confidence. Having reached this stage, a lot of people would probably go nuts with happiness. Among the papers Elvira has brought with her there is a puzzling note pertaining to the births records of the remote town of Quintanaortuño, located about fourteen kilometres from Burgos. I could read in them a strange annotation. The surname "Ser" interrupted by a sharp cut, a clean split in the parchment onto which it is written.

Thunder rumbles right above my head, as if the sky itself had understood the metaphor and was attempting to break through the roof. All activity has abruptly ended on the streets; the screams and yells of several girls who had been playing until now on the nearby swings has ceased, as if a television set had been switched off.

Only the involuntary screams of few people who have not yet evacuated the streets can be heard over the raging storm.

The rain licks the houses, making it appear as though there is nothing but rain and thunder. The latter seems to be flaking and repeating in many echoes and tones, sometimes from a distance, and sometimes signalling the end of the storm, only to return with greater power to shake the moment.

The remainder of the night would be equally turbulent. Every once in a while, the terrifying rumble of distant thunder would startle me awake. My mind was attempting to forget about the parts in that family tree that escaped me; the tangled branches of ancestors and descendants. writhing on paper, mentally going over the notes Elvira had left me.

If it was water I was after, this new piece of information would force this family tree to blossom, revealing the arrangement of its higher branches for our perusal. Perhaps tonight's storm will prove beneficial.

THE PROFESSOR ARRIVED THE FOLLOWING DAY WITH FRESHLY printed material. As usual, the margins were filled with notes and underlining. Some of them were crumpled and wrinkled, suggesting that they had been written by another hand.

"The detective's reports", Arthur mused upon viewing them.

'Look here, fresh information! Our friend Elvira discovered this in the Burgos Cathedral's historical archives. This pertains to volume I, which covers the years from 395 to 1431. Check out this entry! It's priceless!'

Elena and Arthur hunched over the copy of the register, thus indicated and read the fragment the professor had studied the previous evening:

May 26th, 1319, Burgos,

Teresa de Quintanilla Sobre Sierra, nun at Las Huelgas

*monastery, and her son Juan Sánchez, chaplain of the same
monastery, sell their two Manzanillo homes to Sancho García and
his wife Mara Serna for 380 million pesos.*

 At 10 monies, the maravedi".

 Volume 44, folio 4 origin parchment,

'At first glance, it appears to be just a minor transaction, right?'
said the professor, exultant.

'Well,' Elena remarked, looking at the the document Carlos was
holding. 'It looks that way, except for the anecdote of kinship between
the nun and her so-called son, which would startle a casual reader
unaware that marriage was still legal for nuns at the time of this business deal. Besides that, I see nothing here showing this is a clue, as
you point out.'

'Yes, until one realises that that every piece of the game appears
here: Quintanilla Sobresierra, the surname Serna, and the Huelgas
Monastery.'

THE CANON ARCHIVIST LED THE SCHOLARS THROUGH THAT
massive archive undergoing digitalisation, all that accumulated past
of small parishes, and long-forgotten places that had come to rest
here.

Lafuente and Arthur were in the Burgos diocesan archive located
at the Burgos Cathedral. The very place where Elvira had found that
brief reference to a nun from Huelgas Monastery.

The archivist pointed to an old trunk 'See that? That's the so-
called Cid Chest, and not because it belonged to the hero, but
because it's so old that it is presumed to be the same age as the character. It contains the earliest records that have ever been stored in this
cathedral.'

He turned at that moment with some kindness mixed with
amazement at the fact that someone had discovered information that
he had not discovered or volunteered himself.

'I suppose you have been extraordinarily lucky to locate the reference you indicated previously on that Quintanilla nun, but don't expect to learn anything else here.' the man continued in a bored tone 'You see, the birth registrations of Montorio residents contained in this Diocesan Archive begun in the year 1567 and ended in 1926. The one on weddings began in 1561, a bit earlier and lasted until 1925. I am sorry.'

Thus, the non-existence of many of the parish registries was confirmed, despite Burgos being one of the few regions in Spain where they had been gradually digitised and centralised.

Quintanilla Sobresierra.

The name was displayed in large, clear letter on the signpost to their right. No longer was it just a dot on the map, another of those boxes they had been looking at and examining during the previous weeks.

As they approached the village, they discovered Julián González Serna –their local contact—, was already waiting for them on the side of the main road, in a place conveniently close to the canteen. He was wearing a plaid cap and a little melancholy expression. As the two clasped hands, Carlos had an instant sense of recognition.

Quintanilla Sobresierra, just a handful of forty-three inhabitants. A population lost to the west of the Ubierna River Merindad—that local terminology used for the division of the Burgos territory, as if wanting to extricate itself from it. The village they could not visit on their previous trip, despite its proximity to Montorio by only a few kilometres—the hermitage of Las Mercedes located midway between the two towns.

'So you're following in the footsteps of the Serna family,' his acquaintance stated with the same smile he had greeted them with. 'Well, those at Montorio would likely have already informed you of the situation. I'm also a Serna, by the record, should you want to know.'

The man walked with his hands tucked into his vest pockets

shielding himself from the bierzo, that chilly wind that blows from the north in that region, particularly in the evenings.

'I can somewhat relate to what you must be going through. Certainly not as much as you, but close. You see, I'm currently writing a book on my family's history. No rush, you know, but we're hitting it there.' He grinned to himself with the air of someone who doesn't expect to see the outcome of his task and is just immersed in its sheer pleasure. 'That and my dear C.F. Quintanilla are my great passions!'

'We have discovered certain references to Quintanilla people in the Burgos Diocesan Archives,' said the professor. 'We wondered if you could assist us in looking through the parish records. You see, even though we have someone combing through all the nearby towns, I'd like to see some of that data first hand, at least that pertaining to these two villages.'

The patience and selflessness task of this man, dedicated to documenting the history of his family had captured Lafuente's interest from the very first minute.

'When did the last burial took place inside the church?'asked Arthur.

'It was in 1834, I think. Fear of potential plague infections, you know.'

'And the wills and testaments, is it possible to get something out of them?' asked Lafuente.

'Well, that depends on your good luck. Occasionally, they may appear on death certificates, but that was an optional thing, of course. The slightly more important people were registered in the "Notarial Protocols" kept in the Burgos Provincial Historical Archives. Still, if you have already looked there, you've seen everything that can be found. Obviously, should there be a will per se, it would still be possible to know the names of the heirs, and should it have been registered in the notarial protocols, it would still be possible to determine the deceased's assets, which may provide further information.'

Leaving the town and travelling towards the hills revealed an even greater number of these ageless, omnipresent, and silent white windmills covering the horizon. Carlos attempted to envision a cityscape without them.

A voice from behind him murmured, 'Professor?'

It was Julian's.

Lafuente, lost in meditation, had almost forgotten about him.

He was a few steps behind him, waiting, his cell phone at the ready.

'Just got a call from Don Jacinto. He has been in charge of the parish records for quite a long time. He is expecting us. I think we're going to be lucky. Today is one of his best days!'

'HERE THEY ARE,' DON JACINTO REMARKED, RELEASING HIS GRIP on a pile of folders, dismembered books, and loose pages, dumping them on a table. 'I honestly don't know what it is about this that has attracted so much interest. They have been beneath the flooring of my house for longer than I want to recall. My father constantly pushed me to hang onto them. He said that eventually someone could be curious, but who would wish to get some yellowed, tattered, and filthy bits of paper? To be honest I had completely forgotten about their existence until you asked. I was in my last twenties when I last saw them.'

Don Jacinto was a curious man and not nearly as intimidating as Julián's initial introduction might have implied. He had been a petty mayor of Villamayor del Monte, a small hamlet of only fifteen inhabitants. While we were talking he took an old wallet out of his pocket and began fiddling with it, executing a ritual that did not escape Arthur's observation. Don Jacinto kept untangling the wallet's two elastic bands and reattaching them, as if he were about to hand each visitor two banknotes of twenty euros so they may raise a glass to his health in the local tavern.

'You know? I should have left this place years ago.' he said, his eyelids partially closed, his eyes opaque, trying to hide the emotion in his words, 'I always pictured myself taking a leisurely stroll through the centre of Burgos with an umbrella under my arm like a good

Burgos citizen, or through Vitoria, my mother's hometown. And yet, here I am, responsible for running a tiny community of no more than thirty-five individuals.' At that point, he unsnapped the wallet's final rubber. 'Of course, I haven't always been mayor, but when I wasn't, I was the opposition. However, given the situation and the fierce competition, there is no alternative!' At this point, he let out a peculiar laugh that sounded almost like a cough.

His office bore no resemblance to the fierce rivalry he had described; he had convinced himself he had an official position by repeating it numerous times.

A portrait of the King of Spain and a tiny flag behind the table he had brought from home appeared to be in a perpetual battle for space with the chairs in that small room.

Municipal optimism can sometimes go that far.

A brown paint pot in one corner indicated that Don Jacinto was attempting to refurbish the furniture with as little little city funds as possible.

Behind his chair, the whole library of the town hall consisted of a dictionary of the Spanish Royal Academy and a copy of Don Quixote. Should the observer had been more demanding, he would have added in the list the backward copies of the *Marca* newspaper that were placed on a remote chair, hoping to pass unnoticed in order to offer the position held within those four walls a better presentation.

'On the other hand, my business travels to other towns in the Merindades region have caused me great sadness. I see them full of memories. And that's bad. Because, as you no doubt are aware, there's a living memory and a dead one. And if one is advantageous, the other is not so. One ends up hearing the faint screams of people who did not wish to leave. I recall many details of those whose voices were purposefully stifled, either by those who had the information or as a result of sheer barbarism, like in the case of the village of Huérmeces. Its records were looted and burned by the French. The remaining ones would be later collected in the diocesan archives. How would I finish should I have resigned the endless game of chess I've been playing with old Jesus, the baker, for almost two decades? No, thank you, I'm not interested. In addition, I use the party committee as a pretext to approach Burgos and make-believe I am a man of the capital for the day.'

'Huérmeces, you say?' Arthur said, turning to the professor. 'The truth is I have longed to visit it for a long time. It's one of the locations discussed in my thesis. One of the rare places where Napoleon personally supervised his men. Did you know?'

CHAPTER 51

THE EMPEROR'S ROAD

The next morning the man went out to till the land again.

The sky was gloomy. The ox waited, malnourished and emaciated. He had looked moment before in the barn for some of the little feed and fruit he had stashed there after snatching it from the ground before the soldiers arrived to feed the beast one day more.

Ana and the girls would await his return in the cave.

Despite the golden day, the few clouds, and the creamy flowers that covered the hill, Ana and the girls would remain in the cave.

After traversing the Burgos Plain, the Royal Road appeared to weep among the holm oaks after fording the descent from La Varga.

Huermeces was not the same any longer.

The proud tower of the Dukes of Abrantes lifted its silhouette in the distance, casting a shadow across the landscape In an effort to ward off the invader.

The French had set up camp across the entire surrounding expanse. The fields, the firewood, the livestock, everything in the plain had been snatched from the people.

The man did not feel so much concern for Ana as for the two little girls. The smallest of their little screams, their peals of laughter

— laughter that sounded innocent even in this desperate situation—, could ruin everything. Ana would be telling them stories of happier times, such as when she and her sisters visited the nearby town of Sotosierra to dance and play with the other girls. Sometimes the commander or a nobleman used to throw a party to celebrate his birthday in the town square. How distant these memories appeared now to the woman! However, there was something in the little girl's eyes that gave her mother the courage to keep telling these stories, while also giving the peasant the strength to make any sacrifice.

THE SKY WAS GRADUALLY BECOMING DARKER.

'Are you alone?' asked the soldier when he arrived on his horse at the man's height in the meadow. Riding behind him were another dozen or so soldiers.

The peasant kept his head down so he wouldn't make these men angry or arise any negative emotion. He wanted to blend in with the landscape so that he could survive another day.

When it became clear that the peasant was not understanding him, the soldier, who had the appearance of being the captain, continued in a Spanish devastated by the guttural sounds of the Gallic language:

'You're a deaf moron, right? Is there no one else in your household? What, you don't have a woman who can cook some broth soup for me and my men? *N'est-ce pas?*'

The captain dismounted and after violently pushing the peasant to the ground, entered the house.

A few minutes later he came out carrying two or three loaves of bread, the only food the peasant had left in plain view.

'*Cochon de Merde!* These people live in pigstys. How much longer must we have to put up with this shitty country?'

His neighbour, Marcelo, who lived a few kilometres away, had given it to him that morning in exchange for a milk pail.

'Just this, *monsieur?* Bread? Should the Emperor's troops be fed bread?' the captain stated as he took a bite out of the bread, then spit out the morsel he had eaten, threw the remainder of the bread on the ground before stepping on it, amidst his men's mocking laughter.

'Captain, I apologise. It's been a rough year, and other soldiers have been here these last few days.'

"You're nothing but a rascal. You have nothing to offer guests. You have caught me in a good mood today, but the next time we pass through here, you better have something to drink or eat.'

After the soldiers left, the man still sat at the boundary of his property for some time. He had never felt as lonely as he did that night. The cold reminded him he must enter the house. Once inside, he did a thorough search in the dim light, checking every corner of the room, digging into the wall, eventually removing one of the stones. There, concealed behind it lay a small bundle wrapped in rags, prepared there since that morning. He looked carefully around, put the piece in his backpack, and headed for the hills. Tonight, at least the little ones will have something to eat.

~

CHAPTER 52

A MEMORY OF FORGOTTEN VILLAGES

Of how not just locations lose their past.

The next village they visited was Alcocero de las Pueblas, some fifteen kilometres from Villamayor del Monte. Apparently a branch of the Serna family had relocated there in the 1920s.

They were surprised to discover there a large archive.

An archive containing lots of files.

A real archive.

The place aroused the young student's interest as soon as the door leading to it squeaked slightly upon opening, that squeak that arouses the most crazy of fantasies.

It was an old, dusty place. One of those places in which there is no in charge of cleaning the shelves or putting in order the thousands of manuscripts found there. They had been stacked in this manner for centuries. Nobody had perused them to locate a date, a name, or some other information penned by a hand that in turn had been forgotten, lost in the horizons of time.

'It takes some will to give life to these things,' said with a sigh Purificación, the widow of the former town mayor, pointing to a pile of crumpled documents covered in mould and stains in stark contrast to the interest the visitors were showing in them. 'But they look to spring to life the moment one pays attention to them. I like to think that when we do something like that, we are resurrecting our ancestors in a kind of way.'

Carlos merely nodded silently while inspecting the volumes and sheets that the widow was handing him.

'And you've kept the books in this room for all these years?' he finally asked.

She shrugged. 'Given the lack of people interested in them and after what happened to the town and my father during the war, I decided they would not be going anywhere. Give them to the city council or the one in the capital? No, thanks! My grandma told me numerous times about my grandfather's service in one of these big houses. He was one of the few who could read and write—an honest man from head to toe, you know—but even so he was accused of being a fascist. A fascist my grandfather, a good one that! Fortunately, the very same mob that wanted to condemn him saved him in the end. My grandma always kept telling me he should have been more clever and put some money away for his use. She called that being clever! So, when my husband died after years of service in the city hall, I decided he would not be ranked below my grandfather. No, sir! The papers would remain here, and should anyone such as you would come, they would be welcome to them. You see, I was not very misguided. When I was but a young girl I wanted to be town mayor but my father did not want to hear about it. I think it was his way of sheltering me in that world of men in which, if we could ever go to a dance organised by the padre, we considered ourselves lucky. Consider this my revenge. This room is the only remaining place left I can still command.'

Carlos gently squeezed the shoulder of the woman.

'Thanks! You've done the right thing.'

'Now, you can copy whatever you want. I am convinced from what you said before that there are people in those papers worth talking about again. To me, they are just unknown names. names from odd years and things past, but I am confident that you will be able to make some sense of it all.'

Among the first papers that fell into their hands, Arthur had already glimpsed several pages on which the word "Serna" appeared written in clear characters.

THE NAME OF THE TOWN WAS ORBARUEGA DEL DUERO.

At least that was the name written on the little sign buried among the branches of an ancient walnut tree to the right of the road.

A population of approximately twenty dwellings and twenty individuals.

The little square was filled with the pungent odour of cow mingled with the approaching group of sheep that they had observed from the top of the hill a few minutes before entering the settlement. They left the car in front of the steps leading up to the church.

It seemed to Arthur that its interior had a certain sinister air. This first suspicion was reinforced when they entered the building and found a black Christ hanging on an ochre-colored wall behind the altar without any gold leaf, sculptures, or ornamentation other than two candles on either side.

A Christ who was not only crucified, but also sentenced to hang in this church.

A door opened to the right of the altar.

A priest crossed it, dragging a cassock that seemed a few centimetres longer than his size, gathering all of God's and humanity's dust in his wake. A cough preceded him.

'You must forgive me,' he said, pulling a handkerchief from his pocket 'I've been in this state for several days. Due to the construction close to the church and the next town festival, everything is tractors and automobiles going by and kicking up dust.'

He cast a suspicious glance at the professor, ignoring Arthur. The latter, used to this, spent his time instead curiously observing everything in the sacristy

'What do you want? To look at the books? This is not for any television programme, correct? Because I have no interest in appearing in such garbage. What people should do is collaborate more with the church. You kid, for instance, have you already been confirmed?'

Carlos swiftly interjected at that point in order to avoid a theological dispute and told the priest what they want.

'Come with me to the sacristy' he said briefly before walking towards the same door from which he had appeared without verifying if he was followed.

Once in the sacristy and after what seemed like an eternity to both the professor and Arthur, he emerged again, staggering under the weight of two hefty books in a dreadful condition he was carrying in his arms. He coughed loudly before throwing them onto a dark wood table that took up most of the sacristy. The loose and wrinkled pages of one of the volumes would have raised a cry of fear in any Royal Archives civil servant.

'Good thing someone has thought of taking some of this rubbish away!' said the priest, his face still red from the recent exertion.

There, amid the scattered documents on the table, were antique registers arranged in no particular order. The majority of them dated between 1700 and 1800. Weddings, births, deaths and wills all jumbled together in a mishmash.

'My God! These records are invaluable!' the professor remarked. 'Why hadn't you brought this to the attention of the Diocesan archive, my good man?'

' You mean this rubbish? If the parish priests who preceded me didn't care about it, why should I? Anyway, sometimes it's better not to remember things too much, don't you think? Once they have lived, they have disappeared for good. Only His glory matters!'

The man of God slammed the registry book he had been leafing through with mechanical movements as the only sign of farewell. He departed, coughing uncontrollably, pausing only to remove a crumpled handkerchief from his cassock, perhaps with more dust on it now as a result of the manoeuvre. His mind had already pushed the visitors away along with the pile of documents.

In front of them stood the pile of papers the priest had left behind with the same air and speed as if they had been the rubbish of the day dumped in the street for its prompt collection.

THEY WERE IN THE "NORTHERN NORTH" OF BURGOS, A forgotten region. A land full of caves, gall trees, streams, mountains, and valleys.

Many of the populations that Elvira, Arthur, and Lafuente had visited separately during the past weeks were scattered in the so-called Merindades land, a border of difficult demarcation to the west of Montorio.

All those places and populations seemed eager to retreat, to get under a sheet in order to conceal themselves from the sight of the windmills. They were still dreaming of its royal roads, its grassy paths, and lazy strollers. And that's the way they wanted to continue. The nightmare of the *Grande Armée*, of the French 120th Infantry Regiment, had awoken them out of their peaceful slumber. They believed perhaps the moment had come to return to it but just as it is impossible to to pick up where you left off in a good dream, so in vain did the Merindades tried to return to that previous state of mellow slumber.

The Merindades—the place where the name "Castile" originated —had become another term to designate desertion and oblivion. The Merindades, as near to the earth and daily human endeavour as the sky and the sun, and as remote as these two are from each other.

The lands had not been conquered in their day by Napoleon's troops, no. Not even by the speculative bulldozer either.

It had been the silence, yes. They had been defeated by silence and undergrowth.

A total of sixty-five populations boasted now of an intimate relationship with darkness, with the ivy and cobwebs that covered and encircled many of its nooks.

Somehow, they still retain the memory of what they once were. Well inside. Sometimes, as unbelievable as it may sound, they are unaware they possess it. But there it is in any case. In their streets, in their buildings, in the memory of the oldest, and if not there, in the scraps of paper, dusty tomes, and crumpled folios that, along with lost and folded dried flowers kept between the pages of those very volumes, await the touch of the granddaughter or great-granddaughter, of a distant heir or, in the worst case scenario, of an anonymous buyer at an auction, who, ignorant of their reality, would take them home. Then, many years later, at the right time—perhaps after dinner, at that languid hour of the evening, his eyes would land on that neatly folded paper next to the withered rose still holding its petals. Then, upon opening it, he would feel again a sliver of that life contained in those words and perhaps even delude himself into believing he could smell that flower once more.

Today was Hormicedo's day to shine.

THEY HAD LEFT MONTORIO A FEW HOUR AGO IN PURSUIT OF unknown parishes. The diocesan archive in Burgos has, indeed, collected and digitised a large number of their records. But as the detective had warned them, though, many others had not been so fortunate.

The Ubierna River Merindad was left behind. They even paused to contemplate the riverbed, tranquil and serene among the cliffs and gorges that took it far below towards civilisation.

Arthur occasionally murmured under his breath, remembering the professor's words from days earlier. This must be one of those random trips the professor had pointed out "outside the current interpretation of data"

'A beautiful place,' he finally said, looking around after a long period of silence.

Without paying heed to the young man's statements, the professor nodded and turned around.

He surveyed the surrounding landscape, attempting once more not to see the windmills.

It was an extreme case of appreciating beauty by elimination, similar to decorating a home by removing unnecessary items rather than adding ornamentation.

The sky was grey with a short orange and transverse break, resembling a scratch created by a cat, providing that note of hope that Heaven is famous for.

A heavenly wink.

A little bird perched still on the brittle branches of a tree to his left. He looked at it with interest. After a few seconds, its tail twitched ever-so-slightly. Other than the small bird, the only signs of life were his own breath and the sound of a plane in the distance. They were promptly followed by the rumble of a vehicle on the distant highway.

After a few seconds spent in this way, he looked at his wristwatch and—with that simple gesture—, he appeared to regain his sense of time which had seemingly slipped through his fingers. It was time to go back to his own century, to pending chores. It was peculiar how, whenever he went in the countryside, he had the impression that ten minutes spent there seemed like an hour. He felt the day lengthening without urgency, lazy, with no agenda at all, as if true tranquility should need the absence of humans. Tribulations go hand in hand with our nature. To this had been reduced the struggles of a few in their thirst for power; the hardships, wars, and deaths of children, women, the elderly, and powerful men: to a little bird singing his lonely song on a branch.

The branch of a tree that may have been here before any of them. He closed his eyes and recounted the names of the villages they had passed through the day before: Tamayo, Villota de Losa, Valdearnedo, Castell, Icedo, Hormicedo, and most recently Hierro, whose only inhabitant had died in 2017.

From the notes of Arthur Trevelyan.

We descended a stone path invaded by undergrowth. In the distance, the horizon. Silence. What was that sudden noise, almost like a tremor coming from far away? The engine of a tractor like the one in our visit to Montorio? Some sort of bomb? We had not observed on our way down any remnants of planting or farming activity. The noise was getting closer. It turned out to be an aeroplane. What had brought it to the Merindades, anyway? Perhaps to do some geographical reconnaissance, to update the maps of the region?

About thirty minutes later, we reached our destination, a group of houses a little distance below. The water bottles in our black cloth backpacks provided occasional solace on that steep slope.

We had reached Hormicedo.

By this name we intended to refer to the abandoned, demolished church and neighbouring dwellings standing lonely in the landscape. Without a word, we entered through the still-standing semi-circular arch. A smaller door, perhaps added at a later time to facilitate the bringing in of goods and other people, was located to our left. The roof no longer existed.

The main building of the church, which years ago housed the parishioners, their delight at wedding moments, their sadness and compassion in the face of death and the burial of one of their own, was now nothing more than a yawning pit, a scream to heaven. There was a lot of debris lying around, such as beams and rubble, so entering the building was more of an exercise in prudence than investigation.

The tower, with its two windows and side arches, revealed in it the glory and pride of its builders and, with it, the triviality and insignificance of things.

Yes, we were at Hormicedo where the pillars of time still holds back nature without realising that its human inhabitants have long since gone. The stone's deaf ears were unable to hear the roar of automobiles departing one day, laden with people's furniture, clothing, and other possessions. Neither did they afterwards listen to the sluggish and heartless goodbyes with which its residents departed, little by little, in petty, familiar dramas that didn't matter much to the outside world. In Hormicedo, the singing of birds continues the same, only louder now, reverberating in the surrounding silence. They are a constant reminder that there is never absolute silence, that time marches inexorably. Yes, in Hormicedo the bell tower stands proudly, towering over the tree-tops. Since the bells have remained silent for quite some time, however, this assumption is worthless.

In Hormicedo, there is no longer any time on the tower clock since, like a burglar at night, it vanished one day without a trace.

CHAPTER 53

BETWEEN COURTAINS

How the Virgin, like mere mortals, enjoys the Sun.

'There is something we have neglected' Lafuente stated earnestly, looking forward to a respite from this compulsive document searching amid dying parishes. 'Something we found in the text we saw in Huelgas we have not paid proper attention'.

'You mean the remaining text that appears there?'

'Precisely, just have a look at it' Carlos replied, unfolding the Codex copy they had and reading aloud with a voice tinged with the solemnity the passage induced in him with each reading,

"The Virgin Mary is cleaned by the Sun while sitting in her temple."

'This is far more lyrical than the previous one, no doubt about it' said Arthur.

'However poetic it may be, it tells me nothing,' remarked Lafuente.

'Look! It's clearly written in another hand,' Elena intervened with a frown. 'I'd say that both the handwriting, the letters and capitals are more modern, right? My best guess is that they date back to the seventeenth century. Our friend Johannes was very sparing in words in comparison, the poor soul. Look, Carlos, in this sentence.The Virgin Mary's temple is mentioned, but what does it mean by that? What's the nature of that temple?'

'The cathedral, of course,' said the professor surprised himself at articulating that effortlessly.

Indeed, that was it. The temple was the cathedral itself. Her headquarters. Had it not been constructed in her honour?

'However, what about the part about being purified by the sun?' said Arthur.

Carlos looked out of the window. He would have liked to see on that glorious May morning, the silhouette of the cathedral by the river stretching in front of him, inspiring him, in that idyllic encounter of students in tour boats that alternately approached and retreated from the stream. It was difficult enough not to see it when gazing out of the window from home; although in exchange, he had the privilege of seeing the Arlanzón River flow by.

Just a second. That was it.

Burgos had always been a small city.

Everything had been in close proximity.

He recalled the meaning of the term "purification."

'There is such a place, Elena! A place for purification!'

Elena thought his expression now was particularly beautiful. In the last few days, the professor's brain leapt from one argument to another with the agility of a squirrel, connecting strands of grey cells, making unprecedented and unexpected connections.

'Of course, why not?' he said it again and again, as if asserting himself in the idea. 'Arthur, could you please hand me that book to your right on the shelf? The one with brown leather covers?'

Arthur recognised the thick volumen at once. It was the one on the cathedral's stained-glass windows written by Pilar Abad.

The professor opened it to a certain page.

A picture of one of the cathedral chapels appeared before them.

The Constables' Chapel.

'The Constables' Chapel?' Elena said, approaching slowly.

'Yes, also called the Chapel of the Virgin's Purification,' Lafuente added, gazing triumphantly at his colleagues, 'and the finest part of it all is its vault. Look at it!' he said, displaying before them a detailed illustration of the upper part of the chapel. 'A starry dome, a tribute to the Sun, to Light. Dedicated to exalting the light of Christ! At the bottom of this page, the author says that Alfonso Rodríguez Gutiérrez de Ceballos and Felipe Pereda had confirmed precisely that the very place responds to that idea, the exaltation of light!'

'And another thing I have just realised, professor,' said Arthur. 'The very term "purification." The Catholic Church's Feast of the Epiphany, or Purification, is akin to the Jewish festival of Hanukkah, the celebration of light. The builders of the chapel did something more that using the regular procedures for erecting a cathedral. A new reference to what you mentioned Elena you mentioned about the four cardinal directions and how they relate to the temple's architecture? The devout who enter the temple through the west-facing doorways will unavoidably face east. Consider all the details! There's no doubt that Simon of Cologne saw the Codex or at least heard the allusion to the well-known phrase: "From Light shall come Light." Could this, in addition to the hints we've previously looked for, have anything to do with hermetic knowledge?'

'Either way, we must visit that chapel,' Elena said. 'I can't say for certain what we'll find there, but I'm sure it will be crucial.'

'However, there is an issue,' Arthur added.

'Don't tell me, Arthur. It's impossible, right?' said the professor.

'Oh, did you then know about it?'

'No, not really. Simply put, it's just I am becoming used to the notion that every time we are presented with a hint, an obstacle will appear. I see no reason why this time would be any different. Come on, tell me, what's the deal this time?' he said in a resigned voice.

'It was published a few weeks ago in the *Diario de Burgos*. The chapel's stained-glass windows were removed a few years ago following advise from the cathedral architect, as they were in risk of falling off owing to the wind. They're currently in the hands of the glaziers at Barrio's workshop.'

'And...? Nothing is stopping us from going if they are not there.'

'Well, as a matter of fact, they are being prepared for their new placement. The area has been off-limits to visitors since yesterday. It seems art restorers are already at work on a few sculptures and pieces in that area in particular.'

'Perhaps we might rely on the Archbishop's guys to toss us a wire. It's anyone's guess!'

'So now is the Constables' Chapel? What's the matter professor? Have you not had enough with Silos, with bothering all the nuns at Huelgas monastery? I won't say it anymore, Professor Lafuente. I deny you any permission to continue with this, this... The rector here bit his lower lip, his face was flushed, his fists clenched 'this idiocy, this farce. You are a history professor, and as such you were hired by this university. I do not deny that your discovery regarding the musical Codex had some merit, but this, this... Should I have known you had a penchant for the most grotesque of speculations, these ravings more proper of an Allan Kardec follower or a spiritualist group from the advertising section of The Burgos Daily than from a fellow of the university, I would have acted differently. I wouldn't have allowed it. I will not stand by while you put this institution in jeopardy. Did you hear me?'

'Please allow me to explain myself, Mr. Noguer.'

'Did you hear me correctly, Professor Lafuente?'

Was Carlos right in thinking that the rector's pronouncing of "professor" contained a slight hint of irony?

This time it was his turn to chew on his lower lip.

'To further assure me of your collaboration or lack thereof, as you prefer to call it,' Patricio Noguer continued 'I have given instructions to all local and national bodies in matters of heritage, as well as to archives of the archbishopric and monasteries throughout the province, to deny you access to any documentation unless allowed by me. Have I made myself plain, dear Professor?'

At that moment, Carlos Lafuente could hear the silence. A hush so distinct from the stillness of the cloisters and the streets at dusk. Only a dog could be heard barking in the distance. Nothing to do with the silence of his walks across Island's Park, feeling the crunch of dry leaves underfoot. This was a thick, dense void, nearly deafening in its very denial of sound.

The rector made an emphatic gesture with his head as he retracted his arms and exited office. The door was kept ajar.

For several minutes, Carlos did not move from where he stood, the rector's words still reverberating in his head.

CHAPTER 54

ARTHUR GETS INTO AN ADVENTURE

*Of how Elvira and Arthur crossed
the Constables' Chapel, covered by Burgos dusk.*

'Given our progress so far, I bet the cathedral holds some treasures worth exploring. Don't you agree, my dear friend?' Elvira stated, peering at the student through her thick glasses.

The detective's voice resonated around the office where they had been busy filing and organising documents. The two professors had gone for their regular stroll at Island Park.

Arthur, concentrated on his task paid little heed to the detective's words. The young man's smile was nowhere to be found after the decision of the rector.

And, now, right now, after months of complex analysis and research into different sources, doors were closing once again. Was this to be the last destination? Were all their efforts to end here?

'It would be so fascinating to take a tour of that chapel and see whether the guides have missed anything,' Elvira said with a grin that attempted to appear as a catalogue of angelic innocence.

'Elvira, you know very well we have no control over this. Any further investigation into this matter is strictly forbidden by the rector. Besides, the area is closed to the public.'

A malicious look flashed across the detective's face. Her small eyes narrowed. For the first time since he had known her, Arthur felt a certain uneasiness at being alone with her.

'Yes, I am sadly aware of it,' she said, 'However, as far as I am aware, the only staff under the rector's orders are Professors Lafuente and Serna, right? Neither you as a graduate student, nor I as a humble external collaborator, are subject to the same czarist regime, right?'

A slight smile began to appear on the face of the young man. Certainly, should any of the professors continued to undertake any kind of research after the rector's ban, they would be in a very vulnerable position. However, who could prevent any mortal who felt an urge to investigate the same facts on his own? The fact that these individuals should be a graduate student and an eccentric investigator would be nothing more than a mere anecdote, something that would not disrupt the purely speculative reality of the situation.

He shook his head at this bizarre occurrence and went back to his sorting task.

A few hours later, after having put some order in his notes, Arthur heard the little detective entering the office once again. This time, Elvira stood still and silent by the door, staring at the young man as though something had been left unsaid. She remained in that position for a few minutes before finally sitting in front of Arthur leaving her backpack on the floor, all the while throwing intense glances stares every few seconds at the student.

The latter raised his head impatiently, having read the signals in her actions, as if their conversation had not been cut short hours earlier:

'Even so, Elvira,' he said, 'we can't enter the cathedral without a special permit, and I, at least as a student, have no chance to enter certain sites without the university's express permission.'

'Sure, it's true, you're right there,' Elvira answered hastily, with a gesture of sadness that Arthur found sarcastic and exaggerated.

'Why do you make faces?' he finally snapped, clearly annoyed by the ongoing display of facial expressions.

'Nothing, I guess. As you said, we would need permission or at the very least a way to entering the place as you put it, right?'

'Right,' and with that, Arthur turned his attention back to the book in his hands congratulating himself for having convinced the detective so quickly. Reading self-help books about emotional psychology appeared to be paying off. In a few years, he would be an accomplished negotiator.

'To sum things up...' Elvira intervened tirelessly 'You say that should we had that way of entry, we could get in?'

'I already said yes, didn't I?' said the young man on the verge of a nervous breakdown at the insistence of the diminutive detective.

At that moment, Elvira removed an object from her left pocket, silently, with slow and deliberate movements, placing it on the table in front of the young man. A metallic object.

A key.

'Is that what I think it is?' Arthur said, feeling his eyes widening despite himself.

The detective nodded without losing her sneaky smile and peered at him with eyes that were hardly visible under all her wicked facial motions.

'It belongs to a discreet door of the cathedral' said Elvira with a wink.

'How did you get hold of it?'

'I could give you a lot of interesting details about how I acquired it, but it would be, what do they call it in academia? — Oh, yeah! "Something tiresome to disclose", is that the phrase? I'm afraid of boring you with my explanations, boy. So you better move that student's ass and let's put ourselves on the map. Oh! And if I were you, I would bring along that scarf hanging behind you. You may need it tonight. And don't forget to get yourself a good torch! It is not compulsory to announce our presence in the place we are going to, is it?'

'WHAT ABOUT THE SURVEILLANCE SYSTEM? BECAUSE, OBVIOUSLY there must be one, no? CCTV cameras and all that, right?' Arthur muttered once they were out in the street, irritated with himself for not having paid previously more attention to this obvious fact, as well as for the apparent carelessness and speed with which the detective walked in front of him.

'There must be one, I guess,' Elvira said, as she kept checking the contents of her backpack as they kept walking, paying no more attention to the young man's words than if he had remarked on how fantastic the night was or the fact that were few strollers at that hour.

They were approaching the end of Calle Laín Calvo, just before it turns into Calle de la Paloma. On the left, virtually obscured by six small trees encircling that triangle, stood Café Latina and Bar Ambrosia. Next to them was a bronze-sculpted couple who, like the few people in the street, seemed to be defying the wind, the cold and rain, eternally sitting on that bench made of the same material, enviously gazing at the nearby cafe.

Elvira took a scrap of paper out of one of the many pockets of her coat. Some rough lines were sketched on it. Even in that dim light, Arthur could distinguish that despite having being drawn by a shaking and clumsy hand, the drawing bore a striking resemblance to a cathedral floor plan.

At that precise moment, they heard the hammer striking the quarters in the adjacent cathedral. The little automaton was likewise doing its job.

They were approaching the end of Calle Laín Calvo

Elvira pointed to the red dots on the map and added, 'This is the location of the security cameras you asked me about earlier.' she said. 'My friend Esteban is not a particularly talented artist. Poor soul! His work at the Consegur surveillance company, unfortunately prevents him from devoting much time to pursue fine art. But anyway, you can't have everything!'

In the meanwhile, they had reached the end of Calle de la Paloma. Towards their right, not far distant, was the cathedral's cloister. When they passed the Manacor Jewellery store, Elvira signalled Arthur to stop. They were now standing beneath the portico of the building facing the shop, the last one before the cloister. She motioned the student to quickly follow her.

The Flycatcher's bell rang midnight —such was the name given to the old automaton—. Arthur imagined it opening his mouth with no witnesses at that hour.

Currently, they were next to the southern portion of the cloister.

Once in that place, being both of them somewhat sheltered from the light coming from the streetlights hanging from the opposite facade as well as from the gazes of any occasional passer-by crossing at that late hour, Elvira placed her backpack on the ground and, after rummaging through it, drew out what appeared to be a tiny gadget. Without much ado, she applied herself to making some adjustments to it.

'What is that thing?' Arthur said, as he regarded the image of Virgin of la Paloma, who gave the street its name and who, from her niche in the adjacent stone wall, seemed to reproach them for their secret intentions.

The sentence spontaneously sprang to mind,

"The Virgin Mary sits in her temple being purified by the sun."

Elvira was looking at him with the same cryptic smile she had shown throughout the evening. She picked up her backpack again and resumed her stroll.

'Elvira, how long have you been preparing this? This is not a matter of one day, is it?'

'No, in fact, I had hoped to tell your professor about it. I am certain he would have enjoyed this nocturnal adventure of ours,' she replied with a grimace that didn't match the severe image conveyed by her spectacles.

Arthur doubted this would be the case. He grieved, though, that he could not enjoy the moment with his two friends. The very idea seemed stupid to him. To walk through Burgos at night as if they were part of a group of tourists looking for the most beautiful, picturesque and hidden city.

The young man gazed upward. The two towers of the cathedral resembled a pair of tall hats that would be regarde the two of them with suspicion and disapproval, wondering if these newcomers would dare to enter the cathedral and venture into its shadows and secret nooks.

A few lights could be seen in the distance. The silence seemed solid.

They were in Plaza Rey San Fernando.

Before them was the Sarmental Gate.

Two lengthy staircases lead up to two smaller doors with conspicuously placed uppers. How did Elvira think they could enter that place undetected?

'The Sarmental Gate? The Sarmental Gate, Elvira? Are you completely nuts? Is this your definition of a discrete entrance?'

'Just follow me' she answered sharply as she adjusted the knapsack on her back without further words, climbing the steps two at a time toward the doors that awaited them at the top. 'And please, try to behave as if you were checking the visiting hours on that board over there and not like potential thieves!'

Arthur felt overwhelmed to be there at that moment. The situation however did not seem to impress the detective, who proceeded slowly, glued to the walls, scrutinising with her cell phone the little piece of paper in front of her as if she were a tourist following a map under that scarce light.

Why hadn't Elvira considered entering by the Pellejeria Gate that led to the Llanas or through Calle Fernán González using the so-called Coronaria Gate? Even the main door leading to St Maria Gate appeared less exposed to the student than this prominent location at the top of the stairs. For the second time, he questioned the sanity of the action they had taken. He silently cursed the Consegur employee for having advised his nightly companion so thoroughly.

He was about to say something about it when Elvira grinned broadly. She had the little device he had seen minutes earlier in her right hand, concealed under the map. She pressed a side button, and, after a few seconds of looking at the screen, smiled, apparently pleased with what she saw.

Once this was accomplished, Elvira descended the stairs they had just climbed at full speed, under the startled gaze of the young man.

Through his confusion, Arthur observed that the detective was already pointing towards the cloister's left wall. After following her he noticed a little door beneath the steps they had climbed earlier. He had passed in front of it hundreds, thousands of times. It was its disproportion in size with the rest of the building that, in most cases, made it invisible to pedestrians.

The detective left it nevertheless after a few seconds. She walked quickly and in silence, followed by Arthur that attempted to catch up her rhythm.

'But we're returning to Calle de La Paloma! Could you please explain why...?' Arthur began as soon as he realised they were retracing their steps.

He fell silent when he noticed they had returned to the archway where they had stopped earlier. Under the Virgin de la Paloma image, there was an arch. And beneath it, Arthur could see another door. A dark, discreet door.

A smaller door.

"Easier to get in." was the fleeting thought that crossed the young man's mind.

'Please forgive me the little joke, Arthur,' Elvira said. 'I simply didn't want to lose the expression in your face for nothing in the world. I just wanted to show you there are more doors than you thought. Besides, I had some work to do first at the Sarmental Gate.'

Following Elvira's instruction, Arthur tried to mask his intentions in the best possible way. To that effect, he even recalled his recent interpretation of Hamlet in the last play performed at the university; those long rehearsals and lessons inherited from the Actor's Studio in order to accommodate those techniques to the current situation. His role today would be that of a casual stroller.

In the meantime, the detective took the matter at hand in a much more pragmatic manner by directing herself to the wooden door in front of which they were standing and inserting the key without looking back, giving Arthur no time to react, proceeding with the same naturalness as if it were the entrance to her summer flat and she was returning for the weekend.

They heard the spooky, far-off sound of the wooded door creaking open just enough for their bodies to slide inside. Seconds later, after having closed the tight opening, leaving the silent street behind, Arthur became suddenly aware of his surroundings for the first time.

They had entered the cathedral without permission using a duplicate key and bypassing the cathedral's surveillance systems.

Elvira produced a small torch from her pocket and turned it on; It was incredibly powerful and discreet at the same time. Arthur noticed it projected a focused beam, which could be very useful to avoid detection by the security cameras. At least that was what he would say in his statement, should the be arrested.

'Turn that damn thing off, Elvira! It's not the time to announce our little trip in the *Burgos Daily*,' said Arthur, looking around him. 'At least, not yet.'

'In moments of truth, an old thing like this is better than a last-generation iPhone, don't you think?' she answered, a slight hint of professional pride in her voice.

Arthur felt his heart beating faster in his chest, his reflexes quickened, in a way similar to how, towards the end of a boat race, every stroke of the oar is crucial and must be applied exactly where it is required, without hesitation.

'Now, would you kindly explain to me what you have done? I noticed a couple of cameras at the top of the stairs facing the door, right?'

'You asked me before about the placement of the cameras and the device I took out, right? So I'm going to tell you the good and bad news about them.'

'Please tell me the good one first, if you don't mind.'

'The good news is that not every location is monitored by cameras. Apart from the information my Consegur buddy provided, I know many of these things due to the professional pride of the cathedral council itself, which has deemed it necessary to tell anybody who is willing to listen or read between lines about their condition, type, and qualities. both in the media and online sites in order to show how well protected the cathedral was. Mind you! They forgot to mention the brand, price, and Amazon rating,' the detective said with one of her characteristic grimaces. 'I'll have to discuss it with them at some point so they can fix things. Provide guidance on security and such, Arthur. You follow me, right? I'd appreciate it if you wouldn't gaze at me like that. Professionals regularly engage in these practises. Most security cameras these days are connected to a server through Wi-Fi. You only need to identify the IP address of the camera you're interested in and, thanks to my personal inhibitor that every lady should carry along, *voilà!* the camera stops working for a few minutes' she said tapping her knapsack pocket where she had stored the tiny device. 'What I was doing at the Sarmental Gate earlier was exactly that. To get entry you see, I had to compare the IP addresses of the cameras there with those in this area in order to deduce the IP sequence of the cameras.'

'And the bad one?'

'Well, there are two primary kind of cameras here. The first one are motion-sensitive. They activate as soon as they detect movement around fifteen to twenty metres in front of them.'

'However, in the darkness, how...?'

'I see you're not into this, Arthur, or you don't watch many spy movies. Presently, all cameras of this sort use infrared light. You won't look quite as good in them as you would in a colour video, but still be beautiful enough for the police monitor. In most circumstances, however, it is possible to overcome this obstacle.'

'How about the others?'

Elvira pondered for a few moments before stating, 'The others bother me a little bit. They are cameras that record around-the-clock. Fortunately, they don't abound in the cathedral, as I told you.'

'Jolly good then!'

'Their situation will diminish your happiness, however. Some are located in the Cathedral Museum's upper cloister, but I'm not too worried about that because we'll only have to go a few metres there.'

'Great then, huh?'

'I don't think so. The other place containing them is the very Constables' Chapel.'

"I'm ruining my future for a chimaera," Arthur thought, reviewing quickly in his mind what had led him there, beginning with that pile of books, plans, theories, and talks held with the professors about Princess Kristina, the musical Codex, the search for the Serna family, and God only knows what else.

And now this.

"Well, Now that he had come so far," he reminded himself, "We can as well move forward and get rid of doubts once and for all."

And, putting aside those tepid thoughts and anything else other than his immediate concern of treading cautiously in the darkness, he followed Elvira's figure, who was advancing with determination, leaping from column to column. He felt the stone resting against his hands, the faint scent of incense lingering in the cathedral after a day of hectic activity.

They were in the lower cloister. Having been to Silos and subsequently Huelgas, Arthur felt at home in this new location. "When Dad told me I was always cloistered with my books, he didn't realise how close I would come to his prophecy," he thought. The cloister, he recalled his father saying, had been accessible to pedestrians back in his youth. This had been due to the high volume of traffic along Calle de la Paloma at the time. The lamplight of the latter could be guessed through the windows. It seemed to him a long time had passed since they had traversed it. Above them was the upper cloister, built to span the gap between the street and the slope leading up to the castle. It certainly added a ghostly touch to the scene.

Possibly due to how quiet and dark everything was, Arthur felt like he had been transported back to the Middle Ages all of a sudden.

A plaque in the opposite wall indicated they were in front of the Valentin Palencia Room. The lower cloister had been turned into an interpretation centre place where the cathedral's history was explained and where art exhibitions were occasionally held.

A massive sign stood in front of the plaque. In the available light they could easily read:

Sacred art. The thirteenth century in the Burgos Cathedral. From May 15th to May 30th.

Once inside, they walked past stone replicas of some of the sculptures that could be found in the cathedral. Discreetly turned off at that hour, they appeared to be waiting for the new dawn to get to work and pose in the best way before the gaze of incoming tourists.

As they proceeded, Elvira glanced every so often at the drawing showing the placement of the cameras.

'Look!' Elvira exclaimed as she shone her torchlight on one of the displayed models. 'In some sort of way, we have already reached our destination.'

Slowly, Arthur caught up with her, approaching the beam of light.

The torch was focused on a reproduction of the Constables' Chapel, more precisely a section of the interior. They could see that space in miniature with its openwork dome, stained-glass windows, and altarpieces. From the keys in the starry vault to the carvings depicting the apostles and evangelists on either side, Arthur could see that great care had been taken in creating the model. Three Burgos archbishops' coats of arms from the 17th and 18th centuries were depicted next to the windows in the miniature. There, on a small scale, beneath he torch's light, the chapel had nothing to conceal—the recumbent figures of its founders in its centre, the stone shields on the walls, everything easily assimilated and controlled.

Fortunately, although the museum was closed, the emergency lights remained on. Those and the ones existing in some of the exhibit cabinets meant that they could get around safely without having to turn on their torches.

On one wall stacked and leaning carelessly, several wooden boxes lay open. It was, without a doubt, the result of the shipment of pieces brought for the exhibition announced at the entrance. Crates of all shapes and sizes were stacked in the corners, waiting for someone to swiftly remove them so that those nooks and crannies could recover their dreams of antiquity.

'Listen now, boy, and pay attention!' Elvira's voice was suddenly grave and serious. 'Take this as a crash course in security cameras if you want, because you'll need it. These motion-sensor-based cameras can be tricked in numerous ways. The most effective approach is to use polystyrene, but obviously it would have been difficult for both of us to carry two plates of this material around Burgos, so this option was regretfully ruled out. The second, more sophisticated method is, as you may have noticed, by inhibiting their Wi-Fi signals after finding out their IP address. Sliding on the ground, crawling, and strolling close to the walls are the remaining less secure and more pedestrian alternatives.'

'That and to avoid be seen, of course. And how are you so set on the subject, Elvira? And don't give me the lame excuse that Professor Lafuente footed the bill for your CIA training.'

'You're warm there! In 2013, I was lucky enough to attend the so-called Black Hat USA security conference in Las Vegas. The folks at Bishop Fox, the organising company, certainly knew what they were doing. From keypad locks to window and door sensors, we saw it all. But, of course, not every day was going to be spent drinking and toasting with colleagues! The first thing you learn is that every five years, technology becomes obsolete. And I doubt very much that the budget of the archdiocese is as great as the glory of God in keeping them state-of-the-art. Of course, there are other, more challenging cameras to deal with, but I don't believe this to be the case. As soon as I saw those looming outside, I could see they were practically fossils, ancient relics at best.'

'Wow, good job, Elvira. But in the end, though, it all boils down to traditional methods: crawling, moving slowly and keeping glued to the walls!'

THEY ASCENDED THE STAIRS LEADING TO THE UPPER CLOISTER.
Like nocturnal lizards paying their respects in front of the Cathedral Museum, its treasures always on display their silhouettes moved darted swiftly across that huge space.

'Wait!' Elvira said, with an eager gesture, halting in a way Arthur had already become used to. 'Now!' she said, after a little pause, 'You can move on. I was worried about the presence of cameras here. Like I told you, they record continuously. And, by God! Try to keep your torch off, or at least direct its light towards the ground. As you said yourself, we are not interested in announcing our presence to anyone that might be looking from the nearby buildings that there are nocturnal visitors in the cloister. We are doing very well so far, to spoil it foolishly.'

When they were about to leave the cloister, Arthur stopped.

'Did you hear that, Elvira? Some sort of click,' he said, turning and lifting the torch.

'It's nothing, Arthur; nothing at all. We must have kicked a nail from those crates back or something like that. Come on, we still have a long way to go, so don't act like a frightened youngster. And for heaven's sake, don't raise the bloody torch! Nothing is keeping us here. Let's go!'

After examining the chart for a few minutes, the detective exclaimed with a triumphant attitude:

'We stand in front of Santiago Chapel. Its annex is the chapel of St John the Baptist. Next to it is the Constables Chapel—our final destination! From now on, my friend, everything will be easy peasy.'

They cautiously traversed the place with some fear, holding on to the walls and tiptoeing like Elvira had told him previously.

As they turned the corner, the torch beam revealed a massive grilled gate blocking the way.

On the other side, the muted lighting of the central nave seemed to mock their efforts.

'And this grill? It doesn't appear on the map!' Elvira said with a hint of doubt in her voice, which had been absent until that moment.

In vain they projected the light up and down it. As Arthur tried the gate. A slight metallic sound reverberated through the void. He projected the torch of the light to its mid section. A thick chain kept the two halves together. It was tightly closed.

'You attend Mass little, Elvira. Otherwise, you would know that not everything relating to a church is depicted on a map. This grill appears to have been shut for quite some time. Let me see that drawing of yours! I knew my studies of Art History would be worthwhile to me at some point or other.'

And with these words Arthur skimmed the map that Elvira had silently extended him.

After looking at it for a few seconds, he said:

'It's clear as rain. Here we are.' Arthur said, his finger showing the place where they stood, tantalisingly parallel to the unreachable

Constables Chapel. 'We have no choice but to turn around and continue in this direction' he said, tracing with his finger a path that run parallel to the one they had travelled up until being forced to stop at the pre-church.

'Wow!' remarked Elvira. 'I didn't count on that. We must go to the side aisle through the ante-church.'

'Well, so what? What about all that stuff you told me about Wi-Fi jammers and the like?'

'Well, the cameras in the central are equipped with motion sensors. However, unlike the ones we've met before, these are not Wi-Fi enabled. Shit on me! They are of a different model, I believe a modified KRT-33. Although'—she pondered for a few seconds —'there is a way. It's risky, but there is a way.'

THEY HAD REACHED THE SIDE NAVE. THE ENORMOUS CENTRAL transept loomed in front of them, encircled by shuttered gates similar to the one they had previously encountered.

Elvira raised her head from the map.

'The Constables' Chapel is just in front of us, to the left. Listen, boy. As I told you, the cameras facing us at the top of that pillar are the ones with a motion sensor. On the other hand they are set to only detect movement occurring one metre above the ground. They adopted this measure after a cat sneaked into the building and drove everyone half-crazy. Therefore I'm afraid we will have to crawl for a few meters. I'll go ahead with the map. Stay on my trail and follow me as closely as you possible can and please, try to walk as slowly as possible.'

Arthur nodded and gulped.

After saying this the detective proceeded to lie face down on the cathedral's flagstones, as if she were a penitent fulfilling an ancient vow.

The boy followed her, trying to put any other thoughts out of his mind. It was easier to get carried away than to consider the risks involved or the likelihood of being discovered.

Arthur viewed the detective differently at that moment, and not precisely for being the two of them sprawled across the cathedral flagstones. Initially, he had considered using the idiom "in a new light," but he soon realised that this was not the appropriate expression, either, given its scarcity at the moment.

The fact was that seeing her like this, playing her part, literally coiled into a ball that crawled across the slabs of the cathedral, was not the best thing to arouse admiration. Even so, the young man became aware of Elvira's absolute dedication to the cause. The desire that had driven her to travel throughout Burgos province in recent months in pursuit of who knows what. She had surrendered to the cause simply to find out what was on the other side of the thread, whatever that may be. As his metaphysics professor would have stated that figure lying over the cathedral flagstones was nothing more than the living embodiment of matter fighting fate.

Arthur looked back to examine the path they had travelled so far. Then, on looking forward again, he thought for a moment he had lost eye contact with Elvira. It was difficult to see her at ground-level due to the little illumination provided by the electric candles and security lights placed here and there along the central nave, which now appeared immense. This meant that he could only guess the shape of the detective in front of him as he dragged the torch and with it a circle of light that highlighted the pattern of the ground on which he was moving on.

The young man's heart appeared ready to spring from his breast and onto the altar, to be placed there as a last-minute offering. He felt his blood freezing in his veins with every step he took forward. He had the impression that each heartbeat could be heard from hundreds of metres away.

'There's another camera around that column, Arthur,' Elvira whispered. 'This one, unlike the others, utilises the CTV-27 system. I have read they can be disabled for a few seconds after immediately projecting light directly into the lens sensor. Pay close heed to my words. When I count to three, I'll direct the light from my flashlight directly on it. When I remove the torchlight from it, you will have exactly three seconds to cross the nave. Do you understand?' she said, pointing to their destination as if they were marines about to take a hill.

Arthur nodded silently, marvelling at Elvira's decision-making and execution skills in dire circumstances.

'Are you sure the torch's light will be enough to turn it off?' he asked, more to hear his own voice than anything else.

But to his alarm, his words found nothing but emptiness. Elvira was already aiming the torch toward the tiny camera perched on the column's capital, about thirty feet from where they were.

'Come on, Arthur, now!' Elvira said in a voice that admitted no doubt while putting the light away from the camera.

Arthur felt his legs obey blindly, propelling him forward, his eyes fixed on the column in front of him, staring at it with utter concentration, as if in this way he could make it come to him much earlier, as if he could accomplish teleportation, or at least to get confused with the darkness that surrounded him, with the semi-darkness at least, constantly fearing all the time that his presence could be detected at any moment, to hear an alarm reverberating throughout the nave.

Eventually, the stone wall that had seemed so far away became a tangible object in his grasp. They had done it! When he turned back, the detective was already by his side.

Suddenly, he felt an odd wetness on his chest.

It didn't take long for him to realise what it was.

His old friend, his Mont Blanc fountain pen, had apparently given up its soul, spilling a good part of its content over Trevelyan's shirt, due, no doubt to his recent crawling.

'Fuck!' Arthur uttered in despair before prudence forced him to keep silent. Tomorrow was going to be an intense cleaning day, but at this moment, he was not concerned about a future that appeared distant and uncertain.

It was then he experienced a horrible feeling. He felt in the upper pocket of his shirt in an attempt to locate the culprit.

His hands found an empty pocket.

The ballerina not only had sprained her ankle. She had fallen.

'Come on!' Elvira said, gesturing urgently from a few metres ahead, as she focused the torch on the face of her partner: 'What's the matter?'

'I must to go back, Elvira; I must to go back. I've lost my fountain pen somewhere.' The young man's voice was urgent and firm.

'For God's sake, leave it alone! You'll buy another one. Or rather, I'll give you one by Christmas if I ever get paid for my work.'

'No, Elvira. This fountain pen means a lot to me. I have to get it back. I must have dropped it when we passed the cathedral museum. Do you remember that noise I heard before? It had to be it.'

And without waiting for an answer, Arthur turned around, heading back towards the room adjacent to the vestry from which they had emerged a few minutes earlier.

'Okay, I'll wait for you at the Constables' Chapel, then! I'll try to deactivate the cameras there in the meantime to amuse myself. In any case I haven't dated anyone today' But Elvira's words were uttered into the void, to the shadows in front of her, to the spot where mere seconds before the young man had stood. She made a gesture of despair towards the closed grill in front of her, while loosening her backpack. 'I deserve it for taking children to the fair!'

ARTHUR HAD INDEED RETURNED TO THE UPPER CLOISTER, bathed now in that indirect light cast from below onto the exhibits there. A light that, like them, wanted to slither through the area without being noticed too much, barely brushing against the exposed profiles of frames, statues, and altarpieces.

Slowly, he made his way towards the lower cloister, retracing his steps, searching for the staircase they had previously climbed from the Valentin Palencia Room. He racked his brains, trying to remember the precise location where he had heard that sound. Yes, they had indeed halted here, in front of that fifteenth-century statue, or at least a stone replica of it.

He once more stood in front of the crates piled up in disarray, the crates from which so many of the figures had emerged.

He ran the torch slowly, almost like a caress, over the floor tiles, paying special attention to the corners and joints, in case the pen had become lodged between any of them. Following Elvira's instructions, he made sure not to raise the torch any higher than necessary.

No a trace of the fountain pen.

Should he retrace his steps up to the gate through which they had entered?

He leaned against one of the wooden crates. Its cover was leaning against it amid scraps of plastic, pieces of wood, and countless sheets of white cork.

He was on the verge of giving up when he noticed it.

There it was.

His ballet dancer. The ballerina he adored.

It was right next to the poster announcing the imminent exhibition, like the pointer of a tour guide showing the event, exuding the kind of subdued intelligence that only a Mont Blanc could possess at such a crucial juncture. Or was it intent to be shown alongside with the other works on display?

Yes, it had been in this place that he had heard a weird click after ascending from the lower cloister and entering the museum. Yes, Meseguer had correctly advised him, this pen leaked quite a lot, but that same ink had also served as the distress flag raised by this castaway, allowing it to be detected, found and retrieved in the dark of night.

Well, Elvira. Now it's only a matter of getting back on track.

He got to his feet and stoically walked forward.

For a moment, he felt like the hero in an adventure tale. He could imagine the excitement those scientists long ago must have felt when they first discovered the pyramids or Tutankhamen's tomb. A hero posing before the photographers and television cameras, making them fall in love with him.

Those pesky cameras!

For a moment he had forgotten about those infernal cameras and the whole surveillance equipment.

He noticed one of these evil electronic devices outside the

antechamber room, focusing his cold lens on the door, observing, scrutinising the gloom, tirelessly looking for any sign of unwanted movements.

And Elvira must be inside the chapel, patiently waiting for him.

He frantically reached for his cell phone and looked for the detective's number. That little magic trick he'd seen her perform earlier with the torch would be pretty handy now.

After a few seconds he got the message no mobile user ever wants to hear, ever:

"The number you are dialling is not in service at this moment."

He tried calling out her name in a shaky whisper that rose imperceptibly, but was lost in the pitch darkness of the nave.

'Elvira, Elvira! Can you hear me?'

There was no answer.

He didn't dare to raise his voice any higher. As Elvira had pointed out, it was possible some of these cameras might have a voice sensor.

What should he do?

He returned to the pre-vestry. He would try to call Elvira once more from there.

There was no way he could cross in front of all those cameras without the small gadget she carried. Or any of the other options he had been told about.

What was the best of them?

Just a second.

Just a bloody sec.

"You will not embark on the journey alone, Elvira. At least not this time!" he said, with an almost idiotic smile drawn on his face as his photographic memory replayed the brief technical seminar Elvira had given him at the outset of this adventure.

The young man hurriedly descended the stairs two at a time in direction to the lower cloister.

· · ·

THE DETECTIVE WAS STUNNED BY WHAT SHE SAW. SHE HAD unlocked the chapel's gate with another of the keys provided by his friend and spent what seemed like an eternity turning off the cameras monitoring the area. She walked up for the third time to the chapel's entrance, glancing down the aisle, ready to come to the aid of the student and his infernal fountain pen, cursing every few seconds. This time, though, when she looked toward the middle nave, her gaze fell onto what appeared to be a white, rectangular shape moving forward from the pre-vestry towards the central nave. She recoiled, wincing at this unknown form that was creeping silently.

As the shape came closer, she realised it was nothing more than a polypropylene sheet that seemed to advance of its own accord.

When only a few metres separated them, the light of Elvira's torch fell on Arthur's smiling face peering out one of the sides.

Yes, there was Arthur, bearing in front of him as if it were a shield, a large plate of that material he had removed from one of the crates in the museum.

'I remembered your lessons,' he said with a grin as he approached her. 'All that you told me about polypropylene being the only material capable of blocking infrared signals and all that stuff? You see, I pay attention to your lessons.'

THEY HAD FINALLY ARRIVED AT THEIR DESTINATION.

The Constables' Chapel.

They could see the tombs in the centre and in a prominent place: two recumbent figures of the founders made of Carrara marble; Don Pedro Fernández de Velasco and Manrique de Lara, Constable of Castilla and Mrs Mencía de Mendoza y Figueroa, daughter of the Marquis of Santillana whose replica they had previously seen in the model.

"A chapel dedicated to light," thought Arthur.

The light, crucial to every church building. But on this particular night however, the light that had been the key in so many previous occasions had vanished, save for a frail thread detached from Elvira's torch. What a dreadful irony to examine the Chapel of Light in the dark!

They surveyed the area. The stone shields were visible on the walls, swept by the light of the lanterns.

'There it is, The Sun,' remarked Arthur, pointing with his torch to one of the walls. Once again the reference to light: *"From light shall come light."*

Indeed, under the uncertain light of the torches, the image of the solar disk appeared in the centre of the main altarpiece and in the figuration guessed at the top.

They could make out even in darkness the stone shields of the Velasco-Mendoza on the two opposing walls. They resembled two stone giants, ready to fight at any moment. However, now silence ruled supreme. The quiet of authority emanating from the central coffins seemed to be watching every move of the two invaders.

'It also appears in the vault.' Said Elvira pointing skyward with some nervousness in her voice to the openwork plementery eight-pointed star.

'Yes, it's the symbol of St Bernardino of Siena,' said Arthur in a reverent tone.

Undoubtedly, the ancient Masons had studied the science of their day.

"It was the Great Work", Arthur thought, "the Great Work for all to behold, just as the musical Codex had been too. Somewhere lay the solution, the forgotten knowledge forgotten from the Middle Ages, the key to everything that was lost. The professor was right: Keep something in plain sight, and no one will ever notice it." From the large central rose window over the main gate with its two lateral figures to the rest of the ensemble, all that was required was a unique vision of things, some hidden knowledge to read it. As easy or as complicated as that. Like the Egyptian hieroglyphs that had waited for centuries for Champollion and the discovery of the Rosetta Stone.

In silence, in open view for all to see, this extraordinary work had remained there in a parallel and secret world. The two intruders saw —or guessed would be the correct word, under the protective plastic and dim light—the Maria Magdalena portrait attributed to Giampetrino and Leonardo da Vinci.

Arthur considered the irony implied in having arrived here practically crawling. It could be read as a symbolic tribute to the ancient masters of antiquity. Not bad at all.

Little could the intruders suspect that, a few hours before, in that place now bathed in an ashen light, Rus Bermejo, that restorer with whom they had briefly coincided in Valladolid, had been carrying out her daily restoration work.

They could make out some of the tools used by the restoration staff stored in carefully prepared cases. Blueprints and copies were concealed from the explorers' view in adjacent folders.

They were close to the chapel's vestry now, almost obscured from view by the ever present protective plastics and scaffolding that surrounded the entire perimeter, making virtually all the masterpieces and altarpieces invisible to the naked eye.

Under such dire conditions how could they be able to examine anything? It had been a mistake to listen to Elvira only to find themselves in this situation, the whole place shrouded in darkness.

Why had the glaziers at Barrio's decided to reinstall the stained-glass windows from the inside when their removal had been done from the outside? Wouldn't it be easier to have done it in the same way and in this way avoiding any potential danger to the sculptures inside?

What were they hoping to find here? Next to the entrance that led from the chapel to the vestry rested an open toolbox, displaying in a profuse pile all kinds of objects capable of altering, shaping, and also destroying the stone surrounding them. Next to it, nearly undetectable, he observed a weird crack in the wall a few inches from the ground.

They had been in that place for several minutes, lingering among the plastics that covered the walls and tools left behind by the workers, their movement generating that slight whisper that this material emits when perturbed while diffusing the torches' light.

'Well, what now?' Elvira said.

'I don't even know where to begin looking. Anything out of the ordinary, I guess. I don't have anything to go on save the notes I took in class and the ones I borrowed from the professor's office. I feel lost.' Arthur muttered, discouraged as he combed the floor in quest of a clue, an "X" marking the location of the buried treasure.

'You can always write something that will serve as a guide with that crappy fountain pen of yours you went searching for at the risk of sending everything to hell' the detective sneered as she approached to examine one of the figures on the adjacent wall.

A relief caught Arthur's attention. As he approached it, he could see it showed what seemed to be the figures of some alchemists immersed in their task.

It occurred to the young man that probably no one had ever crossed this place before, this immense space, under the light of torches. To provide a similar intensity and hue of light projected onto the walls in this way in antiquity, a large number of candles would have had to be burned at the same time.

The light from the torches paced with studied slowness over the dark walls, sometimes meandering, delaying a trajectory, going back, in a futile attempt to catch sight of anything that might have escaped observation. Arthur perceived the great skylight above their heads. A full moon was visible through it, trying to emulate the sun.

When he looked down, he noticed that the beam of his torch was illuminating a peculiar outline on the wall. He had passed that section of the chapel minutes earlier without seeing anything unusual.

It was the wall next to the vestry door.

'Elvira, look here! I had not noticed this outline before. Observe this nook!'

Elvira approached, projecting her torch on the indicated spot.

'I don't remember having seen this before, either,' she said.

In fact, both of them observed a shadow in the corner between the chapel and the vestry. It began at a column to the right of the door and went across the flagstones, outlining the ashlar masonry close to the small crack they had noticed before.

As Arthur ran his fingertips down the wall, he murmured, 'These stones seem to stand out from the rest.'

'Blimey, it must be result of some recent work, I guess. Recently, a number of altarpieces have undergone restoration. Remember the blue prints yonder? As you know, the cathedral is in a continuous process of restoration.'

'Nope. This is different.' the young man asserted with a strange assurance.

Arthur experienced a peculiar sensation. Something akin to what he had felt in Silos while approaching the old gardener or when he dared to ask the archivist about the duplicate books when both of them were in that basement where volumes of centuries past were stored at a low temperature. The same thrill he felt in Huelgas when he walked through the Claustrillas cloister and, yes, that morning when the musical Codex revealed its secret.

He sensed a peculiar force, a sense of inevitability.

The detective was leaning back, her fingers on the wall, at the precise point where they had seen the slight fissure. She had expected the stone would be loose, but it was not. The torches' light occasionally provided a deceptive feeling of depth, forming shapes and small spaces visible, otherwise unseen in daylight. It was like the flames of a fireplace in the hearth, enlarging figures and familiar objects.

'Perhaps the works have caused some displacement in the walls,' Arthur speculated. 'However, given the security measures implemented for such a restoration, it is doubtful. Let me see' he said, putting his palm on the ashlar near the vestry entrance.

'The wall is moving, Arthur!' Elvira screamed, and her voice echoed throughout the cathedral as she automatically covered her mouth.

Arthur quickly withdrew his, taking a few steps back.

The wall in front of them had effectively moved. Very little, it was true, but just enough to disclose a narrow opening.

They approached, their torches illuminating the gap opening before their eyes.

A cavity.

A passage?

Indeed, it was a door.

A gateway to the past?

If anything, it was a door that had forgotten it had ever been one.

'Wait a minute!' Arthur shouted as looked around to prevent the courageous detective from throwing herself into the cavity.

Nearby were several metal tubes used to form the sturdy scaffolding to access the stained-glass windows. Without hesitation, Arthur chose a couple and crossed them in front of the cavity opened in the wall.

'I will feel more secure that way. I would not like —it if this is what it seems— that the only entrance should close behind us.'

Feeling safer after having placed that obstacle in the small opening, they entered the discovered passage.

A blast of rotten air burst forth from within. They took a step back and waited for a few seconds. Arthur took a handkerchief from his blazer and held it to his nose, realising the air in there had probably been trapped for ages. Even if they couldn't see the past, they were definitely breathing in its stench. It was an overwhelming feeling.

'Come on, Arthur—let's not linger now,' exhorted Elvira, encouraged and energised by the adventure. This was considerably preferable to following unfaithful husbands or workers on sick leave developing other activities.

The floor was covered in dirt; it was clear enough the gallery had not been finished or properly maintained.

It looked like a tunnel. A mere eighty-centimetres wide corridor, just the right width for a thin person to move forward. As they kept advancing, they sensibly felt they were descending little by little.

Everything about the corridor they were traversing, from the uneven ground to the varying elevations along different sections, suggested that it had been excavated hastily, as if the workers were in a race against time to complete it before some obstacle, some unforeseen event paralysed or halted the work forever.

They felt in their noses a damp, stale air, a strong earthy odour, of the kind that seems perpetually humid.

The student took his cell phone out of his pocket and turned on the GPS function. There were areas where coverage was lost, naturally hindered by the cathedral's massive walls beneath which they stood. The gallery appeared to ascend now. It was then that a small line on the left edge of Arthur's cell phone screen indicated the app was once more active.

'Look, Elvira, I think we're in St Esteban's neighbourhood. At least, under some part of it. The professor and I were wandering the area the other day. Blimey! The GPS signal has been lost again! There is no coverage here,' he said, waving his cell phone as if in this way he could get the signal back.

What the young man said was unmistakable. The red circle that had emerged on the screen of his phone pinpointed their position without a doubt.

'Wait, I think I might have what you need,' Elvira said, taking an object from her unfathomable backpack and placing it in her companion's hand.

A compass.

'Thank you, Elvira,' the young man murmured with an appreciative grin, his voice muffled by the beating of his heart. 'Today, old technology wins the game!'

A few steps further, they observed little apertures on either side of the tunnel as they advanced, some slight depressions in the rock wall. From that point forward, they would find them with more frequency.

Arthur walked to the nearest wall and touched it. He felt the earth, the stone.

'I'm sure there had to be other entrances like these coming from many of the neighbouring buildings, or at least from the structures that existed before the new ones were built,' he said to himself, remembering the talk with the professor in Chestnuts's Square.

Some openings on the sides, blinded by stones, appeared to validate this theory. There, rocks had been piled up in disarray. Perhaps they had been tossed out hastily in an attempt to hide a secret that no longer had a reason to be.

'If I'm not mistaken, we must be somewhere under Calle Hospital de Los Ciegos,' Arthur said, looking at both at his cell and the compass, 'However, I can't be more precise. The app does not receive any signal. What could have prompted the construction of this passageway? And above all, why the effort to keep it hidden all this time?'

Arthur stopped and looked at the cellular screen again, scribbling something in the notes app.

The passage rose now. They could see the ceiling descending ahead of them, giving the impression that they were turning to the right.

The light of the torches increased in intensity suddenly.

The cause became apparent shortly after when the light beams suddenly and intensely reflected off an obstacle in front of them. A chalky surface was the cause. A wall formed by an accumulation of stones and earth in rough masonry work blocked the passageway.

Arthur scrutinised this obstacle. There was no fissure in it. It was old work, although not as ancient as the tunnel they were in. Maybe two hundred years? Under the torches dim light, it was impossible to pin down.

The passage had closed in front of them. A wall of rock and earth had been erected in that place—a physical as well as a symbolic barrier. Someone had definitely covered it up.

'Well, this is the end of our trip, Elvira.'

$\sim$

CHAPTER 55

THE STUDENT'S FOULARD

How a rambling stroll through the old streets of the St Esteban neighbourhood, combined with a goose and hide-and-seek game in a fleeting encounter with childhood, transports Arthur back to his elementary school days.

It is wonderful to start a walk in the evening hours, particularly at that time when the evening has no such name, and is instead a sensation. One gets the peculiar feeling the day stretches into indefinite and unending hours in which the rush seems to have left the world, birds sing continuously and children play in the park under the watchful eye of their parents, taken away by that drowsiness sustained by the sun's oblique rays, by that laziness typical of similar evenings.

That dwindling light highlights the objects, clearly delimits each and every one of the leaves on the trees, taking in so doing an X-ray of their internal structure. It also has time to leave its mark on the face of that elderly woman who amuses herself by watching the children hurry past her door while making a gesture with her head that seems to suggest they run like the very devil. Yet this very light bestows majesty onto each of her wrinkles.

The look of the ancient city and its walls is further enhanced by this light. For an instant, the river's surface sparkles and the front of the cathedral is stained gold.

It's an evening perfect for aimless strolls, with no need to think.

There are no words to describe the sensations that bombard us as we pass by, accusing the various sounds such as the muffled door of the house in front of us, the call of a mother in pursuit of that child who has left the house without a snack, or the laughter of a group of teenagers who pass by, oblivious to the world around them, completely engrossed in a parallel world entirely of their own creation.

It is also a time for smells. Floating above all, a peculiar one pervades such an evening. It is composed of a soft fragrance, an imprecise perfume made of a blend of women's aroma, lavender, the freshness of the far-off but identifiable river's clean scent, poplar and weeping willow leaves and, of course, of that chorizo sandwich some child is holding in his hand.

All that exists on evenings like this.

No one notices the lonely figure of a young man who does not appear to be enjoying the evening in the same way as they do. Neither the boy and girl who embrace while gazing into each other's eyes, nor the children who hit the ball in St Ana Square, nor the others jumping next to the wall in Paseo de Los Cubos, nor the idling stroller with the *Diario de Burgos* half tucked in the right pocket of his coat, holding his wife's arm.

This young man is Arthur. On this pleasant Sunday evening, he is walking the same paths as the other strollers, sporting a double-breasted blazer and matching scarf. There is something unique about him however, something that sets his figure apart from the rest of the people illuminated by the violet glow of that hour. His gait is irregular. He pauses now and then, lifts his head, appears disengaged. His attention is not drawn to the group of attractive young women his age who are coming his way. He does not even notice the thorough examination he is put to by one of them, which she seems to share with her friends with laughter after coming across this handsome young man.

In his left hand, Arthur holds his cell phone. Every so many steps, he stops to consult both his screen and the compass Elvira gave him and that he keeps in the breast pocket of his blazer. His gaze is focused and intent. He begun his journey an hour ago starting at Calle Nuño Rosura, but not before taking a cursory glance at the facade of St Maria Church, as if searching for a landmark before proceeding to St Agueda Church. He prefers to remember the latter by its former name, St Gadea, though, closer in connotations to the heroic deeds of the past, to the place where el Cid forced the King swear he hadn't slain his brother.

Arthur has taken a piece of paper from his right pocket and is glancing at it. He looks upwards. Finally he pauses, looks around and after ensuring no one around can see him, he takes lengthy strides as if he were following a treasure trail, the scrap of paper in his hand serving as a map. Someone with a certain romantic background might think he is a bookworm who, like many of James Joyce admirers, is attempting to emulate in the footsteps of Cid Campeador or other heroes of the past.

When Arthur crosses Witches St, the latter appears to be aware of his last night foray. The windows seem to cast peculiar winks at the young man, seeming to say, "We know you were here, boy, but don't you worry; we won't tell anybody."

As he climbs a flight of steep steps in the growing darkness while the streetlights begin their daily routine, Arthur has the stunning realisation he is alone in the area.

Somehow he feels he has returned to the passage, this time without Elvira's talkative comments by his side. At that hour of the evening, when the golden light shines on the facades, giving them a golden glow, it is easy to believe anything.

But Arthur's precautions had not taken into account something essential.

This something is the gaze of childhood, embodied in two little girls, about six or seven years old who are observing him with curiosity from a few metres away as he traverses Paseo de Los Cubos. They appear to be sisters since they both wear double-breasted beige coats with buttons of considerable size. Their parents are about two hundred metres behind. The male component of the equation, engrossed in a devoted and delicate discussion on the most recent match between Burgos CF and Arandina CF. The moms patiently await the outcome of the conversation to resume walking once the world has been fixed for the day.

The extreme immobility of the girls who until that moment had been playing hide-and-seek under the lampposts that line Paseo de Los Cubos is the reason for the young man to be unaware of their presence. They have noticed the boy appears to be immersed in some fascinating and mysterious game. They had followed his evolutions, moves, and twists, his upward glances and his writing in a small brown notebook, as if he were reading the rules of that peculiar game.

'What are you playing at?' the most daring of them finally asks. She seems to be the eldest. The girl wears a crimson cap with a little tassel, under which she smiles nervously at Arthur.

Surprised, the student raises his head and sees these two girls in front of him. He seems to be searching for a suitable phrase.

'No, I just lost something around here the other day and was searching for it.'

'It's not true!' replies the same girl, while the other nudges her— she shouldn't be talking to strangers. 'I've seen you writing things on that notepad. Is that your homework, perhaps?'

'Well, it could be considered as such' Arthur concedes, seeming to accept some the evidence 'I have to show it to my professor.' And with a look that is both apologetic for not telling them more and of shame for having been caught in the middle of his research, he resumes his walk, albeit this time quickening his pace. Women always had the knack of getting all secrets out of him.

THE SKY IS BECOMING GLOOMIER BY THE MINUTE. LIGHT ONCE golden has grown dimmer, then ebony, and is now an inaccurate hue tinged with darkness, occasionally illuminated by the scattered street-lights along Calle St Águeda. The neighbouring alleys, narrow and full of stairs and nooks, seemed to pique an unusual interest in him that day as if he were a visitor who had just arrived in Burgos instead of a student who had spent three years here. After all he and his friends had trod these steps hundreds of times, either going toward the Outside or Inside Llanas in pursuit of a tavern with the clearest beer and the darkest lighting possible. On his descent, he traverses Fernán González Arch; his steps lead him to another region. Was it around here? He is almost certain of it.

The wind that has been attempting to build behind him for the previous few minutes now rises furiously, crossing his hair over his face, but this does not appear to deter the young man from his perusal of the map.

Carlos Lafuente's words from days ago return to his mind. The hidden mysteries under the city's subsoil, or rather the other Burgos, may be forgotten for good, but its joys and sorrows are still there, dormant.

All of them seem to have risen since the night before.

Arthur felt as if he were breathing the polluted air of the dead-end passageway once more.

After a few minutes of inactivity, the screen of his cell phone dims. He touches it and when it lights up again, Arthur searches quickly for the point he had previously marked. He looks at it, pulls out Elvira's compass again, trying not to get distracted by his surroundings. Because he wants to be absolutely sure.

Yes, it was here alright.

He is in that part of the city behind the cathedral. A part that has enjoyed the easily replaceable alterations produced by time and the so-called improvements.

More precisely, he is on Calle Hospital de Los Ciegos, which mixes both modern and historic buildings.

He has been so busy looking at the two instruments to pay attention to his scarf, which, along with a strong gust of wind, pulls itself off his neck and is launched several metres into the air.

Alarmed, he chases after it until he sees with relief that it is finally halted fifty metres in front of him by a metal railing, around which it gets entangled in search of sanctuary.

After picking it up with some relief, the young man looks down and to his right, recognising the stairs leading down the winding alleys that eventually lead to Calle de la Paloma.

On the piece of paper Arthur is holding, he has scribbled down the references that both the GPS and compass provided him the night before, letting him know where he was underground.

Slowly, painstakingly, and taking into consideration a certain margin of error, he has transcribed all the data on a map.

The game is nearly over.

He fears that, as in the goose's game, after being so close to the goal, he could be sent back to the starting square, to jail or the desert.

He does not wish to consider that.

They have lost too many games already.

Articulate and clean, these notes certainly are. He dreads—and longs for—the moment when he may reveal to Elena and the professor what he has seen and confirmed this evening.

Because an old pile rises before him, silent on this Sunday evening.

The right part of the structure has undergone alterations, extensions, and modifications, but its left side still retains the essence of what it has always been, its original character. He looks up. A small virgin observes the solitary stroller, flattered perhaps by this unexpected visit.

What he had least expected was to find precisely that building with a Virgin on its outside wall.

CHAPTER 56

BACK TO SCHOOL

'Arthur, I am far from happy considering the risk you've taken sneaking into the cathedral-like a schoolboy, without permission, and at night, and much less so since you Elvira were also there,' he added, looking at the latter, who immediately began to consult her notes with alacrity and great concentration. 'That and the fact that you should have incited my student to do so is much worse. I simply cannot believe it! I should file be filing a report with the rector. And all this just a couple of days after our previous meeting!'

Here he paused. Arthur's revelations had fallen like a bomb that morning when he and Elvira broke into the sanctum sanctorum spoiling in doing so the coffee the two professors were about to drink after having finished their classes.

The small group sat in silence in front of the wide window. Elvira remained a bit further back, apparently rummaging through her rucksack after having lumped her notes into a messy mess at the bottom.

Arthur had been sitting in the green armchair since the wee hours of the morning. Professor Lafuente had began to make a peculiar sinuous path on the carpet placed in the middle of the office. Sometimes his walk formed an ellipse, others a circle as if he were a bee trying to communicate with another. Elena kept her eyes on the garden. There, small groups of students were already forming under the trees. At times like this, she missed the little secrets of that age, such as concealing the cracked lipstick or noticing that a boy in the class next to hers had been looking at her longer than expected. Instead of that, she found herself listening to an especially incredible story.

'You see, professor?' said Arthur unable to contain his emotions and not paying much attention to his mentor's words, pointing to a cross he had drawn with a pencil on the map spread out on the table. 'On the one hand we have St Gadea, here, Calle de las Brujas, here in the area around the wall, and finally here, Los Cubos Walk at the height of Dona Lambra Tower...' and with each word, he traced circles around each of these spots with the point of his pencil already damaged after so many indications—. 'There's also St. Esteban's Church and the neighbouring Calle Tenebregosa.'

The professor more relaxed after having successfully argued his position and calmed his jitters remained silent as if the previous conversation had not taken place. He stared first at the map, then at the GPS indications on the iPhone screen, and last at the figure of Arthur, who appeared to be gleaming with victory.

'Well, well, I must say that in your circumstances, I might have done something similar, albeit certainly not in the same way,' he said at last. 'In any case, it was a reckless thing to do—and then, looking at the map in front of his student: 'So, all these points according to you...?'

'Yes, Professor, I can't be one hundred per cent sure, of course, since the tunnels were blocked,' said Arthur, rising to his feet with fresh vigour, aware that the professor's wrath was more bluster than substance. 'But it's too much of a coincidence even for us, don't you think? It's not uncommon that passages like this should have been built in troubled times in similar towns on the peninsula, allowing nobles and other important people to escape or, at the very least, seek sanctuary in other parts of the city.'

'Well, it's something to consider, of course, as the rector would say, but I don't quite understand...'

'There's something else, Professor... Elena...' Arthur remarked, looking at the latter for support. The palaeographer had remained silent throughout the whole examination of that piece of paper that had passed back and forth, giving the impression to be a precious incunabulum, one of those codices they had been so used to handle lately, rather than a soiled, crumpled scrap of paper. 'I took the precaution of putting on paper the path Elvira and I followed during our journey, along with each and every blinded passages we found and stops we made, but the most interesting part is the spot where the tunnel ended, forcing Elvira and I to turn back.'

'And why was it so peculiar if you couldn't see anything or get anywhere?'

'As you know the three rivers that pass Burgos, the Arlanzón, the Vena, and the Pico, have caused water levels to rise in ancient times resulting in multiple floods in the city. As a result, the city has been crammed with conduits, bridges, and, sure, why not, tunnels since the Middle Ages. It occurred to me that, should someone have fled to a different part of the city to avoid certain death or any other circumstance that posed a threat, it would be possible to find on the surface a location that related to what we saw underground or at least a clue. Locating our position precisely was crucial. Yesterday, I did just that. The interesting thing, the curious thing, is the building that I found directly above the blocked passageway.'

'You mean...?' said Carlos, scrutinising the map and recognising the structure depicted on it, with a look that tried to decipher something else in Arthur's words.

'Yes, the Saldaña College, or, more precisely, the Colegio Saldaña de Nuestra Señora de la Visitación. Obviously, its construction is more modern than many of the other places we've seen on the map, yet the passageway ended precisely right here. No doubt about it' Arthur's restless finger tapped again and again on that point on the map. 'Although its foundation and subsequent construction took place in the 17th century, there were already buildings in this area initially used to house the college in its earliest days. Do you get it?'

'This is extremely intriguing,' the professor remarked, taking in his hands the map hastily drawn by Arthur. Elena followed him with her eyes as he past her on his way to the library. The professor, perched by now at the top of the stairs, was already immersed in a train of thought. From one of the shelves, he removed an old volume that revealed to be the *Chronicles of Burgos*, written by the Marquis of Fisones in 1885.

'We know the chapel was built centuries after the completion of the cathedral in 1460,' he stated, after perusing the tome for a few minutes. 'That much is certain. However, if we take a closer look, we can read that Saldaña and Villegas founded the school in 1674, using in the meantime some houses owned by Villegas near the current location of the school, right?'

A pause. A fresh approach to the window.

'That tunnel, passage, or whatever the heck it was...' said the professor, 'Its presence there doesn't make any sense after all the renovations and constructions being made in Las Llanas area throughout the years. Hundreds of archaeological excavations have been done there. I tell you it's impossible. I can't imagine that connection.'

'And yet, Professor, Elvira and I were in one! Moreover, 16th-century house foundations were discovered during the excavations you mention. Perhaps the corridor passed beneath one of them. Remember Elvira and I found constant level changes!'

'Even so, the rationale for the creation of that passage between the Constables' Chapel and the school remains a mystery. The fire that engulfed the archbishop's palace in 1812 caused the loss of many important documents from the Burgos Archives. A great deal of records were lost forever. Then, following that, as I never tyre of reiterating, Napoleon's destructive forces did their thing too.'

'What do you think the purpose of the passage could have been then?'

'Perhaps we'll never know for sure, Arthur. Believe me, I've never felt so frustrated. However, if there is one thing I am willing to hazard a guess at, it would be that the purpose of these tunnels was to provide a means of escape from enemy attacks, as you have previously mentioned. But I would like to point out that you demonstrated two very significant things yesterday. Once more, you've established that this was the chapel of light. Once again, light shone through the darkness, even if this time it was only the feeble beams issuing from the flashlights of a student and a renegade detective.'

On saying this, the professor cast a glance at Elvira, who promptly lowered her head, putting it back in her backpack. 'Oh! And one more thing; I've been leafing through the existing chronicles pertaining to this school of yours. Again, we find here barbarism, the gratuitous and extreme savagery of humans destroying humans. The fires, massacres, rapes, and plundering of the French in Burgos, particularly during the battle of Gamonal, gave many people the chills. Even a French general was appalled by the memory of the events. The local government, in an attempt to protect the wall surrounding the castle, had several buildings in the neighbourhood destroyed. It is not too far fetched to assume that among them there should be a certain number of the college buildings, and that some of them could be the final destination of one of those passageways.'

'Whoever built them had assumed in advance a lot of circumstances, variables of what we now would term Plan B, only they also had a C, D, and so forth,' Elena said. 'In short, escape routes established so that someone could flee, either from any of the neighbouring houses, the school, or the cathedral itself. Escape routes.'

'Escape routes, you say, but why? What for?' Arthur said.

'Not what for Arthur. It would be wiser to inquire for whom.' said Lafuente guessing Elena's argument. 'From what we've learned so far someone took a great interest about the princess's offspring.'

'The same people who were responsible', Arthur intervened quickly, 'not only of writing with special ink in the musical codex but also of establishing rules, guardianships, and benefits for the family left in charge. I don't think it will be going too far if I suggest that the Masonic lodge itself may have been involved.'

'Freemasonry?' Elena said. 'You really think so, Arthur?'

'Yes, I am not an eminent expert on the subject, of course, but as you know better than myself, Freemasonry was not a kind secret organisation or cult back then, as we like to imagine; it also preserved a certain know-how, certain techniques to achieve what they termed the Great Work. I have told you many times, professor,' he said, addressing the latter, 'that the same Gothic cathedrals, as blessed Fulcanelli said, were nothing more than a book written in stone, transmitting all the knowledge of antiquity. According to him, both humanism and the Renaissance were only periods limited to copying art. It was during the Middle Ages that ancient wisdom was worked on and then lost.'

'Forgive me for interrupting you amid so much speculation,' said Elena, 'but I think it would be interesting to remind you, in line with what Arthur just stated, that it was in the fifteenth century, during the time of Bishop Don Luis de Acuña, that an alchemist's laboratory existed on the third floor of the cathedral cloister.'

'But it's a proven fact the school took nearly six years to be finished since the Marquis of Villegas and Saldaña himself began the project.' Lafuente said.

'Yes, it's true, almost as long as it would take to build such a passage, don't you think, professor?' smiled the young man with a certain malice, 'a whole six years following Saldaña's initiative. Why the long delay? Were they perhaps waiting for the passageway's completion prior to its inauguration? And if so, was it a joint idea of Saldaña and Villegas or just the latter? The initial plan I guess would have been to expect and anticipate the changes of time, distrusting the rulers in order to transmit knowledge by other means, outside of established organisations and the establishment. Freemasonry knew a great deal about that. It had created its own means of communication. Somewhere, all that knowledge is waiting to be discovered. Some studies and theories suggest the Holy Grail itself may be buried somewhere in the triangle formed by the towns of San Pantaleón,

Criales, and the temple of St Maria de Siones in the northern part of the Burgos province.'

'The North of Burgos once more,' Carlos stated in a low, thoughtful voice. His face was worn, serious, although nevertheless affable. He was looking at his student with some respect, sinking again his gaze into the volume he had taken from the shelf while his companions were talking. After examining it for a few minutes, he raised his head, pointing with his index finger at the page in front of him.

'¡Wow!' he exclaimed 'You will definitely appreciate this. Marquis of Saldaña included among his friends a certain Baron Miralles de Santa Cruz who, curiously enough, appears to have been the anonymous collaborator who took part in the foundation of Saldaña College. And do you know what his family name was before receiving his title? — De la Serna,' the professor added, punctuating his words with a dramatic silence to highlight his words. 'And yet another thing I've just read here. According to writers Jeronimo de Villa and Jorge de Montemayor among others, the surname origi-nated mostly in the Palencian village of La Serna. Can you guess in which judicial district?' And, after seeing the startled expressions on his interlocutors's faces, he continued unperturbed, 'Well, in Saldaña's, of course! Why does that last name ring so much in my ear? Too many coincidences if you ask me. This gets curiouser and curioser. That, plus the fact that the institution was founded as a home for orphaned girls from low-income families.' After saying this, he took the jacket that Elena had placed carefully at the back of his chair. 'Anyone for a walk? I've longed to return to school for quite some time. Come on Elena, let's give the pair of transgressive investi-gators a break from their efforts!'

Carlos Lafuente had lived in Burgos for over twenty years. During his time he never had allowed himself to be carried away by his feet to the neighbourhood of St Esteban except on rare occasions. Pedestrian streets that must have caught the attention of someone given to thoughtful walks like him. A mistake. A serious blunder. He never stopped discovering new things in his daily routine, whether it was a new store in the neighbourhood where he had grown up, a new restaurant down a street he've walked hundreds of times, while running for an errand for his mother against his will, in search of an ice bar for the refrigerator, always in search of that quarter and a half, which he never quite understood what it was. Was today going to be one of those days?

There was nothing particularly noteworthy in their arrival at Saldaña College coming from Calle Hospital de Los Ciegos, at that time in the evening outside school hours, nothing particularly epic either. There was no life-changing epiphany waiting for the two academics. Nothing changed or shook the expectations both of them might have had that day. But on this particular day of their adventure, Carlos had Elena alongside to share his effort with. That beautiful and elegant dark-haired woman, a companion he could not have foreseen on the first days of this research, leaving behind her the trail of her hair, the trace of her steps.

Elena was thinking how odd it was for her to be precisely here at the school where her aunt had attended college as a young girl many years ago.

Su llegada al Colegio Saldaña no tuvo nada de épico.

'Good evening!' said a middle-aged woman with short hair, as the school door was opened for them. 'Are you the ones who phoned earlier, right?' And after ushering them in this way, she walked ahead of them with quick, hurried steps, halting every so often as if she thought she'd forgotten his house keys in the car and was going to go back for them before realising, at the last second, she had them in her right pocket.

They entered the headmaster's office. The room was small but functional, with a picture of the king and the Spanish flag hanging behind the desk. There was no trace in the place of the religious past of the institution. Should one of the orphans of old welcomed by Marquis de Villegas and his co-founder, Mr Saldaña, had entered the premises that evening begging for alms, a bed, or shelter, she would have recognised here anything remotely resembling the house in which she had stayed, slept, and worshipped hundreds of years ago. Thankfully, time had taken them away so that they would not suffer any such disappointment with the places they formerly called home.

The headmaster, Don Esteban Márquez, was a man in a grey suit, a shade of grey that defied description; a grey not even comparable to that of a leaden sky or the one covering the ashes of a fire-place after it has been burning for hours, revealing the embers of the heat that had been contained within just a few hours earlier. It was rather a worn floor type gray, the kind that awaits the arrival of the cleaning lady to scrub it after a long day's work. After listening to what the two professors had to say and looking through his files, he addressed the visitors with a weary expression.

'Sorry, but we've looked over all of our records since you phoned and I have been unable to find anything pertaining to that passage you mentioned. On the other hand, believe me, the argument of following a surname is of no use to us. Besides, there is the fact that the Data Protection Law currently in force prohibits us from using any information related to the families without their expressed autho-risation and consent. Hundreds of people throughout history have shared that surname. Here, as at any Burgos school, the same holds true. You probably already know that the Sisters of Charity took with them a substantial amount of paperwork when they left. Among them, of course, the entire school's records. It's fine with me what you intend to do in researching up the genealogy from the 13th century onwards, but I seriously doubt you will get anything that way. Look here; the school is called Saldaña, that is correct. Unfortunately, however, very little of the institution you are looking for is left. Between the new regulations, pedagogical changes, the departure of the Sisters of Charity and a long list of other factors, is nothing short of miraculous that the very building should be standing.'

The headmaster remarked this, unconsciously overlooking the premises as they were walking through the courtyard, dodging in the process several children who were playing there outside school hours. The mouldy old structure stood to their left, history dripping off its walls. The sports court, situated in the centre of an odd "L" offered the facilities to the gaze of any flock of birds that might be flying through the sky at the time. The recent downpour had darkened the exposed modern brick classrooms to their right. It was this a desolate, dreary building with crimson bars blocking the view from the street. Unfortunately, this architectural style—somewhere between

welcoming and educational, has been making its way across the country, gradually chipping at our memories everywhere in doing so.

AS SOON AS THEY RETURNED TO THE HEADMASTER'S OFFICE, THE
latter turned to face the supervisor who had followed them. She
appear to be eagerly awaiting the outcome of the interview so that she
could inform of it promptly at the butcher's while waiting in the long
queue to be served. After some trepidation, she went up to the headmaster and whispered something in his ear. At first, he seemed
surprised, with that kind of surprise that results from not having
thought of the very idea himself. Suddenly, he looked up, grabbed a
pen and a piece of paper, and said to the visitors:

'Something has occurred to me. As distant partners in the sphere
of education, so to speak, I think it would be beneficial if I were to
lend you a hand. The supervisor here has just brought to my attention there is a person who might have some information about the
recent Saldaña's past. At least she is the only one we know. On occasion, she has sent her niece in her stead to represent her at the school,
whether it be for an event or an anniversary.'

He shook his head and looked back at the supervisor for confirmation before speaking any further.

'She worked as a teacher throughout the forties and part of the
fifties, I believe. The Sisters of Charity always mentioned her
favourably. She retired many years ago, and despite been repeatedly
invited to come when some commemorative events have been organized in the school, she has flatly refused. Whether or not she is still
alive is a mystery to me. She was not in particularly excellent health,
poor soul, but in any case, perhaps her niece keeps some important
documents or information. Maybe she could provide you with
intriguing details on the old school. I'm afraid I have only her address.
Nothing else was ever left for us to get in touch with her.'

He handed a note to the two professors on which he had scribbled a name in short, choppy strokes, along with some "I's" that
seemed to fall into the void:

Silvia Cruz
35 Calle Hermitage
Sotopalacios (Burgos)

The sky was darkening, and the hues of twilight were beginning to cast a shadow on the college's front entrance.

The man in the grey suit escorted them to the exit with precise movements.

As they descended the gradual slope that forms Calle Hospital de Los Ciegos, the professor stopped briefly to take one more look back at it. To that enclosed street that promised to lead to the summit, up the hill, all the way into the realm of dreams, and beyond. Instead, he saw, to their right, the houses that had been built after the street collapse in 1977, with their blackened, exposed walls made even darker by the way the light was fading. Above them, the figure of the grey man watched their descent into the town centre, perhaps with some degree of envy before he turned his back on the recent visitors and merged with his surroundings.

CHAPTER 57

THE FORGOTTEN DRAWING

Or, why going to night classes or performing other chores associated in the dark is not a wise decision.

'Aunt Silvia, the university professors I told you about have arrived.'

The old woman was sitting next to a stretcher table wrapped in a shawl. Despite the ominous omens of the school's headmaster, she still lived. "She must be around ninety", thought Elena. When the visitors entered the room the old lady greeted them a kind and sweet smile, the kind of smile that quickly transports one back to childhood. The look of someone who has dedicated her best years of her life to teaching. There are people like that. Time seems to stand still when speaking with them. For a moment, Lafuente felt himself again a shy boy, reverting to his awkward self, sitting alone in the corner watching his classmates playing football while eating a sandwich.

As soon as Elena entered the room she noticed some charcoal drawings on the walls. In one of them, three girls were playing with a rope while a funny looking little dog was looking at them. In another, a young woman smiled, throwing inviting glances from behind a pink parasol.

'Sit down, sit down, you must be chilly,' said the old lady with a smile that conveyed the warmth lacking outside, beckoning them to sit down and proceeded to cover herself further with the skirt of the stretcher table.

'Ana, could you please bring some coffee for our guests? Because you would you like a cup of coffee, right? You're interested in the portraits, aren't you?' she then asked Elena upon discovering the latter's interest in the in them. 'I painted them in my youth,' she said, a particular tone of pride in her voice. 'Except for that one with the horse,' she said, pointing to a beautiful picture of a colt in a landscape. A small dog wearing a cape seemed to be contemplating the scene with interest. 'That was a holiday present from a school nun in 1965.'

'Yes, I enjoy painting very much.' Elena replied with a smile. 'They are certainly beautiful drawings.'

'Aunt Silvia, our guests have been to Saldaña College,' said her niece and, addressing those present in a low voice, 'Despite central heating, there has been no way to get her away from her old brazier.'

'Well, well,' murmured the old woman regarding them with a suspicious look that appeared to have descended upon her face like a curtain that slides after the cords holding it are unfastened upon hearing the school's name. She first regarded Elena, then the professor, and finally Arthur. As her gaze landed on the latter, a particular brilliance seemed to appear in her wrinkled eyes. That radiance Arthur had noticed on the face of the Silos monk as well as on Sister Amalia during their visit to Huelgas.

'I'll tell you a story about the old school,' she eventually whispered after listening to their reason for the visit, 'It's not much. Possibly, it would be useless to you, you know. With age, one becomes confused with dates and images. By dint of remembering them, things get beautified. They cease to be what they once were to become the memory of a memory', she pondered with a sad smile as she surveyed the artwork on the wall. 'Perhaps we are all like one of these drawings hanging here, the reflex of something once perceived.'

After saying this, Aunt Silvia paused for a moment, closing her eyes before continuing in a weak voice that gradually gained strength as she advanced in her story. She seemed to be searching in the recesses of her mind, casting a glance to absence,

"I could't say for certain what year it was, but if I had to guess, I would say that it was around 1945 or 1946. But winter it was, this much I am certain. Christmas was drawing near, and formal classes had already been dismissed for the holidays, so the memory is clear in my mind in that respect. A few weeks before, the diocese had informed the nuns that the main structure of the building would be undergoing restoration and repair works, as well as renovations to the chapel floor and presbytery. The decorating of the chapel included, among other things, the placement of marble and various arrangements, that sort of thing. Something was mentioned about the possibility that foundations of certain areas could potentially collapse, or something to that effect. In the weeks that followed, most of the nuns moved to other convents and seminaries in preparation for the school's temporary closure. The following day, masons and carpenters would fill everything with their machines. Only the library and a couple of modern areas would remain untouched by the workers' footprints, rubble, and plaster. Everything had been arranged to cause as little disruption as possible to the internal running of the school in the interim.

I had been working at Saldaña School for more than ten years at that point, ever since I returned to it as a teacher after having completed my education in France preceded by a brief stay in Madrid testing my luck there before finally coming home.

Ten entire years full of joys and sorrows! Of joy whenever I saw my students' grateful faces and felt their love. The affection and gratitude I received from my students was truly one of the greatest joys of my life. And then, of course, there is the heartbreak that comes with watching them leave for the "world" or "life," as the nuns used to put it. Little girls came, and —after what seemed a brief span of time —, left as women. Such is the course of things!

I never in a million years would have guessed that one day I would return to the school of my childhood, my beloved college. Indeed, there had been a time when I was one of those girls.

There were not many non-religious teacher at the time. I was one of them. I had been looking forward to my Christmas holidays more than ever. I had well used the planning of my chores, reviewed all the examinations on time and carried out other clerical duties. At last the day had come!

To commemorate the occasion, I had prepared a wonderful present for my mother: a sketch I had drawn in the afternoons spent in the teachers' lounge while the rest of my colleagues sipped coffee, knitted, or read romance novels.

A charcoal painting.

It was a likeness of my father in his prime. Mom would be overjoyed.

I had rented a little flat in the southern part of Burgos, next to the train station. The constant rumble of trains passing did not bother me at all, quite the contrary. It was a great way to wake up, getting me ready for the day and focused on the task ahead of me. As soon as I entered the flat, I placed the key on the table and headed straight for the kitchen to brew myself some tea. It wasn't until that point that I became aware of something that in my eagerness to get the day over with had not noticed.

I had forgotten the drawing in the classroom, wrapped and propped up against the professor's desk.

I distinctly recalled having placed it there, with that clarity of the retrospective, almost cinematic vision that we use in order to recreate an event when no solution is readily available. My, what a fool I'd been! Precisely today when the school was about to close its doors! I would have to go back. Fortunately, I had a key to the rear door. Back then, we teachers still enjoyed that rare privilege of having a copy of the college key, trust in hand, allowing us to come and go as we pleased in a city many of us were unfamiliar with on a lonely fall evening. It was the gateway to a moment of one's own, a place I could control, sitting in front of the pupils' work, recall their familiar faces, and have the feeling of being surrounded by hundreds of little voices.

On that particular day, however, things were going to be different.

The evening had changed its tones, revealing a bleak, clouded sky. The upper part of the St Esteban's neighbourhood had the appearance of a postcard issued from some Romanian city, the day dying in front of me, filling the cobblestones I was walking on with a million different shades of grey. It began to rain. It started off as just a few drips, hitting first on the toe of one of my brand-new shoes and then on the rest of my body. It was entirely my fault. I should have foreseen this and worn different footwear. Today was going to be the day of absent-mindedness. If only I had looked at the clear signs of the changing atmosphere before leaving home! At least I had grabbed my trusty heavy ivory-handled umbrella which served both as a protection against undesirables as to hold back the rain. As I said, I was trying keep my small, inappropriately-shod feet from stepping on the many countless puddles that were forming by the minute. I jumped over them every few yards, looking for the slight promontory, the fortuitous flagstone that would allow me to remain dry a little longer.

The sound of thunder could be heard in the distance, announcing the approaching storm.

I raised my head. I had reached my destination. I was in front of the Milkman's Gate, so called after the professional who used it daily in days of old.

I had not noticed its proximity until that moment as I had been paying close attention to my path and especially where to set my feet as I climbed the steps that led from the lower streets to Calle Hospital de Los Ciegos, focusing on the much-needed coordination required to leap the puddles with dexterity; my mind busy, concerned only with getting the drawing.

Of course, given the rain, I would have to find something to protect it. Should I have got my driving licence like the rest of my colleagues, things would have been simpler. Every Monday morning upon entering the teachers room, the first topic of conversation was without exception the various trips they had made during the weekend, either with their boyfriends or families. Some had travelled to Santander or Madrid; others to Salamanca.

Yes, I loved entering through here whenever it was possible. This part had endured the vagaries of time and so-called progress. It was the school's beating heart. On the contrary its south flank, facing Calle Hospital de Los Ciegos, had, suffered the blindness of both architects and city planners.

I gazed up towards the Virgin set in her niche, barely visible at that time save for a weak beam of sunlight, paying its respects after having kissed her cheeks, apologising for having to leave so early and promising to return the following day at the same hour.

The Milk Gate —provided it has not been altered by later street improvements that could have been made since then—, could be found at the end of a fifty-meter-long alley. Crossing it one gained access to the vacant, gloomy and grey courtyard, which at that hour was practically invisible due to the darkness that was already engulfing everything.

The two basketball hoops appeared to droop like silent, slender cranes, perplexed by my presence there.

The second door I used led into complete darkness. It reeked of emptiness, of silence.

I knew there was switch on my right. Even so it took me quite a while to find it.

After extending my hand with the confidence that such a daily routine affords, I found it. However, after hitting the button, darkness remained. I pushed it once more. Nothing. The electricians were likely installing new fixtures and had disconnected the wires in preparation for the job ahead.

I thought, "They certainly seem eager to start working right away." However, some teachers claimed that a full-fledged restoration had already been carried out in the building between 1908 and 1910, which had meant, in fact, a new construction resulting from it. Almost the entire building was demolished, leaving just a few inner master walls, along with a few worship spaces for the congregation. It was from this arrangement that the current building, the one that encased me, took its final form.

There was still enough light to illuminate my steps as long as I tread cautiously. I tried to stay away from any chance of meeting a loose wire. A faulty connection in the dark was not something to be desired at that moment. I remembered then I kept a torch in my desk drawer in case a power loss might cause the predictable commotion in the classroom.

Certainly there is nothing scarier than the sight of a large space intended for the use of many people when they are not there. Such is the case with a hospital, a prison, an old mansion, or even an elementary school in a case as prosaic as this. The ears, used to the sound of daily screaming, laughter, games, and countless feet dashing in all directions, seem to sharpen expectantly, looking anxiously for the missing sound.

Acknowledging that absence only appears to create more uneasiness. A restlessness we do not dare to reveal to anyone, but restlessness anyway.

And so we put contemporary furnishings and cover old spaces with bright colours and plastics, install aluminium shelves to replace stone and aged wood in an effort to modernise and change the atmosphere. However, we are quite wrong. The old place is still there, in some form or another.

Slowly, I made my way to the end of the corridor, towards the staircase leading to my classroom. On both sides images of the school's promotions adorned the walls; prints and frames that, during the day, conveyed the illusion of life, hope for the future cherished by the school's previous generations as they smiled at that camera that mirrored and reinforced the friendships and aspirations of that bunch of girls. But this evening, though, those same paintings, those blurred, unrecognisable faces, without identity in the dark, reminded me more of the portraits of noble ancestors peering out from the walls of an ancient English manor.

A dim light trickled in through the windows at the top of the stairs; this was especially pleasant on that overcast afternoon, given how poorly lit this area of the building was.

I felt as though the portraits stared from the walls at me as I passed in front of them.

Under that peculiar evening light, the faces of the portraits seemed to emerge from the darkness, from the solitude of the corridor at that odd hour only to return to it after having presented an enigmatic, different, and unsettling face. As I got closer to the stairs, I could make out a small glow coming from the top of them. Apparently someone had left a light on despite our having received clear instructions to double-check everything before we left.

It seemed the electrical outage had affected only the ground floor.

The corridors—that old staircase, those signs of another time— seemed to speak to me of other steps, other presences that for generations had traversed them, now rushing, now sauntering, or with determined steps, as the case might have been. I presume this is the destination of all places with a certain historical past. It was difficult to escape from these pervasive presences that permeated everything.

But now I had to take care of my drawing.

As I ascended the stairs and passed beneath the image of Our Lady of the Visitation on the first landing, I realised the light I had previously noticed came from the library. This was located them at the end of the corridor after passing the school chapel and dining room.

My classroom was located at the far end of the corridor, a few metres before reaching the library doors.

As I ascended the steps and passed beneath the picture of St Tecla...

I passed the windows that looked out onto the cathedral. At that moment, under that light, its towers appeared to be two golden fingers ripping the sky.

I proceeded along the corridor, flanked on both sides by classrooms shrouded in darkness, save for a few strands of light filtering through the windows. I noticed on my way that a few of them had been opened by the rising wind, leaving a small, invasive puddle beneath them.

I stopped to shut them.

As I passed near the toilets I heard the sound of running water. I paid attention. There was a dull thud. A drip? Yes, it certainly was. I spotted the offending faucet as soon as I entered. It froze for a moment upon my entrance, like a student caught at fault, and then, blatantly, continued its spaced dripping in a very brazen manner. I closed and double-checked it before leaving the place. No other accomplice appeared to be involved. Someone had left a comb on the large central marble table. One or two buckets had already been placed in some of the classrooms; clearly in anticipation of the rain the radio had announced for the coming days. Reforms were unquestionably required.

I reached the library.

The Library.

Whenever I passed through its doors, I had the odd feeling that instead of finding the place full of books, tables, and chairs, I was going to find it replaced by the old workroom, where, up until quite recent times, girls could be seen hunched, not over books but needlework and embroidery. Such had been the purpose of this spacious room before I became a student here.

When I entered that bright space, almost expecting to see it full of students under the tutelage of the nun in charge lugging stacks of books from one point to another. I was taken aback precisely by the fact of not seeing anyone. What had I expected to see? That strange girl, Maria Angustias sitting in a corner reading Homer, or that other, Rosa de las Heras, translating Herodotus? I smiled to myself.

The first thing I noticed was that comforting aroma emerging from the books, that the effluvium of years, possibly centuries in some cases, that accumulated knowledge waiting to be rescued. I had forgotten that sensation. Do books, like flowers, release a stronger fragrance as dusk falls? Perhaps the pages of one of those volumes still contain that note I wrote when I was but a young girl, a nervous first-grader. God forbid that someone might find it! What a weird notion to leave it between one of those pages! The folly of youth! Randomly composed poetry written in a state of ecstasy. What volume could it be? My mind has wandered to that question many times while dozing. Perhaps I put it in an atlas, one of those I liked to consult in order to recreate scenes from my readings? Or rather in the Monitor Salvat Encyclopaedia between the words "giraffe" and "Panama" or between "Disney" and "dyspnoea." Perhaps in a Salgari, Louise May Alcott, or Enid Blyton book? Hard to say. Perhaps someone, someday, might come across that hieroglyph, that piece of the past, without a name or signature.

Little from that time period remains in my memory, but as I stood in the silent library, the image of a piece of purple paper in my hand came to mind. I remember I had my hands clad in little lace-embroidered gloves. My mother undoubtedly gave me those on my birthday. But why was I wearing them at school? Memory is peculiar; I don't remember any of that, yet I can vividly evoke the pressure of my finger pressing down on the paper, brushing against the lace.

As my finger sped through the phrases drawn by the fountain pen, I had the unusual impression that the letters and their meaning were tripping, revealing themselves to the world. I remember yes, the shy girl sitting in front of one of those very windows in this library on rainy evenings. That pupil recently arrived to school with no friends. And now here I was, back again in the school where I had studied.

I took a look around.

The nicely arranged chairs surrounding the long tables in the centre of the room appeared to be waiting for someone to remove them, in preparation for the upcoming prom to be held. The dais flooring supported this impression. The window shades had been drawn to keep the outside world out. There was in addition a statue of the Virgin of the Visitation as well as several rusty, outdated white radiators. Now, in the peace and quiet of the night, the four white-painted iron columns completed the nineteenth-century touch only broken by the ceiling's rectangular panels of glaring light.

Then I realised there was something different. Something that shouldn't be there. At least not today.

On one of the tables in the centre of the library a huge volume lay open.

It appeared to be an old codex—a thickly bound volume.

Besides it, there were a few pages on which a few characters had been scribbled here and there. At first glance, I was unable to comprehend what their meaning. They resembled names. Strange. A list of names. The book and a rubber nearby were the only objects on the study table.

Someone had gone to the trouble of retrieving this volume from the school's old archives, which had been kept on the premises ever since its foundation, back in 1650. I had heard of them before, but had never been in such close proximity to one. The careful and delicate calligraphy as well as the detailed figures recreated in the capital letters aroused my curiosity.

All of these folios had been painstakingly written or, as I would prefer to say, drawn, painted over the course of months, maybe years. Who could have left it here, on this table, instead of returning it to the archives? Precisely today when everyone had left the school?

Images of those visits at dusk that I had witnessed many years ago came flooding back. It had been one those days when I used to stay up late in my class reviewing my pupils' papers. It was around 8 p.m. when I saw, or thought I had seen —because everyone insisted the following day it was all in my head—, those two priests with tall figures and long cassocks sauntering through the court-yard below, passing by the statue of the Virgin placed there, deep in conversation while casting occasional glances around them. From my window I could only see one of them was fair-headed, while the other had an odd pointed white beard. I remembered the nuns' closed-door meetings in the principal's office a few week before, meetings to which the rest, non-religious teachers were not invited. On the other hand those gatherings were not a source of envy as the vision of the attire of the sisters of Charity in those years encouraged more to running away than to piety.

Years later, upon revisiting photographs of those years, my initial impression was confirmed: many of the faces depicted in them seemed to lack a propensity for any type of piety, if not compassion. Or was it just my impression based on the events of that evening? In any case after the mysterious meetings we paid no more attention to it. One gets used to the nuns' manias, always imagining that going to the butcher's to purchase York ham is a God-given task that must be carried out with great care and only after solemn reflection.

I was still staring at the peculiar volume in front of me when I was startled by a loud bang followed by the sound of rain entering the building. It seemed to come from one of the classrooms used by the senior students at the end of the corridor, near the stairwell.

I left the book and went out, eager to pick up my drawing once and for all. After all, what did it matter to me the secrets of some crazy nuns?

Upon leaving the library, I noticed the sound I had heard came from the classroom next to mine.

One of the windows had blown open by a gust of wind. As I crossed the threshold, the rain began to pour in unrelentingly, falling on the teacher's desk, drenching the chalkboard and the first benches, filling the small holes allocated for the inkwells on the benches nearest the windows. Should Sister Irene, the current headmaster, have seen it, she would have cried out aloud for sure. Since joining the school's management in 1946, totally aware of its recent legalisation as a primary education centre, she had endeavoured to honour her position through strict disciplinary and administrative supervision.

The shutter blades kept opening violently, as if pushed by a supernatural force. When I finally got hold of them, I used all the strength I was capable of, using both arms, fighting against the wind and the invading rain until I finally could shut them, putting the pin firmly in place to prevent the incident from repeating itself.

I finally reached my class. Picking up the drawing was being quite an adventure.

There it was, propped up against the desk, precisely as I had left it. I surveyed the classroom, checking the windows. There was at that moment no attentive little head bowed in concentration performing her menial chores. Nobody save the benches would know I had been there that evening.

Only the benches.

After wrapping the sketch it in one of those colourful papers we used to do handiwork which I discovered in one of the class-room cabinets, I took the drawing with me. I was ready to go.

I caught a brief flash of light out of the corner of my eye, but by the time I turned around, it was gone.

It seemed to have come from the corridor.

The library lights once more?

The electrical installation, those outdated plugs, those twisted cables that broke and shattered so easily, those leads so exposed to adverse weather had undoubtedly caused some bad connections that came and went every once in a while. Well, I'll double-check it on my way out. The most likely explanation was the workmen had paid no attention to it as they had not planned to carry out any work in this part of the building. If the headmistress found out that someone had left the light on despite all the warnings, she would be quite angry. I opened my drawer and retrieved the torch I kept there. It would be quite useful in negotiating the lower floor area as dusk was approaching.

I decided to approach the library once more and turn off the lights.

It was beyond my ability to comprehend how anybody could have built a school against the slope of the castle hill, preventing the rooms in that wing of the building from having access to natural light.

But when I got back to the library door, I could see its two white wooden doors were firmly closed.

I must have closed them without noticing when I rushed out of it to close the windows. How curious the actions we can do auto-matically!

Through the glazed door glass, I could see the lights were indeed off. The reflection must have come from the street outside. In spite of it I entered and turned on the lights to make sure no window was open. I did not desire to repeat these procedures indefinitely and wanted to return home. The weak light from the bulbs once again lighted the library. Everything seemed in order. I crossed the library in order to move a chair away from the window. Somebody had put it there. The force of custom, I guessed. The books continued dozing on the shelves, irritated by all these interruptions. It was almost dusk. I noticed that weird feeling again as if I was an undesired visitor interrupting something.

I tucked my artwork tightly under my arm and headed for the door. What a surprise my mother was going to get! It may not have been as complete and intricate as the images in the antique book I had just viewed, but it was undeniably a labour of love. God knew it had cost me time and effort. My father's face was hard to capture on paper in any circumstance.

The old book...

I looked at the table on which I had seen it open with its glowing letters, next to those notes and that pencil crossed over them.

However, there was nothing on the table.

I looked at the neighbouring tables. Perhaps I had been confused about the place where I had seen it.

No, it had been this one for sure. I looked more closely. There was something on its surface, a kind of thin, elongated thread. When I touched it with my hands, I recognised the familiar old feeling.

Rubber.

I gasped for air.

I'm not a person easily frightened or startled, but suddenly, there, at that moment, I felt something strange.

Something clicked in my head. The image of those two priests elongated forms I had seen many years ago traversing the courtyard while dragging their cassocks behind them came flooding back to my mind for no apparent reason. After a few seconds, I realised it was not an idea. It was a thought.

No, that wasn't what I experienced either. It was more like an impulse, an unreasonable one.

Get out of here!

Get out of here for Christ's sake!

It dawned on me that that if anyone else was been in the building at the time, they would probably were unwilling to be discovered for some strange reason. Under normal conditions, I would have understood everything. The reasoned and detailed explanation, precise like a diagram, as exact as the chemical or mathematical formula exposing cause and effect. But not that evening. Not at that time. I had no explanation for my experience. I suppose that, nearing my prime, I was accumulating manias.

It seemed as though my rational thinking had got trapped. I cannot recall anything else. I have tried numerous times since then, but I am unable to remember how I got out after taking my drawing under my arm. Nor do I recall how I left the corridor and descended the flight of stairs to the ground floor, how I passed the first doors that I found in my path.

I did, however, realise something.

The torch beam fell on the painting that hung on the stairwell landing in front of me. It depicted St. Thecla gazing upwards. Her face was not particularly threatening. However, her eternal tranquillity seemed somewhat disturbing—another effect of the torchlight.

Soon after, I was surprised to feel the chill of marble beneath my hand.

It was the pink marble balustrade. It was then that I realised my mistake.

I was not on the staircase that ascended from the Milkman's Gate; I was rather on the so called St Luisa stairway that led directly from the library to the inner chambers of the school.

In my haste I had come down the wrong way, placing myself even further from the exist than ever before.

If I wanted to avoid walking through the entire dark school

towards the front door at the opposite end of the building, I had no choice but to turn around and go back.

And that meant crossing the library once more.

I don't remember how I did it. I suppose the old expression that feet can fly came true on that occasion. I remember, yes, having a clear view of the Milkman's Gate after making a hasty decent down the right stairway. The door did not seem to get any near, seeming to keep always in front of me in spite of all my efforts. It was like one of those nightmares in which try our best to get somewhere, but no matter how fast we run, we never move more than a few feet away from where we started. As I rushed, I guessed more than seeing the paintings of the saints that, stalking in the corners seemed to emerge out of nowhere as the focus of the torch fell on them by turns, only to vanish again into that world of shadows from which they had emerged momentarily.

The wooden planks in the section leading to the exit became the ultimate test. The thumping of my feet gliding over them still rings in my mind every so often.

The door was opened by hands that didn't look like mine, and I was finally able to leave the building.

The Milkman's Gate fell like a heavy curtain behind me, generating echoes inside the building. Had anyone inside it harboured doubts that someone had been in the school, they certainly would have been dispelled at this point.

I remember, yes, jumping fearlessly between the puddles that had already formed in the narrow spaces of the existing alley on my way to Calle Hospital de Los Ciegos. When I reached the latter, I jumped repeatedly toward the stairs leading down towards the city centre, all the while under the heavy rain that poured mercilessly. Thunder rumbled. The storm raged with more force. It was certainly going to be a rainy night. I looked up, bracing my umbrella firmly in the face of this downpour, against the curtain of rain that had formed in front of me. My walking became a race, not caring for once about the condition of my poor footwear. But through my haste, anguish and that peculiar feeling I had not yet named, emerged the idea that I must protect the drawing at all costs. Lightning struck between the cathedral's two towers. For an instant they resembled the lengthy shadows of old priests hunched over an ancient, secret book. The thunder I had been waiting rumbled above.

I slipped on one of the last steps. I tried to keep my balance while sliding forward. At that precise moment, just as I was getting ready to feel the humidity of the cobbled street and the hardness of the stone on my back, my right hand, letting go of the umbrella, could hold on to the nearby railing. I rose to my feet. I recognised the building in front of me. It was the comforting and reassuring glow of the window display at number 18, Quintanilla's Antiques on Calle de la Paloma.

I took a deep breath; the air filled my lungs, forcing out the sensation of suffocation that had been with me for the past several minutes.

The cathedral clock struck ten o'clock. I had inside for only half an hour. Why did I have the incredible feeling that it had been longer? And why did I get the impression that I began to get older that night?

I never returned to Saldaña School after that term. I never went back to Burgos again, except for infrequent business trips. Something had occurred that evening I was not prepared for.

Nobody had had to tell me twice that some parts of life don't require too much investigation. I suppose you would call that intuition.

Only once before had I had a comparable experience being a little girl. I was thirteen then and alone at home. My parents had gone out to spend a few hours with some friends. I had spent the evening reading horror stories and as a result of that, I found myself with a lingering feeling of unease, the natural result of such practices. That's when I had the bright idea of turning on all the lights in the house. This certainly would drive away shadows, fears, and my own overactive imagination. With the light, the phantasmal forms and presences would vanish, disintegrate into nothing.

And so I did, but a few minutes later, when I saw the result of this display of lights, furniture, rooms and items cut out clearly in front of me, my confidence began to waver; My awareness of the "possibility" of unseen beings moving through the other rooms increased and fear presented itself in reverse. Thus, I imagined shapes that, much like the giant amoebas I had discovered that week in my Science classes, would be silently gliding through them.

My mind became blank. The next time I looked around, I noticed that I was outside on the street. Apparently I had gone out, slamming the door behind me. Sitting on the sidewalk the road, facing the traffic. And there I remained, awaiting the arrival of my parents, all the lights in the house on as if we were getting ready for a magnificent ball that would never take place, those guests who would never arrive. Years later, when I read some of Lovecraft's works, I was immediately transported back to that primordial, ancestral terror."

Tears found their way between the creases of the elderly woman's eyelids as she repeatedly opened and closed the book.

'My school, my school...' she was muttering in a low tone, her eyes lost in a classroom that her visitors were unable to see.

'Excuse me, but as you can see, my aunt is really distressed,' her niece said, gently caressing the woman's hands. 'I haven't seen her in such a state for quite a long time. She should not have talked so much. I beg your pardon. We do our best to keep her from dwelling too much on her school days. I am the first one to be surprised that she wanted to tell you that old story in her own words.'

A few minutes later, after bidding goodbye to the old lady, they were escorted to the door by her niece. At the last moment, before uttering the last farewell, Elena turned to her.

'Do you know by any chance what became of the drawing she

picked up?' Elena said, almost choking on her words as she realised how simple the question seemed.

'Well, I know she gave it to my grandmother, certainly, but she has never wanted to see it again. Perhaps it reminds her too much of that evening. After she moved in with us, I placed it in a chest along with the rest of all of her things.'

THE SMALL GROUP GATHERED THAT EVENING AT CARLOS Lafuente's residence remained silent, motionless, each of them bent over their respective notes.

The ticking of the clock alerted them to the passing of time.

It was the professor, as usual who stood up and walked through the study unable to repress any longer the unease that had been building up inside him.

'Strange story... such a strange story' he said once and again.

'The lady is quite old.' Elena stated 'There is certainly the possibility she has embellished her story over time, as she herself said, and the truth might bear little resemblance to what she finally remembered.'

'Yes, yes absolutely, but as you point out, we have to ponder her perception of the facts, the way she lived them. Possibly, the explanation could be something as simple as someone forgetting the book, just as she did with her father's drawing, right? Due to the lateness of the hour, this person probably didn't want to be seen either. That doesn't count as a sin, does it?'

'Did you just hear those words coming out of your mouth? Who on earth would buy that? It doesn't sound to me at all like a ghost story or a coven at nightfall. Anyway it's still an odd and unsettling tale at that. What I can glean from it coldly is that something was being prepared that evening at school, taking advantage of the fact that there would be no one there, much less an absent-minded teacher coming to retrieve a personal item.'

'The more I examine this case, the more I feel the presence of a sort of secret organisation,' Arthur whispered, more to organise his thoughts than to get any confirmation from the others.

'And what about the book? What do you two think about the book she found there?' Carlos pointed this out, looking at Elena without seeming to have heard Arthur's impromptu argument. 'If you ask me, that obscure book that no one had heard of before or after, has some bearing to the Musical Codex and the mystery we are investigating. It relates both to the mystery of the princess and the Serna family we are tracking. I'll shoot pool with Patricio Noguer if leaving codices unlocked in school libraries is a common practice.'

Arthur, lost in thought, said nothing, nervously scratching his crown repeatedly. By performing this motion over and over again during the evening, he had finally succeeded in lifting a tuft of hair in it, which would now require both love and money to tame again.

'From my point of view, there are certainly more things concealed under the school's troubled history than we are able to perceive with the naked eye,' he said. 'Unfortunately, the modifications it has suffered over history do not help us much, I'm afraid—too many principals, too many charities.

The only thing in common is the name of the institution and the building it occupies, no matter how hard they have tried to sell it to us in another guise.'

'Well, we can only carry on from where we left off. And hope that our daring and intrepid little detective might achieve something,' Carlos said, gathering his things, indicating by that gesture that the meeting had come to an end.

Elena, however, did not want to consider the matter settled and, placing a hand on the papers that she was organising pulled out of it an early twentieth-century Burgos chronicle.

'And don't you believe,' she said after giving her notes a cursory look over, 'that the crucial clue, the name of the family that held the secret at that specific moment, could have been precisely lost during the confiscation?'

'Could be,' Lafuente replied shortly. 'There is also something more you have not considered. That teacher appeared to know the school like the back of her hand. However, someone had sneaked in there without her knowing it. At least she did not hear any doors opening while she was there.'

'That goes without saying. Unless the individual or individuals were already inside,' Arthur replied.

'I don't think so. Taking into consideration the amount of time that had passed, the memory lapses, as well as the manner in which she told her story, should there be someone inside, they came out quietly, almost right under her very nose , possibly making use of some of the blinded passages you discovered—someone who had a habit of entering the school in any way they pleased. The question that needs to be answered now is why someone would wish to enter at that hour? We must look at the current events to get any hints. From what I have seen in the local newspaper archives and our own notes, Burgos passed through a number of changes.between the years comprised 1963 and 1965. Do you recall that in the same year the stained-glass windows of the Huelgas monastery were moved to their current location? Remember, as well, that the princess' tomb was found in Covarrubias in 1958, just a few years earlier, just when the eighth centenary of her arrival in Spain and her subsequent wedding was approaching.'

'Take a look at this,' Elena said, flipping through a history book, and revealing the section covering the year 1905. 'Remember what the teacher said about substantial arrangements made at the turn of the twentieth century? According to this paragraph, they were fully supervised by a jesuit priest from La Merced school.'

Carlos examined the book Elena had handed him.

'Nothing about this remodelling strikes your attention?' she asked after a few minutes. 'There's no doubt this same priest was responsible for the blueprints and instructions. There was no room for improvisation, and he seemed to be in a haste to complete the task. Over sixty workmen, fifteen carpenters, and eight stonemasons laboured against the clock to complete in just a year and a half what had just been named an unofficial primary school. Too much attention for a simple school, in my opinion.'

'Well,' Arthur said, reading the old chronicle himself 'Even so, they were not happy with the result; I also read here that a few years later, in 1914, the school chapel was restored after some experts deemed it to be in a state of ruin. Why didn't they see this when the centre was renovated?'

'Yes, too many changes in such a short period of time,' the professor continued, 'and if your theory regarding the passageway is accurate, the works undertaken at that time or shortly before meant possibly the end of the entrances to the few remaining buildings in the St Esteban neighbourhood.'

'The recent changes seem to point to another reason, of course. Not simply a means of escape but also of defence,' Elena said.

'Defence?' said Arthur, in response to the palaeographer's suggestion. 'But if I'm not mistaken, the passageways were already blinded by that time. If I understand you correctly someone would want them to continue protecting the secret.

'If we make a parallel with our modern world,'said Lafuente 'when someone protects himself, it is out of fear or awareness that he could be attacked.'

'So you're saying...?' Elena inquired, carefully getting from her chair and approaching the two of them.

'Yes, I have a terrible feeling we are not the only ones looking for the lost ancestry.' said Lafuente. 'If Silos was in any way a necessary part in this complete mess, I wonder what the former abbot, Father Serna, would have said about it. Unfortunately, if he knew anything about it, it is lost by now."

Fate had played her vanishing trick on him, his unfair magic in plain sight under the form of the Alzheimer's that now afflicted the old abbot. Nothing around here, nothing around there.

And as he said these words, the professor shook his head and felt silent.

～

CHAPTER 58

THE SALDAÑA GIRLS

How a girl traversed mist and faced the adventure of life.

It is a foggy day in Burgos. It stretches over the winding alleyways, covering the river, but it is no match for the towers of the old lady who, pricking her cloak, soars victorious above it. Some courageous passers-by feel elated upon reaching their destination. Alberto, the night watchman, one of the last in his trade, feels it on his walk, the cold numbing the hand that grips the keys as if it were a glove.

The fog creeps over the ground, filling Calle Hospital de los Ciegos, giving the buildings an eerie appearance, a foreboding look. It walks lazily up and down the street, looking for discarded scraps, rags of mist forgotten on some steps. Once this is accomplished, it reverts to makes it way up the street, knocking on the doors of the old grey school standing there, begging it to open its doors; hoping against hope that some devout nun inside, sensing its presence, would open at that ungodly hour so it can sneak into the building, walk the corridors and flood the classrooms, as if possessed by an unquenchable thirst for knowledge... the most advanced student of them all!

The fog and Saldaña school have been friends for quite a long time. They have played together in the cool mornings before anyone disturbed them. Their friendship begat at the very first instant when, after the construction of the school, the latter was invaded by such an incursion. The college, due to its sober and gloomy appearance, seems notwithstanding, older than the mist itself.

Obviously, the fog has other friends. One of these is the cathedral, but so are Las Huelgas Monastery and St Gadea Church. On this particular foggy morning, it would not have been surprising to see the figure of El Cid leaving the latter after having made the king swear he had nothing to do with his brother's death.

In that invisible landscape it would be possible to see, despite the early hour and fog, looking at the lofty towers a figure standing out above the surrounding mist. It is the sculpture of a stone angel that appears to pray for the city, for the souls of the citizens waking up at that hour.

The first pupils arrive with the light of dawn, their tiny figures carrying their bags in their hands, their happy outlines tearing through the mist, some of them giving small jumps. Others, more subdued, drag their feet and bags over the cobblestones, much to the subsequent annoyance of their parents once they see the tear and wear caused by this constant, repeated manoeuvre, carried out day after day.

They are the Saldaña girls, as they are commonly referred to. They feel on their faces the morning freshness which the mysterious air fog infects, gives and distributes.

Among them, among that bunch of students, are the Serna sisters, laughing, despising the cold, with the only concern in their hearts that the day ahead will reveal the faces of Sister Josefina or Sister Vicenta upon discovering the undone homework, the question poorly answered. The Serna sisters embody in their small bodies what statistics call in certain registers—in less affectionate and much more prosaic terms—, the six to ten per cent of "military families" attending the institution.

The Saldaña school—or, more precisely, the School La Visitación of Our Lady—could be found in the St. Esteban neighbourhood, more specifically at 26 Calle Hospital de Los Ciegos, not far from the cathedral. The ancient building is at the crest of the slope that makes up the street, displaying in the extension of its main building that bunker-like aspect of exposed brick with which several similar establishments were built or remodelled at the time of its construction. The school seemed to retreat inwards showing its friendlier side in that portion of the yard where the name "Saldaña Public School" is clearly visible. Only a few windows and the aforementioned brick walls of the ugly concrete basements with its red bars can be seen from Calle Hospital de Los Ciegos. Since its founding in 1674 by the archdeacon of Treviño, Don Francisco de Villegas, under the name of Our Lady's Visitation, it has behind it a history of nearly three centuries.

None of this was on Sister Elena's mind that morning when she raised her head from the geography book she was holding in her hands, and fixed her gaze on the pupil in front of her.

The girl was staring, as she had done countless times before at the silhouette of the city visible from the two classroom windows. From there the cathedral towers appeared to touch the school. It was raining outside.

'Serna, you seem particularly interested today in the cathedral's view, isn't it?'

The girl jumped and stopped nibbling the tip of the pencil she was holding between her lips, surprised at that pleasant task by the nun, turning tomato red.

True to form, she found it difficult to pay attention in geography class, so she had decided instead —as she had done countless times before—to focus her attention in a more productive manner contemplating the cathedral towers that could be glimpsed in the distance through the two windows.

'You know what day is tomorrow, right?' Sister Elena continued, ironically.

'Yes, Sister Elena, it's the Day of the School.'

'And wouldn't it be better if you applied yourself to your task instead of admiring the cathedral's architecture, great as it is? You'll have more time for that in the next grade! We are already aware not all of you can be as studious as the school's boarding students, but we can still strive for excellence, can't we? What would Our Lady think of girls who do not apply themselves with due respect to their studies, just the day before the Day of the School?'

The girl dropped her head at this unexpected scolding. She had been merely looking how the sun's rays were landing on the cathedral towers, the clouds creating a unique pattern around them. Sunrises, cloud formations, and the play of light in the sky had always piqued her interest.

'Tomorrow you will know the punishment that corresponds to you for your lack of attention, Serna.' sentenced the nun.

The look of Sister Elena, according to the angle of vision she exerted, was quite enough to maintain the discipline of the entire class, certainly more than enough for the addressee to know what she wanted to convey.

Since she first arrived at the school in 1954 from Jaén —a fact she had never stopped remembering to anyone who might question her identity—, Sister Elena had not ceased to be surprised by some of her pupils.

In any case, enthusiastic and dedicated to her job as she was, she always called her students "great girls."

Even though other teachers were in charge of the remaining classes, it was impossible to escape Sister Elena's presence. She had the strange gift of ubiquity, being in charge not only of gym, science, geography, and history, but also of language. So it was tremendously painful to see the girl trying to escape both study time and schoolwork.

She couldn't stop thinking about the nun's words as she left the school that evening, descending the stone stairs by the side of the cathedral in the company of her sister.

Would she remain grounded again, as the previous week, writing lines upon lines of phrases, or, worse still, recopying the map of Spain and its provinces?

· · ·

'Tomorrow we shall go on a field trip to the castle,'
Sister Josephine had announced that afternoon before the bell rang.

Well, another one of those trips to the castle... by far the most
exotic and uncharted spot they had ever visited! At least they
wouldn't be exposed to religious movies. They had already seen the
likes of *The Holy Robe* and others in the previous term. An excursion
to the castle promised at lest a certain degree of exoticism. She made
the sign of the cross thanking Jesus for sparing them from another
cinematic journey. Sister Valentina always emphasised the need of
giving thanks to Jesus for life's blessings. Didn't she? So there was
nothing sacrilegious about her actions. Quite the opposite.

Such outings were endorsed under a worthy name: nothing more,
nothing less that "Education Community Field Day."

The old ruins of the castle could be seen from afar, above the
cathedral. There, races, rope games, and other activities would be the
order of the day.

There was a heaviness in her gait as she walked down the red
marble stairs. How distant seemed the days when she and her friends
had descended them sliding down on their little behinds before St
Tecla's stern glance, which seemed to scold them for their lack of
academic seriousness! And down they went those rounded edges
steps, perfectly adapted to their mischievous bodies.

When they sallied forth to the yard and passed in front of the
sculpture of the Miraculous Virgin they could verify the image was
already draped with long ribbons in preparation for the Day of the
School. The girl had entirely forgotten about the punishment.

Her buddy Clara was already waiting for her at the main gate.

'Can you invite me today to sweets, please?' she asked her friend.
'My mother has grounded me and hasn't given me any pocket money.
She found out about the disco, you know? A chore,' she concluded
with a shrug.

'Pierre et Madeleine vont a la campagne, Est-ce que Pierre
va a la campagne? Oui...Pierre...'

'No, no, Serna! Position your tongue properly to pronounce the "r" as I explained before... *Allez!! Allez!!*'

Unspoken giggles erupted as the questioned girl faced herself again with the pleasant refrain. She had spent the night before copying sentences and memorising the verbs *"être"* and *"avoir"* for the umpteenth time. Despite the fact that Sister Josephine was born in France, she seemed incapable of expanding her grammar to include more than these two verbs!

But revenge was not long in coming.

And so, two days later, when the young woman was wondering if it would be better to purchase more or less sour sweets, or whether her favourite TV show was airing that day or, even better, whether her Madrid friend would bring new comics to Quintanilla that week-end, the teacher's penetrating voice was heard, breaking the silence:

'Serna, to the blackboard, if you please!'

The girl flinched. She had entirely forgotten about the task she was supposed to be performing at the moment. She did a quick review in her mind. Was it the verb *"avoir"* or, on the contrary, was it the *"étre"* or one of those convolutions of the *"passé compossé"* with which the nun tortured them every other day?

'Come on, try writing in French for a change: "Today is a very sunny day."'

The girl looked at the teacher and then at the class attending expectantly and finally at the white piece of chalk in her hands. She stood there, her back to the blackboard. Seeing that she could not deduce the solution from the expression on the face of Sister Josephine or her classmates, nor from the chalk in her hands, she courageously faced the future, scribbling on the blackboard:

'*Aujourd hui le soleil est beaucoup de fort.*'

'No, no Serna!' Exclaimed the exasperated nun, as she swiftly corrected the text on the blackboard with mathematical speed. She accomplished the task with a stroke of chalk on the blackboard. That stroke, standard fare for any self-respecting teacher, was carried out with professional air, the sophistication of the French language and culture made it all the more fitting.

'*Et voila!* This is the correct phrase, *mademoiselle.* I really hope you will remember it *pour* next time. ¿*Comprenez-ça?* I want you to copy that sentence ten times for tomorrow.'

'*Oui, soeur* Josephine!' This phrase, repeated every few minutes, was the one with the greatest possibility of success for our poor students to get right.

It seemed, due to one of those special circumstances of existence, that the further away the girl was from the didactic explanations, the closer she was to a certain inner spiritual world she was satisfied with.

The numerous attempts made by her teachers to obtain a higher level of attention from her had been of no use. Everything came to a grinding halt before that sweet smile.

'WOULD YOU COME WITH ME TO BUY JELLYBEANS?' MARIBEL invited her downstairs.

After making their purchase, they would go up to the school terrace to smoke, a more pleasurable task than reviewing the upcoming math or French lesson.

'You know something? I am looking forward to the holidays. I'm going back to Quintanilla you know,' the girl confessed to her best friend. 'This year, the classes have been more burdensome than usual.'

'I'm bored as an oyster, too. Luckily, my sister has bought a house near Valencia so we will spend the long vacation there,' she said.

The young girl nodded approvingly, comforted by that shared thought, taking solace in that fact and looked out over the horizon, toward the unavoidable cathedral that claimed visual attention.

There was a certain satisfaction in skipping class once more. She would later inform the teacher she was not feeling well and had needed to use the bathroom. She must jot down her excuses in her notebook. She'd used the last one a few times in the previous few days.

The spacious terrace on which they where ran the whole length of the modern wing providing sweeping views of Calle Hospital de

Los Ciegos. The city could be seen from that vantage point from various angles and perspectives. Its surface was also safe to play games and run along it without worrying about being hurt. Also, one could make comments about the other students with whom they shared that space at a safe distance and without danger of being overheard.

Later, once classes were over, the young girl and her friend Maribel would return to the kiosk to get a pack of cigarettes and some lollipops, both of which essential items if you wished to have a relatively carefree adolescence. To modern eyes, the combination would appear incongruous, but from the perspective of these two young ladies, they were the two things most forbidden at the time: eating sweets and smoking.

CHAPTER 59

A CHALET IN THE ATTIC

Of castles in the air, sketches, mercurochrome, organ music and other mundane items discovered that can be discovered within the walls of an old school.

The eighth-grade classroom was deafeningly quiet.

Only the sound of a single fly hitting the glass in a desperate attempt to escape.

Sister Dolores, the art teacher, was savouring one of those rare quiet moments when, being her students absorbed in their daily tasks, the afternoon seemed to sink into a peculiar slumber. The nun would have described it as almost mystical, but she discarded that sinful thought as soon as it entered her head.

'You are free to draw whatever you like. The topic is free, but for that very reason, I am going to demand more from you '—the teacher had said with her unmistakable Andalusian accent moments before.

One of the girls was showing exquisite concentration on the view outside the window. The teacher stood up silently.

The fly seemed to buzz more intensely, perhaps warning the girl to the presence of Sister Dolores.

The latter approached slowly, with lazy movements, her interest piqued by the extreme concentration of the twelve-year-old girl, who, leaning her body over her drawing, concealed its execution from prying eyes.

The first thing the nun could glimpse over the girl's shoulder were those two towers, drawn in astounding detail, and —next to them—, the sloping roof of the school. In the foreground as if to remind her of where she was appeared the thick and hated French dictionary.

Yes, that parallelism of forms was unmistakable.

The girl had chosen to draw the view from the window, in which she was a consummate expert.

Yes, that wonderful cathedral was worth the assaults of the educational process on her flesh. It had witnessed her blank gaze as she contemplated what she would do after class. She projected onto her towers the face of the boy she liked, the adventures she read about in her novels, and even the simple exploratory wanderings of a cat on the surrounding rooftops.

Sister Dolores smiled at the dedication and concentration shown by the girl. At times like these she had no regrets whatsoever about having traded the sun of her native Andalusia for the snow and chill of Burgos.

THE GIRL SCREAMED NERVOUSLY AS BLOOD GUSHED FROM HER thumb: 'I think I've cut myself!' She had suffered a fall during recess. She struggled to rise from the ground.

Her friend Maribel reacted quickly.

'Let's go to Sister Dolores's chalet!' she exclaimed, seizing control of the situation.

Within the vast and intimidating structure that housed the Saldaña School at the time, there were hidden places concealed from everyday sight. Corners that might appear ordinary but possessed a special allure. To reach them it was necessary to pass through innumerable doors, possibly climb several flights of stairs, and pass beneath venerable portraits. There were entire areas that were off-limits to students, areas with access to the adjacent and always mysterious hill on top of which the castle rested; here one could find enormous paintings that were actually access doors to private areas of the congregation... an enchanted place not lacking in hidden passageways.

It was to one of these places the girls directed themselves that morning, one of them looking in ecstasy over the blood that flowed from her finger, as if she were St Tecla reincarnated, attending her own beatification.

They eventually reached the attic, getting curious glances here and there from a few nuns and a couple of students in the hallways who stood still and watched the girls pass by, fully aware of their destination.

Maribel and her friend came to a halt in front of a wooden door. The former tapped it lightly.

'Come in, come in!' said a voice from within. 'Who is it? Ah, it's you. What's the matter now? Oh, I see. Let's take a look at your finger. Wow, wow... doesn't it look like a morning mishap? I believe we can fix it, I think we can fix it'—continued Sister Dolores, always on the ready for such situations leaving aside the painting she had been working on until that moment. She went to the place where the mercurochrome was.

The girls took advantage of the opportunity to glance around her.

The so-called "chalet" was a place that commanded both reverence and respect. It was an old shed with large wooden beams supporting the roof and small windows in the ceiling allowing natural light to enter.

It wasn't the first time the girl had been there.

Both she and her sister were fascinated by this place. The prospect of seeing one of the nuns painting with such mastery, and working as a nurse on the side for any of the fifteen hundred students at the school who had some minor ailment or headache made the prospect of going there—under any circumstances or pretext—, something to be contemplated with expectation and emotion.

Calm reigned there.

Students loved this place full of paintings. That morning, three or four easels in the centre of the room displayed works in various stages of completion. Landscapes of Andalusian fields, portraits, and flower vases of various compositions and hues. Many tubes of oil paint with a distinct turpentine odour with esoteric names like "sienna yellow" and "indigo blue" lay on a nearby table. Three or four pots with brightly coloured flowers had been placed between the trestles and the window, lending the space an air of Andalusian elegance.

In one of the corners, separate from the other paintings, Maribel observed a work-in-progress.

'Just look at that painting!' said she in hushed tones, pointing to the canvas flooded in reddish tones, as if a former student in search of a cure, had placed her bleeding finger down its entire length.

'Yes, it looks like blood,' the girl replied, motioning her friend to lower her voice since Sister Dolores was already approaching them with the mercurochrome bottle in one hand and cotton in the other.

'By the way, are you drawing something at home?' the nun asked the girl, pretending not to notice the curiosity aroused in the girls by her work as she squirted what appeared to be mercurochrome on the bruised finger. 'Your drawing of the cathedral turned out beautifully.

'Yes, Sister Dolores,' the girl admitted, 'but I couldn't paint as well as you.' She said pointing to the canvas the nun was working on.

'Of course you can paint that way honey, honey if you really want to. It's just a matter of patience, of using your observation gifts.' the nun said as she finished applying a bandage to the girl's finger and checked to see if the cut was still bleeding. 'And I know you're not short on it either. Sister Isabel also told me you were hard at work in the choir in preparation for the school holiday. Is that right?'

The girl spotted another artwork tucked away in a nook.

It represented a poet serenading to his lady. The latter was standing on a balcony and listening attentively. Next to the impro-vised troubadour and a nearby tree, hidden behind it and apparently also enthralled by the verses of his master, there was a small dog wearing a cap and a green cape.

'And this dog? Why is he dressed in a cape? I've never seen dogs wearing capes before,' the girl said, pointing to the curious animal.

'That's only an example of what you can do in painting, in all art. You can create anything you want, even things that don't exist, but that you'd like to see in the real world nevertheless.'

On one of the walls was displayed a framed drawing, clearly the work of a different artist. There was a legible and careful signature at the bottom: "Silvia De la Cruz."

'It was painted by a teacher who worked at Saldaña many years ago,' Sister Dolores explained, noticing the gaze of the two students. 'She had a lot of talent' and after saying these words, she lowered her head.

Upon noticing the nun was not paying attention, the girl walked up to smell the turpentine boldly touching the oil palette that had been left aside when the girls came in. She then examined her finger, stained with vermilion as a result of her brief experiment.

'Okay, and here ends your art class. I'm very sorry, but you must return to class,' Sister Dolores said, ending the visit.

And so, in this almost heavenly environment, illuminated by the light that bathed their silhouettes after having passed through the narrow windows placed at the top, with her band-aid and her mercurochrome smear, the girl noticed—like the rest of her companions who had come to Sister Dolores's chalet—, that all ills had vanished.

She walked yes, back to her eight-grade class, proud of herself for having passed the adventure with flying colours, looking proudly at the other students she met in the corridors.

* * *

It was five o'clock in the afternoon in the College's chapel. Before the clock struck the hour, the girl was already standing at the choir stall, score in hand, waiting for the organ to burst forth under the expert and precise fingers of Sister Isabel.

Sure enough, it was the Day of the School. She knew it well

without Sister Elena having to remind her of the fact. Not in vain she had spent a substantial chunk of that term practising with the other chosen kids under the cautious eye of their music teacher, and it had paid off.

From where she stood she had a good view of the benches, the smiling faces of her classmates and the encouraging one of her sister, sitting among the older girls.

At a nod from Sister Isabel, after having thrown the latter a glance at the figure of the Virgin, as she had been in the habit of doing, as if waiting for her mute approval, the first notes sounded and the song began.

Gounod's *Ave Maria* had been chosen for the occasion.

The students' music and voices filled and widened the beautiful Saldaña Chapel with their sound.

Sister Dolores and Sister Josephine smiled at each other as soon as it began. They would never have told her directly, but the girl's sweet voice, her little hands holding that sheet music in her hand was a source of pride for both of them, a reward after the hurried preparations of the previous days. The good mothers knew that this was the subject in which the girl excelled, being that the reason she had been chosen to sing in the choir in all the school celebrations.

Sister Isabel's fingers slipped across the organ, as she swayed in a musical trance, as if she were in some sort of private mystical connection. A strange tic in her right hand caused her to involuntarily contract her little finger at the most inopportune moments, but her fast fingerwork with the rest allowed her to make up for this, bringing the musical verse to a successful conclusion.

The beautiful voice of the young girl rose, drowning out her memories of the day's pranks, French classes, and the normal dryness of mathematics. Her singing blended with the choir's and echoed down to the pupils seated on the floor near the altar.

CHAPTER 60

A VIEW FROM THE WINDOW

Patricio Noguer gets a painting lesson.

'You claim that I am a slave to my fantasies. What a pleasant and precise way to choose words! You know, I envy people who, like you—with your Jesuitic education and all that—have used the word to shape the world to your reality. Although you are not looking for the truth exactly, are you?'

The professor spoke with assurance. He kept his eyes fixed on Patricio Noguer's face. He had been surprised by the unexpected visit in his office while he had been busy reading Montesquieu's memoirs. However it wasn't just that the professor showed up out of the blue but the discovery that the latter's apparent submission had mutated into indignation.

'How dare you!' exclaimed the rector as he rose from his chair, his cheeks flushed and leaving the cigar he was about to light on the ashtray, still dazed.

'Yes, you are devoted to a task, as you repeatedly say, but it's not the one that everyone expects from you, is it? The university is only a façade. The bits, phrases, and words I have heard from your mouth in the past few months have not escaped me. Neither your determined effort to minimise each and every step I was taking to investigate and verify the the authenticity of the manuscripts discovered. You have exhausted all efforts to stop me. On the other hand I know you've always wanted to know behind my back the results of my research. Why the fervour if you said it was pointless, if it wasn't science but mere speculation? Why so many prohibitions? The obstacles and the paperwork? Finally, I realised you are pursuing something quite different.'

'Quite different? What do you mean?'

A pause.

A lengthy pause.

'It's obvious, isn't it?' Lafuente finally remarked, staring Patricio Noguer dead in the eye, 'the work of white freemasonry. You're an Opus Dei servant, right? In what grade? collaborator? Oh no, that is not acceptable at all! That would be insufficient. A supernumerary, of course!'

'You are mad. Get out of my office!'

' I expected you to deny it. It's part of the secret code of practise which no member recognises, is it not ? "Ask me, and I will give you the nations as an inheritance," ' said Carlos, reciting the brotherhood's creed by heart, "and I will expand your dominions to the limits of the earth. You will rule over them with an iron rod and break them like a potter's vessel... " I'm terrified of you. You claim I'm crazy. If by that you mean that I understand and love history in these crazy times, that I surrender to the truth of the events that occurred, yes, I am totally nuts. But I belong to the club of benign nuts. You, with your piousness, your faux wisdom, have done more damage to the world than many of the most dangerous insane.'

The professor had spoken almost without pausing to breathe. He looked around at the desk, at the mahogany earth globe, the figure of the rector in front of him, and finally at the large windows and the recreated world that could be seen through them.

'Perhaps you, too, should dream, even if just a little bit at first,' he continued. 'However, make sure you're tuned in to the appropriate station. Your problem, the problem of people like you is that you refuse to acknowledge you have become history yourselves. No, not of the sort that can be learned from a book. But of the other, the one that is forgotten, that fades away into oblivion. You've been so busy making this closed and flawless world that you haven't realised it's just a toy,' he remarked, pointing with his right arm to the gardens. 'And you know what? In times like these, it's crucial to have a historian on hand. Even better if it's a palaeographer to interpret the signs no one recognises anymore. I will not charge you for the advice, although I will follow yours nonetheless. My resignation will be on this table by tomorrow morning.'

Lafuente was already on his way out. Behind his interlocutor, the poplars and weeping willows were already being illuminated by the setting sun. That same light had been there before the professor entered the room. The scent of freshly cut grass and the orchids below the window could be smelled. However, by that point in the evening, they had lost some of their intensity.

'On the other hand,' the professor said, turning with impeccable dramatic timing, 'you've always told me I was too cautious, too restrained, remember? Well, perhaps you were right, but today I'm going to make an exception. You and your pragmatic view of higher education can go to hell today!'

'How dare you!' Don Patricio repeated, rising from the table, his eyes wide as he became tense, his fists resting on it, clearly unable to articulate other words. "In addition" and "something to contemplate" came to his mind at that time, but he realised they were irrelevant in the current situation.

Lafuente was standing by the door. His attention drawn to the painting that dominated the space, the fictitious and unattainable vision of a Burgos reproduced in a dislocated perspective to be viewed from heights only believable through creative vision. That idealised landscape, that picturesque setting, with no contemporary windmills in sight and a river meandering beneath the university buildings. Despite the objective beauty of the arrangement, the magnificent sunset appeared false, distorted, and ugly that evening to the professor. The walkers in it appeared frozen, hieratic in their attitudes. Unfortunately, neither the city's architects or topography itself did have the deference to create this privileged panorama, so Noguer had been forced to recreate it using his influences, like a modern-day Frankenstein.

'Ah, and another thing,' said the professor, 'despite all the shady dealings you may have engaged in with the powers that be in this city, those perks that you have obtained for yourself and the more or less covert manoeuvring. Yes, yes, do laugh!' he exclaimed, detecting a certain rictus on his interlocutor's face; 'Nonetheless, despite having made this stretch of the river navigable at the expense of wasting a lot of public money for your capricious and egotistical ends, there's one thing you will never obtain. Arlanzón River runs through Montanilla and directly in front of this fucking university. Even if I tried, I couldn't deny it. A university where students might pursue their wildest ambitions, the kind of lofty goals that only come to fruition in the carefree years of youth when one has the luxury of devoting one's life to learning. I will regret not being able to witness that dream, but that's the truth, and I have no choice but to grieve. But I pity you because no matter how hard you try Mr. Noguer, the cathedral cannot be seen from your window! 'he said, pointing to the picture of dubious romantic aesthetics. 'No matter what you want or desire, geography will never submit to your whims and fancies. The cathedral's domes will never be visible from your window. But I realise that's a *boutade*. You've already demonstrated to me on several occasions that you can't see even the tip of your nose!'

CHAPTER 61

THE SENTINEL WITCH

Of roads, flying witches, and regattas.

The boathouse was behind Arthur as he prepared the canoe for storage. He didn't see Elena approaching across the campus, a cigarette in her left hand.

'Hello, how do you feel? A little nervous about the regatta? Only two days left, I'm afraid,' she said.

The boy turned and smiled upon seeing his friend.

'To be quite honest, I haven't given it much thought between one thing or another' he lowered his gaze to put the rope under the canoe. 'I consider myself fortunate to have been able to train for these two years. Still I have to carry on with the thesis and all that.'

'At least the weather will be fine,' Elena said, and then cocked her head as if daring the sky to disagree with her.

A tight knot around the oars completed the arrangement.

'On top of that,' Elena continued, 'you've been assigned the role of supporting Watson. I know Carlos can be quite persistent at times.'

'Yeah, sure, I don't know... Perhaps I should have studied something else in Santander, in the first place. Maybe business administration like my father. I might be by now on the verge of joining one of the major corporations or significant banking groups, who knows?'

'You? With your imagination full of elves and paranormal legends mixed with historical facts? Please let me laugh.'

They were sitting on the riverbank.

'Elena, you know I'm right. I doubt history is of much use nowadays. Just look at us. So much effort for so little reward! What a waste of time and energy!' said Arthur dipping his left hand into the stream and fraying the surrounding grass with wet fingers.

Elena continued to stare at the water, saying not a word. A couple of canoes raced ahead in front of them, spraying water over the shore, the oars rising and falling in a rhythmic motion.

'Beware! The pragmatic side is out! But look at me. I also have my hidden side, you know? I was also on the verge of shooting it all during my last term at Deusto University. My friends and I were not satisfied with our privileged and expensive education, oh no! We were daddy's girls, always attentive to Morgan's fashions, the latest trends, dresses, and so on. We felt the world owed us something. Simply the best. But the magical side of life appeared to me then, you know? I haven't told this to many people. You see, when we came to Burgos for the summer, my aunt used to take us to the castle. It was on one of those days when I heard for the first time the story of the Sentinel Witch.'

'The Sentinel Witch?'

'Well, at least that's what my aunt called her,' Elena said, her face aglow with a childlike grin. 'Apparently, if we looked carefully at sunset from the point in the castle we were that evening, we could make out the figure of a woman flying from the left tower of the cathedral toward the opposite one, high above the rooftops. My aunt claimed she lived in the upper part of the towers, watching over and keeping the city safe from evil spirits.'

'Wow, what a tale! ' Artur replied with a grin he couldn't suppress. 'I've never come across that before.'

'Since then, whenever my sister and I went up to the castle for whatever reason with our cousins, we remembered the Little Witch and gazed over there,' Elena continued, pointing her finger toward Burgos as if she could see the towers from there. Then, with a look lost in memory, she added 'I guess we were seeking for evidence that the city was protected. And if you ask me, now that your professor Lafuente is not here, I would never say too loudly that magic, or the occult, is sheer nonsense.'

'But one changes,' said Arthur. 'The things that we used to believe in at a given moment do not stay that way. One grows, I guess. One matures.'

'Well, even so, just consider how influential youth is, along with all the things that drive us that whenever I see the cathedral, whether I'm near or far from Burgos, or see it reproduced in a book or on television, that thought comes to my mind. I know of course it's stupid, silly, and idiotic; nonetheless I can't get away from that thought. Assuming the city is safe makes me feel more secure and at ease. Of course, I never saw the little witch, but that doesn't make her non-existent. There's a good chance that she wouldn't have wanted to go out precisely on the days my sister and I expected her to. Free will stuff, right? And now, young man, the time to fantasise about fairies is over! You're done with rowing, and unfortunately it's back to the books and eventually to genealogy, I'm afraid. But before you get wet and ruin the professor's rare books, you should go change your clothing.'

THAT EVENING OF THE LAST DAYS OF MAY, PROFESSOR Lafuente's office displayed an unusual feature. A wooden plank supported by two poles had been placed in front of the wall opposite the window, concealing most of his paintings and butterflies. Pins and papers covered its entire surface. A casual onlooker might be fooled into thinking he was at a police station, while watching an inspector deeply involved in the process of resolving a case, balancing facts, figures, and circumstances. The papers placed on the white panel looked uniform and tedious. They contained only names and dates. In each of them, the name "Serna" had a significant, obsessive place.

So far, over three thousand surnames have been looked into, closely scrutinised, confirmed and rejected. Along with that, birth dates, marriages, sales of land, inheritances, and any other human transaction recorded in the different populations they had visited. Texts whose very existence had surprised the professor and his friends.

A list was prominently displayed in the centre of the board. A brief list in comparison to the documentation that surrounded it, deceptive in its apparent simplicity. Written on it was a list of names that Lafuente reread repeatedly, his eyes questioning it, looking for an answer that the panel did not volunteer.

The oldest entry stood out at the top of the board,

MARCOS DE LA SERNA MARTÍNEZ Montorio, son of Ambrosio
(Montorio) and María (Montorio)
married to CATALINA GONZÁLEZ RICO
Quintanilla Sobresierra, daughter of Diego and María. (Both from
Quintanilla) married on May 2, 1632.

MARCOS DE LA SERNA, Montorio
6-6-1635 of the above, married to BEATRIZ DE LA CUESTA SOL,
Montorio 4-8-1639,
parents, Alonso and Catalina.
Married on 9-6-1658

Nine generations followed below it, each meticulously annotated with the year and place of birth —which used to be Montorio in almost one hundred per cent of the cases—for both spouses. Couples that had married either in their place of birth or in the neighbouring town of Quintanilla.

The final entry was highlighted with a red marker,

ISAÍAS SERNA GONZÁLEZ Montorio on 7/29-1895-
MARIA GUADALUPE DIEZ PÉREZ Quintanilla Sobresierra on 1-
13-1900 married in Quintanilla Sobresierra on 5-20-1922 died in the
latter.

All of them crossing paths, without losing the family name thanks to the successive links between families, such as Gómez Serna and Serna Gómez, crisscrossing over and over in their footsteps.

After that a vast, blank space appeared. The professor's tired eyes had settled on it.

A blank representing an entire generation.

Lafuente had been staring at the panel for what seemed like minutes to him but actually had been more than a half-hour. Arthur walked over to Lafuente and put his hand on his shoulder, sensing his frustration and guessing the thoughts that might been passing through his mentor's mind.

Other names and dates were listed below the board:

Julián María, Serna Diez, González Alonso and González Serna.

These had no apparent connection with the genealogy. All of them the result of Elvira's hard work; her pilgrimage, the dust accumulated on her corduroy pants; the many scrapes she got while climbing over country fences she had been forced to cross to reach an isolated shepherd's house or a sullen neighbour confined in his home for decades.

A Serna family shield from the Palencian branch hung in front of them, displaying gold-banded weapons in the sinople field. The professor had got it from the Hispanic Blazoned Community's repertoire, courtesy of the Salazar and Castro Institute.

'Arthur, are you aware this represents a year's worth of work? Months of it! We have taken the ancestors out of their graves, disturbed their privacy and that of their families, roused the mice in church basements and records and combed through the rubble of abandoned villages in search of books, only to arrive at this conclusion. It all comes down to names on a piece of paper. Is this what we were looking for? Names on a piece of paper... and a huge blank!'

"So close yet so far away. I get your point, professor.'

'I no longer know where to look. It's ironic that the message has passed down for eight centuries, that we should have discovered the name of the host family only to have the records suddenly vanish within a few years due to the damned Civil War. It would have been much better not to have found anything.' he said as he walked away from the window, the extinguished pipe in his hand, continuing to move his arm as if the pipe would alight on its own owing to this peculiar technique.

'Don't say that, professor! That at least proves our efforts were worthwhile! We've come a long way, and we know for certain the family survived, that its descendants continued somehow until now.'

"Yes, I appreciate your concern, Arthur; and, objectively speaking, I do not disagree with your point of view, yet, nothing can ever make me forget we'll never be able to go all the way due to the lack of a generation or two.

Arthur had never seen the professor so upset. The lock of hair fell freely across his brow; his pipe lay unattended on the table.

'And somewhere, in some bloody place,' Lafuente added, 'The facts, the date, and the names are written. How do you think I felt last time we were in Montorio? As we entered the pub for a cup of coffee or saw an elderly woman sitting at her door, I couldn't shake the feeling that we might be facing the last descendent, the last link. If we had conducted our research in a far away place like Kenya or Lasa, I probably wouldn't care as much. In that instance, it would have been more like an abstract concept, an unresolved issue. In our situation, though, it has become something else; an unsolved reality, a reality just around the corner. A conundrum I'll never be able to crack. There is no solution at the end of the newspaper or gamebook.'

AFTER ELENA'S EVENING LESSONS CONCLUDED, SHE JOINED THE group, and the three of them went for a walk around campus. It was a lovely afternoon, but the willows there seemed to have a particular reason to cry that day.

As he walked with Elena's hand in his, the professor mused, "I've been playing a fool for a full year. The moron!" He wondered if he had given in to his impulses in the vain hope of making a name for himself in academia. But, no, that had already been discarded a long time ago. Trying then to validate a theory that seemed original to him, like a desperado? To inject new life into History's stale research methods? That was one of the many things the had stressed to Arthur over and over again; along with the importance of paying homage to those who had gone before us, to the hundreds of thousands of souls who, to borrow an immortal metaphor from Venerable Bede, had entered through a window from the cold, snowy night of non-being, crossed that great hall of life, and exited through the opposite window.

He raised his head once more. He was determined not to let defeat get the best of him this time. He'd done the right thing, according to his conscience. In that respect, he sided with his friend Ernesto Santos. One had to believe in life, in all of it, past and future.

The plain truth was that the Civil War and the destruction of many parish records had muddied the trail, leaving the researches only with doubts. Each of them would have to assimilate it in different ways. The threads that move the world had left a few strands untied; that was all. What had been tight before was now loose. Had it once been a ball? A lamp? The most stunning gem? There was no way to tell now. The only solace was the reality of a world in which the Serna surname still flourished, a world in which the songs contained in the musical Codex were sung on a daily basis to comfort the tortured souls of both Ernesto Santos and Carlos Lafuente.

'That Silos librarian was right,' the professor said aloud. 'Do you remember our old friend, Arthur?'

'How could I ever forget him?' he replied with a sly grin while tossing pebbles from the bridge parapet where they were standing at the time.

'What animosity he showed to that novelist for coming to Silos in search of documentation! And how did he manage to throw him out of bounds? Alas, this is not a novel. Here, events cannot be altered at will. Perhaps Fray Anselmo was right. Fiction, both in novels and films, has conditioned us to look for and hope for perfection or at the very least, closed endings, in a certain way.'

'Yes, I agree or as we say in the rowing world, everything is just a matter of effort and training, right?'

Arthur remained silent after these last words, alone with his thoughts, recapitulating much of the professor's reasoning.

It was in this manner, after having exhausted all search methods, files, addresses, and phone numbers, making numerous enemies, that evidence began to pile up.

There was an absent connecting node.

Perhaps only a mere notation, a marriage record, or a will were missing from the records as the professor had pointed out. At most, a couple of them. But, like in the Darwinian evolution theory, it was the missing link that connected the first documents to the last branch of the Serna family, from that glimmer of hope that leaked one day in the chapter house of Huelgas Monastery.

And only by a miracle could they find it.

∾

CHAPTER 62

THE VOYAGE OF KRISTINA

*How a princess wrote a love letter and a monk responded to it
centuries later.*

A newborn's wail pierced the calm of the cloister on that
Christmas Day.

The Jewish physician had left the monastery quietly
and discretely. Making use of one of the privileges granted by King
Sancho IV, Burgos monks could make use of the Semites subjected to
the abbess's jurisdiction in their capacity as doctors in order to treat
the nuns' diseases.

His steps had disturbed the cloisters, quiet and sunk in their
eternal sleep under the warm January light, while daily prayers still
drifted in the air and the bells rang for Matins.

Mother Abbess, Doña Elvira Fernández was crossing at that hour
the Claustrillas, the inner courtyard.

'Forgive me, mother,' the foreign girl had said a few minutes
earlier in her bed in a broken Spanish, all the world's sorrows on her
face. 'I cannot tell you anything else you don't know already. I would
offend my father, King Haakon. He placed so much faith in me!
Everything depended on me... everything! He desired the union of

our kingdoms with such fervour! That's no longer possible now and it has been entirely my fault. I didn't know what to do, mother. Throughout the journey here, I prayed for a miracle to happen.' she murmured, lowering her head. 'A miracle! During my voyage some of my courtiers informed me you were a powerful person. Your king, though kind and wise, would not understand. To be honest, I don't think I understand it myself. But I couldn't find the strength to find a solution to my lot during the entire trip with...' At that moment she looked at the tiny bundle next to her from which little moans came, 'Oh! Mother! What can I do? What can I do? I'd like to die.'

DOÑA ELVIRA WAS ALONE.

She knew she couldn't turn to anyone for help. Prior to entering the convent, she had always counted on her father to help her through any tough situation. Her father, Don Alonso Fernández de Valladares, Commander of Navarra, —his brother none other than the queen Berenguela's majordomo—, placed her on his knees with a decisive, gentle gesture before giving her some advice or other:

'Elvira, you must be aware that there will be times when you will not know how to act,' her father had told her the day she declared her wish to serve God. 'You might believe you understand what's right and what's not. There will be occasions, however, when your loyalties will be tested. The day will come when you must pause, close your eyes, and pay attention to the message your heart is sending. Many times facts contain the answer in themselves so long as we do not impose our will on them to change their tone, their inner truth. It took me a long time to realise that, my child. In that way you will serve God as well or better than those who claim to do so for their own gain. Always keep in mind the origin of your name,' he urged. 'The name of our family is associated with illustrious deeds. The entire city, not just the religious community, will be watching you. Truth will illuminate your path.'

The facts.

A child had been born on Christmas Eve. Fatherless. Her mother had sought refuge and assistance in this community.

A woman who had crossed borders carrying a child in search of refuge in another country.

The facts.

After removing names, titles, and other embellishments, these were the facts.

The story kept repeating itself.

Dona Elvira reflected on her birthright, the sacred vows she had taken, and her responsibility as Mother Abbess. Her predecessor Doña Inés Laynez, had come from the Tulebras monastery, a distant descendent herself of Don Diego Laynez, the father of Don Rodrigo Díaz de Vivar. She, too, had set a good example.

Yet there was an additional, more compelling reason. Why didn't she want to put a name to it? How come she couldn't trust the truth inside her? Why had she been seen all morning and early afternoon pacing and praying near the Claustrillas?

Still perplexed, she attended Vespers. May God forgive her, but she was not putting her senses into the liturgy. She was oblivious to the pungent aroma of incense that had fascinated her since childhood, didn't notice the intricately carved figures, nor did her gaze fell on the founders' tombs set in front of the altar, as she had done since being named Mother Abbess. The chaplain's religious reading scarcely penetrated her consciousness. But little by little, a picture was taking shape in her head, certain paragraphs were making sense, drawing her in, pleading to be addressed.

THOSE VERSES FROM CORINTHIANS 13:2 REACHED HER consciousness:

"And if I had the gift of prophecy, understood all mysteries and knowledge, and should I have the faith to move mountains, but lack love, I would be nothing. And if I give away all my possessions to feed the poor and let my body to be burned, but have no love, it is useless."

'Oh, God, give me the courage to follow my heart!' the abbess prayed.

She knew this was the moment she had been anticipating and dreading. Everything she'd heard for years about God putting her to the test had nothing to do with the seclusion, nor the isolation from the outside world to devote her life to Him, regular prayers, mass attendance, low-voiced blessings, or exhausting work in the monastery. No, it meant something like this. This was the real test. She realised something else. She was aware of the responsibility her position entailed.

This was the opportunity, the time to use it wisely. There was more to her job than just punishing chaplains for small offences or removing idle workers from their positions.

The cloister was deafeningly quiet. Even the small birds that normally gathered there at this hour had stopped chirping. Doña Elvira was alone. And alone she would be required to make a decision.

Something inside her was calling. The little woman that had always been there, inside her.

Clara.

Her sister Clara, who had left her so soon when they were both little girls.

After a week of games, fun, and laughter, she had left.

They had been carefree girls, naive to the troubles of the world.

Clara had bolted from her that day, laughing all the while clutching in her arms the fruit basket they had just bought at the market.

Her path was crossed by that horse, mounted by a hasty rider.

She sank to the ground at the mount's feet.

Upon reaching the muddy path where her little body lay surrounded by the apples that had fallen from her basket, snatching her from the people who had come to her aid, she could see her sister's lips slowly moving.

Her small face still displayed a faint smile. She had no right to be laughing at this time. Elvira didn't want to see the gap in her head;

she didn't want to remember her little sister like that. Clara's small brown eyes looked directly into hers, pleading forgiveness for the trouble she'd caused by running away.

'Please forgive me, Elvira. It was all my fault,' That was the last thing she said, one of the apples still clutched in her right hand.

Her death had been fast; that was the only consolation Elvira had.

How was she supposed to act now as Mother Abbess? To return the newborn infant to the world in the same manner as those who refused to receive the Virgin Mary into their homes? The symbolic nature of the situation did not pass unnoticed to her.

She was aware her position offered her power to correct injustices, or at least to prevent them from happening.

This was going to be one of those days.

She had been staring at the Claustrillas central fountain. By the way she approached and retreated after having touched the surrounding columns and capitals, any sister who may have witnessed her at that hour would have concluded she was evaluating the quality of their carving.

She realised what needed to be done. Yes, she possessed authority. As far as she knew no woman had ever held such power within the church. The capability to do good, to punish, but also to be charitable. Thousands of thoughts raced through her mind at that time.

But suppose...

Just suppose...

She quietly summoned Sister Urraca, who had been always willing to assist her with any of the daring enterprises she had performed since assuming control of the monastery with varied degrees of success.

'Dona Urraca,' Mother Abbess said upon seeing the approach of the latter. 'Please follow me! God requires us to perform a charitable act. It's about the Northern Princess.'

'Poor soul! May God help her!' exclaimed Sister Urraca, aware of the princess's precarious situation.

'Please make arrangements for Sisters Engracia and Ines Laynez to be at the chapter house in half an hour.'

Infected by the abbess's gestures, Doña Urraca rushed out of the cell in quest of the mentioned nuns.

THAT NIGHT, IN THE THIRD HOUR, WHEN THE REST OF THE congregation was fast asleep, four figures, four shadows stole through the cloisters and gathered in a small chamber close to the scriptorium. They arrived at ten-minute intervals coming from various locations. In that chamber, by candlelight, a pact was made. A covenant of faith. A genuine religious alliance. Those sisters, united by a shared experience, by a common formation in Tulebras Monastery before being assigned to Huelgas, made a solemn vow.

The sisters had already decided. The princess's ladies-in-waiting were promptly summoned.

The infant would be taken care of. It would be looked after by the monastic order, the monastery itself. They all agreed on the one hand that it was vital to conceal his ancestry in order to prevent jeopardising future negotiations between the two crowns, and on the other hand, the delicate balance in Europe. They were also cognisant of the irreversibility of such a decision.

Later it would be necessary to locate a foster family to protect and care for the child. This family would be subjected to an essential vow of silence under the supervision of the monastery. In exchange for that circumspection and attention, that family and their descendants would receive privileges and special favours from the monastery, not being subjected to the payment of any tribute. It was only fair.

The image of the young woman to whose bed they had gone that night had ceased to be a crowned head for those nuns. She was no longer the Norwegian princess, just a kind young woman suffering and in need of assistance.

The medical examination that would follow her introduction to her future husband was also taken into account. Women were well-versed in many secrets, they certainly knew how to trick men into believing what they wanted them to believe. And if this was the salvation of a pure and innocent soul, there was even more reason to leave it in God's hands.

She knew just what to do. Her doubts were now of a different nature.

There was nothing objectionable about her decision. But how could she make it endure in time and in the hearts of the sisters who would succeed her? That would be something to be considered at a later time.

THE PARCHMENT HAD ALREADY BEEN STAMPED WITH THE abbess's unique with its richly detailed internal watermarks, many of which had been created solely to divert attention away from the document itself, causing the reader to pay more attention to the stamp, the detail, rather than the text itself.

The horses chewed eagerly on the Outside Compass as they waited. The entourage was ready to continue their journey to Valladolid.

Before the official farewell, the abbess had visited young Kristina in her cell.

'My dear daughter, your sin,-- if you insist on calling it in such severe terms--, may be one in the eyes of men, but not to God. We will not see each other again in this world, but in times of doubt and unease, trust, always trust! Providence is mysterious. You have loved and sacrificed yourself for the sake of your family, father, kingdom, and daughter. There are no more significant values than those, little one.'

'I feel so weak and confused, mother. Throughout these months traversing France, I firmly believed I'd have the strength to tell the truth before your king and, perhaps, just perhaps, be able to return to my homeland. But what would I say to my father then? My beloved would be exiled, if not worse. I know my decision was not the right one, and I am ready now, as I was when I left my land under what I believed were different circumstances, to never see Bergen again, even if the sound of the very name breaks my heart.'

'The monastery will look after your daughter. Do not be scared. Wiser hands than mine are doing what is required for her.'

'Did you know? I named her Teresa. My father would have wanted it that way... a Spanish granddaughter with a Spanish name,' she said sadly, her father's last words still ringing in her ears,

"Give me a Spanish grandson Kristina, so that our family may endure beyond the horizon, beyond our times."

When Mother Abbess retired to pray that night, she thought she could see again the tiny eyes of her little sister closing her lids, smiling.

That is how the plan got underway.

Kristina was lying in bed. About three years had passed since her arrival in Spain. She was feeling exhausted. Her depression and weakness have worsened over the past few weeks. Next to her was a scroll on which she had written a few love poems addressed to no one in particular.

That day in Seville was suffocatingly hot. It was indeed a very different climate from the crisp air of Bergen and even Burgos and Soria, those cities she had met on her outward journey.

Burgos...

If only she could have stayed in that northern Spanish city where the loving nuns had so warmly welcomed her! The abbess's words still echoed in her mind from time to time.

"As long as these feeble hands dare to defend what is right under the Sun, and we may serve God to the maximum of our strength, God will take care of your daughter and her descendants. She must not lack shelter, care or education."

Only a few hours before the abbess had been an unfamiliar face in a faraway land, but by the time they had finished talking, she felt as though she had known her forever. In addition to the few Latin phrases that functioned as a means of communication, her gentle face made her understand the meaning of those foreign words. That gaze, fixed on her figure as she left the monastery with her retinue had never left her. Undaunted, she stood at the sanctuary's gates, surrounded by the rest of the congregation, as the horses eagerly stamped and beat the ground. This image came to mind now, and it soothed her like a balm. The image of a distant friend.

The expected union of the two crowns had not taken place. Had been her sacrifice in vain? Nonetheless, out of it something survived, something continued to exist.

That something was the promise of four women, the hidden, truly Christian act of kindness born in a nativity in that year of the Lord of 1257. Her thoughts wandered back to the landscapes of her childhood, to her beloved Bergen. She remembered her father, whom she hadn't seen in years, and her eyes filled with sorrow. Life had been so cruel!

He noticed her eyelids closing, how life was leaving her, but that vision remained before her the entire time.

With that pleasant image she closed her eyes slowly, a smile on her face.

As the years went by, each new abbess kept the promise made by their ancestors.

It was in 1320 when Mara González de Agüero, Mother Abbess at the time, concerned about the best way to transmit the instructions for the care and guardianship of the offspring of that family for as long as Nature —not very lavish in those hard years with children—, would allow. She devised a way to ensure that the passage of time and the fallibility of human nature would not be a stumbling block in transmitting the message.

It had been one evening while listening to the choir perform, that inspiration struck her.

She remembered hearing some sisters coming from other religious centres speak about a certain exceptionally skilled scribe.

She'd seen examples of his talent in the codices and manuscripts loaned by monasteries such as Yuso, St Domingo de la Calzada, or Cañas. Master Roderici was without a doubt an exceptional artist.

'As you are aware, Master Roderici,' Doña María González stated to him that morning, 'you've been entrusted with composing a codex containing the music used in our liturgical services. Do you know of any method that could avoid prying eyes from reading some parts of it, or, in other words, to reduce the number of eyes that might read it?'

"Dear mother, there are numerous ways to hide something that should not be seen. Those who have their doors closed will not see the light,' he stated cryptically.

'Don't make me dizzy with your words, Master Roderici. I only need your assurance that you will not use evil arts to achieve your purpose.'

'I can assure you, Mother Abbess, I will only use the oldest science known since the dawn of time. Forgotten techniques, yes, but already existing when the Son of God stepped into this world.'

'If so, begin as soon as possible. And may God bless the endeavour you are about to undertake.'

MASTER JOHANNES LOOKED UP MOMENTS BEFORE WRITING IN the codex with the unique ink he had laboriously prepared, his gaze fixed on an indeterminate point in the scriptorium. The rest of the monks surrounding him kept their heads down in strange, unearthly concentration. Just the occasional cough here and there, just the sound of scrolls being shuffled. The time had come to build the phrases, relationships, the accumulation of knowledge he had learned from the alchemists and sages of his time. And ultimately, to condense this information into a few brief lines in a single determined effort.

It must appear simple and effortless. And deep within, that incomprehensible message he had pledged not to share under penalty of excommunication. The abbess's gaze was eager, urgent. He'd never seen such determination before.

A dull, persistent exhaustion had set in on him. It was a weariness that crept into his soul gradually. But his doom was already sealed in those inks, whose mercury, in varied concentrations, had already killed a number of his colleagues. No, his fatigue stemmed from a reality that he couldn't comprehend. He had begun his life in this craft alongside his father, who had taught him to read and write from an early age. He had taught him to trust the codices and manuscripts rather than men. He found in the latter an extraordinary truth, the truth that others had so frequently betrayed. There he found solace, joy, and hope.

When he took the quill and the dyes and set the scroll to illuminate before him, he knew he could control that. He also knew that someone, somewhere, someday, would seek the the knowledge contained within. And he, like a master cathedral builder, would have been part of it.

He inhaled deeply. He had to concentrate. He needed to remember all the old tricks of the trade, the seemingly effortless line, the tiny picture embedded inside the capital letter. He had the mysterious notes to transcribe besides him along the more technical ones indication how much ink to use, the properties of the mixture, and how dense it should be.

In the scriptorium beside him were several shards of red glass that had aroused the misgivings of one monk. However, no one asked him about their purpose. They all knew very well and respected the quiet laws that governed their work.

He would take one of them apart now and then, bringing it closer to the paper, changing it again for another before repeating the process. Finally, he would shake his head, reapplying the ink he had meticulously prepared.

The tower bells could be heard at that moment. The abbess had specifically excused him from attending the church service. He must finish the work as soon as possible. There would be time later to apologise for the zillion thoughts that had raced through his mind at the sight of the content of the message he was composing.

He finally stopped and leaned back, staring at the scroll in front of him.

He smiled.

The task was completed. He put his signature at the bottom, made the sign of the cross and rose from the scriptorium.

The other monks kept their heads bowed over the different miniature codices in front of them, unaware of old Johannes' little secret.

Tomorrow, he would return to the scriptorium, but it would be then a different man and a different day. For tomorrow, it would be an older man who would be sitting there.

Because his crucial days, his mission, as he liked to call it, had ended to the sound of the bells still ringing when he left the room. For this was the day he was to present the Codex to Mother Abbess.

"It had been a magnificent job," he thought proudly after having delivered his work, as he headed toward the neighbourhood where the guild of copyists and illuminators clustered, hoping to lose himself among the maze of streets in search of a much needed rest.

He had one secret regret, though. Better said, two.

The first was knowing he could show no one the perfection of his art.

The second was of a more disturbing nature.

What if he had made it too perfect? What if no one ever read it?

CHAPTER 63

GOLDEN DAYS

Party day at Golden Mount, followed by another one in Covarrubias.
Ernesto is brought up to date —Montorio.

That evening on June 23, Elena, Arthur and Carlos sauntered through the Montorio streets on their way to the cultural association after having parked in front of Balbina Inn.

It was strange being here again, feeling the sun on face and arms while crossing the street, with no other concern than feeling its warmth thought Lafuente. He closed his eyes, keeping his hands in his pockets, fiddling with the inner fabric.

As they approached the "Golden Mount" headquarters, they could see it had become a veritable whirlwind since the last time they had been here. Their arrival had coincided with the prime point in the town's festivities waited expectantly for an entire year by all Montorians. The upcoming preparation for the Cultural Week organized yearly by the association only added to the increasing excitement.

Inside the premises, Honorio, leaning on the bar, watched with a child-like smile as a group of kids were taking among peals of laughter planks, fabrics, chairs, and many things with uncertain shapes out of the warehouse. All that in preparation for the dance, games and cultural activities that would take place in the following days.

'Wow! Glad to see you here again. Thanks for coming! With so much ado, I had almost forgotten about you,' said the veteran member jokingly upon seeing the group entering the place with some difficulty, shaking hands with every one of the newcomers.

The premises of about seventy square meters were being filled by a population that seemed to emerge from nowhere. The long tables and benches had already been prepared for the occasion. The pellet stove —both witness to lively meetings during the last winter and an uncomfortable memory of the cold— was now relegated to a corner, the need for it forgotten. In the spacious library attached to the living room, children, members and locals came and went, some with newspapers and books, others with games, in a creative whirlwind that was amusing to contemplate due to its very hodgepodge. To that number one had to add friends from the neighbouring towns, as well as the return of others who after having left long ago were returning like the prodigal son.

'We've been in high demand lately, if you know what I mean, professor,' Honorio said. 'That writer friend of yours and his girlfriend were here some time ago. We haven't seen so many people pass through town in recent months since the reconquest and the French invasion.'

They were now at the door of the premises. Honorio was greeting the many neighbours and friends who were approaching. A couple of youngsters who used to spend the rest of the year going up and down the street on their bicycles with bored faces had left them leaning against the green bench, the latter accustomed and resigned to such use. Yes, the rest of the year the road was an obligatory path for young people who, like those who had just passed, undertook that cycle route over and over before heading towards the consoles that awaited at home. But, unlike those of the professor's youth, these youngsters had been expelled by their parents, condemned to go out into the open air and enjoy it against their wishes.

From the back of the room raising their glasses and beer cans as a way of greeting the newcomers could see among those present some members of the local potato cooperative, dedicated to the tireless cultivation of potato crops and responsible for the tractor traffic they had witnessed in their last visit. In a few seconds, Arthur and his friends hurried to take some photos with them.

'Don't let anyone dare to say 'potato' or I'll kill him!' — said Sara Serna, a member of the cooperative in a plain reference to their daily chores during the rest of the year.

Her brother Nico gave a laugh not directed at anyone in particular, born of the moment and the day.

Arthur looked around him at such boiling and movement.

Only two or three cars had dared to park on the street, thus reminding the occasional traveller he was in the 21st century.

Behind the few houses facing the association, the mountains and hills spread themselves, dotted here and there with some buildings. In this place landscape reigned, as was well attested by the very name of the street on which they stood.

'One of the members took a great photo of a sunrise from this point,' Sara said. 'I think is still on Google.'

'Yes, I've seen it, as a matter of fact,' Carlos said. 'I must confess my interest for Montorio reached that point. An excellent picture, if I may say so. Of course, I also realised the name of this member was Soledad Serna. Well, Honorio,' he said, feeling the moment for farewells had arrived, 'we will always remember you. Elena was right when she told us the first time this was indeed a golden hill,' — and in saying this, Carlos could see the sun peeking out from behind the clouds that had initially given the impression of spoiling the day.

ELENA RAISED HER HEAD FROM HER DESK AND SMILED AT THE couple that had just entered her office. Ernesto and Clarissa had been looking for Professor Lafuente in vain after having arrived to Burgos that very morning. After greeting them, Elena sat back in her chair with deliberately slow movements throwing her hair backwards.

'By the way, while you wait for Carlos, I think you must be interested in knowing about the Codex fate,' she said, trying to add an ill-concealed touch of drama to her sentences. 'I'm sure he would have preferred to be the first one to break the news, but you can't have everything, can you? We do not have all the information yet as the proceedings are in court under summary secrecy. Still, apparently, the alleged owner,-- our dear Count Dabrowski--, had found the manuscripts on his estate a long time ago without having revealed their existence. No family heirloom or anything like that. A pure tall tale, as we suspected. A shaggy dog. A way to get easy money for a declining estate. We don't know yet how they ended in the family, anyway. Possibly someone stole them from Silos or Huelgas. But we do know that the count tried to sell them through Sotheby's of London, despite the final opinion of their authenticity. Fortunately, his attempt was discovered in time by Interpol, and the manuscripts are now in Huelgas where they should be under the careful supervision of our friend, Mother Abbess.

'Amazing. Should I have written it, you would have told me it would be a far-fetched story,' Ernesto said. 'I guess that settles once and for all the matter of the MS And what about your relations with the rector? I hope they have improved after the recent events.'

'Yeah, you can't imagine how well they're going. Let's say the events have developed unexpectedly for him.'

'Unsuspected? What do you mean?'

'Yes, you see, after Carlos presented his resignation to the University a few days after his additional report to National Heritage, your invaluable articles on the Codex following shortly after, things began to happen. Well, to make a long story short, both the university board and the foundation realised they had been close to losing the original manuscripts forever. Of course, their reaction was not a very favourable one. The rector's attitude did not seem to create a friendly atmosphere at that meeting. There were also other things, you know....'

'Other things? Apart from the report, you mean?' Clarissa said.

'Yes. It seems our friend kept in his safe certain documents that showed— how should I put it? A certain misuse of his functions as head of the university. It is unclear how, but the details of these circumstances reached the Board' Elena continued, looking at her friends with what seemed a mischievous smile. 'Well, to sum things up, the result of it was that the Board strictly applied the principles of rectitude and protection of the monumental legacy of the building, as well as of the scholastic tradition that the very rector had always highlighted and emphasised, but had not practised enough in the real world.'

The palaeographer continued recounting the useless protests of innocence that Don Patricio Noguer had raised in his defence, the outbreaks of fury, absolute or feigned that kept his secretary and personal advisers away from his presence throughout that week, suddenly indisposed or busy. Trying to locate them, either by phone or in person, was a useless task. All the official contacts on his agenda were of no use either. The assistant professors became suddenly flooded with work on their tutorials, theses, research assignments, classes and so on, which made their presence in the corridors, labyrinths and passageways of the venerable university relatively scarce...

Mr Noguer's bicycle did remain in its usual place in those days, leaning against the wall covered in Boston ivy, that, continuing its climbing and growing between the front wheels of the vehicle threatened to incorporate it into the garden vegetation. It wasn't until a few weeks later that it was finally removed by two gardeners who, without a word, and perhaps just a glance at each other, rescued the poor velocipede from its vegetable prison.

Finally, after a week of investigations, both the University and Mogueroles governing Boards met in an extraordinary session, a session that lasted throughout all day and had the primary purpose of examining the bulky and detailed file voted unanimously for the sudden dismissal of the rector. The new position fell unanimously on a surprised Carlos Lafuente, who was slow to assimilate such an appointment.

'Congratulations, professor!' Arthur said, all smiles, approaching him half an hour after the appointment had been made official, 'I just heard the news!'

Gossip spread about how strange the whole procedure had been, to the curious and almost ghostly way in which those mysterious documents had appeared on the Board's table, namely inside a thick envelope dotted with oil stains containing names, figures and precise notes pointing out to sundry irregular activities of the rector.

There were some who, given these marks, pointed to Elvira as a mediating agent in the events that ruined the prospects of the previous rector. When these suspicions first arose, there was no way for Professor Lafuente — now rector—, to find her in order to corroborate those rumours. The detective's phone appeared always out of range and there was no way to see her for love or money. One day Arthur had the impression of having seeing her as he was climbing the stairs that led to the Outside Llana with a group of friends, but with his usual prudence he had judged better to let things go their way. There were mysteries that, unlike the one they had been dealing with for over a year, it was better to let rest.

The young man knew the little detective had always acted out of the greatest affection and respect for the professor and the mission's objective, as she had always said when mentioning this search for her particular Grail.

It had indeed been an intense year.

As expected, Arthur had finished his master's degree.

But not only that.

In front of him, facing the bay window and the river that had made it possible, hanging from a vermilion ribbon, between the photos of Cracknell and Pérez, was a medal on which was reproduced St Maria Gate enclosed in a white shield on a maroon background. It had been designed by a local artist marking in so doing a breaking point in the history of the city.

The rowing Blue, the Burganda Blue.

'Burganda my friend. We are going on vacation' Arthur said before packing his suitcase to go on a well-deserved vacation to Italy.

The boy's perseverance, the long evenings spent on the river, had paid off. Yes, he had got the much-coveted medal of that first regatta between the two universities held last April; a victory that had been the result of the concentration and effort applied that afternoon, while being splashed by the Arlanzón waters, all his attention put in directing his team, in the precise blows of each movement of the paddle. Finally, they had brought their canoe to the finishing line only a few seconds ahead of the rival team.

And that April afternoon — despite T. S. Eliot—, had not been part of the cruellest of months for the young man.

As for Meseguer, it can only be said briefly that Daddy's wallet ceased to supply freely and in grand opulence the whims of his first-born son. Under those circumstances, this budding genius was forced to leave the university and try better fortune in his uncle's mechanical shop, located two streets down from his father's glass-enclosed offices.

A familiar silhouette crossed the Montanilla campus with short, determined steps.

Another figure with uncoordinated movements met her.

'Greetings, my fair lady. Can I do something for you?'

'To begin with, you can keep your medieval dialectic to yourself until I finish my classes. Nothing less than a whole new bunch of students for me today! I will have to convince them of how splendid it is to look into the past and all that,' Elena said, as she kept walking, carrying some books in her crossed arms as if she were one of those students recently arrived that term.

'I'm sure you'll do fine. Just tell them about the wonders of hunting butterflies in the moonlight, and you will have them aboard. Remember, coffee later in my suite!' Carlos replied with a wink, leaving without waiting for an answer.

They both used to have long chats with their colleague, Professor

Abad, who had done so much to clear up the mystery, although unconsciously, due to her patient and dedicated work. While they had these conversations, they sometimes recalled the curious fact they were in an area that — although now part of the Burgos University, had been the King's Hospital--, owned by Las Huelgas monastery and where most of their adventures had taken place. A fitting end to the time spent on it.

These three had created what only a few months back was difficult to contemplate — a healthy camaraderie between the two universities.

From Ernesto Santo's notes.

Covarrubias, July 24, 20 ...

It had dawned a splendid day for the occasion.

We had arrived the evening before in a repetition of the cultural trip we had made to this place long ago. Once again, we were in Covarrubias after having rested from our long journey. Today an event was to be held in honour of Princess Kristina. This year, however, it was going to be something special. It no mystery that Montanilla University had been conducting intensive studies on the princess. Local newspapers and organisations had not skimped to sign up to this trend that brought novelty, interest and perhaps a huge extra income to the annual celebration.

Clarissa and I accompanied Carlos and his team in all the pilgrimages and tributes with that *sprit de corps* that had characterized our small group. They were, in any case, private and quiet tributes, far from the hubbub and noise that filled the village. We thus went to the collegiate church and laid flowers before Kristina's statue. We verified we had not been the only ones in doing so as the ground was already shining with colour due to other offerings.

The Norwegian music band was preparing their instruments in the central square on an improvised stage, at the foot of the town hall we had visited last time we were here. Some vendor stalls had been prepared, surrounding the square, showing tiny wooden dolls on display and sundry objects that no one would have conceived could exist so far from their land. Once again, I was reminded of Pinocchio's tiny hamlet.

At that moment Hans, our old acquaintance approached us along a corpulent figure with a blond beard who stood by the side of both the mayor and the councillor for Tourism, Mr Ramón Valverde.

'Mr Birk Larsen is the Norwegian ambassador to Spain,' said Hans, making the introductions,

'Why, if they are no others than the Norwegian Grail seekers,' said the Consul in English, 'I have to congratulate you gentlemen for such an admirable job. It was brilliant of you to think of choral music as a transmitter of the message. *Veldig dyktig!*

'He said it was a brilliant thing.' Hans translated after we left the ambassador.

Carlos and Elena were smiling and talking to some of the press attending the event when the former, searching for Arthur found that the young man had disappeared into thin air.

'Devil of a boy! He is never found when he is needed!'

We soon were concentrated on another task as beer mugs came to us, held by Hans's firm hands.

'I bring this for you on behalf of the Norwegian Legation. Let's say it's the Norwegian way of thanking you for your work,' he said with the same smile he had shown us the first time we arrived in Covarrubias. 'As we use to say, *"Kemst Tho haegt fari"*, which is something like "you will arrive even if you saunter."'

'Thank you, Hans,' Carlos said, taking the jug he was offered and passing the other to Elena while I did the same with Clarissa. 'After reading so much about ancient Norway in the old manuscripts and chronicles, it's glad to relate to the contemporary country for a change, I must say. I was about to think you were still wearing medieval headdresses and such stuff!'

'That reminds me Pub La Serna where we met last met had to close its doors for good. A pity!' said the Norwegian.

'Wow,' said Lafuente, 'I'm sorry. Right now, it would have been very appropriate to meet there for a few drinks. Symbolically, and given the course of our research, it would have been the most appropriate thing to do.'

'I know,' said Hans, 'but the owner couldn't resist the fact that fewer people were coming to town now. *Skol!*' he said, raising his mug.

Arthur smiling then, holding the hand of an old acquaintance. This was none other than Remedios Ponciel, that young lady from Las Huelgas Carlos had told me about some time ago and whose movements had captured the student's attention from the first time he saw her.

I looked at all the people surrounding us, at the musicians playing, at the girl in purple glasses laughing by the side of a boy in an extravagant shirt, and at an elderly couple, eminently Norwegian, showing a contagious joy. All of this motivated because one day, long ago, Princess Kristina had put their feet on this land. Although brief, her life had been meaningful, within that incessant chain of cause and effect that had created this auspicious moment.

I raised my glass to that old friend I had got to know in a way. A strange sense of familiarity washed over me.

'To Kristina!...'

We toasted in silence.

The solemn moment for speeches had arrived.

Carlos Lafuente ascended swiftly the small stage set up in the square, his figure facing the clock on the facade of the town hall, that seemed busy in an eternal race against time. Once there, the professor stood next to the musical instruments that would later resonate with the performance by the rock group "Los Águilas", already announced on the festival programme.

'Eight centuries ago,' the professor began, staring at the clock as if he were addressing his speech, not to the group of people in the square, but at the very Time, 'a Norwegian girl began a journey full of illusion, uncertain about her destiny, thinking of being the queen of a new empire. We have traced that past, that distant past, looking for some evidence of her, of her truth. We have gathered here today next to her grave, after an adventure that has taken us months to go through. We want to pay tribute to her in this place, precisely here, her last resting place, where not only her body but her dreams and hopes remain. It's the least we can do for her. To quote the Alicante poet Miguel Hernández, she is nothing more than dust now, but dust in love. Actually, from our humble little-ness, we can do little for those historical figures that members of her entourage and the people who welcomed her would not have already done in a daily tribute.'

Today, the press and television present here—as well as the social networks no doubt, will know that we were in this place, but for those of us who have been involved in knowing her figure more closely, she will live not only for these moments. She will remain within us somehow. We who interpret history, must be the ones to honour her truth. Not only the truth of those who lived centuries ago but the truth of the average person, of the man in a grey coat who buys cigarettes for the festival on an autumn afternoon, of the boy who flies his balloon through the main square bound for home. In this way, these stories, these little daily stories, will be of some use.'

'Congratulations on your speech, professor! It was superb,' Arthur said as Lafuente left the platform.

'It has no merit, Arthur, believe me. It was pure Lincoln!' Lafuente said with a grimace.

Those moments spent in Covarrubias have confirmed me there are stories worth undertaking, worth living for, even if the road ahead is hard and dark. Events apparently unimportant, banal, but neces-sary to tell we have lived even if fatigue and discouragement arise throughout them, like those wounds borne on our anatomy, on our knees and elbows, after playing along with our childhood friends on long summer afternoons, running up the stairs to the castle. Yet, those stories are the ones that —in a strange sort of way—, mark us, make us better, make us enjoy having lived them. At the road end, we will look back at those memories and be grateful for having come across that series of people who accompanied us part of the way. Together we saw unique landscapes or even these being the same, the gaze will be different, the vision unusual, the perception ever-changing, and the result always, always surprising.

The Covarrubias fair had taken place on July 24 and the visit of my friend Carlos to Montorio a month earlier, on June 24. Of course, nothing more than one of those significant coincidences I was already so accustomed to.

As I said all these are just memories now, brief snippets of a year we have lived in a kind of trance; impressionist brushstrokes, blurred, like a landscape seen through a misted glass. I suppose these are the moments one treasures, rewinds in memory. It is nice to pause and enjoy the authentic pleasure of keeping your mind blank and feeling, simply feeling that everything possible has been done in that daily effort, in that constant decision-making thing that constitutes existence.

CHAPTER 64

A FAREWELL

Anyone strolling down the Espolon Walk could have noticed in a shady part of it, two unmoving figures resting on the parapet, gazing out at the river.

The sunlight rays, filtering through the cloud that had veiled the picture for a minute revealed them to be none others than Carlos Lafuente and Ernesto Santos.

The location where they were so intently observing the river was close to the professor's residence. Around them, the Espolón Walk continued its normal routine. People walked by without casting a single glance in their direction. A family, leading by the hand a freckled girl in a yellow coat and a striped hat. Some dogs strained on their leashes in a futile attempt to sniff her at her approach.

During that evening stroll, they had passed previously the Royal Theatre on their way to this gorgeous location. A few metres away, on a river-facing corner, was a clothing store franchise. This certainly detracted from the scene part of its romanticism and showed that Burgos was still thriving and well in the modern world.

In front of them stood the old Espolón Bookstore, a quiet witness to previous walks in the area. Inside it, Pilar, its owner, would be spending one day more looking over the new acquisitions.

'Practically everyone in Burgos has entered it at some point or another,' Carlos added, recalling his many visits to the location.

'It's also a significant spot for me,' Ernesto said, looking through the bookshop window. 'That's precisely where my first novel, *The Perfumed Institute*, was sold a couple of years ago. I'm delighted to see it hasn't lost any of its unique charm.'

'Well, I guess we've succeeded marvellously, if we may return to our subject. It's difficult for me to acknowledge that it has been far from flawless; it's true.' said the professor, staring out at the river. 'But as the old adage goes: "never ever celebrate a victory or lament a failure." It cannot be denied that it's in our DNA to value thing more the harder they were to achieve. I have always liked coming to this bridge when I needed to think, meditate, or put my life in order. This is actually my favourite spot. It feels odd to be here today without having the same level of concern as other times. At least not with the same uneasiness, not in the same way.'

'Everyone meditates as best they can, given the circumstances. Of course, some people prefer walking for doing so, which is the most common thing.'

'I guess I'm more complicated. Whenever I was feeling down, I would come and stand here and stare at the waters at low tide. I would sit beneath those weeping willows that convey a certain melancholy, and, before leaving, I always made a point of touching the bridge with my hands, delighted to feel its sturdiness, its fixity, if you will. Except me, everything seemed to be moving. I felt the stone's hardness, the heat of summer days, and the winter chill.'

So it was. The professor must have watched the sparse underbrush heave into the stream and slip before his eyes countless times during that sleepless reveille. The soothing sounds and gentle motion of the river flowing down from one place to another, eventually disappearing from his line of sight.

The river showed gray, green, brown, a thousand different colours of water, but it always, always silky. Tangled, appearing out of nowhere, on their journey to an unknown location. The stone, the moisture on his hands, something tangible to grasp. Stable and consistent.

More than one evening after dinner, he would come here with his pipe and spend the hours standing in the spot he so wonderfully had described to his friend, oblivious to the time, twisted as the very waters.

And for a short time while doing this exercise and puffing on his pipe, he felt at ease.

'I believe an important stage begins for you now,' said the professor, pausing to study the Arlanzón waters and looking his friend in the eyes. 'If I remember correctly, you said you were crossing the pool to Canada, didn't you? I wish you both the best of luck. We'll be keeping the old pile here. Elena has come up with a few ideas for restoring it inside. I believe she wants to bring her private collection of landscape paintings to complement my seascapes and butterflies.'

They exchanged silent glances for a few seconds.

They shook hands.

There was no need for words this time.

~

CHAPTER 65

LETTERS READ AT DUSK

From Ernesto Santos's notes
Prince Edward island
December 21st

It started raining a little while ago. The rain keeps striking the covered roof where I am working, hitting it repeatedly. It's like being hit over and over with a hammer, with the force always changing. I have adjusted myself to this routine before I start my evening writing.

'It's quite common around here. It won't take long for you to get used to it,' I was reassured by the bartender at the Duke of Cornwallis, the pub around the corner the first time I patronised it.

And yes, that much was true; it didn't take me long. And so, here I am, awaiting the hour, that space of time between five and six o'clock in the evening, when I will once again hear thunder rolling and lightning flash once more through the study windows as something necessary before beginning my daily task.

Therefore, this was a fantastic day. We'd wait for the rain to become heavier, the sound outside the windows to increase, the world's darkness beyond the windows bringing memories of so many downpours, so many evenings spent watching the lightning, the dense undergrowth green, the trees, grateful for each and every one of those raindrops falling from above.

The best way to get in touch with the divine is to sit in a storm and watch the lightning flash and the thunder roll.

And then it ended as abruptly as it had begun.

Will it continue later? Nature writes her own thriller novel, keeping us on our toes. Our human nature, being more primary, cannot do otherwise. And as with all natural wonders, there is a part of us that is alarmed, fearful; a part ready to flee should the situation cross a certain threshold.

Yes, on evenings such as this, I would remember those friends I made along the way, across the ocean, Carlos Lafuente, Arthur Trevelyan, and, of course, Elena. We had accomplished something extraordinary as a group. We had tightened the strings of the possible, the invisible threads that intertwine destinies, as invisible as a spiderweb until one becomes entangled in it. So, when I'm by myself, I raise a glass and toast silently to our friendship, to our meeting, and to the unique role each of us played in that web of chance encounters, scientific breakthroughs, and, yes, also miracles.

A letter arrived in my mailbox not long after the occurrences described in the previous pages. The Montanilla University logo was prominently displayed on it. It was a bulky envelope, the type that inspires some dread, due to the fact that its size suggested it would contain critical information rather than a quick note of courtesy, invitation, or professional regard.

I tore into it with keen anticipation. It was signed by Elena Serna, our old friend.

Burgos, December 15th, 20...

Dear Ernesto,

As I promised I'm writing to fill you in on the latest developments outside of the official Serna genealogical inquiry we've been undertaking.

No need to tell you that neither Carlos nor I have given up and that we occasionally consult old chronicles, various historians' books, and a thousand theories, aside from those given to me by my colleague Carlos Ensiñar, from Deusto University, although of course not with the same zeal. I have also been in touch with a couple of companies specialising in tracing family lineages. Nonetheless, while it is certain that the Serna line was maintained in Montorio and the surrounding area before a sizeable portion of the population relocated, the final segment, from the nineteenth century onwards, is more patchy and less clear.

I've included photocopies of all relevant documentation. Many branches came to an end due to lack of new registers, while others converged and intertwined in an arabesque that seemed to point us in the right direction.

It is quite frustrating that one of the particular genealogical lines we were pursuing, namely the one documented in Isais Mendoza Carmona's *Burgos Chronicle*, written in 1895, has yielded no results. On the other hand, the historian Francisco Quesada Villegas, who wrote a history of the local surnames, zeroes particularly on Montorio and the surrounding area in his work. One can only speculate, and as you know, this task is dangerous.

I'm sorry this information isn't more useful to you or myself. The absence of chronicles, of reliable written documents, leads us to a dead end. Due to the partial burning of numerous civil records during the Civil War, the genealogical line suffers a significant documentary loss. Carlos, Arthur, and I have all agreed the fact that the musical Codex is still around today is nothing short of a miracle.

Two of our old acquaintances, Clemente Násera and Rufio Colmenar, remain in contact with us. They are interested in our advances or, more accurately, the lack of them as well as about your professional career—with that persistent curiosity that characterises both of them.

In any case, our journey has been both amazing and unsettling, and I, too, believe that hard reality has pushed us to face a dead end.

As historians, we're used to being jolted out of our slumber on a regular basis. I would like to give in to the yearning for knowledge and, like you, fill those unknown voids with creative desire, but my training unfortunately precludes me from doing so.

A hug,

Elena Serna Serna

History Department

Montanilla University

There was another letter signed by Carlos Lafuente alongside the first. Although it was dated earlier than Elena's, it had shared the same envelope. There was no doubt that Sweet Sofia, the university secretary, had indeed acted frugally. My two friends had agreed to bring the old Burgos closer to my new home.

Burgos, December 18th, 20th

Dear friend,

One has to know when evidence, along with the reality offered by our five senses and that seldom-applied common sense, demands vehemently, but persistently, that we pay attention.

I have worked relentlessly for months to persuade a large number of people to join me. My days, thoughts, concerns, and future projects have all been placed at the foot of this illusion. For nearly two years, we have drunk from the princess's dream, from her memory. I have no regrets, however. Elena and Arthur share with me the firm belief we have done everything our effort and scientific knowledge can do and, yes, also, our friend's paranormal sciences may have played a minor role along the way. Perhaps some time from now, another generation will take over and continue the race. Each of us has a purpose to accomplish in life. Elena observes me as I write this letter. She deserves a little peace.

I see her leaning against her easel, attempting to mix the

colours once more, shape an outline here and there on the canvas, sketch an idea, and compose poetry once more. And I will be there.

The missing link, if it exists, if it is humanly possible to find it, will be found. But I have already realised it will not be me. It is only sensible to acknowledge one's own human fallibility. Nonetheless, you and I have every reason to be pleased. We've both chased a dream, which is in and of itself a success. It is, in some ways, what makes us great.

Elvira is still thinking about the while thing since the very day she began working with us. For months, the detective remains calm. Then, all of a sudden, a word, the name of a town, a short mention in the *Burgos Daily* about some forgotten village, an old tradition or the mere mention of a forgotten local family, sets her off, putting her behind the wheel of its Opel Kadett which, after emitting some peculiar noises, drives it up again along unknown routes and adventures burning inside her. Elvira is already a slave to this inner dream, this nightmare that the quest for knowledge means, both torment and blessing for those of us who suffer from it. That fever, I believe, will always burn within her after having come too close to the spark of inquiry kindled in this office. She has been too close not to be an inseparable part of it.

I have already given up discouraging her with these inquiries. I know too much about what inner search entails to even attempt it.

What about Arthur, the newest recruit at Montanilla University? The new professor has received a large number of tutorials, not only because of his good looks and demeanour, but also because of his exceptional work and the personal magnetism he exudes in his classes and seminars, conveying to his pupils his love and passion for knowledge. Elena now occupies, of course, the chair of the Palaeography Department.

Together, we have learnt to live with our limitations, and from time to time we listen to some of the new information Elvira brings us. Clarissa and Kristina, our four and three-year-old daughters, thank us with their devotion and questions regarding the time we sacrificed in pursuit historical secrets.

But we will never forget that amid so many others, it was this one that brought us together. The one which made us realise that genuine wisdom, like the true secret of this story, can only be understood as a divine gift.

I left the letters on the table.

I took a long look at the wall in front of me, then at the open window, and last at the forest that opened before my eyes.

My computer screen was filled with the manuscript I had been working on for the past few hours.

On that drowsy afternoon, the island appeared strangely devoid of historical concerns, chimaeras of bygone ages, and concealed mysteries. Was that really the case, though?

CHAPTER 66

LAFUENTE LOOKS AT THE SEA

In Santander, December 21st, 20 ...

After writing the letter to Ernesto, I felt I had accomplished a kind of duty. The separate land mentioned by John Donne in his poem was getting closer.

What were the words I had used in my letter?

That it would require a miracle, a divine gift to find the truth, the lost connection?

Only my instinct, that relentless drumming in my head, those strewn-about historical clues had encouraged me to continue. Arthur has taught me to trust my intuition, as well as to start jotting down ideas in my notebook.

Somehow, I had known about the story of the Norse princess. Had it all been by chance? By sheer coincidence?

All that information had fallen in my lap unexpectedly, without looking for it.

The parallels and symbols had been there, waiting to be discovered.

The Monastery's Chronicle, which the abbesses kept secret and only shared with her successors on her death bed.

The love letter discovered in the coffin, possibly addressed to an unknown lover and the creature she had left behind.

I could not get out of my head the image of that child lost in Huelgas, in northern Spain, while her mother invoked her presence through the centuries.

I would certainly never know the truth. Just a beautiful romantic chronicle lost in history, in the alliances and wars of a Spain not yet formed.

Who knows? perhaps my enhanced sensitivity would have made me a better pamphlet writer than a historian.

After working for a few hours on the book I was writing on mediaeval Burgos, I went in search of Elena. She had gone for a walk after leaving the kittens some food.

I walked a few steps behind the house in her search.

Her bike was nearby. She couldn't be far away.

Yes, I found her a little further on, in the little cove next to the lighthouse, sitting on a rock, gazing out to sea.

She was engrossed in contemplating the flight of the seagulls, her eyes following the ever-changing movements of a landscape she never tired of. She would occasionally pull out the camera I had given her for her recent birthday. From where I was, I could hear the familiar click of the camera's shutter immortalising some of those creatures.

At that hour of the evening, the sea sounded rough. The violet light had begun to engulf her, outlining her silhouette against the horizon, against the leaden ocean.

I smiled.

I stopped and stared at her in silence for a few moments. It was this an experience I never grew weary of.

She was at that moment the living embodiment of a mystery that should have decided to go for a walk in the evening.

I took the path that led to our house. I didn't want to disturb her. Not today, not right now. I had to do something before. I wanted to capture that memory, that moment.

. . .

THAT'S HOW I LIKE TO REMEMBER HER ON THOSE RARE occasions when, for work reasons, I have to absent myself from the place to attend a symposium or a book presentation.

It was useless to tell her about the supernatural intuition I had experienced one day, or whatever I wished to call it. It made little sense, even to me. It had been a journey of inner exploration, of self-discovery. I positively knew it was now my turn, my moral obligation to take care of her, of that mythological inheritance, if you will.

Yes, that's how I want to remember her, fixed on my retina forever. May that memory come to visit me in my final moments, bringing peace to my soul. With all the strength of her DNA, looking North.

Elena, watching the horizon, had transformed herself into a new person. Obviously, my senses told me she was still her, but I knew, or perceived that something more was at stake here. Something I did not dare to name. Perhaps one day I will.

Or perhaps never.

I no longer had any restlessness in my heart. As if by magic, the emotion from months before had vanished.

Yes, as I once told Arthur, this was life, not a story whose conclusion could be chosen at our discretion. Even so, this was the end I had hoped for in my life, despite the imperfections proper to our humanity.

And I felt that way evening after evening, watching the leaves fall, new or old, with the same colours of the previous season, as they would do year after year, century after century; the identical shapes, the same scent, as if the world had not altered at all in the intervening years.

A part of me converses in silence with this ancestor through the centuries. That woman with a sad and melancholy look.

I feel indebted to her and some nights, before I close my eyes, I can hear a kind of whisper in my ear:

'Thanks!'

The two princesses of Arlanzón River.

Elena had completed the task. She was already a genuine princess of the North, rising as a figurehead on that rocky promontory facing the sea.

～

EPILOGUE

A MONTORIO STATUE

Montorio has suffered a slight variation in its urban landscape. As a result of it, any motorcyclist approaching the town hoping to cross it quickly on his way north will run into an obstacle in doing so. A minor obstacle, but enough to force them to slow down through the town centre.

Between Calle Burgos and its expansion, Calle Félix Rodríguez de la Fuente, there is now a little roundabout. A bronze statue stands in its centre.

It is a modest and small sculpture but —like many of these monuments—, oh! so full of meaning.

It has been made possible thanks to the initiative of the cultural association and the new mayor, Roberto Costa—a close friend of the former—as well as the collaboration of the Norwegian legation through the Princess Kristina Foundation and the equally valuable collection of signatures carried out by Montanilla students.

The statue represents a girl.

A girl depicted in the sculptor's imagination contemplating the setting sun, perhaps recalling those other infants appearing in the works of Flemish and Dutch painters, in those paintings drenched in an evening light filtering through windows at the end of long corridors. She raises her right hand, showing on it a little bird standing between her gaze and the horizon.

A little golden plaque at its base reads:

To the unknown Serna,

In remembrance of the lost descendants of Princess Kristina who lived in the environs of Quintanilla and Montorio between the 13th and early 20th centuries.

And following that, there is a brief sketch of the sad end of that Norwegian princess sent on a strange mission to Spain.

At the base of the monument there is always a small group of flowers, which some neighbours take care to change frequently owing to the the wind, rain, or the occasional thug's act.

Honorio, the association's president, is proud to show it to the many visitors who come to Montorio for the Virgin of Mercedes festivities or any other local event.

Parades include now a quick tour around the statue before proceeding up the street, while all the time the bronze girl appears to smile gratefully.

REGARDING THE STAINED GLASS WINDOWS AT HUELGAS Monastery and the secret of their making, as well as the composition of the ink used to write the mysterious words on the codex, we are aware that they are currently the subject of extensive research by a number of scholars, among whom—aside from our friends at Montanilla University—, the name of Pilar Abad, the UBU professor who is reporting the progress of her research in a number of conferences and articles published in academic journals, stands out. There are numerous grey places that Professor Lafuente's research did nothing but highlight, removing the corner of the painting's protective cover, if not the entire image. Such has been the case since ancient times, in those alchemical secrets transmitted in codices similar to the Musical Codex through the architecture of cathedrals, convents, and monasteries.

CHAPTER 2

MOTHER ABBESS REMEMBERS

Mother Abbess found solace in her daily walks through the garden and adjacent vineyards. A balm that could not be recognised as such. It was a scorching August morning and the first mass had just finished. On that clear day she appreciated the diaphanous clarity, the faint presence of clouds. She enjoyed walking through the garden and, on occasion, sneaking out into the Outside Compas before the daily arrival of visitors and National Heritage staff, allowing herself to be swept away by the privilege of spending her days here.

If no other sister was present, she dared to pray in the Claustrillas or, after crossing the Conversas Passage, reach the Infant's Garden with a similar goal.

She had recently heard from some sisters they had witnessed a young blonde wandering alone at night, her silhouette barely outlined behind a set of columns. Just for a moment—perhaps a second or two. She had also shared that vision once, but realised upon paying more attention it had been but an illusion.

Despite this, this so-called illusion had repeated itself several times.

On such a morning, when the only sound was the chirping of

some lost bird searching for its tree, of some sparrow or a late black-bird exploring the nooks and crannies of the closed cloisters in quest of food, it was easy to imagine oneself in another age.

She got a peculiar sense of foreboding when she viewed the wall opposite these windows, knowing that behind it were computers, cables, and contemporary technology, as well as the staff of National Heritage. A fact very far, yes, very far removed from the frequent walks, the repeated explanations of guides, not-always precise, summarising a complicated story in a few brief phrases.

Cars seemed to have forgotten to drive down the cobblestone street on such a day.

She was in a state of deep concentration. She had lived very diverse and, at the same time, very intense experiences over the last few weeks. The old epistolary formula that headed the letters of her predecessors since the Middle Ages came to mind: *"In Santa Maria la Real Monastery, near Burgos..."* Yes. The monastery had paid a high price for being so close to the city. The Cistercian order had stipulated that monasteries should be built far from urban areas so that the sisters could pray and gather. The one in Burgos had been an exception, and now, centuries later, that exception was being paid for.

She jerked her head up. She had just exited the Low Counter, which housed the abbey offices and was now beneath the five-barred arches of the Porter's Lodge. A lattice separated this confined realm from the outside world. In days of yore, an iron chain with five golden enamelled artichokes had been here, strung from column to column, forming an arched tassel, the symbol of the abbess's civil authority. For a brief moment, she thought that if she closed her eyes and reached out her hand, she would be able to feel the cold of iron. In front of her, on the patio, was the fountain, constantly throwing water through its spout in a repeated, ceaseless, different, and identical noise. A car had just pulled in.

Someone should forbid these monstrous, gleaming, metallic machines from entering the compound, breaking the spell and silence. Couldn't all these restorers and scholars hired by Royal Heritage see these vehicles destroyed any basic sense of aesthetics besides the disrespect caused to the monastery itself? How could you possibly match the metallic red colour of one of these cars with the tones of ancient stone? The sound of a horn on the Inside Compass, no matter how involuntary, with the tolling of the bells? She could sense the presence of technicians and other officials behind the walls, with their computers, cell phones, photocopiers, and fax machines; rush, if not boredom, written in their gestures, the daily tedium produced by a job that was always the same as the day before. An almost empty yard their sole source of amusement.

She hoped she wouldn't have to deal with the monastery's future for very much longer. She was aware other similar settlements had perished and she considered it a privilege that Huelgas had survived all the previous tribulations and invasions.

She noticed something strange in the light surrounding her at that moment. A sense of *déjà vu* washed over her; it was a sensation similar to the one she had experienced that dawn in the chapter house when the sun's rays pierced the stained glass window of St John, falling on the Codex. She felt an uneasy, unsettling apprehension. She had no idea where it came from or what caused it. She took a look around. There were no sisters near the gate at the time.

Then, she remembered it. That perception. That strange sensation she had previously felt.

It had happened the year before, in front of her, on the opposite side of the gate. A small group had just entered the Compass. A man and a woman, accompanied by a young man. The woman, with medium-length hair, wore a green bonnet to one side. But there was something else. Something unusual.

Yes, there was something peculiar about her.

She noticed the figures. Just tourists, like so many others she saw on a daily basis; looking around, taking in the walls, the main gate and the fountain for the first time and remarking on how beautiful they were. The woman moved away from the group and approached the founding plaque built on a side wall commemorating the yard's construction. On it was inscribed the name of the abbess who had commissioned its construction. Under it, the small stream continued to sing.

The woman dipped her hand in the falling water and passed it over her face. After that, she gazed absentmindedly towards the place where the abbess was. The latter instinctively took a step back, having been caught off guard.

Something about that woman's gait struck Mother Abbess. She appeared to glide across the ground rather than walk properly. Silently, quickly, and precisely, like a feline. When she looked again, she had returned to the group.

A few minutes later, the latter entered through the admission and ticket sales gate, disappearing from sight.

Why had she shuddered when she saw that woman?

Many times in the years that followed, being an old woman now with a hunched back, she sensed the impending moment of meeting her Saviour. Nonetheless, deep down, she felt gratified by that secret she had shared with that group of Montanilla University researchers.

The image of that stranger in the courtyard occasionally entered her consciousness.

"How very peculiar," she told herself, dismissing the thought. "Even though I had she sitting in my office, I didn't recognise her upon her return, nor even that day at the chapter house."

She realised how the other sisters must have felt when they thought they had witnessed that young blonde in the Claustrillas at twilight.

Over the course of her life she had learned to control her curiosity. This discipline had remained almost intact, except for the expectation the visit of the Montanilla professors had aroused in her soul. But her curiosity, though, would last until the end of her days. She could only hope one day our Lord would lift the veil on this and other concerns she had carried throughout her life.

'Hail Maria, Mother Abbess,' said a sister approaching from the monastery garden, 'I hadn't seen you around here.'

'Good morning, Sister Mariana; I was simply taking in the beauty of the day. Don't you think it is brilliant?'

'Yes, it's a day fit for a princess,' Sister Mariana replied as she walked away in the inn's direction.

CHAPTER 3

THE LOST LINK

An old Mozarabic tower, almost demolished, stands on a hilltop. This is a place where hardly anyone treads anymore. It only houses now bird nests left behind a frosty morning after their inhabitants migrated to warmer climates, intending to return the following winter.

A few trees surround the fallen walls, overcome by the undergrowth that penetrates them. The path leading to the entrance is no longer even a memory, which explains why, every now and then, a nature-loving stroller, one of the few who usually makes it here, stumbles over some remaining tile or beam hidden by the high vegetation.

The Burgos Council has not yet reached out in this direction with development plans or new infrastructure.

A twisted iron cross on its roof proclaims its former use as a place of worship.

There are few places quite like this parish, like this old church with a shaky, creaking wooden porch that threatens to collapse with every gust of wind, to crumble completely over the rest of the population every time a storm approaches. In fear, the rural mayor and parish priest have tried to raise funds for its restoration but their efforts have only succeeded in securing a temporary shelter to celebrate the religious service. The priest has even increased the frequency of his prayers in a vain attempt to prevent the worst from happening.

Yes, there are not many places like this one, where leafless trees surround it, spreading their branches almost over their roofs, like hands trying to prevent the sky from collapsing on it, trying to make it last one day more, one month more, one more year, like a mother trying to protect her child's sleep in a dark night by keeping a single light in the window, a light that serves as a symbol of protection and home warmth, for both the child and herself.

There aren't many parishes like this one, where the paths have been erased by overgrowth over the years. Fern and creeper roots have grown through old tiles upon which children formerly used to play tag or other games until they themselves were covered in turn by larger tiles in the local cemetery.

The church is not completely alone. There are a few more structures nearby that have withstood the worst of the storms; but even them have suffered damage, their walls crumbled and their glassless windows left open to allow even more air to flow through its roofless rooms. A nearby stream can be heard along with a chirping song, like a cricket delighted to be visited by a group of its own kind.

Sometimes a small bird or similar animal come seeking refuge, daring to enter the tower's interior. There, beneath a half-collapsed section of the cornice, is a marble slab erased by time, moss, and oblivion. Its surface bears a name. Only one name, sole survivor of everything previously marked on its surface.

Just one word.

Serna.

And beneath it, some erased dates, of which only a few numbers can be read, accounting for the years: 15—16.

There, in that old church, under the old, forgotten altar—in case the future archaeologist had not found the previous plate—, a double tile sealed in the ground conceals a small cavity, just a few feet long and one foot deep. In that tiny hole, there is a rotten box containing a few torn pages.

Some stains appear on the surface of those parchments that have endured the cold of hundreds of winters, fighting and resisting the external humidity. There are a few brown spots on its pages—similar to ants running from one end to the other. Signs that only vaguely recall their former selves. A path. A path to knowledge. Letters. Sentences.

In some corner, should anyone be able to see this relic under the right light, they might be able to guess—with some effort—the name "Kristina" and, a few lines below, the words "Norway" and "infant."

The surname "De la Serna" appears twice or three times in those pages.

And at the bottom, right at the bottom, a clear signature drawn with energy and intent.

The signature and seal of Mrs Maria Teresa Zabarce De Aramburu, Abbess of Las Huelgas, followed by an illegible name and a date: "1905."

A few pages, just a brief remnant awaiting for the scribe, palaeographer, or archaeologist who would never lay eyes on them.

But the troops did get here, as did the cries of hatred years later, hatred between brothers. Before them all, in front of them all, the scrolls resisted. They did so for centuries, waiting for knowledge.

But, as with many unknown human efforts, the final foe overcame them, insidiously and covertly.

Time has defeated them.

Because nobody, no one will read those pages.

And there, far away, the city of mist witnessed once more how, at dusk, the sinking rays of the setting sun were finally filtering through its shadowy alleys, passages, corridors and stairs, illuminating and filling them with light.

～

Serna

ACKNOWLEDGMENTS

Every book is born from a simple premise, from an idea.

Before me other authors had written about the figure of Kristina from Norway. In my case, it all started with a question.

A basic question. A query of the "What if...?" variety."

From there all I had to do was follow the trail —the clear path left by the very concept. I needed simply to seek out the shadowy nooks of history—the unexplained sections, the unresolved questions.

The starting point, the premise, was certainly ludicrous, but, like those incoherent dreams we sometimes have in the middle of the night, I followed its trail until I reached an inevitable conclusion that, I believe, surprised me as much as the potential reader of these humble ravings.

The list of thanks is—and should be in a novel like this— necessarily long.

My heartfelt gratitude goes to the following people in order of appearance:

To Professors Sonia Serna Serna of Burgos University and Elena Rodriguez Diaz and Margarita Gómez of the University of Seville, who were instrumental in getting this project started. They gave me valuable advice on the "mode of operation" of palaeographic procedure, guiding me in this new world to better comprehend the principal character's activity.

During a trip to Burgos, Covarrubias, and Silos for both pleasure and research, I had the good fortune to meet Begoña, a tour guide, who, during a busy visit to St Domingo de Silos assisted me in entering the hidden and restricted library only accessible to scholars. I had previously notified Father Norberto, the monastery's librarian, of my impending visit by email. Unlike the fictional Fray Anselmo, he welcomed me with genuine kindness and Benedictine patience, showing me the files and rooms and saying wise words upon my departure that one of the novel's characters will use later: 'I hope you will make good use of what you have seen here.' I believe I have followed his advice and can repay his kindness with this work.

To Don Juan José Alonso Martín, director of the General Archives of Palace and Heritage, who enlightened me on the protocol for consulting the archives held by that agency at the Huelgas Abbey.

The small towns of Montorio and Quintanilla became a reality in these pages in part thanks to the hard work and dedication of Honorio Serna in the former, who virtually opened me the doors of the "Golden Mount" association over which he presides, and Julian Gonzalez Serna in the latter, who assisted me with the genealogy of these two villages.

To Rosa Mari, friend and collaborator of the aforementioned association, for her understanding and support.

To the local Covarrubias Tourism Office, which supplied me photographs of the interior of the now-defunct pub "La Serna."

In Soria, I was fortunate enough to find a guide whose name I regrettably do not recall, but to whom I am eternally grateful for his recitation of Machado on a bridge parapet, thus allowing me to discover the poet in a new light beside the Duero River.

As the plot thickened, my encounter with the book written by Burgos Professor,Pilar Alonso Abad from Burgos University on the history of Las Huelgas monastery, as well as her studies and discussions regarding the so-called "Burgalese Red," shed a great deal of light—that protagonist's light—as well as the essential novelistic thrill for my purposes. One of the book images depicting the chapter house of the monastery provided me with a clue to one of the plot's final events.

Very important too was the help of Belinda Peña, an exceptional tour guide who, despite the pandemic, found time to answer my impertinent messages while providing me with the essential advice to make Elvira and Arthur's midnight stroll through Burgos Cathedral possible.

My appreciation also extends to the Burgos Union Circle and, in particular, to its president, Mr. Arévalo, who, with his warm words of welcome for this small accomplishment, permitted Carlos Lafuente to reside in the association's building.

To the Saldaña school staff, and Miss Itziar in particular, for sending me photographs of the school's interior, which, coupled with the few works published works about it, allowed me to become familiar with the premises.

Thank you also to the civil servants of the Burgos Municipal Archive for their kindness, professionalism, and friendliness in granting me permission to use that magnificent engraving of St Fernando's Cloister on the back cover of the book.

The Montorio potato cooperative also deserves credit for preserving the so-called "Serna Gene."

I'd like to thank everyone who contributed in any way to the creation of this work, including those who didn't initially, because they forced me to find an alternative approach to tell this story. Throughout the documentary phase, many of my interviewees shown an almost childlike and lively excitement, which spurred my determination to complete the assignment.

And, above all, to Rus, my wife, who became a renowned art restorer in the novel, for her love, support, and advice, as well as for finding the title that the work required, which, like the mystery itself, had been there all along, and who patiently endured my afternoon as a budding writer, with her personal creative touch and charm.

To Irene, my dear daughter and my wife Rus who were so patient and understanding with the many corrections and whose editorial revision was incredibly helpful to me.

ABOUT THE AUTHOR

Enrique Terol was born in Alicante in 1958.

An inveterate reader from early childhood, a hobby that combined more bad than good with math and physics classes, and passionate about stories of all kinds since he started drawing comics in childhood, he went on to try to write small stories that left unfinished. He let himself be carried away in his teens by the desire to shoot small shorts in Super 8 in which he tried to recreate with the few means available to him at the time the cinematographic world with which he had been born. In 1978 he collaborated in the creation of the comic "Mocha el anti-Trocha" together with the then nicknamed Juan Prestón, future creator of Norma Editions. He also collaborated as an atypical film critic of that loving transition in the magazine The Alicante Guide during the years 1986-87.

"Elena's smile" is his first novel.

Eternal mythomaniac and Anglophile, continues in Alicante, although eternally dreaming about the countries and regions of the north, about rainy and snowy landscapes.

9 780645 005882